D1081783

Don't miss Gregg Hurwitz's

TRUST NO ONE
ISBN: 978-0-312-38956-7

"I guarantee that once you read the first page of this
terrific novel, your hands will keep ripping pages
until there are none left."—David Baldacci

Available from St. Martin's Paperbacks

"Invasion of privacy reaches sinister new levels in thriller maestro Hurwitz's latest....With cinematic pacing and strong echoes of countless other twisty suspenses, this one is a natural for the big screen."

—*People*

"Turns with equal skill and mastery down the nightmarish road paved by Harlan Coben...Hurwitz's grasp of Hollywood noir is firm and his command of his story makes *They're Watching* riveting in all respects."

—*Providence Journal-Bulletin*

"[A] labyrinthine thriller...full of twists and turns and unexpected revelations. Hurwitz frequently sets us up to expect one thing but delivers something entirely different. He keeps us constantly on our toes, and—this is especially good—he keeps us guessing right until the very last pages about exactly who has targeted Patrick and why. Highly recommended, especially for fans of Dean Koontz, Linwood Barclay, and Harlan Coben."

—*Booklist* (starred review)

"You'll be gripped by this terrific read from page one."

—*The Sun*

"*They're Watching* is a thrilling novel, dripping with mystery, suspense, violence, and even a little romance. It contains all the ingredients for a bestseller."

—*New York Journal of Books*

"Scary fun, handled with skill by veteran Hurwitz."

—*Library Journal* (starred review)

"Combines action, strong characterization, and a genuine, mesmerizing mystery to produce what is arguably his best and strongest novel to date."

—Bookreporter.com

TRUST NO ONE

"With *Trust No One*, Gregg Hurwitz deservedly takes his place at the forefront of suspense writers. I guarantee that once you read the first page of this terrific novel, your hands will keep ripping pages until there are none left."   —David Baldacci

"Gregg Hurwitz weaves a tangled web of political deceit that will keep even the savviest thriller readers guessing until the very last page."   —Brad Thor

"*Trust No One* is as fine a thriller as you will read in this or any other year. But mostly, it's in a class of its own: magnificent."   —Christopher Reich

"One of the best thrillers of the year."   —*Daily Beast*

"Do NOT start *Trust No One* at the end of a long day when you have to get back up early the next morning. This is the only warning you get…I read until I went blind...Hurwitz grabs you by the throat with this one, and he doesn't let go till he's finished with you."

—Denver Times

"Well-drawn, appealing characters and propulsive narrative...Unlike many authors in the thriller field these days, Gregg Hurwitz understands the craft of writing. His characters, even minor ones, have personalities. His descriptive passages are vivid, never distracting. His prose is crisp and driving."   —Chicago Sun-Times

"At the top of this year's must-read list."

—Bookreporter.com

"Gregg Hurwitz has emerged as one of today's most exciting thriller writers...his ninth novel takes a cue from the best of Alfred Hitchcock."

—The Sun-Sentinel

"The plotting is masterful. The story moves like a bullet as Hurwitz deftly interweaves his hero's soul-searching with his race to untangle a conspiracy reaching to the highest levels of government. Exciting all the way."   —Andrew Klavan

"In a briskly paced case that blends action with insight, Hurwitz puts the clues on the table, then plays the shell game with the reader and wins."   —*Kirkus Reviews*

"Page-to-page suspense and breakneck pacing....a slam-bang beginning to a fast-paced thriller."

—*Booklist*

"Blasts new life...an intelligent thriller...provides plenty of excitement."   —*Publishers Weekly*

"The breathtaking pace of this thriller is set from the opening scene."   —*Sunday Telegraph*

"Hurwitz writes brilliant, highly original thrillers."
—*Weekend Australian*

"Starts out with a bang...a thriller with heart...Nick's personal journey will hook genre fans as surely as the fast pace, cutting-edge technology, and political machinations."   —*Library Journal*

"A political thriller of considerable ambition and tension. Gregg Hurwitz is a rising star among thriller writers, and *Trust No One* is going to make that ascent brighter. [He has an] extraordinary mastery of his genre's demands."   —*January magazine*

ALSO BY GREGG HURWITZ

The Tower
Minutes to Burn
Do No Harm
The Kill Clause
The Program
Troubleshooter
Last Shot
The Crime Writer
Trust No One

THEY'RE
WATCHING

Gregg Hurwitz

St. Martin's Paperbacks

THEY'RE WATCHING

For information address St. Martin's Press, 175 Fifth Avenue, New York, NY 10010.

ISBN: 978-1-250-10031-3

St. Martin's Press hardcover edition / July 2010
St. Martin's Paperbacks edition / May 2011

St. Martin's Paperbacks are published by St. Martin's Press, 175 Fifth Avenue, New York, NY 10010.

To Kelly Macmanus,
who provided my introduction to the town

Nothing is foolproof to a sufficiently talented fool.

—Anonymous

Navigating a hairpin turn, I gripped the steering wheel hard and did my best not to slide in the driver's seat. If the butcher knife tucked beneath the back of my thigh shifted, it would open up my leg. The blade was angled in, the handle sticking out toward the console, within easy reach. The acrid smell of burning rubber leaked in through the dashboard vents. I resisted the urge to flatten the gas pedal again; I couldn't risk getting pulled over, not given the deadline.

I flew up the narrow street, my hands slick on the wheel, my heart pumping so much fear and adrenaline through me that I couldn't catch my breath. I checked the clock, checked the road, checked the clock again. When I was only a few blocks away, I pulled the car to the curb, tires screeching. I shoved open my door just in time. As I retched into the gutter, a gardener watched me from behind a throttling lawn mower, his face unreadable.

I rocked back into place, wiped my mouth, and continued more slowly up the steep grade. I turned down the service road as directed, and within seconds the stone wall came into sight, then the iron gates that matched the familiar ones in front. I hopped out and punched in the code. The gates shuddered and sucked inward. Hemmed in by jacaranda, the paved drive led straight back along the rear of the property. At last the guest quarters came into view. White stucco walls, low-pitched clay-tile roof, elevated porch—the guesthouse was bigger than most regular houses on our street.

I pulled up beside the cactus planter at the base of the stairs, tight to the building. Setting my hands on the steering wheel, I did my best to breathe. There were no signs of life. Way across the property, barely visible through a netting of branches, the main house sat dark and silent. Sweat stung my eyes. The stairs just outside the driver's-side window were steep enough that I couldn't see up onto the porch. I couldn't see much of anything but the risers. I supposed that was the point.

I waited. And listened.

Finally I heard the creak of a door opening above. A footstep. Then another. Then a man's boot set down on the uppermost step in my range of vision. The right foot followed. His knees came visible, then his thighs, then waist. He was wearing scuffed worker jeans, a nondescript black belt, maybe a gray T-shirt.

I slid my right hand down to the hilt of the butcher knife and squeezed it so hard that my palm tingled. Warmth leaked into my mouth; I'd bitten my cheek.

He stopped on the bottom step, a foot from my window, the line of my car roof severing him at the midsection. I wanted to duck down so I could see his face, but I'd been warned not to. He was too close anyway.

His knuckle rose, tapped the glass once.

I pushed the button with my left hand. The window started to whir down. The knife blade felt cool hidden beneath my thigh. I picked out a spot on his chest, just below his ribs. But first I had to find out what I needed to know.

His other hand came swiftly into view and popped something fist-sized in through the open gap of the still-lowering window. Hitting my lap, it was surprisingly heavy.

I looked down.

A hand grenade.

I choked on my breath. I reached to grab it.

Before my splayed fingers could get there, it detonated.

CHAPTER 1

In my boxers I stepped out onto the cold flagstones of my porch to retrieve the morning paper, which had landed, inevitably, in the puddle by the broken sprinkler. The apartments across the street, Bel Air in zip code only, reflected the gray clouds in their windows and sliding glass doors, mirroring my mood. L.A.'s winter had made a late entrance as always, slow to rise, shake off its hangover, and put on its face. But it had arrived, tamping the mercury down to the high forties and glazing the leased luxury sedans with dew.

I fished out the dripping paper, mercifully enclosed in plastic, and retreated back inside. Sinking again into the family-room couch, I freed the *Times* and pulled out the Entertainment section. As I unfolded it, a DVD in a clear case fell out, dropping into my lap.

I stared down at it for a moment. Turned it over. A blank, unmarked disc, the kind you buy in bulk to record onto. Bizarre. Even a touch ominous. I got up, knelt on the throw rug, and slipped the disc into the DVD player. Clicking off the surround sound so as not to wake Ariana, I sat on the floor and stared at the plasma screen, rashly purchased when our bank account was still on a northerly heading.

A few visual hiccups jerked the image, followed by a placid close-up shot of a window framed by plantation shutters, not quite closed. Through the window I could see a brushed-nickel towel rack and a rectangular pedestal sink. At the edge of the frame was an exterior wall, Cape Cod blue. The view took only a second to register—it was as familiar as my reflection, but, given the context, oddly foreign.

It was our downstairs bathroom, seen from outside, through the window.

A faint pulse came to life in the pit of my stomach. Apprehension.

The footage was grainy, looked like digital. The depth of field didn't show compression, so probably not a zoom. My guess was it had been taken a few feet back from the pane, just far enough not to pick up a reflection. The shot was static, maybe from a tripod. No audio, nothing but perfect silence razoring its way under the skin at the back of my neck. I was transfixed.

Through the window and the half-open bathroom door, a slice of hall was visible. A few seconds passed in a near freeze-frame. Then the door swung in. Me. I entered, visible from neck to knee, the shutters chopping me into slices. In my blue-and-white-striped boxers, I stepped to the toilet and took a leak, my back barely in view. A light bruise came into focus, high on my shoulder blade. I washed my hands at the sink, then brushed my teeth. I exited. The screen went black.

Watching myself, I'd bitten down on the inside of my cheek. Stupidly, I glanced down to determine what pair of boxers I had on today. Plaid flannel. I thought about that bruise; I'd banged my back standing up into an open cabinet door just last week. I was trying to recall which day I'd done it when I heard Ariana clanking around in the kitchen behind me, starting breakfast. Sound carries easily through the wide door-ways of our fifties open-plan two-story.

The DVD's placement—tucked into the Entertainment section—struck me as deliberate and pointed. I clicked "play," watched again. A prank? But it wasn't funny. It wasn't much of anything. Except unsettling.

Still gnawing my cheek, I got up and trudged upstairs, past my office with the view of the Millers' much bigger yard, and into our bedroom. I checked my shoulder blade in the mirror—same bruise, same location, same size and color. In the back of the walk-in closet, I found the laundry basket. On the top of the mound were my blue-and-white-striped boxers.

Yesterday.

I dressed and then went down to the family room again. I pushed aside my blanket and pillow, sat on the couch, and started the DVD once more. Running time, a minute and forty-one seconds.

Even if it was just a tasteless joke, it was the last thing Ariana and I needed to deal with right now. I didn't want to upset her, but I also didn't want to withhold it from her.

Before I could work out what to do, she walked in carrying a breakfast tray. She was showered and dressed, a mariposa lily from her greenhouse shed

tucked behind her left ear, the flower a striking contrast with the chestnut waves of hair. Instinctively,
I clicked off the TV. Her gaze scanned over, picked
up the green light on the DVD. Shifting her grip
on the tray, she flicked her thumbnail against her
gold wedding band, a nervous tic. "What are you
watching?"

"Just a thing from school," I said. "Nothing to worry
about."

"Why would I worry?"

A pause as I worked out what to say. I managed only
a contrived shrug.

She tilted her head, indicating a thin scab across
the knuckles of my left hand. "What happened there,
Patrick?"

"Caught it in the car door."

"Treacherous door lately." She set the tray down
on the coffee table. Poached eggs, toast, orange juice.
I paused to take her in. Caramel skin, the mane of
almost-black hair, those big dark eyes. At thirty-five,
she had a year on me, but her genes kept her looking
at least a few younger. Despite her upbringing in the
Valley, she was a Mediterranean mutt—Greek, Italian, Spanish, even a little Turkish thrown in the mix.
The best parts of each ethnicity had been distilled
into her features. At least that's how I'd always seen
her. When I looked at her, my mind drifted to how
things used to be between us—my hand on her knee
as we ate, the warmth of her cheek when she awakened, her head resting in the crook of my arm at the
movies. My anger toward her started to weaken, so
I focused on the blank screen.

"Thanks," I said, nodding at the breakfast tray. My low-grade detective work had already put me ten minutes behind schedule. The edginess I was feeling must have been evident, because she gave a frown before withdrawing.

Leaving the food untouched, I got up from the couch and stepped out the front door again. I circled the house to the side facing the Millers'. Of course the wet grass beneath the window showed no marks or matting, and the perp had forgotten to drop a helpful matchbook, cigarette butt, or too-small glove. I sidestepped until I got the perspective right. A sense of foreboding overtook me, and I glanced over one shoulder, then the other, unable to settle my nerves. Gazing back through the slats, I felt a surreal spasm and half expected to watch myself enter the bathroom again, a time warp in striped boxers.

Instead Ariana appeared in the bathroom doorframe, looking out at me. *What are you doing?* she mouthed.

The ache in my bruised knuckles told me my hands were clenched. I exhaled, relaxed them. "Just checking the fence. It's sagging." I pointed at it like an idiot. See, there. Fence.

Smirking, she palmed the slats closed as she set down the toilet seat.

I walked back into the house, returned to the couch, and watched the DVD through a third time. Then I removed the disc and stared at the etched logo. It was the same cheap kind I used to burn shows from TiVo when I wanted to watch them downstairs. Purposefully nondescript.

Ariana passed through, regarded the untouched food on the tray. "I promise I didn't poison it."

Grudgingly, I smiled. When I looked up, she'd already headed for the stairs.

I tossed the DVD into the passenger seat of my beater Camry and stood by the open door, listening to the quiet of the garage.

I used to love this house. It was at the summit of Roscomare Road near Mulholland, barely affordable and only because it shared the block with those cracked-stucco apartments and a neighborhood shopping strip. Our side of the street was all houses, and we liked to pretend we lived in a neighborhood rather than on a thoroughfare between neighborhoods. I'd had so much pride in the place when we'd moved in. I'd bought new address numbers, repaired the porch light, torn out the spinsterly rosebushes. Everything done with such care, such optimism.

The sound of steadily passing cars filtered into the dark space around me. I clicked the button to open the garage door and sneaked under it as it went up. Then I circled back through the side gate and past the trash cans. The window overlooking the kitchen sink gave a clear view of the family room, and of Ariana sitting on the arm of the couch. Steam wisped from the coffee mug resting on her knee. She held it dutifully, but I knew she wouldn't drink it. She'd cry until it got cold, and then she'd pour it down the sink. I stood nailed to the ground as always, knowing I ought to go in to her but blocked by what little remaining pride I had left. My wife of eleven years, inside, crying. And me out here, lost in a haze of silent devastation. After a moment I eased away from the window. The bizarre DVD had pushed my vulnerability up another notch. I didn't have it in me to punish myself by watching her, not this morning.

CHAPTER 2

For me, growing up, there was nothing like the movies. A dilapidated theater within biking distance had second-run matinees for $2.25. As an eight-year-old, I paid in quarters I earned collecting soda cans for recycling. Saturdays the theater was my classroom, Sundays my temple. *Tron, Young Guns, Lethal Weapon*—through the years those movies were my playmates, my babysitters, my mentors. Sitting in the flickering dark, I could be any character I wanted, anyone other than Patrick Davis, a boring kid from the suburbs of Boston. Every time I watched the credits roll, I couldn't believe that those names belonged to real people. How lucky they were.

Not that movies were *all* I thought about. I played baseball, too, which made my father proud, and I read a lot, which pleased my mom. But most of my childhood daydreams were celluloid-induced. Whether I was shagging fly balls and thinking of *The Natural* or pedaling my Schwinn ten-speed and praying I'd lift off like in *E.T.*, I owe the movies for imbuing my rather ordinary childhood with a sense of wide-eyed wonder.

Follow Your Dreams. I heard it first from my high-school guidance counselor as I sat on her couch gazing down at a glossy admissions pamphlet from UCLA. *Follow Your Dreams.* It's scrawled on every celebrity-signed eight-by-ten, regurgitated by every Oprah success story, flop-sweating valedictorian, and for-a-fee guru. *Follow Your Dreams.* And I did, all the way across the country, a carpet cleaner's kid, trading one puzzling culture for another, rocky shorelines for smooth ones, buttoned-up Brahmin lockjaw for surfer drawl, ski sweaters for tank tops.

Like every other wannabe, I started typing a screenplay within the first week of my move, hammering away on a Mac Classic before I bothered to unpack into my dorm room. As much as I loved it at UCLA, I was an outsider from the start, nose up against the glass, a window-shopper. It took years for me to realize that in L.A. *everybody* is an outsider. Some are just better at nodding along to the music we're supposed to be hearing. *Follow Your Dreams. Never Give Up.*

My first stroke of luck came early, but like most priceless things it was entirely unexpected and not at all what I was looking for. A freshman-orientation party, lots of too-loud laughter and teenage posturing, and there she was, slumped against the wall by the exit, her disaffected posture betrayed by lively, clever eyes. She was, impossibly, alone. Steeled with a cup of warm keg beer, I approached. "You look bored."

Those dark eyes ticked over to me, took my measure. "Is that a proposition?"

"Proposition?" I repeated lamely, stalling.

"An offer to unbore me?"

She was worth getting nervous over, but still, I hoped it didn't show. I said, "Seems like that could be the challenge of a lifetime."

"Are you up to it?" she asked.

Ariana and I got married right out of college. There was never really any question that we wouldn't. We were the first to get hitched. Rented tuxes, three-tiered frilly cake, everyone dewy-eyed and attentive, as if it were the first time in history a bride had step-pause-stepped down the aisle to Handel's *Water Music*. Ari was stunning. At the reception I looked over at her and got too choked up to finish my toast.

For ten years I taught high-school English, writing screenplays on the side. My schedule gave me ample time to indulge myself—out at 3:00 P.M., long holidays, summers—and every now and then I'd mail a script out to friends of friends in the industry and hear nothing back. Ariana not only never complained about my time at the keyboard but was happy for the satisfaction I generally got out of it, just as I loved her devotion to her plants and design sketches. Ever since we'd fled that orientation party together, we'd always kept a balance—not too clingy, not too aloof. Neither of us had an interest in being famous, or all that rich. Mundane as it sounds, we wanted to do things we cared about, things that made us happy.

But I kept hearing that nagging voice. I couldn't stop California dreaming. Less often about red carpets and Cannes than about being on a set watching a couple of actors mouthing stuff I'd devised for better actors to say. Just a low-budget flick to limp onto the sixteenth screen at the multiplex. It wasn't that much to ask.

A little more than a year ago, I met an agent at a picnic, and she was enthused about my script for a conspiracy thing called *They're Watching,* about an investment banker whose life comes apart after he improbably switches laptops on the subway during a blackout. Mob heavies and CIA agents start dismantling his life like a NASCAR pit crew. He loses his perspective and then his wife, but of course wins her back in the end. He returns to his life battered, wiser, and more appreciative. Not the most original plot, certainly, but the right people found it convincing. I wound up getting a good chunk of change for the script, and a decent rewrite fee on top of that. I even got a nice write-up in the trades—my picture beneath the fold in *Variety* and two column inches about a high-school teacher making good. I was thirty-three, and I had finally arrived.

Never Give Up, they say.

Follow Your Dreams.

Another adage, perhaps, would have been more apt.

Careful What You Wish For.

CHAPTER 3

Even before the footage of me showed up in my morning newspaper, privacy had been hard to come by. My one haven—an upholstered interior, six feet by four-and-change—still required six windows. A mobile aquarium. A floating jail cell. The only space left in my life where someone couldn't walk in and catch me covering the tail end of a crying jag or convincing myself I'd make it through another workday. The car was pretty banged up, the dashboard in particular. Dented plastic, cracked faceplate over the odometer, air-conditioner dial barely holding on.

I slotted the Camry into a space in front of Bel Air Foods. Walking the aisles, I gathered up a banana, a bag of trail mix, and a SoBe black iced tea, which came loaded with ginkgo, ginseng, and a handful of other supplements designed to kick-start the bleary-eyed. As I neared the checkout lane, my eye caught on Keith Conner, gazing from a *Vanity Fair* cover. He reclined in a bathtub filled not with water but with leaves, and the headline read CONNER TRADES GREEN FOR GREEN.

"How's Ariana?" Bill asked, cuing me to move

along. A flustered mother with her kid was waiting behind me, grinning impatiently.

A plastic smile flashed onto my face, instinctive as a nervous laugh. "Okay, thanks."

I set my items down, the belt whirred, and Bill rang me up, saying, "You got one of the last good ones, that's for sure."

I smiled; Flustered Mom smiled; Bill smiled. We were all so happy.

In the car I pinched the metal post where the button used to be and twisted on the radio: Distract me, please. Down the hill I veered around the turn onto lurch-and-go Sunset Boulevard, and the sun came on bright and angry. Lowering the visor, I confronted the photo rubber-banded into place. About six months ago, Ariana had discovered an online photo site and had tortured me for a few weeks by reprinting flashes-from-the-past and hiding them various places. I still found new pictures now and then, vestiges of play-fulness. Of course, this one I'd discovered immediately. Me and Ariana at some intolerable college formal, me wearing a shoulder-padded blazer with, alas, cuffed sleeves, her in a poofy taffeta contraption that resembled a lifesaving device. We looked uncomfortable and amused, painfully aware that we were playacting, that we didn't belong, that we didn't really fit in like everyone else. But we loved that. That's how we were best.

You got one of the last good ones, that's for sure.

I hit the dashboard to feel the sting in my knuckles. And kept hitting. The scab cracked; my wrist stung;

the air-conditioner dial split. With smarting eyes, my chest heaving, I looked out one of my six windows. An older blonde in a red Mustang studied me from one lane over.

I cranked that plastic smile onto my face. She looked away. The light changed, and we drifted back off into our private lives.

CHAPTER 4

After I sold my screenplay, Ariana was even more elated for me than I was. The production got fast-tracked. Dealing with studio executives, producers, and the director, I was intimidated but determined. And Ariana pep-talked me every day. I quit my job. That gave me plenty of time to obsess on the project's almost daily ups and downs—interpreting the nuances of each two-line e-mail, having meetings about meetings, taking a cell-phone call on a sidewalk while my entrée went cold and Ariana ate hers alone. Mr. Davis, tenth-grade American lit teacher, was out of his depth. I had to choose roles, and I chose wrong.

Follow Your Dreams, they say. But no one ever tells you what you have to give up in the process. The sacrifices. The thousand ways your life can go to hell while you keep your eyes on the horizon, waiting for that sun to rise.

I was too distracted to write—or at least to write well. As *They're Watching* progressed through development, my agent reviewed what I was putting out now, and it didn't catch her fancy any more than the scripts that had been moldering in my desk drawers. I sensed a slow leak in my aspirations, like a tire with a nail through it, and my agent, too, seemed to be running out of steam. My lack of focus built to full-blown writer's block, and still I couldn't seem to find the time to pay proper attention to the people around me. I was lost in the typhoon of possibilities, unsure if the movie was actually going to move forward, if I had what it would take, if I was, at bottom, a fraud.

Ariana and I never quite found our footing again after the shift our relationship took following the script deal. We harbored silent resentments, misread the currents of each other's emotions. Sex grew awkward. We were too far in for lust, and falling out of love. We'd lost the connection, the heightened awareness. We couldn't get it started, and so we stopped trying. We buried ourselves in routine.

Ariana had forged a friendship of commiseration with Don Miller, our next-door neighbor—coffee twice a week, the occasional walk. I told her she was naïve to think he didn't have a thing for her and that this wouldn't affect her relationship with his wife, Martinique. Ariana and I had never been controlling with each other, so I didn't press her on it, but that reflected my own naïveté—not about Ariana, but in how far she and I could let things slide.

Hard as it was to admit, I checked out on everyone but myself for the better part of that year. I lost sight of everything but the movie, which finally entered preproduction, and then production.

Shipped to frigid mid-December Manhattan to fulfill my obligation for production rewrites, I had a kind of time-release panic attack. The director's cellphone ban on set made things worse, since I was way too timid to use the lines wired to the important people's trailers to talk to my wife. Even though Ariana was worried about me, I managed to return her calls only a few times, and even those conversations were cursory.

On the set, it rapidly became apparent that I'd been hired not as a production rewriter but to take dictation from the twenty-five-year-old lead, Keith Conner. Sprawled on his couch in his trailer, slurping a lumpy green health drink and yakking half the day on the sole ban-exempt cell phone, Keith offered endless notes and dialogue changes, interrupting them only to show off photos of naked, sleeping girls he'd snapped on his Motorola RAZR. The high weekly rate they were paying me was not for ideas. It was for babysitting. Tenth-graders were a lot less work.

After a little more than a week of eighteen-hour days, Keith summoned me into his trailer to say, "I just don't think my character's dog would have a squeaky toy. I think he'd have, like, a *knotted rope* or something, you know?" To which I'd wearily replied, "The dog didn't complain, and *he* actually has talent."

The friction that had built up between us gave way like a crumbling of tectonic plates. Jabbing a finger at me, Keith lost his footing on the rewrite pages he'd thrown on the floor and banged the counter with his well-defined jaw. When his handlers rushed in, he lied and said I'd hit him. There were major contusions. Having the star's face in that condition would mean shutting down the shoot for at least a few days. Given the Manhattan location, that would cost about a half a million per day.

After realizing my lifelong dream, it had taken me just nine days to get fired.

As I waited for the taxi to arrive to take me to the airport, Sasha Saranova empathized with me in her trailer. A sometime model from Bulgaria, she had a knee-weakening accent and natural eyelashes longer than most Hollywood prenups. Playing opposite Keith, she'd endured his personality in close-up. Her visit was motivated more out of self-concern than genuine friendship, but I was shaken and didn't mind the company.

It was just then when Ariana called the set. I had been off the radar with her, not returning phone calls for three days, worried that if I heard her voice, I might just crumble under all the pressure. And Keith happened to be on hand to grab the phone from the production assistant. Still icing his swollen jaw, he told Ariana that Sasha and I had withdrawn to her trailer, as we did every evening after wrap, and our standing instructions were that we were not to be interrupted. "For *anything*." It may have been his best performance.

Ironically, I left Ariana a message on her cell at almost the same time, breaking the news and reciting my flight information. Little did I know that Don Miller had dropped by with the enrollment paperwork from the Writers Guild, accidentally messengered to his doorstep. I'd imagined her many times in the sweaty, regretful aftermath, listening to the voice mail from me and putting my miserable explanation together with Keith's little ruse. A stomach-turning moment.

I had a long and reflective flight home to L.A. Pale and shaken, Ariana was at the Terminal 4 baggage claim, waiting with even worse news. She never lied. At first I thought she was crying for me, but before I could talk, she said, "I slept with someone."

I couldn't speak for the ride home. My throat felt like it was filled with sand. I drove; Ariana cried some more.

The following afternoon I was served with my very first legal complaint, filed by Keith and the studio. Errors-and-omissions insurance, it turns out, doesn't cover tantrum-inflicted injuries, so someone had to be held accountable for the shutdown costs. Keith had sued me in order to back up his lie, and the studio, in turn, had jumped on board.

Keith's version of the story was leaked to the tabloids, and I was smeared with such cold proficiency that I never felt the guillotine drop. I was a has-been before I'd really *been,* and my agent recommended a pricey lawyer and dropped me like a sauna rock.

No matter how hard I tried, I could no longer find the interest to sit at the computer. My writer's block had become fixed and immobile, a boulder in the middle of that blank white page. I suppose I could no longer suspend disbelief.

Julianne, a friend since we'd met eight years ago at a small-time film festival in Santa Ynez, had thrown me a lifeline—a job teaching screenwriting at Northridge University. After long days spent avoiding my stagnant home office, I was thankful for the opportunity. The students were entitled and excited, and their energy and the occasional spark of talent made teaching more than just a relief. It felt worthwhile. I'd been at it only a month, but I was starting to recognize flashes of myself again.

And yet still, every night I went home to a house I no longer felt I belonged in, to a marriage I no longer recognized. And then came the legal bills, more listlessness, the mornings waking up on the downstairs couch. And that feeling of deadness. The feeling that nothing could cut through. And for a month and a half, nothing had.

Until that first DVD fell out of the morning paper.

CHAPTER 5

"Do it," Julianne said, rising to refill her mug from the faculty lounge's machine. *"One time."*

Marcello riffled his blow-dried hair with a hand and refocused on the papers he was ostensibly grading. He wore tired brown trousers, a button-up and blazer, but no tie. This was, after all, the film department. "I'm sorry, I'm just not feeling it."

"You have a responsibility to your public."

"For the love of Mary, relent."

"C'mon. Please?"

"My instrument isn't prepared."

Standing at the window, I was checking *Variety* since I'd gotten distracted from the *Times'* Entertainment section earlier. Sure enough, page three carried a fluff piece on *They're Watching*—production had just wrapped, and anticipation was through the roof.

I said, over a shoulder, "Marcello, just do it so she shuts up already."

He lowered the papers, letting them tap against his knee. "IN A WORLD OF CONSTANT NAGGING, ONE MAN STANDS ALONE."

The voice that launched a million movie trailers. When Marcello uncorks it, you feel it in your bones.

Julianne clapped, one hand rising as the other fell to meet it, a hee-haw display of amusement. "That is so fucking fantastic."

"IN A TIME OF OVERDUE GRADES, ONE MAN MUST BE LEFT ALONE."

"All right, all right." Wounded, Julianne came over and stood next to me. I dropped *Variety* quickly to my side before she could see what I was reading, returning my gaze to the window. I should've been grading papers, too, but in the wake of the DVD I was having trouble focusing. At a few points in the morning, I'd caught myself studying passing faces, searching out signs of menace or masked glee. She followed my troubled stare. "What are you looking at?"

Students poured out of the surrounding buildings and into the quad below. I said, "Life in progress."

"You're so philosophical," Julianne said. "You must be a teacher."

The film department at Cal State Northridge draws mainly three kinds of faculty. There are those who teach, who love the process, turning young minds on to possibilities, all that. Marcello is such a teacher, despite his well-cultivated cynicism. Then there are the journalists like Julianne, wearers of black turtlenecks, always rushing from class, on to their next review or article or book on Zeffirelli. Next, the occasional Oscar winner enjoying the dusk of his career, basking in the not-so-quiet admiration of adoring hopefuls. And then there's me.

I watched the students below, writing on laptops and arguing excitedly, their whole disastrous lives in front of them.

Julianne pushed back from the window and said, "I need a smoke."

"IN AN AGE OF LUNG CANCER, ONE SHIT-HEAD MUST TAKE THE LEAD."

"Yeah, yeah."

After she left, I sat with some student scripts but found myself reading the same sentence over and over. I got up and stretched, then walked to the bulletin board and flipped through the pinned flyers. There I stood, perusing and humming a few notes: Patrick Davis, the picture of nonchalance. I was acting, I realized, more for my own sake than Marcello's; I didn't want to admit how much I was disquieted by the DVD. I'd been numbed for so long by dull-edged emotions—depression, lethargy, resentment—that I'd forgotten what it was like when sharp concern pricked the raw skin beneath the calluses. I'd had a rough run, sure, but this footage seemed to be signaling a fresh wave of . . . of *what*?

Marcello cocked an eyebrow but didn't glance up from his work. "Seriously," he said. "Are you okay? The screws seem a little tight. Tighter than usual, I mean."

He and I had forged an accelerated intimacy. We spent a good amount of downtime together here in the lounge, he'd been privy to plenty of my and Julianne's conversations about the state of my life, and I found him helpful in his sometimes brutal and always irreverent incisiveness. But still, I hesitated to answer.

Julianne came back in, cranked open a window irritably, and lit up. "There's a parent tour. The judgmental stares wear on me."

Marcello said, "Patrick was just about to tell us why he's so distracted."

"It's nothing. This stupid thing. I got a DVD delivered to my house, hidden in the morning paper. It kind of weirded me out."

Marcello frowned, smoothing his neatly trimmed beard. "A DVD of what?"

"Just me."

"Doing what?"

"Brushing my teeth. In my underwear."

Julianne said, "*That's* fucked up."

"Probably some kind of prank," I said. "I don't even know that it's personal. It could've been some kid skulking around the neighborhood, and I was the only jackass taking a leak with the shutters open."

"Do you have the DVD?" Julianne's eyes were big, excited. "Let's look at it."

Minding the fresh divots on my knuckles, I removed the disc from my courier bag and slid it into the mounted media unit.

Marcello rested a slender finger on his cheek and watched. When it finished, he shrugged. "A little creepy, but hardly chilling. The production quality sucks. Digital?"

"That's what I figure."

"Any students you've pissed off?"

That hadn't occurred to me. "No standouts."

"Check if anyone's failing. And think if there are any faculty members who you may have rubbed the wrong way."

"In my first month?"

"Your track record's hardly been exemplary this

year," Julianne reminded me, "when it comes to . . . well, people."

Marcello waved a hand to indicate the building. "Department full of folks who make movies. Most of them just as accomplished as that one. Suspects abound. I'm sure it's nothing more than someone having a little mean-spirited fun." Losing interest, he returned to his papers.

"I don't know. . . ." Julianne lit a fresh cigarette off the end of her last. "Why *inform* someone that you're watching them?"

"Maybe they flunked spy school," I said.

She made a thoughtful noise in her throat. We watched students trickle out of our building below. With its giant windows, colonnades, and a metal swoop of roof, Manzanita Hall always struck me as oddly precarious, seeing that it was a product of the rebuilding effort after the '97 quake.

"Marcello's right. It's *probably* just harassment. If so, who cares? Until it becomes something else. But the other possibility"—she blew a jet of smoke through the window slit—"is that it's an implicit threat. I mean, you're a film teacher and a screenwriter—"

Over his papers, Marcello volunteered, "Screen-*wrote*r."

"Whatever. Which means whoever did this probably knows you've seen every thriller in the Blockbuster aisle." Wrist cocked, elbow to hip, cigarette unspooling—she looked like a film noir convention in her own right. "The recording-as-clue thing. It's *Blowup*, right?"

"Or *Blow Out*," I said. "Or *The Conversation.*

Except I didn't accidentally happen upon this. It was delivered to me."

"But still. They'd have to know you'd pick up on that movie stuff."

"So why do it?"

"Maybe they're not after the usual."

"What's the usual?"

"To reveal a long-buried secret. To terrorize you. Revenge." She chewed her lip, ran a hand through her long red hair. I noticed how attractive she was. It was something that took effort for me to notice. From the first we'd had a sibling-like rapport. Ariana, even with her southern Italian sensibilities, had always been notably unjealous, and justifiably so.

"Someone at the studio could be behind the DVD," Julianne added.

"The studio?"

"Summit Pictures. There is this little matter of a lawsuit. . . ."

"Oh, yeah," I said. "The lawsuit."

"You have a lot of enemies there. Not just executives but legal, investigators, the whole posse. One of them could be fucking with you. And they've certainly made clear they're not on your side."

I mused on this. I had a friend in Lot Security who it might be worth risking a visit to. The DVD *had* been hidden in the Entertainment section of the paper, after all. "Why not Keith Conner?"

"True," she said. "Why not? He's rich and nuts, and actors always have plenty of time on their hands. And shady entourage members to do their bidding."

The chimes sounded from the library, and Mar-

cello exited, giving us a parting bow at the door. Julianne accelerated her inhales, the cherry glow jerking
its way down the cigarette. "Plus, you *did* punch him
in the face. I've heard movie stars don't like that."

"I didn't punch him in the face," I said wearily.

She watched me watching her smoke. I must have
had a longing expression, because she held out the
butt, ash up, and asked, "You miss it?"

"Not the smoking. The ritual. Tapping down the
pack, my silver lighter, a smoke in the morning, in the
car, with a cup of coffee. There was something so
soothing about it. Knowing you could count on it. It
was always there."

She ground out the cigarette against the edge of
the window frame, her eyes never leaving mine. Puzzled. "You trying to give something else up?"

"Yeah," I said. "My wife."

CHAPTER 6

When I pulled in to our driveway, Don Miller strode out his front door. Like he'd been waiting. It was just before ten o'clock—popcorn and Milk Duds for dinner at the Arclight cineplex. I'd promised a student I'd go to this pseudo-indie film he was ripping off for his assigned short, which was good because I'd seen all the other releases. It beat time at home.

As I walked over to grab the mail, Don met me at the curb. A broad, confident guy, ex-athlete handsome. He cleared his throat. "The . . . ah, the fence at our property line is falling down. Section in the back there."

I shifted the dry cleaning slung over my shoulder. "I'd noticed that."

"I was gonna have my guy fix it. Just wanted to make sure that's okay with you."

I looked at his hands. I looked at his mouth. He'd grown a goatee. Animal hatred bubbled to the surface, but I just nodded and said, "Fine idea."

"I . . . ah, I know things have been a little thin for you lately, so I figured I'd just cover it."

"We'll cover half." I turned to head inside.

He stepped forward. "Listen, Patrick . . ."

I looked down. His boot was across the pavement line, in my driveway. He froze and followed my stare. His face colored. He withdrew his foot, nodded, then nodded again, backing away. I watched until his front door closed behind him. Then I continued up my walk.

I went inside, dumped the mail and dry cleaning on the kitchen table, and chugged down a glass of water. Leaning against the sink, I ran my hands over my face, doing my best to ignore the mounting stack of dignified taupe envelopes on the counter, from the Billing Department of my lawyer's firm; his evergreen retainer had dipped beneath its thirty-thousand-dollar threshold yet again and needed refreshing. Beside it sat a forgotten dry-cleaning tag, set out by Ariana yesterday; in the morning commotion, I'd neglected to grab it. Despite everything, we were still trying to split our chores, maintain civility, dodge the mines floating beneath the calm surface. She needed that suit for a big client meeting tomorrow. Maybe by some miracle, the dry cleaner had pulled it with our other laundry. As I crossed to check, the little mound of mail caught my attention. The red prepaid Netflix envelope looked different, altered somehow. Blood moved to my face, warming it. I walked over, picked it up. The outside flap had been lifted and retaped. I tore it free, tilted the envelope. A blank sleeve slid out.

Inside was another unmarked DVD.

My hands shook as I fed the disc into the player. I was doing my best not to overreact, but my skin had gone cold and clammy. As much as I hated to admit it, I was as creeped out as a kid listening to a camp-fire ghost story, the ragged unease starting in my bones and moving outward, eating me up in reverse.

Falling back onto the couch, I fast-forwarded through footage of our front porch. It's weird how dread turns to impatience—can't wait for the ax to fall. Same shitty picture quality. The oblique angle, I slowly realized, had to be from the neighboring roof.

Don and Martinique's roof.

I'd made up the couch like a bed this morning, but already the sheets were shoved around from my fidgeting. Fists pressed to my knees, I waited, watching the screen to see what the action would be.

Sure enough, it was me again. The sight of my face sent a bolt of ice down my spine. Watching spy footage of me going about my clueless business was something I doubted I'd adjust to anytime soon.

On-screen, I stepped into view and glanced around nervously. The clothes I was wearing were the same ones I had on now. I appeared gaunt and not a little unwell, my expression sour and troubled. Was that really how I looked these days? The last year had taken its toll on me. How much younger I'd seemed in that bright-eyed picture they'd run in *Variety* when my script had sold.

As I stepped off the porch, the picture wobbled a little to keep me in frame. I went blurry, then came back into focus.

This effect, however minor, set my nerves on edge. The angle on the last DVD had been static, fixed; it suggested that someone had set up the camcorder and gone back to retrieve the footage later. This new clip left no doubt: Someone had been behind the camera, actively tracking my moves.

I watched myself walk around the house. Studying the ground, my head bent, I paused by the bathroom window. Adjusted my position. Inspected the wet grass. The Millers' chimney edged into the shot. I looked around, my gaze passing disturbingly close to the camera's position, Raymond Burr in *Rear Window,* only oblivious. A slow zoom to a close-up found my face drawn and angry. I said something to the window, and then the slats closed, pushed down from inside by Ariana's invisible hand. I trudged back to the porch, disappearing into the house.

The screen went black, and I realized I was standing up halfway to the TV. Breathing hard, I stepped back to the couch and sat again. I shoved a hand through my hair. Sweat dampened my forehead.

Ariana was in bed upstairs; I could hear the TV through the floorboards. When I wasn't there, she liked to have a sitcom keep her company; she didn't like being alone, as I'd painfully learned. A few cars zipped by on Roscomare, their headlights brushing the family-room blinds.

Too agitated to sit still, I rushed around the downstairs, closing blinds and curtains and then peering through. Was there a camera trained on our house right now? My emotions were a blur—concern bled through anger into fear. Scored at intervals by the laugh track from the television upstairs, my movements quickened, grew a touch frantic. First the Entertainment section of the newspaper. Then Netflix. Both seemed to point to Keith or someone at the studio.

But the on-set altercation had happened months ago—an eternity ago in Hollywood time, so someone outside the industry might have read about it and decided to make use of it to misdirect me.

A light shone in the Millers' bedroom. Their roof was dark. I thought about how Don had popped out of his house when I'd pulled up. And the new video *had* been shot from his roof—this morning, when it would have been tough for someone to sneak up there unseen. He was the obvious choice.

I started out for his house but balked at the brink of the street. It struck me that I might be gravitating toward Don because that was reassuring. He was familiar, a known entity. An asshole, sure, but what reason would he have to film me?

I went to the front of his house, staying a step back from the curb. Still couldn't make out whether there was a camera set up on the roof. Scrambling up there to search for it was my logical next move. So, clearly, not what I should do.

Spinning in a full circle, I peered across the other rooftops, the windows, the parked cars in the shopping strip a half block up. I imagined lenses peering back from every shadow. From what I could see, no stalkers or hidden cameras were in evidence, waiting to watch me climb onto the Millers' roof. But I couldn't see very well.

I needed to find a better vantage to see if the camera was still up there. The apartment balconies across the road would offer only a partial view onto the Millers' roof. As would the nearest two streetlights and a telephone pole. And the roof of the grocery store was too far away. Maybe I could see up there from another position on the ground? I hurried up and down the street, trying different perspectives, getting winded. But the pitch of the Millers' roof was too flat to allow a clear glimpse of the spot from which I'd been filmed. It became apparent that the only unobstructed view would be from our own roof.

I jogged back to our house, more deliberately now. As I pulled myself onto the low eaves over the garage, the unchecked wind was strong, cutting through my shirt, rising up the cuffs of my jeans. An elm blocked the yellow throw from the nearest streetlight. I tried to minimize the noise of the shingles under my sneakers. Crossing to the slope above the kitchen, I hooked a leg up over the second-story gutter.

"Hey!" Ariana, in the driveway in sweatpants and a long-sleeved T, hugging herself. "Checking that sagging fence again?" More irritated even than sarcastic.

I paused midclimb, my leg still up past the gutter. "No. The weather vane's loose. It's been rattling."

"I hadn't noticed."

We were almost shouting. The idea of the stalker's camera capturing Ariana—let alone our exchange—made me all the more uneasy. My shoulders tensed, a wolf's hackles rising protectively. "Look, just go inside. You're freezing. I'll be down in a minute."

"I have to be up early. I'm going to bed. So that should give you plenty of time to come up with a better story." She disappeared under the eaves. A moment later the front door closed, hard.

The pitch was steep, and I lowered my body, keeping a knee and a forearm in constant contact with the shingles. Scuttling like a crab, I worked my way up and diagonally to the highest peak, near the Millers' house. I eased around our chimney.

There was no camcorder on the Millers' roof.

But the view onto the balconies, streetlights, and other rooftops was pristine; this was the best vantage yet to search out hiding places. Houses, neighboring trees, backyards, vehicles, telephone poles—I scrutinized them until my eyes ached.

Nothing.

Sagging against the brick, I exhaled with mixed disappointment and relief. I turned to start back. That's when I saw it, glinting in the dim light. Way at the edge of the east-pointing run of roof extending out over my office, raised elegantly on a tripod and looking alertly at me, was a digital camcorder.

My heart seized. I felt a calm terror, the kind that comes in a nightmare in which horror is mitigated by the suspicion that you're only dreaming. The tripod, a few feet down from the peak, had been adjusted for the slope. The rise of roof behind acted as a windbreak, the trembling weather vane just above attesting to the necessity. Whoever had placed the camera there—aimed not at Don's roof but at where I would come to *look* at Don's roof—had planned my move for me, had thought through everything I had and come out one step ahead. Across the rutted stretch of dark shingles, the blank lens and I regarded each other, gunslingers on a dusty boomtown street. The wind whirred in my ears, Ennio Morricone on the upsurge.

My rubber soles gripping the rough surface, I left the safety of the chimney, heading toward where the rooflines met. Getting on all fours, I worked along the spine. My mouth had gone dirt dry. The two-story fall looked higher from up here, and the wind, though hardly gale force, didn't help. As I reached the brink, the drop confronted me dizzyingly. I hugged the rusty rooster weather vane, getting my first up-close view of the camera perched barely out of reach below.

It was mine.

The swung-out viewfinder framed the stretch of roof I'd just come across. No glowing green dot, so my passage hadn't been recorded.

Cars whined by on the turn below, light streaming fluidly across metal, disorienting me further. I leaned down and snagged the unit. The digital memory had been wiped. And the camera hadn't been set to record. So why was it here? As a decoy?

The light in the Millers' bedroom switched off. Fair enough—it *was* ten-thirty. Yet I couldn't help but find the timing suspect.

Awkwardly hauling the camcorder—a cheap Canon I hardly ever used—I worked my way back along the roof's ridge and then jumped from an interior corner to our bed of ivy.

I hurried inside and sat at the sleek, dark walnut dining table—one of Ariana's designs—and turned the camera over in my hands. With optical zoom, extended battery life, and a straight-to-DVD recording option, it was fairly idiotproof.

I got up, shoveled water over my face, and then stood with my hands resting on the lip of the sink, staring blankly at the closed blinds two feet from my nose.

Finally I went upstairs to my office. A chipped desk, bought at a fire sale, predominated. I checked the cabinet where I stored the camcorder, stupidly confirming that yes, it was missing. Downstairs, moving with purpose, my thoughts burning like a fuse. Collecting the two discs, I compared them. Identical. I forced myself not to take the stairs back up to my office two at a time, which would wake Ariana.

I retrieved the spindle of blank DVDs from my office bookshelf. Same cheap kind, all right. Same *exact* cheap kind, down to the write speed, gigabyte capacity, and the brand stamped on the polycarbonate. Since I'd started burning shows from TiVo last year, I'd used maybe a third of them. The plastic cover said *Paquet de 30.* A quick count showed that nineteen remained, stacked unused on the spindle. Could I account for the missing eleven?

Downstairs once more—this was turning into a workout. In the entertainment center, I found four discs containing reruns of *The Shield,* two *24*s, and a *Desperate Housewives* (Ariana's). An *American Idol* from the Jordin Sparks season bore visible beer-glass rings. So eight total. Despite the fact that I rarely rewatched shows, I'd yet to throw away any of the DVDs once I'd burned them. Which meant three were unaccounted for. *Three.*

I scoured the cabinets beneath the TV again, then craned to see if a disc had fallen behind the unit. Nothing. Three missing DVDs, of which I'd received only two back.

I checked the porch, letting in a blast of cold air. No magical delivery had shown up. I closed the door, dead-bolted it, set the security chain. I peeped out the peephole. Then I turned and put my back to the door.

Was the third DVD en route? Had I been caught by *another* camera from somewhere else as I'd recovered my own from the roof? Was that why my Canon had not been set to record?

The obvious finally hit me, and I laughed. It wasn't a laugh of amusement, not at all. It was the kind of laugh you let out when you lose your footing and fall down concrete steps, the kind of lying laugh that says everything's okay.

I crossed to the kitchen. I sat at the dining table. I popped the loader on the camcorder.

The third DVD was inside.

CHAPTER 7

Fade in on the rear of our house. Horror-movie low angle, a few branches adding menace to the nighttime view. Cutting into one side of the frame was the green corrugated-plastic wall of the shed where Ariana cultivated her flowers. Advancing, the point of view pushed through the brushy sumac and began a psycho-killer crawl toward the other side of the wall I sat facing, the wall holding the flat-screen I was staring at. The sound track, were there one, would have been shrilling strings and huffy breathing. Silence was worse. Through patches of shadow, images loomed—here a solar-powered garden light, there a patch of grass caught in the cone-throw of a porch lamp. Moving up on the house, the angle stayed low, approaching the windowsill, then creeping north to take in the family-room ceiling, dimly lit by the flickering of the TV.

My back was slick with sweat. My eyes moved involuntarily to the window. Through the semi-sheer sage green curtains, the black square of glass stared back, giving up nothing. Until that moment I'd never grasped the stale phrase "knotted stomach." But I felt my fear sitting there, deep in the pit of my gut, dense and unyielding. Every second my eyes were off the screen caused a rise in my panic. Surreally, the TV seemed to contain the present threat, and the window itself—outside which someone could be lurking at that very minute—seemed fictitious. The screen reclaimed my absolute attention.

Growing bolder, the perspective rose above the sill. Brazenly sweeping the interior through the window, it settled on a form slumbering beneath a blanket on the couch.

As the camera pulled back, I heard the low rush of my heart shoving adrenaline through my veins.

The image bounced along, moving parallel to the wall, toward the kitchen. A rapid swing to our rear door, autofocusing from the blur. My breath stopped.

A hand gloved in latex reached out and twisted the knob. It turned. Despite Ariana's reminders, I often forgot to relock that door after running trash out to the cans. A gentle push and the intruder was inside, next to our refrigerator.

My eyes pulled frantically to the kitchen, back to the screen.

The point of view floated farther into the kitchen, not hurried but not cautious either. Crossing the threshold to the family room, it angled toward the couch, the couch on which I lay sleeping, the couch where I now sat, stupidly willing myself not to look over my left shoulder for a camera on its way, grasped by a gloved hand.

I couldn't move my eyes from the screen. The angle dipped. The intruder was standing over me. I slept on. My cheek was white. My eyelids flickered. I stirred, rolled over, curling an edge of blanket around a fist. The camcorder zoomed in. Closer. Closer. A blur of REM-shifting eyelid. Closer still, until the flesh was no longer distinguishable, until all bearings were lost, until only the twitching remained, as detached as lines of static across the bleached screen.

Then darkness.

My hand was curled in the blanket, just as in the clip. I swiped a palm across the back of my neck, wiped the sweat on my jeans, leaving a dark smudge.

I ran upstairs, heedless of waking Ariana, and pushed open the door of the darkened master bedroom. She was there asleep, oblivious. Safe. Her mouth was slightly open, and her hair fell forward over her eyes. Relieved, I felt the rush of adrenaline drain from me, and I sagged against the doorway. On the TV, Clair Huxtable was riding Theo about his schoolwork. I had an urge to go over and wake Ari, just to check, but I contented myself with the rise and fall of her bare shoulders. The new bed, an oak sleigh with hand-carved scrolls, looked solid. Protective, even. She'd replaced our old bed last month. The mattress, too. I hadn't slept on either.

I stepped back into the hall, eased the door closed, and put my shoulders to the wall, exhaling hard. It made no sense that she'd have been harmed, of course; the footage was shot last night at the latest, and I'd seen Ariana less than an hour ago. But rationality was about as helpful right now as it had been when I'd braved my first post-*Psycho* shower.

I went back downstairs. To the couch where the intruder had pointedly shown me sleeping apart from my wife. The foldout couch that I'd steadfastly refused to fold out for fear that would add a level of permanency to the current arrangement. In the clip, the blanket covered whichever boxers I'd been sleeping in, so more laundry forensics wouldn't help me deduce when it had been shot. Bracing myself, I picked up the remote and clicked "play" again. Seeing that grainy approach to the house sent another jolt through my system. I tried to detach myself and watch closely. No gauging how recently the lawn had been mowed. No fresh scratches on the back door. The kitchen—no plates in the sink showing the remains of a meal. Trash! I punched "pause" and studied the full can. Empty cereal box. A crinkly ball of foil stuck in the mouth of a yogurt cup.

I rushed into the kitchen. The trash in the can matched the screen snapshot precisely, in content and composition. Nothing on top of the cereal box or yogurt cup. Today was Tuesday—Ariana had worked late as usual and probably ordered takeout to the showroom, so she'd added no new trash since yesterday. I checked the coffeemaker, and sure enough the soggy filter from this morning was still parked inside.

The footage of me sleeping had been shot last night. So that clip, on the third DVD, had been shot before the second clip, which in turn showed me checking out the location of the first. Pretty good planning. I almost had to admire the care being taken.

I checked the back door. Locked. Ariana must've caught it this morning. I wouldn't require any more reminders to throw the dead bolt. Handling the DVD, as before, with a tissue, I snapped it into a spare case.

Julianne's nicotine-fueled commentary in the faculty lounge took on fresh significance. Clearly this had gone beyond harassment. Three DVDs like this in under eighteen hours constituted a threat, and that scared me. And pissed me off. It seemed certain that, as Marcello has intoned in innumerable trailers, this was only the beginning. I would have to tell Ariana now, that was certain; for all its shortcomings, our marriage had a full-disclosure policy. But first I wanted to cross Don, the obvious red herring, off the list.

I headed out, turned left at the sidewalk. The night was brisk, the clean air and bizarre mission making me light-headed. Just a neighborly visit.

A bus rattled by, unnervingly close, a behemoth on creaky joints. It carried a coming-this-summer ad for *They're Watching:* a figure in a raincoat, made blurry by Manhattan rain, descending into the subway. He toted a briefcase, his shadowy face peering over his shoulder with a furtive panic that implied paranoia. As the bus passed, I skipped back to the curb, dodging a slapstick obituary.

The chimes sounded unusually loud inside the Millers' foyer. Charged from fear, the night air, my proximity to their house, I shifted from foot to foot, composing myself. An interior light clicked on. A shuffling, some grumbling, and then Martinique at the front door. Don's long-suffering, beautiful wife, with her sad eyes and contrived L.A. name. The flesh at the backs of her arms was feathered, loose from the sixty pounds she'd dropped. Her waist now looked like you could fit a napkin ring around it. Stretch marks formed half-moons emanating from her belly button, the lines of a cartoon explosion. They were faded, microdermabraded into submission, and looked soft and feminine. Even roused, she looked impeccable—her hair shiny and brushed, satin pajama bottoms matching her burgundy halter camisole. She was aggressively competent—ethnically appropriate holiday cards, morning thank-you calls after our infrequent dinner parties, twigs and raffia adorning neatly wrapped birthday presents.

"Patrick," she said, casting a wary glance over her shoulder, "I hope you're not going to do anything you'll regret." She clipped some of her words, only barely, but enough to broadcast that she was Central American instead of Persian.

"No. Sorry to wake you. I just stopped by to ask Don something."

"I don't think that's a great idea. *Especially* right now. He's wiped. Flew back this morning."

"From where?"

"Des Moines. Work. I think, anyway."

"How long was he gone?"

She frowned. "Just two nights. Why—did she take a trip, too?"

"No, no," I said, trying to hide my impatience.

"Someone lies once, you know. How am I supposed to believe he went to Iowa?" She was standing quite close. I felt her breath on my face. It smelled faintly of mint toothpaste. It seemed odd to be close enough to a woman to breathe her breath, and it brought home how long Ariana and I had been keeping our distance from each other. "It's hard, isn't it?" she said. "They'll never understand. We were the victims here."

I balked at the word "victims" but didn't say anything. I was trying to figure out a good segue into asking for Don again.

"I'm sorry, Patrick. I wish we all didn't have to hate each other now." She spread her arms, her perfect nails flaring. We embraced. She smelled divine—faded perfume, feminine soap, sweat mixed with lotion. Hugging a woman, really hugging her, brought back a flood of sensations—not quite memories, but impressions. Impressions of my wife, of another time. Martinique's muscles were tighter than Ariana's, more compact. I patted her back and let go, but she clutched me another moment. She was trying to hide her face.

I pulled away. She wiped her nose, looked around self-consciously. "When Don and I got married, I was beautiful."

"Martinique. You *are* beautiful."

"You don't have to say that."

I knew from experience there was no winning this battle with her. My fingers drummed involuntarily against my forearm.

"You guys all think because you only value us for what we look like, that's what we value in ourselves. It's kind of pathetic how often you're right." She shook her head, hooked a wisp of hair back over an ear. "I gained so much weight after we got married. It's hard for me. My mom's huge, and my sister . . ." She drew her fingertips along her lids to remove smeared eyeliner. "And Don lost interest in me. He lost his *regard* for me. And now I understand. Once it's lost, it's lost."

"Is that true?"

She looked at me anxiously. "You don't think so?"

"I hope not."

And then, abruptly, he was there at her shoulder, nervously cinching his bathrobe. His bare chest was wide and sported a salt-and-pepper scattering of hair. The muscles of my lower back tightened instinctively, pulling me into a harder defensive posture. The air took on a different charge.

"Martinique," he said firmly, and she withdrew, padding down the hall, casting a glance at me over her shoulder. He waited for the bedroom door to close, and then his big, handsome head bobbed on his thick neck, his eyes darting to my hands. He looked as nervous as I felt, but he wasn't letting on. "What do you want, Patrick?"

"Sorry to wake you. I know you're tired from your trip." I studied him, looking for some poker tell that he hadn't really been out of town but instead tiptoeing around rooftops with camcorders like a perved-out Santa Claus. "Someone's been surveilling our house. Have you seen anything?"

"As in watching you?" He looked genuinely confused. "How do you know?"

I held up the unmarked DVD. "They sent this. And the POV on it seems to be from your roof. Have you had any workers at the house or anything?"

"Patrick, you're starting to concern me." He put a thick hand on the door, ready to slam if I lunged.

"Let's skip past this part," I said. "We both know this script. You push the buttons and I'm supposed to respond."

"I'm not pushing any buttons, but it sure seems

like you're responding." He started to swing the door closed.

I put my hand out, stopped it. Gently.

I said, "Look, I'm not storming over here making threats. I'm not calling the cops. I just want to ask you, calmly—"

"The cops now? I don't know what you're trying to set up here, Patrick, but I'm not going for it. I'm gonna shut the door now."

I removed my hand. Not taking his eyes from mine, he slowly closed the door. I heard the dead bolt clunk, the chain fuss into the catch.

I walked back home. Locked the front door behind me.

Ariana was sitting on the couch. Those dark eyes lifted, looking straight at me. And then she raised her hand, holding two of the DVDs. "What the hell is this? Are you paying someone to watch our house? To keep an *eye* on me? Or is this Martinique's doing? She spies on me while you spy on Don? Not even getting into how fucking invasive this is, I thought we were beyond this."

"Whoa, wait a minute. Those recordings are of *me*—"

"They're *surveillance*. So a few clips caught you. How many others are there? What have they been watching me do?"

"I have *no idea* who's behind those videos."

I took a quick step forward, and she recoiled in fear. I froze. She'd never flinched from me before, not ever. We stood in the still house for a moment, both of us horrified by her reaction.

She brushed a lock off her forehead and flattened her hand against the air, willing us both to calm down, slow down. "You're telling me you're not part of this."

"No. *No.* Of course not."

She looked away, took a deep breath. "Patrick, you're starting to scare me here. You've been like a coiled spring. And now it's as if you've gone off the deep end. You're snooping by their fence, up on our roof spying on them, now you go storming over there. I didn't know what to do. I thought this whole thing was going to blow up on their porch. Don has all those hunting rifles. This is gonna get you killed, and then *I'm* gonna have to feel guilty."

"Get me *killed*?"

"I thought Don was going to shoot you." She gave a dark little cry, half anger, half relief. "And if *anyone's* gonna shoot you right now, it should be me."

I held up the third DVD. "You need to see this one."

Still using the tissue to preserve any prints, I slotted it in, and the blue screen quickly gave way to the shaky view of the back of our house. As the clip ran, Ariana pulled her legs under her, distressed, and pressed a cushion across her thighs. She gasped when the latex glove materialized to grip our doorknob. For the first time, I noted the black sweatshirt covering the brief flash of the intruder's wrist.

The footage ended, and Ariana said hoarsely, "Why didn't you tell me about this? Why didn't you go to the cops?"

"I didn't want to scare you." I held up a hand. "I

know. But I just found this one tonight. On our roof. I was coming to tell you, right now. But I wanted to rule Don out first, for obvious reasons."

She said firmly, "There's no way this is Don."

"I agree. But still, the cops aren't going to do any good."

"What do you mean? Someone came *inside our house*."

"It's creepy, but it's not proof of a crime. They'll say they don't have a way to know who did it. They'll say it could've been you."

"*Me?* Patrick—"

"They won't be able to do anything. 'Contact us again if there's further trouble. Blah, blah, blah.' "

The doorbell rang. She froze. "Shit, oh, *shit*," she said. "You might not want to answer that."

CHAPTER 8

I opened the door, revealing a vast, pyramidal woman with oval, plastic-frame glasses. Her hair, a touch puffy, was center-parted and feathered. The pooch under her belt said she was a mother, and she had the brisk, no-nonsense demeanor to back it up.

"I'm Detective Sally Richards. This is Detective Valentine. He'll give you his first name if he's feeling social."

A slender black man stepped out from behind her. His hair was about two inches deep all around—no shape, no notched part, just a uniform rise of dense black curls. His mouth twitched, his mustache undulating. Like her, he wore slacks, a button-up, and a blazer.

Behind me, Ariana said faintly, "Detectives? I assumed they'd just send a couple patrolmen."

"Bel Air service." Richards hoisted her belt, weighed down with a hip-holstered Glock and a flashlight. "The surveillance tape sounded bizarre, so Dispatch kicked it to us. Plus, we're bored. West L.A. station. There's only so much Starbucks you can drink. Even the doughnuts aren't doughnuts. They're gourmet cupcakes."

Valentine blinked twice, displeased.

Ariana had called them to protect me from Don's guns, but now that they were here, they required an explanation of some sort. I ushered them in. We sat at the dining table like it was some sort of social visit. Richards's gaze caught on my bruised knuckles. I dropped my hand quickly into my lap.

"Would you like something to drink?" Ariana asked.

Valentine shook his head, but Richards smiled brightly. "I would *love* something to drink. Glass of water. With a spoon."

Ariana arched an eyebrow but brought both over. Richards plucked three Sweet'N Lows from her inside lapel pocket and shook the pink packets down. She tore off the ends, dumped the sweetener in, and stirred. "Don't ask. It's a fucking diet so I can fit into a boat tarp by beach season. Now, what's going on here?"

I ran through it all for them, Richards quietly noting Ariana's surprise at some of the revelations. Halfway through, Valentine got up and stood at the kitchen window, staring out despite the fact that the blinds were closed. After I finished, Richards knocked the table twice and said, "Let's take a look at these DVDs, then."

I fed in the first disc, Richards and Valentine exchanging a glance over my tissue-handling of the evidence. We stood before the flat-screen, all four of us, arms crossed, scouts watching batting practice. After the last one finished, Richards said, "Well, well."

Back to the dining table. She sat, and Ariana and I

followed suit. Valentine stayed in the family room, poking through the cabinets. Ariana glanced over her shoulder at him a few times, nervously. I realized, with approval, that Richards had taken a chair on the far side so Ariana and I would wind up sitting with our backs to her partner as he snooped.

Richards smoothed her hands across the lacquered surface. "This one of your designs?"

Ariana said, "How did you . . . ?"

"Stacks of trade mags on the table by the front door. Sketch pad on the stairs, there. Charcoal smear on your left sleeve. Lefty—creative. And your hands"— Richards reached across the table, took Ariana by the wrists, like a fortune-teller—"rougher than sub-urban. These hands work with abrasives, I'd guess. So: a furniture designer."

Ariana withdrew her hands.

Valentine was behind us. "You keep a house key outside somewhere? Hidden?"

"Fake rock by the driveway," I answered. "But like I said, I probably left the back door unlocked myself."

"But you're not certain," he told me.

"No."

"Alarm? You got two signs out front, stickers in the windows."

"Just the signs. From the last owner. As deterrents. We dropped the service."

Valentine made a noise in the back of his throat.

Richards asked, "Why?"

"Expensive."

Valentine looked around with pursed lips, presum-ably at the nice furnishings.

"Okay," I said, "we'll call the company, get it hooked up again."

He asked, "It work by code or keys?"

"Both."

"How many keys?"

"Two."

"You still have 'em?"

I walked over, pulled them from the back of the silverware drawer. "Yes."

"Anyone else know where those keys are?"

"No."

Valentine took them from me and dropped them into the trash can. "Get new ones. Change your code. Don't tell anyone. Not the cleaning lady, not your Aunt Hilda, nobody." His flat stare was unreadable. "Only you two should know."

Richards stood, winked at me. "Let's take a look outside, Patrick." Ariana started to stand, and Richards said, "It's cold out there. Why don't you wait inside with Detective Valentine?"

Ariana eyed her a beat too long. "Fine. I'll go get the key in the fake rock, then."

Richards gave me an after-you flourish of the hand, and we went through the rear door. Outside, she crouched, studied the knob.

"Detective Richards—"

"Please. Sally."

"Okay, Sally. Why was he wearing latex gloves?"

"Leather ones leave distinctive marks, just like fingerprints."

"So if the guy used leather gloves twice, you'd be able to ID them."

She cocked her head, taking me in from an angle. "Screenwriter, yeah?"

I grinned. Her Sherlock routine in the kitchen with Ariana's charcoaled sleeve was probably just stage dressing on a Google search. "Teacher, really."

" 'Guy,' " she noted. "You said 'the guy.' "

"Better odds for an intruder. Plus, the gloved hand looked masculine."

"Just a little big, really. Maybe it's a woman retaining water."

I crouched next to her. "He used his right hand to open the door. So I'm guessing he's left-handed."

She paused in her examination of the doorframe, just for a split second, but I knew I'd surprised her. "Ah," she said, "because you figure he'd use his dominant hand for the camcorder." Another sideways glance at me. "Glad to see you're not obsessing about this."

A faint mark in the thin layer of dirt on the rear step caught her attention. The edge of a footprint. She swept me back and leaned over it, fists on her knees.

My heart quickened. "What can you tell?"

"It was made by a Mexican male, six-two, goes about a buck ninety, had a backpack slung over his right shoulder."

"Really?"

"No. It's a fucking footprint."

I laughed, and her eyes crinkled a bit at the edges; it seemed she found me as amusing as I did her.

But there'd be no lingering in our joint fondness. "Lemme see your shoe," she said. "No, take it off."

I tugged my sneaker off. She held it over the imprint. A perfect match. "Square one."

"How 'bout that."

She stood, arched to crack her back. It didn't crack, but she got in a good groan. Clicking on her Mag-Lite, she started along the wall, reversing the course the camera had traveled. "Any problems with your left-handed wife?"

Don and Martinique's bedroom light was still on. "All couples have problems," I said.

"Any serious disputes with anyone else?"

"Keith Conner. And Summit Pictures. There's a lawsuit—it was all over the tabloids. . . ."

"I don't read *The Enquirer* much. Tell me about it."

"The judge issued a gag order until the matter's resolved. The studio didn't want any bad press circulating."

She looked mildly disappointed in me, as if I were a dog that messed the carpet. "Maybe that's not so important right about now."

"It's so stupid you wouldn't believe it."

"I probably would. I had to arrest a director last month for taking a dump in his agent's pool. I can't mention any names, but it was Jamie Passal." She looked at me flatly, not pushing.

I drew in a breath of cool air. Then I told her about the confrontation with Keith, how he'd slipped and banged his jaw on the counter, how he'd lied and said I'd hit him, how the studio had joined him in suing what was left of my ass.

When I finished, she looked unmoved. "Money disputes are our bread and butter." She looked at me, then added, "And stupid domestic disputes." She ran her fingers along the wall, as if checking for wet paint. "So this thing with Summit and Keith is ongoing."

"Right."

"And expensive."

Right.

"Seems like a pretty elaborate and time-consuming method for an actor or a studio to harass you," she said.

I pressed my lips together and nodded. I'd considered the same.

"Besides," she said, "what would they hope to gain by this?"

"Maybe they're wearing me down in preparation for a demand of some sort."

It sounded thin, and Sally's face showed that she thought so, too.

"Let's get back to Ariana." Sally had maneuvered our exchange so we were looking through the window into the family room. "She have any enemies?"

We stood side by side, a big-screen view of the blanket and pillow on the couch. I took a deep breath. "Aside from the neighbor's wife?"

"Okay," Sally said. "I see." A pause. "I'm not gonna find out anything about those bruised knuckles that makes me mad, am I?"

"No, no. I hit the dashboard now and again. When I'm alone. Don't ask."

"Make you feel better?"

"Not yet. I don't know of Ariana's having any real enemies. Her only sin is being overfriendly."

"Often?" she hazarded.

"Once."

"People can surprise you."

"All the time." Following her out across the lawn to the sumac, I stayed on the underlying question. "Ariana doesn't lie well. Her eyes are too expressive."

"How long until she told you about the neighbor?"

We'd established an easy rapport, Sally and I. She seemed trustworthy, genuinely interested in my take on the matter at hand. Or was she just a skilled detective at work, making me feel special so I'd keep flapping my mouth about personal matters? Either way, I heard myself answer again: "About six hours."

"What took so long?"

"I was on a flight. She picked me up at the airport. After I didn't punch Keith."

"Six hours is good. I wonder if she's taking longer to tell you something else." She shoved aside the sumac branches. No footprints on the spongy ground beneath. She shot the light through the plastic sheeting of the greenhouse shed. Row after row of flowers poking up from the sagging wooden shelves. "Lilies?"

"Yeah. Mostly mariposas."

She whistled. "Those are hell."

"Three to five years from seed to grow the bulb up. Everything eats them."

"Plant 'em a foot deep and pray."

"Like the dear departed."

"Progressive the way you take an interest in your wife and her activities." She hoisted her considerable frame onto our rear fence, peered across at the quiet street beyond. "Could've hopped over from here."

I nodded at the other fence, the drooping one dividing our backyard from the Millers'. "Or there."

"Or there," she conceded. She dropped back down with a huff of breath, and we started along the property line.

"Now what?" I asked, a bit anxiously.

"Neighbor's name?"

"Don Miller." Saying it made my mouth sour.

"It *was* shot from his roof. I'll have to talk to him."

I stopped in my tracks, looking across at the Millers' property. "Shouldn't be hard."

"Why's that?"

"He's still awake." I pointed over the sagging fence at his silhouette in the bedroom window.

He stepped away from the curtain, but Sally kept her stare on the house. "We'll be back in a jiffy, Patrick. Go be with Ariana. She's scared. Those expressive eyes." She turned her back on me politely, starting for our house to retrieve her partner.

Ariana and I watched the DVDs again, all three, one after another. The hand in the latex glove *did* look masculine. The cuff of the black sweatshirt had been tucked into the glove so no skin would show, but I freeze-framed forward just to make sure.

"I'm sorry I called the cops without talking to you. You lied to me, but still. I thought you were out of your head and going to do something stupid that would get you shot." Ariana was pacing around the couch, her hands laced on her head. "It's amazing how little it takes to make someone suspicious. A misinterpretation, a white handkerchief, and a few well-placed nudges, right?"

I watched the scoop of tan skin at her neckline. "Is there anyone you can think of . . . ?"

"No. Please. I don't know anyone that interesting."

"I'm serious. Are there any other men who—"

"Who *what*?" Pink crept along her throat into her face. When Ari got flustered, she was usually a half step away from anger.

"Who've taken an interest," I said evenly. "At the showroom, the grocery store, wherever."

"I don't have a *clue*," she said. "He was prying at me about that. Detective Valentine. Who the hell *does* something like this? It's gotta be someone from the studio. Or that asshole Conner." More pacing. A glance at the clock—it was nearly 2:00 A.M. "They're gonna take the DVDs into evidence. We should copy them." She held up a hand to stop me. "I know, I'll handle them with an oven mitt."

While she picked up the disc carefully by the edges, I went upstairs and searched the Internet for Keith Conner. It didn't take long to find a picture that included his hands. He wore a great old Baume & Mercier on his right wrist, so he was likely left-handed. I pulled an image into Photoshop and enlarged his right hand. Was this how celebrity stalkers whiled away their lonesome evenings? Keith's hand looked like most men's, like the hand used to open my back door. But even if he *was* behind this, he would have outsourced the break-in.

Ariana's voice startled me. "You're not gonna believe this." She cradled her silver laptop, open. "Look at this." She tried to play the loaded DVD. Blank. "I dragged the icons to my desktop, but when I went to burn them, the disc drive made this sound"—she demonstrated—"and then I double-clicked on the icons, and they all vanished."

"DVDs don't erase themselves," I said.

Her stare hardened. "Well, these ones do."

I looked at the two other DVDs, in a Ziploc bag. "And you dragged them all to the desktop before burning. So you're saying they're all blank now."

She nodded. "I guess they were designed to erase as soon as someone tried to copy them."

I gritted my teeth, shoved the heels of my hands into my eyes.

The doorbell rang.

I swallowed, trying to moisten my throat. "Ari, let me handle the detectives. Pretend you went to bed." She started to say something, but I cut her off. "Just please trust me on this."

She ejected the last disc, carefully put it in the Ziploc with the others, and handed it to me without a word. Tense, I jogged down the stairs and opened the front door.

Sally said, "Come in?"

"Of course. How 'bout Valentine?"

He was sitting in the passenger seat of the Crown Vic, jotting notes. Sally shrugged. "As I said, he's less social."

We went inside. I said, "Make you a cup of tea or something?"

"You have that chai stuff?"

I zapped two mugs in the microwave and brought

them over. She shook a packet of Sweet'N Low into hers, and then another. She curled her hands around the mug. "You're lonely, Patrick."

"Yeah. You?"

She shrugged—it was something of a tic. "Sure. Single parent. Female detective. It's a lot of time with people who don't talk back. Or do. You know?" She pulled off her plastic-frame glasses, buffed a lens on her shirt. "Don was out of town last night and this morning, when—according to you—the second and third DVDs were shot. He was attending a due-diligence meeting for a mutual fund in Des Moines. Sounds too soul-destroying to make up."

"He doesn't have the imagination to do this."

That same shrug. "I'm not a child psychologist. So I asked him to show me the boarding passes. Plus, he's right-handed." She took a sip. "Maybe the wife was in on it."

"No, she's a sweetheart. Harmless."

"Yeah, I don't see her tottering up on your roof in spikes."

I laid the Ziploc full of discs on the table between us. "I just tried to copy these. They deleted themselves."

"Did they, now?"

"I know what it looks like. Don't start."

Through the steam of her tea, her eyes held steady on me. Yellowish brown, dull, not particularly keen. As deceiving as the rest of her.

"And guess what else?" I asked.

"What else?"

"I'm thinking the only fingerprints on those DVDs will be mine and my wife's. And?" I waved her on.

"And now, all of a sudden, the footage no longer exists." Her fingertips tapped the jewel cases. "Because these are magical self-erasing DVDs."

"Like I said, I know what this looks like. But someone broke in to my house, took my camcorder, my DVDs, videoed me sleeping in my own family room. You and your partner both saw the videos."

"Yes, but we didn't have the opportunity to analyze them, did we?" She offered an affable frown, as if we were two scientists puzzling over the same theorem. "I'll add that it didn't look like the intruder broke in. Looked like he turned a knob that was unlocked and came into your *and your wife's* house. But okay. So let's think about the next question: Why?"

"How do I know?"

"Aren't you a screenwriter or something? Why would someone do this in a movie?"

"To show that they can."

"Or to show you *and your wife* that they can." She matched my frustrated expression. "I don't have the answers. Valentine and I read signs. The signs here all say the same thing: domestic. Now, I don't mean that makes it simple, but we know not to waste a lot of time once a couple closes ranks."

"Here's the part where you tell me there's not much you can do."

"There's not much we can do."

"That I should contact you if anything else out of the ordinary happens."

"You should contact us if anything else out of the ordinary happens."

"I like you, Sally."

"Hey, I like you, too. How 'bout that." She stood, gulped the last of the chai, and shook her head. "Needs real sugar."

She set her mug gently on the counter. Outside, she stopped on the walk, Valentine waiting in the car. "Here's what I'm saying, Patrick. If you wanna dig, we're ready to come back here with a backhoe, compliments of the county. But you gotta make up your mind if you wanna know what we might turn up."

CHAPTER 9

In the family room, I plugged in my camcorder to recharge. A creak on the stairs startled me, but it was Ariana, descending.

"Well, that went just like you predicted," she said. "So there's nothing we can do but wait for the next installment?"

"I don't want to wait," I said, "because we don't know what's coming next."

Ariana tugged at her hair in the back, then realized she was doing it and stopped. Her hands tapped her hips nervously. "They questioned Don. So now he's officially pulled into it. If he tries to talk to me about this, what do I say?"

"I don't like setting rules."

"Implication: You *should* just be able to trust me."

"Ariana. Someone is menacing us. Do you think I give a shit whether you talk to Don?"

She made an exasperated noise and went into the kitchen. As she filled a glass with slow-filtering water from the fridge, I watched her back. The smooth skin of her shoulders, framed by the tank top she slept in.

For a brief stretch there, Ariana and I had been a team again. The familiar closeness, forced to the forefront by crisis. But now the detectives had gone, and there was just us with all the old problems and a handful of new ones.

Ariana sat at the dining table, fingers around her glass, facing away. Her shoulders, hunched, looked frail and bony. Without turning, she said, "In the movies the guy cheats. Before a wedding, whatever. He feels awful, sleeps outside her door, humiliates himself in romantic fashion, and is forgiven. But never the woman. *Never* the woman."

I said, "*Ulysses.*"

"Yeah, but it didn't do box office." She sipped her water, set it down on the table. I walked over, sat across from her. She didn't look up at me. Her lips were trembling. "Why didn't you ever yell?"

"At who?"

"Anyone. Me, him."

"He's not worth it," I said.

"I thought maybe I was."

"You want me to yell?"

"No, but maybe you could figure out some other way to show you give a fuck." She laughed. One bitter note, and then she wiped her nose with the back of her hand. "Look, I make overpriced furniture and sell it to people who mostly don't appreciate it. They gonna carve *that* on my gravestone? I'm thirty-five. Most of my friends are busy with car pools and play dates, and the ones who aren't have developed exercise disorders or stay on vacation. It's a weird age, and I'm not handling it so well. The world closed in on me in a hurry, and my life doesn't have a lot of what I hoped it would. The one thing I have that feels special is you." Her voice cracked. She chewed her lip, trying to recapture the thread of her thoughts. "Is it the end of the world you don't feel that way about me? No. But it still sucks. So when I talked to Keith, and he told me you were with Sasha . . ." She pulled a tissue from her pocket and blew into it heartily. "And then Don came over, and maybe I thought I could still surprise myself, surprise you. To jar us out of whatever shitty place we'd gotten ourselves into. I don't know." She shook her head. "The sex was miserable, if it's any consolation."

"Some." I'd fought every instinct in my body not to ask about what happened, not to torture through the beads one by one—who wore what, who put whose hand where. I was at least smart enough to know that the more I knew, the more I'd want to know, and the worse it would get.

I reached a hand awkwardly toward her on the table. "I neglected you. I get that. Keith hit you when you were vulnerable. When you were primed to believe it. But what I can't get past is that you didn't talk to me first."

"I'd been trying to talk to you for days, Patrick."

"I was barely holding it together. I couldn't cut it. Keith was just my excuse to bail out." I couldn't manage to meet her eye. "The notes—the stupid rewrite notes morning after night." I stopped myself. "I know, you've heard it all already. But I was . . ."

She sensed the change in my tone. "What?"

I looked at my hands. "I made so many compromises and *still* wound up a failure."

She looked at me silently, her dark eyes mournful.

"I never knew that," she said. "That you felt that way."

I said, "So I wasn't there for you. Fine. A marriage should grant you the right to be uselessly self-absorbed for a period, like, say, nine days before your spouse goes jumping in the sack with someone. It's not as if I didn't have opportunities. I was on a movie set, for Christ's sake."

"Yeah, as the *writer*."

I had to laugh.

She bit her lip, tipped her head. Smoothed a hand across the varnish. "Look at this walnut, Patrick. Chocolate brown, open-grained, even-textured. We quartersawed it to pick up a prettier angle on the annular rings. You know how hard it is to get wood this fine? Problems everywhere. Splits. Shakes. Decay. Pitch pockets. Honeycombing. Blue stain from fungi." She knocked it with her knuckles, hard. "But not here. I chose the best."

"But?"

"Give me your hand." She ran my palm slowly across the tabletop. I sensed the faintest bulge toward the center. "Feel that? That's warp. Look overhead."

I did. The heating vent, breathing from the cornice down onto the table.

Her eyes were waiting for mine when I lowered my head. "Seam of stored moisture in the wood, maybe. You can't catch everything."

I said, "I'd never noticed it."

"It catches the light differently, bends the sheen. I see it every time I come down the stairs. And here"—she traced my fingertips across the slight bump of a dark circle—"we varnished over a knot. It was smooth here just three months ago. Having a knot in there's a risk, too, but some defects make it more beautiful. You want uniform, go to IKEA." She took my other hand, too. "You can't see all the flaws. But it's a good goddamned table, Patrick. So why throw it away?"

"I'm still here, aren't I?"

"Technically." She pressed my hands together, like I was praying, except hers were clasped over mine, gentle across my bruised knuckles. As she leaned forward, her dark hair curved to crowd her face. "This isn't good for either of us. Whatever steps we have to take, I'm willing to take them with you. But I'm not doing this anymore. Whatever that means for you, I'll have to find a way to live with."

She shoved out her chair, stretched across the lacquered surface, and kissed me on the forehead. Her footsteps moved up the stairs, and the bedroom door closed quietly.

CHAPTER 10

I had an excess of energy, the kind that tends to overtake me the morning after a wakeful night. Desultory, slightly frantic, edged with desperation. For four dizzy hours, I'd fussed under a twist of blankets on the couch, distracted by stairway creaks, bobbing tree-branch shadows, the dark yard beyond the semi-sheer curtains. Ariana's last words to me had left me with plenty more to gnaw on in my more lucid moments of unsleep. She'd called me out on the inevitable: Stay or leave, but do one properly. Even in those brief spells where I'd drifted off, I'd dreamed of myself lying on the uncomfortable couch, frustrated and unable to sleep. Several times I'd gotten up to peer out the windows and check the yard. Just after 6:00 A.M., when the *L.A. Times* landed, I'd searched it anxiously but found no DVD lurking inside.

Now I positioned my camcorder by the front window of our tiny living room, angling the lens out onto the porch and walk. I'd tucked the tripod behind a potted palm so the camera was lost among the blunt-tipped leaves. The strategically drawn curtains left only the necessary slice of view. Slurping my third cup of coffee, I checked the setup yet again and pressed the green button, recording onto the well-advertised 120-hour digital memory.

Ariana's voice startled me. "Is that what you've been doing down here?"

"I woke you?"

"I was up already, but I sure heard you thunking around." She yawned, finishing it with a feminine roar, then nodded at the hidden camcorder. "Giving them a taste of their own medicine?"

"I hope so."

"I'll call the alarm guys today."

"That doesn't sound like a vote of confidence."

She shrugged.

I went up to my office, where I shuffled my lecture notes into the soft leather briefcase I'd bought to look more professorial. When I came back down, Ariana was leaning against the sink, a desert mariposa behind her ear. Vibrant orange. I contemplated this. The color of lily she wore in her hair gave away her mood. Pink was playful, red angry, and lavender, lavender she saved for when she was feeling particularly in love. So . . . not in a very long time. In fact, for months she hadn't gone with anything but white, her safety color. I'd forgotten which mood orange broadcast, which ceded my advantage.

Ariana shifted her grip on her coffee mug, uneasy under my gaze. I was still focused on that orange bloom. "What?" she asked.

"Be careful today. I'll keep my cell phone on, even during class. Just . . . watch out for anything weird.

People. Anyone approaching your car. Keep the doors locked."

"I will."

I nodded, then nodded again when it was clear neither of us was sure what to say next. Feeling her eyes on my back, I headed out to the garage and knuckled the button. The door shakily rose. I dropped my briefcase through the open passenger window and leaned over, my hands on the sill. Her words from last night returned to me—*I'm not doing this anymore.*

In a sealed clear plastic bin on one of the overburdened shelves, I could make out Ariana's wedding dress through its transparent wrapping. Like her, modern with traditional flourishes. Again came the seesaw tilt, betrayal and pain, anger and grief. That goddamn in-good-times-and-in-bad gown, preserved for a future we might not have.

I walked outside, past the trash cans, and peered in the kitchen window. Ari sat in her usual spot on the arm of the couch, clutching her stomach as if to quell an ache. Mug resting on her knee. She wasn't crying, though; today her face expressed only disillusionment. She plucked the flower from her hair and twirled it, staring into the orange folds as if trying to read the future. Why did I feel let down, pushed away? Did I *want* her to cry every morning? To prove what? That she was still hurting as much as I was? I hadn't known it, not consciously, and revealed to me, it felt petty and foolish.

Given the DVDs, I didn't want to startle her if she looked up. Just as I was about to step back, she crossed to the kitchen door. Contemplated it. Then she unlocked the dead bolt and set it again, firmly.

I stood there a moment after she'd disappeared upstairs.

CHAPTER 11

The Formosa Cafe was a Hollywood haunt long before Guy Pearce's Ed Exley mistook Lana Turner for a hooker there in *L.A. Confidential.* At the bar beneath black-and-whites of Brando, Dean, and Sinatra, I gulped a scotch, gathering my courage. At least I had fortifying company. The throw of buildings that composed Summit Pictures loomed in the west-facing windows, as did a tall-wall ad for *They're Watching*— Keith Conner's overblown face adhered to the side of the executive building. From Bogart to Conner with a half turn of the head. Except Bogart was an eight-by-ten and Conner a high-rise. Poetic injustice.

The six-story ad dwarfed the passing cars. They'd redone it—I could tell from the missing square of banner at the bottom that revealed the old version beneath. Keith squinting in inflated close-up, ready to take danger head-on, had replaced the image of the hazy figure descending into the subway. Principal photography on the movie had barely finished, and a trailer hadn't even been cut yet, but the early buzz had jumped Keith to the next tier, made him worthy of an ad campaign built around his face. He was now an A-lister in waiting. Which was partially my fault.

The barkeep paused from topping off the mixers to collect my glass. Recognizing me as a former regular, he'd waved me in, though they'd yet to set up for lunch. He didn't ask if I wanted another.

Using my cell, I called the Summit switchboard. "Yes, can I please have Jerry in Security?"

Jerry and I had become friends when I was at the studio every day during preproduction. We'd met in the commissary and before long were having lunch together a few times a week. Of course, we hadn't spoken since things went sideways.

Each ring sounded like a countdown. Finally he answered. My voice was dry when I said, "Hey, Jerry, it's Patrick."

"Whoa," he said. "Patrick. I can't talk to you. You may have noticed that you're in the middle of a lawsuit with my employer."

"I know, I know. Listen, I just want to ask you something. I'm across the street at Formosa. Can you give me two minutes?"

His voice lowered. "Just being *seen* with you could land me knee-deep."

"It's not about the lawsuit."

He didn't respond right away, and I didn't push it. Eventually he blew out a breath. "It'd better not be. Two minutes."

He hung up and I waited, my heart pounding. After a time he scampered in, giving a nervous glance around the empty restaurant. He slid onto the stool next to me with no greeting, none of the gruff conviviality cultivated by his stint in the marines.

"The only reason I'm here is because we both know

you caught the raw end," Jerry said. "Keith is a prick and a liar. He tangled us all up. Be honest with you, I can't wait to get out of this racket." An irritated gesture at the window and studio lot beyond. "Get back to real security. An *honest* dishonest living."

"I heard you guys just signed Keith for two more."

"Yeah, but the idiot's doing some bullshit environmental documentary next. Mickelson tried to get him to wait until he had another hit under his belt, but it had to be *now*." He smirked. "I guess Mickelson told him the environment'll still be up shit creek in two years. I don't think that won him over." His broad shoulders lifted, then fell. "But he's with us after that." He reached for my untouched glass of ice water and took a long sip. Peeked at his watch. "So . . . ?"

"Someone's been messing with me. Videotaping me. Came into my house at night, even. I was thinking it might be someone from the studio going off the tracks. I know you're overseeing the investigative files. Anyone you think has taken an extracurricular interest?"

"No, man." The relief was audible. "Look, this lawsuit's a mess, but it's not anything they don't deal with all the time. It's business."

"*This* business at least," I said. His stare stayed level. Uninterested. "So as far as you know," I asked, "no one here seems bent out of shape enough to want to make it personal?"

"As far as I know. And I know pretty far, Patrick. I monitor e-mails, sweep for bugs, interface with Legal, all that shit. You know how this type loves security. I'm the in-house tough guy and the good daddy all in one. Someone chips a nail, they call me bawling. A valet's gaze lingers on the wrong set of legs, I have to go have a conversation. That kind of bullshit. It's a complicated world now. But one thing's still like the old days—if they wanted you ruffled, I'd be the guy they'd call."

I wasn't sure what I expected. Certainly Jerry wasn't going to come clean if the studio *was* running a harassment campaign. But I looked him in the eye and I believed him. Whatever was coming down on me, it wasn't studio business.

He glanced nervously at the door. "Anything else?"

"Can you tell me Keith Conner's new address?"

"What do you think?" he said. I held up my hands. He asked, "You really believe Keith Conner would sneak into your house?"

"Not personally, but he's got plenty of money and underlings and what looks like a vindictive streak. I need to talk to him."

"I think that's the *only* thing his lawyers, your lawyers, and our lawyers all agree on. You don't talk to him. Ever." He shoved back from the bar and walked out.

CHAPTER 12

"Is Keith Conner as hot in person?" Front row, blond, sorority sweatshirt. Shanna or Shawna.

"He is fairly handsome," I said, pacing in front of the class, chewing gum to cover that nerve-settling morning scotch. Some tittering up and down the rows of stadium seating. Introduction to Screenwriting—you couldn't cross city limits without enrolling. "Now, are there any questions about *screenwriting*?"

I glanced around. Several of the kids had digital camcorders on their writing tablets and atop their backpacks. Even more students typed notes on laptops equipped with embedded cameras. A guy in the middle used his phone to snap a picture of his buddy next to him. I tore my attention away from the myriad cameras and found a raised hand. "Yes, Diondre."

His question was something about talent versus hard work.

I'd been distracted all day, finding myself searching out hidden meaning in student remarks. During the break I'd gone through past assignments to note how many fails I'd handed out. Only seven. None of the students had seemed to take the grade personally. Plus, anyone who was doing poorly was still well within the deadline to drop the class, which had to cut the odds further that my stalker was an aggrieved student.

I realized I hadn't been paying attention to what Diondre was saying. "You know what, since our hour and a half's up, why don't you stick around and we can get into that?" I made the little half-wave to dismiss class. You'd think it was an air-raid warning the way they dispersed.

Diondre lingered behind, clearly upset. He was one of my favorite students, a talkative kid from East L.A. who usually wore baggy Clippers shorts, a do-rag that even I knew to be dated, and a crooked smile that inspired immediate trust.

"You okay?"

A faint nod. "My mama said I'll never make it, that I ain't no *filmmaker.* She said I'd just as soon be a Chinese acrobat. You think that's true?"

"I don't know," I said. "I don't teach Chinese acrobatics."

"I'm serious. Man, you know where I'm from. I'm the first person in my family to finish high school, let a-*lone* go to college. All my relatives are up on my shit for studying film. If this is a waste of time, I gotta give it up."

What could I say? That despite fortune cookies and inspirational posters, dreams aren't sufficient? That you can dig down and do your best but in real life that's still not always good enough?

"Look," I said, "a lot of this comes down to hard work and luck. You keep at it and keep at it and hope you catch a break."

"Is that how you made it?"

"I didn't make it. That's why I'm here."

"What do you mean? You done writing movies?" He looked shattered.

"For now. And that's okay. If there's one piece of advice I'd offer, and you shouldn't listen to it anyway, it's to be sure this is what you want. Because if you're pursuing this for the wrong reasons, you might get there and realize it's not what you thought it was."

His face was pensive, empathetic. Pursing his lips, he nodded slowly, took a few backward steps toward the door.

"Listen, Diondre . . . I've been receiving some weird threats."

"Threats?"

"Or warnings, maybe. Do you know of any students who'd want to mess with me?"

He feigned indignation. "And you askin' *me* 'cuz I'm black and from Lincoln Heights?"

"Of course." I held his stare until we both laughed. "I'm asking you because you're good at reading people."

"I dunno. Most of the students are fine with you, from what I've heard. You don't grade too hard." He held up both hands. "No offense."

"None taken."

"Oh." He snapped his fingers. "I'd watch out for that little Filipino kid. What's his name? Smoke-a-bong?"

"Paeng Bugayong?" A small, quiet kid who sat in the back row, kept his head down, and sketched. Figuring him for shy, I'd called on him once to draw him out, and he'd taken an aggressively long time before finally offering a one-word response.

"Yeah, that one. You seen that kid's drawings? All fucked-up beheadings and dragons and shit. We joke he gonna go V Tech up in here, you feel me?"

"V Tech?"

"Virginia Tech." Diondre made a pistol of his hand and shot it around the empty chairs.

"In my day," I said with a grimace, "we called it 'postal.'"

"Goddamn it," Julianne said. "Someone broke the swing-out thing."

"INCONSIDERATENESS ABOUNDS. AND THE FATE OF MR. COFFEE HANGS IN THE BALANCE."

"Knock that shit off, Marcello. I'm getting a no-caffeine headache."

He looked to me for support. "One day they can't get enough, the next you're old news."

"Town without pity," I drawled.

We had the faculty lounge to ourselves, as usual. Marcello was kicking back on the fuzzy plaid couch, thumbing through *The Hollywood Reporter,* and I was rereading the few assignments Paeng Bugayong *had* handed in, mini-scripts for shorts he could shoot later in a production class. So far he had a castrating wizard who targeted jocks, a serial vandal who kidnapped Baby Jesuses from Christmas nativity scenes, and a girl who had resorted to cutting because she was so misunderstood by her parents. Standard disaffected adolescent fare, half goth, half emo, and all seemingly harmless enough.

When I'd asked the department assistant to pull Bugayong's student file for me earlier, bumbling out some pretext about wanting to make sure he wasn't recycling skipped-attendance excuses, she'd held eye contact a beat too long. My nervous grin had frozen on my face even after she said she would put in a request to Central Records.

"Either of you teach a kid named Bugayong?" I asked.

"Odd name," Marcello said. "On second thought, that's probably like John Doe for Korean people."

"Filipino," I said.

Julianne banged the coffeemaker with the heel of her hand. It appeared unmoved. "Little weird kid, looks like he's always sucking a lemon?"

Marcello asked, "So Pang Booboohead is your lead stalking suspect?" He was starting to take an interest in the updates. Or didn't like being left out. "Is his writing troubling or something?"

Julianne said to me, "If someone read *your* scripts, they'd think you were paranoid."

"Good thing no one reads them, then." Marcello, ever supportive.

Julianne came over, stirring coffee into hot water. Not freeze-dried instant, but ground. She said, "I know," took a sip, then retreated and dumped it into the sink.

"A student of mine told me he's a little loose around the hinges," I said.

"And they're such good judges of character at this age," Marcello said.

"Bugayong's a wuss," Julianne said. "I'll bet you a new coffeemaker that he pees sitting down."

I tested one of the scabs on my knuckles. "I know. It's not him. He's got the imagination for it. I doubt he has the nerve."

"And your neighbor has the balls but not the imagination," Marcello said. "So who's got both?"

Simultaneously, Julianne and I said, "Keith Conner."

Her zeroing in on the same name unsettled me. Not that any of the prospects were good ones, but given Keith's resources, his targeting me was a pretty chilling scenario to contemplate.

Julianne sank into a chair, picked at her flaking black nail polish. "You never really think about it," she said. "How thin the line is that separates everyday resentments from obsession."

"The stalker's obsession or mine?" I headed for the door. I wasn't sure what I hoped to accomplish, but if my scuttled career had taught me anything, it was that a protagonist has to be active. I wasn't gonna sit around and wait for the next escalation—the intruder, inside my house, with a camcorder *and* a claw hammer.

From behind, I heard, "ON FEBRUARY NINTH, PATRICK DAVIS HAS. *NOWHERE*. LEFT. TO HIDE."

I said, "Today's the tenth, Marcello."

"Oh." He frowned. "ON FEBRUARY TENTH—"

I closed the door behind me.

CHAPTER 13

I found Punch Carlson in a lawn chair in front of his ramshackle house, staring at nothing, his bare feet up on a cooler. A scattering of Michelob empties lay crushed next to him, within ape-swing of his arm. Punch, a retired cop, worked as a consultant on movie sets, showing actors how to carry guns so they didn't look too stupid. We'd met several years ago when I was doing research for a script I never sold, and we stayed in touch over the occasional beer.

Bathed in the glow of the guttering porch light, he took no notice as I approached. That blank gaze, fixed on the house, held an element of defeat. It occurred to me that maybe he dreaded being inside. Or perhaps I was just projecting my feelings of late for my own house.

"Patrick Davis," he said, though I couldn't tell how he knew it was me. He was slurring, but that didn't stop him from cracking a fresh brew. "Want one?"

I noticed the script in his lap, folded back around the brads. "Thanks."

I caught the can before it collided with my fore-head. He kicked the cooler over at me. I sat and took a sip. It was good as only bad beer can be. Punch lived four blocks from a seedy stretch of Playa del Rey beachfront, and the salt air burned my eyes a little. A plastic flamingo, faded from the sun, stood at a drunken, one-legged tilt. A few lawn gnomes sported Dada mustaches.

"What brings you to Camelot?" he asked.

I laid it out for him, starting with the first DVD showing up unannounced in yesterday's morning paper.

"Sounds like some bullshit," he said. "Leave it alone."

"Someone's laying the groundwork for something, Punch. The guy went inside my house."

"If he was gonna hurt you, he would've already. Sounds like an elaborate crank call to me. Someone trying to get a rise out of you." He looked at me pointedly.

"Okay. So it worked. But I want to know what it's about."

"Leave it alone. The more attention you pay to it, the more it'll turn into." He waved at me. "If you remove a woodpecker's beak, it'll pound itself to death. It doesn't know, right? And it keeps bashing its little woodpecker face against the tree. So—"

"Is that true?"

He paused. "Who gives a shit? It's a metaphor— ever hear a' them?" He frowned, took another sip. "Anyways"—he struggled to recapture his momentum—"you're like that woodpecker."

"A powerful image," I concurred.

He took a healthy swig, wiped the dribble from his stubbled chin. "So where do *I* come in on this little boondoggle?"

"I want to talk to Keith Conner. You know, given our whole fiasco, he's my top contender. But he's not listed. Obviously."

"Try Star Maps."

"It still shows his Outpost address," I said. "He's in the bird streets now, above Sunset Plaza."

He flipped halfheartedly through the script. It seemed he'd zoned out.

"What do you say?" I pressed. "You think you could dig up an address for me? And nose around on him a little?"

"Police work?" He raised the script, let it fall back into his lap. "If I was any good, you think I'd be doing this shit?"

"C'mon. You always know the right moves, who to talk to to get something done. All that LAPD-brotherhood stuff."

"Going official routes never got anything done, my friend. You do it all *unofficially.* Call in a favor here, return another there. Especially when you're shooting a movie. You need a street permit, some asshole needs to rent the SWAT chopper, whatever. You're on a deadline." He smirked. "Not like, say, when you're trying to catch a serial rapist."

I could read his tone, so I said, "And?"

"A tired dog like me, I only got so many favors. I gotta spend 'em for rent."

I stood, drained the beer, dropped it on the lawn beside the others. "Okay, thanks anyway, Punch."

I went back to my car. When I closed the door, he was at the window. "When did you start givin' up easy?" He jerked his head toward the house.

I got back out and followed him across the front yard and into the kitchen. Dirty dishes, a dripping faucet, and a trash can overstuffed with bent pizza boxes. A strip-club magnet pinned a child's drawing to the fridge. A crayon depiction, nearly desperate in its cheer, portrayed a family of three, all stick figures, big heads, and oversize smiles. The requisite sun in the corner seemed the single spot of color in the dingy room. I couldn't blame Punch for having retreated to the front lawn.

I looked for somewhere to sit, but the sole chair was piled with old newspapers. Punch poked around for a while before producing a pen. He tugged the drawing off the fridge, the magnet popping off and rolling beneath the table. "You said he's on the bird streets?" he asked.

"Blue Jay or Oriole, maybe."

"An asshole like Conner probably put title of his new house in the name of a living trust or whatever to make him harder to track down. But someone always fucks up. DirecTV or DMV registration or something goes in his name. Wait for me outside."

I went out and sat in his lawn chair, wondering what he thought about when he contemplated the same view. Finally he emerged.

With great ceremony he handed me the crayon drawing, an address now scrawled on the reverse. He snickered. "Nice part of town your boy took up in." He waved me out of his chair. "I'll ask around a bit about Conner, see if anything comes back."

Something about actually having the address made me uneasy. As a movie star, Keith Conner seemed like fair game, but of course that was bullshit. Digging into his life was invasive. And the past two days had retaught me the meaning of the word. My actions—and my motives—gave me sudden pause. But I folded the paper into my pocket anyway. "Thanks, Punch."

He waved me off.

I took a few steps to the car, then turned. "Why'd you help me out? I mean, with everything you were saying about calling in favors?"

He rubbed his eyes, hard, digging with his thumb and forefinger. When he looked up, they were more bloodshot than before. "When I had the kid in the minute and a half before I fucked it all up and Judy lowered the boom on custody, that time he got jammed up in school? You helped him. That book report."

"It was nothing."

"Not to him it wasn't." He trudged back to his lawn chair.

When I pulled out, he was just sitting there motionless, watching the facade of his house.

My apprehension grew on my way home, rising with the altitude as I crawled up Roscomare in evening traffic. All the lights were off at the Millers'. I pulled in to the garage next to Ari's white pickup, then went back and checked the mailbox—lots of bills, but no DVD.

I let go a breath I hadn't known I'd been holding. Don and Martinique were minding their own business, our mailbox was clear, and all was momentarily right with the world.

When I opened the front door, an alarm screeched through the house. I started, dropping my briefcase, papers sliding out across the floor. A door shoved open upstairs, and a moment later Ariana thumped down the stairs, wielding a badminton racket. Taking note of me, she exhaled, then jabbed at the keypad by the banister. The alarm silenced.

I said, "Lawn party?"

"It was the first thing I could grab in the closet."

"There's a baseball bat in the corner. A tennis racket. But *badminton*? What were you gonna do, pelt the intruder with birdies?"

"Yeah, and then he'd slip on your papers."

We took a moment to smirk at our feeble reactions.

"The new code is 27093," she said. "The new keys are in the drawer."

Tonight, if I wanted to check the property, I'd have to remember to turn off the alarm before going outside. We stood there looking at each other, me with papers across my shoes, her with a badminton racket at her side. Suddenly awkward.

"Okay," I said cautiously. Her implicit ultimatum from last night hung between us, clogging the air. I knew I had to say something, but I just couldn't land on it. "Well, good night," I offered lamely.

"Good night."

We regarded each other some more, not sure what to do. In a way the strained politeness was even worse than the standoff atmosphere that we'd been inhabiting these past months.

Defeated, Ari forced a smile. It trembled at the edges. "Want me to leave you the racket?"

"Given the size of his hands, I think it would just aggravate him."

She paused by the banister and punched in the alarm code to rearm the system. A moment later, through the open bedroom door, I could hear rerun-reliable Bob Newhart.

Even after the door closed, I stood at the bottom of the dark stairs, looking up.

CHAPTER 14

I slept fitfully on the couch again, rising for good when the morning light once more accented the futility of semi-sheer curtains. Swiftly, I got up and raced to the front of the house, anxious to see if another DVD had been folded into our morning paper. I yanked the door open, forgetting about the alarm until I heard the blare of it in my skull. Racing back to the pad, I turned it off. Ariana was at the top of the stairs, hand pressed to her chest, breathing hard.

"Sorry. Just me. I was checking outside for . . ."

"Is there one?"

"I don't know. Hang on." The front door was still open. I jogged across to retrieve the newspaper and searched it, dropping rumpled sections all over the foyer. "No."

"Okay," she said. "Okay. Maybe this whole thing'll just blow over." She reached out, knocked drywall superstitiously.

I had my doubts, but so did she. No need to say it.

We moved through the morning routine on autopilot, tamping down panic, doing our best not to pause and acknowledge the threat hanging over us. Shower, coffee, brief polite exchanges, mariposa from the greenhouse. Orange again. I wondered what to make of that.

After checking my pseudo-security footage of the porch and walk, then repositioning the camcorder in the lady palm, I hurried out, eager to keep moving. Once again I stood in the garage, the slanted sheet of sunlight through the open door capturing the trunk of my car, the wedding dress peering out at me through the clear side of the plastic bin. For the first morning in recent memory, I didn't want to sneak around to watch my wife. It took me a moment to figure out I was afraid. Afraid that she'd be crying, and maybe more afraid that she wouldn't.

I climbed into the Camry, reversed out into the driveway. Cars whizzed behind me, the morning commute well under way. On bad days it could take me five minutes to back out onto Roscomare. I tapped the wheel impatiently; I had a full schedule of classes in front of me. And the piece of paper on the passenger seat had Keith Conner's address scrawled on it in Punch's hand.

Movement next door caught my attention. Don strolling to his driveway-parked Range Rover, talking into a Bluetooth earpiece. He was focused on his conversation, gesturing, as if that would help drive home his point. A moment later Martinique came running after him with his forgotten laptop carrier. She wore workout clothes, spandex to show off the new body. It was practically her uniform; the woman worked out four hours a day. Don paused to take the laptop. She leaned forward to kiss him good-bye, but he'd already turned to climb into his truck. He pulled out, taking advantage of a break in traffic I'd been too distracted to notice. Martinique stood perfectly still in the driveway, not looking after him, not heading back to the house. Her face was surgery smooth, expressionless. Her eyes moved, just slightly, focusing on me, and I could tell that she knew I'd watched what had just transpired. She lowered her head and walked briskly inside.

I sat for a long time, the beat-up dashboard looking back at me. My eyes pulled again to the paper in the passenger seat with the address. I flipped it over so Punch's kid's crayon drawing was faceup. A big, sloppy sun, stick figures holding hands. A heartbreaking picture, primitive and wistful.

I put the car in park, climbed out. When I came in, Ariana was sitting where she always sat when I left, on the arm of the couch. She looked surprised.

I said, "I have spent six weeks trying to find any way not to be in love with you."

Her mouth came slightly ajar. She lifted a shaking hand, set her mug down on the coffee table. "Any luck?"

"None. I'm fucked."

We faced each other across the length of the room. I felt something budge in my chest, emotion shifting, the logjam starting to break up.

She swallowed hard, looked away. Her mouth was quivering like it wanted to smile and cry at the same time. "So where's that leave us?" she asked.

"Together."

She smiled, then her mouth bent down, and then she wiped her cheeks and looked away again. We nodded at each other, almost shyly, and I withdrew back through the door to the garage.

CHAPTER 15

I brought Julianne a Starbucks from across the street, which I held before me like a sacrificial offering as I entered the faculty lounge. She and Marcello sat facing each other, but at different tables to maintain the pretense that they were working.

She regarded me warily. "What do you want?"

"Cover my afternoon classes."

"I can't. I don't know how to write a screenplay."

"Right. You're the only person in Greater Los Angeles who actually knows she doesn't know how to write a screenplay. You're already overqualified."

"Why can't *you* teach?" Julianne said.

"I have to look into some things."

"You're gonna have to do better than that."

"I'm going to talk to Keith."

"Conner? At home? You have his address?" She clasped her hands with excitement, a girlish gesture that looked about as natural as a Band-Aid on Clint Eastwood.

"Not you, too," I said.

"He is sort of dishy," Marcello offered.

"Perfidy everywhere."

"Why don't you just go see him after work?" Julianne said.

"I have to get right home."

"Home?" she said. "*Home?* To your beautiful wife?"

"To my beautiful wife."

Marcello, in monotone: "Halle-fuckin'-lujah."

"That's all I get?"

"ON FEBRUARY"—Marcello checked his watch—"*ELEVENTH,* PATRICK DAVIS DISCOVERS THAT THE MOST IMPORTANT JOURNEY . . . IS THE ONE THAT TAKES YOU HOME."

"That's more like it." I waved the Starbucks cup in Julianne's direction, letting her attack-dog nose pick up the scent.

She eyed the cup. "Gingerbread latte?"

I said, "Peppermint"—she sagged a little with desire—"*mocha.*" Her head drooped wantonly. I walked over and extended the cup. She took it.

I heard her slurping contentedly as I walked out. Classes were in session, the halls empty. My footsteps seemed unnaturally loud without bodies there to absorb the echoes. As I went by each classroom, the voice of the teacher inside rose and fell like the whine of a passing car. Despite the full classrooms all around, or perhaps because of them, the preposterously long hall felt desolate.

There was a clap like a gunshot, and I jumped, my files spilling all over the floor. Wheeling around in a panic, I saw that the noise had been nothing more than a kid dropping his binder, which had struck the tile flat on its side. I mock-grabbed my chest and said, too loudly, "You scared me."

I'd intended it lightly, but it had come out angry.

The student, crouched over his binder, glanced up lethargically. "Relax, dude."

His tone got under my skin. I said, "Hold on to your stuff better, *dude.*"

Two girls paused in the intersecting hall, rubber-necking, then scurried away when I glanced at them. A few students had collected at the far end also, by the stairwell. I was breathing hard from the scare, still, and from my reaction now. I knew I was handling this poorly, but my blood was up and I couldn't find my composure.

The kid nodded at my spilled papers. "You, too"—he turned to walk away, coughing into a fist to mask his last word—*"asshole."*

"What the *hell* did you just say to me?" My words rang down the corridor.

A teacher I vaguely recognized stuck her head through the doorway of the nearest classroom. Lines of disapproval notched her forehead between her eyebrows. I stared her back into her classroom, and when I refocused, the offending student had vanished into the stairwell. The others milled and gestured.

Embarrassed, I gathered my papers swiftly and left.

CHAPTER 16

Vast iron gates greeted me a mere two steps from the curb. A ten-foot stone wall ran the length of the property line. The only point of access was a call box with a button, mounted on a pillar beside the gate.

Though it was three o'clock—and February—the cold had given way to a hot snap, the sun harsh off the concrete. I was supposed to be in class discussing dialogue, not chasing down movie-star litigants.

Before I could push the call button, a screech jerked me around—a door rolling back on a beat-up white van at the opposite curb. The clicking of a high-speed lens issued from the dark interior. I froze, nailed to the pavement. Leading with a giant camera, a man emerged and walked deliberately toward me, snapping pictures as he came. He wore a black zipped hoodie pulled up so the camera blocked out his face; there was just a lens protruding from the hood like a wolf snout. I could see the dark amoeba of my reflection in the curved glass. My thoughts revved as he neared, but I was caught off guard, my reaction lagging.

Just when I'd balled my hand into a fist, the giant zoom lens lowered to reveal a sallow face. "Oh," he said, disappointed. "You're not anybody."

He'd mistaken my immobilization for apathy. "How'd you know?"

"Because you don't give a shit if I take your picture."

I took in his scraggly appearance, the multipocketed khaki shorts weighed down with gear, and finally put it together. "*National Enquirer*?" I asked.

"Freelance. Paparazzi market's gotten tough. Have to sell where you can."

"Conner's a big catch now, is he?"

"His price has gone up. Hype over the upcoming movie, you know, and the paternity suit."

"I hadn't heard."

"Some club skank. She threw up on Nicky Hilton, made her stock rise."

"Ah. Got herself a media profile."

"They're paying twenty grand for a clear shot of Conner doing something embarrassing. Nothing like a sleaze-success cocktail to stoke a bidding war."

"Cocktails that stoke. I could use one."

He looked at me conspiratorially. "You a friend a' his?"

"Can't stand him, actually."

"Yeah, he's a dickhead. Kneed me in the nuts outside Dan Tana's. Lawsuit pending."

"Good luck with that."

"Gotta get them to hit you, not the other way around." He eyed me knowingly. "He'll settle."

I hit the button. Asian chimes. The crackle of static told me the line had gone live, though no one said anything. I leaned toward the speaker. "It's Patrick Davis. Please tell Keith I need to talk to him."

The guy said, "*That*'s your game plan for getting inside?"

The gates buzzed. I slipped through. He tried to follow, but I stood in the gap. "Sorry. You need your own game plan."

He shrugged. Then he flicked an ivory card from his wallet: *Joe Vente*. Below, a phone number. That was it.

I tilted it back at him. "Spartan."

"Call me if you want to sell out Conner sometime."

"Will do." I pulled the gate shut, making sure the lock clicked.

The Spanish Colonial Revival was spread out with no regard for the price of L.A. real estate. To my left, the row of garage doors was raised, presumably to vent the heat. Revealed inside were two electric coupes, plugged in, three hybrids, and various makes of alternative-fuel cars. A private fleet for conservation; the more you spend, the more you save. The front door, sized for a T-Rex, wobbled open. A waif, made waifier by the giant doorway, waited for me, holding a clipboard. She had impossibly pale skin, a neck that looked like she'd stretched with tribal rings, and a model's expression of perennial boredom.

"Mr. Conner is out back. Follow me, please."

She led me across a house-size foyer and through a sitting room and a set of double doors open to the expansive backyard. Stopping at the threshold, she waved me on. Maybe she'd ignite in direct sunlight.

Keith bobbed on a yellow inner tube in the middle of the pool, a black-bottomed monstrosity interrupted by a confusion of waterfalls, fountains, and palm trees sprouting from island planters. He said, "Hi, asshat," and started paddling in. Then he shouted past me, "Bree, the pool bar's out of flaxseed chips. Think you can get them restocked?"

The waif jotted a note on her clipboard and disappeared.

Two rottweilers frolicked on the far lawn, all fangs and cords of saliva. Knotted ropes—of course—abounded. To my right, a woman reclined on a teak deck chair, filling out a yellow one-piece and reading a magazine. Her blond hair, turned almost white by the sun, tumbled down around her face in a Veronica Lake peekaboo. She looked far too refined for the company, and too old—she was at least thirty.

Keith collapsed onto the chair next to her and lit up, of all things, a clove cigarette. I hadn't seen one since Kajagoogoo clogged the airwaves.

"Meet Trista Koan, my lifestyle coach." Keith set a hand on her smooth thigh.

She unceremoniously removed it. "I know. The name's a laffer. My parents were hippies and shouldn't be held accountable."

"What's a lifestyle coach *do,* exactly?" I asked.

"We're working on reducing Keith's carbon footprint."

"I'm gonna save the whales, dawg," Keith said. His teeth appeared seamless; the sun off them was squint-inducing.

My expression made clear I was missing the connection.

"L.A. is all about environmentalism, right?" he said on the inhale.

"And hair restoration."

"So we gotta get people thinking that way *every-where.*" Inspired, he swept his arm to indicate, presumably, the world beyond the park-size backyard. The grand gesture was undercut by the jet trail of clove smoke left behind. "It's about constant awareness. I was all into the electric-car thing first, right? Even ordered a Tesla Roadster. Clooney ordered one, too. They inscribe your name on the sill—"

"But the problem is . . ." Trista said, keeping him on track.

"The problem is, electric cars still plug in to the grid and suck energy. So then I bought some hybrids. But they still use gas. So I switched to"—a glance to Trista—"what're they called?"

"Flex-fuel vehicles."

"Why not take a bus?" I thought it was pretty funny, but neither he nor Trista laughed. I said, "Whales, Keith. This started with whales."

"Right. They're using this high-intensity sonar, it's like three hundred decibels—"

"Two thirty-five," Trista corrected.

"You know how many times louder that is than the level that'll hurt humans? *Ten.*"

"Four point three," Trista said, with faintly disguised irritation. I was beginning to understand her role better.

"That's as loud as a rocket blasting off"—he paused to look at Trista, but evidently he'd gotten this one right—"so it's no wonder whales are beaching themselves. Bleeding out their ears, around their brains. The sonar also gives them, like, air in their bloodstreams—"

"Emboli," I said, figuring Trista might need a break.

"—so imagine how much other sea life is killed we don't even *know* about." He was waiting for my reaction with an almost sweet eagerness.

"The mind boggles."

"Yeah, well," he said, as if that were something to say. "So I'm a dumb-ass actor. I'm twenty-six, and I make more money in a week than my dad made his whole miserable working life. It's a miracle, and I know I don't deserve it, because no one does. So what? I can still tune in, make a difference. And this movie's really important to me. A passion project." He looked to his life coach for approval, which Trista withheld.

He'd leapfrogged our animosities, momentarily, for a pitch and some pious confabulation. He was using me to work out his new material, the green-friendly repackaging of Keith Conner, which would give him the edge on the red carpet, where it really mattered. But now playacting was over and it was time to get down to business. Sensing this, Keith held out his arms. "So what the hell are you doing here, Davis? Aren't we suing each other?" He flashed his camera-ready smile. "How's that going, by the way?"

"I'm here to take possession of the house."

Trista didn't look up, but she touched a fist to her lips. Keith smirked and beckoned for me to talk.

"I have something of yours." That got his attention. I removed a DVD, a matching one from my office, and held it up.

"What is it?"

"It looks like a disc, Keith," Trista said.

I liked her as much as I liked looking at her.

"Yeah, but what's on it?" he asked.

"I don't know," I said. "Didn't you have someone leave it for me?"

"Me send you a DVD? Davis, I haven't *thought* of you since you got kicked off my movie." He gestured around, appealing to an invisible supporting cast. "They said you were a little nutty, man, but hell." His stare hardened. "What's on it? Is this some bullshit from that paparazzi ass-suck who's stalking me? You here to fucking *extort* me?"

Maybe he was a better actor than I gave him credit for. "No." I flipped the case to him. "It's blank."

Trista was finally interested enough to set the magazine down on her tan knees.

Keith was getting worked up. "What'd the delivery guy say?"

I rolled with it. "That he was told to bring it by, since you were shooting pickups in New York."

"No, I've been right fucking here, cranking preproduction on *The Deep End*. It's a race against time, man."

I said, "*The Deep End*?"

"I know," Trista said. "Keith's manager's title. We had to agree to it before Keith came on board and got us the green light."

I said, "Producer–lifestyle coach? That's an unusual hyphenate, even for this area code."

Keith said, "She's hooked in with the environmental group behind the production company. She knows *everything* about this stuff, so they flew her in as a, you know . . . resource."

The picture resolved, their relationship finally becoming clear to me. Trista's job was a new version of my old job. Monitor Keith so he didn't get caught looking too hypocritical or saying anything too stupid. I'd rather push a boulder uphill in Hades, but maybe that's why I was teaching screenwriting in the Valley and Trista was reading glossy magazines next to an Olympic-size tiki pool.

Keith tossed the jewel case back over, giving me a nice clean set of prints. I wanted them on record in case he vanished behind locked mansion doors or hopped a carbon-free jet to Ibiza.

"I wouldn't send you shit." He leaned forward. "Not after you assaulted me."

For the thousandth time, I replayed what I'd reconstructed of the phone conversation between him and Ariana. I pictured the words going in, straight to the pit of her gut. Everything that had followed. Until I lowered my guard and took a step back, I didn't realize how badly I'd wanted him to go for me so I could knock in those shiny teeth. I wanted it all to be his fault.

I slid the DVD case into my back pocket, careful not to smudge it too much with my own fingerprints. "Don't get worked up, Keith. I'd hate to see you lose another fight with a countertop."

He nodded at the double doors behind me, where Bree had materialized, a clipboard-wielding apparition. "She'll see you out."

CHAPTER 17

An officer accompanied me up to the second floor, where Sally Richards sat at a desk, intently focused on her computer screen. I crossed and set a Costco box of Sweet'N Low beside a picture of her holding a toddler.

She glanced over at my offering and bobbed her head, amused. "Great. That'll get me through lunch tomorrow."

"This a bad time?"

"Sorta." She nodded at the monitor. "A Japanese guy pulling a live snake through his nostril on You-Tube." She shoved back and folded her arms. "A new disc show up on your doorstep?"

"No. Did you manage to retrieve anything off the old ones?"

"Totally wiped. Though our tech-head could tell there'd been something burned on them once. He said the data was totally obliterated by some self-devouring software program. He's never seen anything like it."

I chewed on that dread-inducing tidbit a moment. "Any prints?"

"Just yours. Your wife's. You're in the database for

background checks for community service you guys did in college?"

I nodded.

She continued, "And the discs have some marks consistent with latex gloves. In other words, fucking smudges."

I handed her the DVD case from my back pocket. "This has Keith Conner's fingerprints on it."

"Wonder what you could get for it on eBay."

"I was hoping you'd pulled a partial and we could use this for a match."

"A *partial*? Easy there, Kojak."

I pressed on: "Even if Keith had someone else do the drop or break-in, I figured he might have touched the disc at some point. He's not the brightest bulb on the string."

"You don't say." She followed my gaze to the picture of her with the toddler. "Artificial insemination, since you asked. Miracle of life, my ass. The nausea alone." She whistled. "If I had it to do over again, I would've adopted from China like any self-respecting daughter of Sappho." Her voice rose. "Now, Terence there, Terence has four boys. *Four.* Imagine that." Valentine paused at the top of the stairs, regarded us with sad, tired eyes, then trudged up a corridor. Sally said, "He *loves* having me as a partner. Makes him the envy of the squad room."

"I would've thought it was his ready smile."

She said, "Sit."

I obeyed, easing into the humble wooden chair at the end of the desk. On her blotter was a to-do list. *Call gopher guy. Rebate on dryer. Sitter for Tues night shift.*

The glimpse into the cogs and gears of her life struck a chord. Perhaps it resonated with the banal tasks I'd been crossing off my own checklist while my insides crumbled.

I kept my gaze on the floor. "Ever feel stuck?"

"Like that U2 song? Part of being a grown-up, I suppose."

"Yeah, but you always hoped it wouldn't be you."

She smirked. "The only new surprises are you can't eat Indian on an empty stomach and how expensive patio furniture is."

"Just how it goes, I guess. It's okay. If you like where you are." I looked away quickly; I'd revealed more than I'd wanted to. "No prints at all? Maybe you should've dusted the camera and tripod."

She noted my discomfort, the rushed segue. "Sure. We could shoot an episode of *CSI* at your house. Maybe call in FBI profilers."

"Okay, okay," I said. "You have limited resources. As of now it's still a camcorder prank."

"Not just that, Davis, but the guy wore latex gloves. The jewel case, sleeve, and discs are totally clean. If we believe your version, the DVDs auto-erased like something out of a Bond film. Whoever's behind this went to great care. He's not suddenly gonna push a 'record' button with a bare thumb." She poured water from a bottle into a mug and busted into the Costco box, digging out a few pink packets and dumping the crystals. "Now, I shouldn't tell you this, but you *did* bring me Sweet'N Low. . . ." She used a pencil to stir. "You have any other cops to the house?"

"That's a question, Sally. You didn't actually tell me anything."

"How 'bout that."

"Why are you asking about other cops?"

She took a sip, leaned back in her distressed little chair. "The boot print came back—"

"Wait a minute. *Boot print?*"

"From the mud patch by the leaky sprinkler in your front yard. We saw it when we went over to talk to your neighbor." She tugged open a drawer, then tossed down a file in front of me. Numerous photos spilled out. A decent impression of a thick worker's sole, pointed toward the street. Left behind, I guessed, when the intruder split the premises. In a few of the shots, the print was illuminated by a Mag-Lite flashlight, just like Sally's, lying in the grass to give a sharp angle.

"When did you take these?" I asked.

"I didn't. Valentine did when I went back to talk to you."

I pictured Valentine waiting out in the Crown Vic and then her sitting with her tea, holding my attention and keeping me turned away from the front window.

"It's a nice three-dimensional track," she said. "Severe sole wear on the outside by the ball of the foot. Pebble wedged deep in the ridges here in the heel. See?"

"Did you cast a print?"

"Like I said, Kojak, we can't roll criminalists because someone sent you a spooky home video."

"Great. So we'll get slaughtered in our bed and *then* you'll send a van."

She lifted an eyebrow. "First of all, *you'll* get

slaughtered on your couch. And yes, then we would send a van."

I thumbed through the photos. One was taken from directly above, Valentine's radio lying beside the print. "The radio's for scale?"

"No, for period atmosphere. Yes. Scale. The print's from a size-eleven-and-a-half Danner boot. The make is Acadia, common uniform footwear, eight inches high at the ankle. They're comfortable as hell, and you can resole them. Cops love 'em, but they're twice the price of Hi-Tecs or Rockys, so you don't see them around as much. They're a field boot, for patrolmen or SWAT guys. Detectives wear bad dress shoes." With a grunt, she set her long-suffering loafer on the edge of the desk. "Payless if you're on a single-mother budget."

"So it's a law-enforcement boot?"

"But anyone can order them. Just like handguns. And we all know how deranged members of our society have been known to fetishize police gear."

"Especially when they're already working in law enforcement."

"Don't look at me. I wanted to be an astronaut."

My eyes wandered around the squad room, taking in the black boots of various makes attached to various officers. "What size shoe is Valentine?"

Her lips pursed with irritation. "Not eleven and a half. And he was on shift with me when that footage of you was taken. Surely you can do better than that, Inspector Clouseau."

"Well, there haven't been any cops to our house that we know of. I think ever."

"Like I said, it could be a cop in a cop boot, or it could be a wackjob in a cop boot." She stood, pulled on her jacket, bringing the conversation to a close. "If you want to be doing something useful, you should be thinking about who you've pissed off lately. Or who your lovely wife has."

"I have been," I said. "Where else am I supposed to look?"

"There are rocks everywhere," she said. "We just usually don't kick 'em over."

CHAPTER 18

Heading back up Roscomare, I called Ariana at the showroom. "I'm going home early."

"You're not going to the movies?" she asked.

"I'm not going to the movies."

"Okay. I'll finish up here, too."

There was a courtship excitement to our exchange, unspoken but understood, like we were smitten teenagers planning a second date. It hit me how rarely these past six weeks I'd come home before she was in bed for the night. And now I was nervous but eager, unsure what the evening with her would hold.

Simmering unease eroded my optimism. Ariana's meeting—the one I hadn't picked up the suit for—was supposed to be in the afternoon. So why had she been at the showroom when I'd called? For a half block, I actually debated calling back and checking with her assistant. As Ariana had pointed out, it doesn't take much more than a white handkerchief and a few well-placed nudges. My paranoia, I realized, was bleeding outward, making me question—however stupidly—everything going on around me.

I passed the shopping strip, and the reception bars blinked off the cell-phone screen, offended by the altitude. As I slowed for the driveway, a sense of fore-boding seized me, and I couldn't help but crane to see if a new surprise was waiting. The front yard looked normal, and the doorstep was empty. But a ripple at the curtain snagged my focus. I caught a flash of a white hand before it withdrew. Too white.

A latex glove.

It was so odd, so out of place, that at first it stunned me into a kind of mental blankness. Then, through my rising alarm, I registered the figure behind the curtain, shadow-smudged like a fish in murky waters.

My body had gone rigid. But I didn't slow the car further; I rolled right past my driveway and the house next door before pulling over to the curb. I debated hooking back to the grocery-store pay phone to call 911, knowing that the intruder would likely be long gone by the time the cops arrived. Gripping the door handle, staring at my fist-battered dashboard, I fought with myself for several prolonged seconds, but my fury—and burning curiosity—won out.

I climbed out and jogged back. Cutting up the drive-way, I slid along the fence, reaching the door to the garage. I paused for a silent twenty-second freak-out, my fists shoved against my head, and then I regained what composure I could muster, slipped my key into the door, and pushed it tentatively open. The garage's walls and ceiling seemed to amplify my rapid breath-ing. My eyes darted around, settling on the golf bag languishing beneath a veil of cobwebs, where it had lived since my then-agent bought it for me to celebrate the screenplay sale. My hand fussed across dusty club heads, upgrading from wedge to iron to driver.

The door leading into the dining nook had a creak. I knew this. I'd been meaning to WD-40 the hinges for months. I was in the garage; why not do it now? I found the blue-and-yellow can, sprayed the hinges until they dripped. Under the guidance of my white-knuckle grip, the door swung in, slowly, without complaint. I realized, too late, that it could have sounded the alarm, but the intruder had disarmed the system.

A bead of sweat held to the line of my jaw, tickling. I slipped inside, easing the door shut behind me. Setting down my feet as silently as I could, I led with the club, holding it upright, a yuppie samurai sword. I inched around the cabinets, my view of the kitchen opening up.

Across the room the back door finished a slow opening arc, stopping halfway.

I bounded over to it. At the far edge of the lawn, a large man in a ski mask and black zip-up jacket stood perfectly still, facing the house, arms at his sides.

Waiting on me.

I froze, my heart lurching, my throat seizing up.

His gloved hands floated at his sides like a mime's. He seemed to register me not with his dark irises but with the suspended crescents of white that held them.

He turned and ran almost silently through the sumac. Enraged, terrified, I followed. In the sane quadrant of my brain, I noted his bulk and almost military efficiency. And his black boots, which I would've bet were size-eleven-and-a-half Danner Acadias. He bounded from an upended terra-cotta pot to the roof of the greenhouse shed as if off a trampoline bounce, then whistled over the fence. I hurled the club at him, but it hit the wood and rebounded back at me. I slammed into the fence and hoisted myself onto it, shoes scrabbling for purchase. Hanging, the slat edges digging into my gut, I looked up the street, but he'd vanished. Into a yard, a house, around the corner.

I dropped back down with a grunt, fighting to catch my breath. Had I surprised him by altering my schedule, skipping the movies? If so, he sure hadn't seemed concerned. Judging by his build and adroitness, he could have dismantled me. So hurting me wasn't his aim. At least not yet.

I trudged back inside, collapsed into a chair, and sat, breathing. Just breathing.

After a time I rose and checked the kitchen drawer. Both new tubular keys to the alarm were there. Nothing appeared to have been touched. At the base of the stairs, I stopped to stare at the alarm pad as if it had something to say. I continued up, checked our bedroom and then my office. The cover had been removed from the DVD spindle and set beside it. A count confirmed that one more disc was missing. I went back downstairs and into the living room. The intruder had pulled the tripod clear of the lady palm and tugged the curtain closed. My camcorder's digital memory had been erased. I walked numbly into the family room.

The DVD player tray was open, a silver disc resting inside.

I thumbed the tray closed and sank into the couch. The popping of the TV turning on struck me as unusually loud. I kept getting a blank screen, so I fussed with the buttons, clicking "input select," "TV/video," and the other usual suspects.

At last there I was. On the couch. Wearing my clothes. From today.

I stared, waiting. I chewed my lip. My on-screen self chewed my on-screen lip.

The blood in my veins turned to ice. I tried to swallow, found my throat stuck.

I raised a hand. My double raised a hand. I said, "Oh, Lord," and heard my voice come out of the surround sound. I took a deep, shaky breath. My double took a deep, shaky breath. He looked utterly dumbstruck, blanched, his face an ungodly shade of pale.

I got up and walked toward the TV, my image growing like Alice. I tugged the flat-screen off the wall and set it, trailing wires, on the floor. The same perspective of myself stared up at me. Shoving and pulling the tightly stacked equipment had no effect on the shooting angle either. Leaning into the top shelves, I ripped out a few plugs and snapped off the outlet covers. Nothing. I yanked out discs and books, used a paperweight to punch a hole in the drywall near a ding and the fireplace poker to pry around further. Finally I reached down and swung open the glass door of the cabinet protecting Ariana's teenage record collection. The TV image at my feet spun vertiginously.

I crouched. A tiny fish-eye lens clipped to the top of the glass. I rotated the door open, closed, the room swaying correspondingly on the TV. I unclipped the little lens. A wire trailed back, across the dusty cover of *Dancing on the Ceiling*. I tugged. It came, giving some resistance. At the end, hooked as neatly as a rainbow trout, was a cell phone. Some shitty prepay model that you'd buy off the rack at 7-Eleven. Clenched in my shaking hand, the crappy cell phone, of course, showed full reception. Unlike my three-hundred-dollar Sanyo.

I took a step back, and then another. Stunned, I mounted the stairs and retreated to our bathroom, the farthest point in the house from the fish-eye lens. I was acting automatically, like an animal, a zombie, and my actions made about as much sense. I turned on the shower, cranked it to red, and let steam fill the room. I wasn't sure if the sound of running water provided cover from whatever other bugs had infiltrated our house, but it always worked in movies and seemed like a good idea now.

In a flash of lucidity, I went over to my office, where I grabbed a digital mini-recorder to document any call that might come in. I trudged back and sat with one arm resting on the toilet, the fuzzy oval rug wrinkled up beneath my shoe, the cell phone precisely centered on the floor tile where I could keep an eye on it. One knee was raised. I wasn't cowering in a corner, but it might have looked that way to an impartial observer. The water drowned out my thoughts; the steam cleaned my lungs.

I don't know how long I'd been sitting there when the door banged open and Ariana came in. Her face was red, her hair frizzy; she clutched a butcher knife like a crazed soprano. At least she'd upgraded from the badminton racket. The knife clattered into the sink, and she sagged against the counter and pressed a hand to the slope of her bosom in what seemed a genetically conditioned response.

I felt more protective of her in that moment than I could ever remember.

Her gaze took in my expression, the throwaway cell phone, the mini-recorder I'd left on the counter. "What . . . The TV . . . What . . . ?"

My voice sounded dry and cracked. "I came in on an intruder. Ski mask. He ran away. There's a bug in the house. A hidden camera. They've been recording us. Every *fucking* thing we've . . ."

She swallowed hard, her chest jerking, then crouched and picked up the phone.

"It was hidden," I said, "in the cabinet under the TV."

"Has it rung?"

"No."

Working her bottom lip with her teeth, she punched a few buttons. "No incoming. No outgoing. No saved numbers." She shook it, frustrated. "How . . . how'd he get in?"

"The back door, I think. He must've picked it. Or he has a key."

"And turned off the alarm?" The air was thick with steam, moving in wispy sheets. Condensation clung to her face, mimicking a good sweat. "*The cops.* They saw where we hide the alarm keys. They're the only ones who know besides us."

"That's what I thought. But then I realized. The house is bugged. So when you told me the new code, someone was—"

The cell phone shrilled. Ariana jerked back against the counter, dropping it. It bounced but did not break.

It rang again, rattling against the tile. I reached across and turned off the water. The trill seemed amplified. As did the silence.

I pointed at the mini-recorder, and Ariana snatched it from the counter and tossed it to me. The phone rang again.

"Jesus, Patrick, get it, just *get it*."

Readying the recorder, I pressed the phone to my cheek. "Hello?"

A voice, electronically distorted, made the hair rise along my arms. *"So . . ."* it said, *"are you ready to get started?"*

CHAPTER 19

The next statement was just as chilling. *"Turn off the tape recorder."*

I obeyed and set it gently on the toilet seat, glancing apprehensively at the walls and ceiling. My voice was hoarse, shaky. "It's off."

"We know that you stopped by Bel Air Foods Tuesday morning to buy a bag of trail mix, a banana, and an iced tea. We know that you watch your wife cry most mornings through the kitchen window. We know you went to the West L.A. police station today at four thirty-seven, that you saw Detective Richards at her desk on the second floor, that you spoke to her for thirteen and a half minutes." Cold. Steady. Scrubbed of emotion. *"Do you have any question as to the range of what we can find out about you or anyone else?"*

"No."

"Do you have any question as to our capability to reach into your life and touch you where we want?"

The electronic filter made the voice flatter, the utter lack of modulation all the more unsettling. My mouth felt gummy. "No."

Ariana was leaning toward me, hands on her knees,

her eyes wide and wild. I tilted the earpiece away from my face so she could hear better.

"Do not go to the police again. Do not talk to the police again." A pause. I rotated the mouthpiece up so the caller couldn't hear how hard my breath was coming. *"Stand up. Leave the bathroom."*

I exited, Ariana ahead of me walking backward, stumbling over books and strewn clothes. The bedroom air iced my face, a bracing contrast from the lingering steam of the shower.

"Go out into the hall. Watch your shin on the corner of the bed. Turn right, pass your office."

Ariana was now scurrying alongside me as I marched, my cheek sweating against the plastic.

"Is there anything I can do to make you stop?" I asked, but the voice forged ahead.

"Pass the M movie poster. Down the stairs. Pass the alarm pad. Hard left. Watch out for the table. Right. Left. Rotate. Another forty-five degrees."

I was standing with my back to the TV, facing my meager puddle of blankets.

"Open the couch that you've refused to fold out."

I flung the cushions aside, my heartbeat kettle-drumming in my ears. What was inside? What had I been sleeping on top of?

The vinyl loop handle slipped from my hand, and Ariana stepped in to help pull. My other hand pressed the phone to my ear, a shock connection I couldn't break. We tugged and the contraption opened, an insect unfolding from its shell. Ari grabbed the metal brace, which creaked and thumped to the floor, the bottom third of the weary mattress still folded back.

Hiding something.

With a numb hand, I reached out and nudged the mattress, which flipped over. It landed flat, setting the crappy springs on twangy vibration and revealing a manila folder and a black wand, maybe four feet long, with a circular head like that of a metal detector.

"That folder contains a floor plan of your house. The red circles indicate where we have planted surveillance devices. The instrument beside the folder is a nonlinear junction detector. It will help you locate those devices and search for any others you believe we may not have indicated on the floor plan."

I didn't have to examine the folder itself to know it had been taken from my desk drawer upstairs. Inside, as promised, two printouts, one for each floor of the house—JPEGs from our contractor that I'd saved in my computer after we'd opened up the fifties bathrooms a few years ago. Down the center of each page ran a faded stripe from my mostly spent toner drum— they'd been printed in my office recently. But that's not what sent the wave of panic-nausea through my stomach.

It was the dozen or so red circles pockmarking each sheet.

Placing the pages side by side, I tried to process the scope of the intrusion. All this time I'd thought my life had turned into *Fatal Attraction*. But I was really in *Enemy of the State*.

Ariana mopped hair off her forehead and let out something between a sigh and a groan. Slowly, I tilted my head and took in my disused proofreading marker, tucked into a year-end edition of *Entertainment Weekly* at the edge of the coffee table. With shaking hands I retrieved the pen and drew in the margin of the top page, the frayed felt tip tracing a matching, distinctive circle.

Ariana stepped back, her eyes darting around the walls, the furnishings. With a glance to the printout, she trudged over and stuck a finger into a tiny dent in the plaster just below a framed Ansel Adams she'd had since her dorm-room days. "It can't . . . They can't . . ."

The voice startled me out of my stunned reverie; I'd forgotten that the call was still live. *"A Gmail account has been set up for you, patrickdavis081075"*—my birthday. *"Password is your mother's maiden name. The first e-mail will arrive Sunday at four* P.M., *telling you what's next."*

The *first* e-mail? The phrase intensified my controlled panic into full-blown terror. I was a fish newly hooked, my journey only beginning. But I barely had time to shudder when the voice said, *"Now walk outside. Alone."*

Forcing my feet toward the door, I gestured for Ariana to stay put. She shook her head and trailed me, chewing at the side of a thumbnail. I stepped out onto the walk, Ariana waiting behind, shouldering against the jamb and tugging the door tight to her side so only the front sliver of her was exposed.

"End of the walk. You see the sewer grate? Just past the curb-painted house numbers?"

"Hang on." I stopped ten feet shy of the grate. "Okay," I lied, "I'm standing right on top of it."

"Lean over and look at the gap."

So they weren't watching *all* the time. The trick was to know when.

"Patrick. Patrick!"

With dread, I turned to see Don making his way over from his driveway, toting a box of office files. I muttered, "Wait a second," into the mouthpiece through clenched teeth. And then: "This really isn't the best time, Don."

"Oh, didn't see you were on the phone."

"Yes. I am." Out of the corner of my eye, I sensed movement at the front door, Ariana easing back and shutting it to barely a crack.

"Don't stall us."

Don was stammering at me, "Listen, I just . . . felt I should apologize for my role in . . . everything, and—"

"You don't need to. It's not between me and you." My face burned. "Listen, I'm on a critical call. I can't get into this right now."

"Get rid of him. Now."

"I'm trying," I muttered into the phone.

"Well, when, Patrick?" Don asked. "I mean, it's been six weeks. For better or worse, we *are* neighbors, and I've tried a number of times—"

"Don, I don't need to discuss this with you. I don't owe you anything. Now, get out of my face and let me finish this call."

He glared at me and took a few backward steps before turning for home.

"Okay," I said, "the curb drain . . ."

"Once you've removed the devices from the house, put them in your black duffel bag on the top shelf of

your closet and drop them down there. All lenses, cables, even the nonlinear junction detector. At midnight tomorrow. Not a minute before. Not a minute after. Say it back to me."

"Midnight tomorrow, sharp. Everything down the grate. Sunday at four P.M., I get an e-mail."

Until then, live with dread about what that e-mail might hold.

"This is the last time you will hear my voice. Now set the phone on the ground, smash it with your foot, and kick it down the sewer grate. Oh—and, Patrick?"

"What?"

"This is nothing like what you imagine."

"What do I imagine?"

But I was talking to a dead line.

CHAPTER 20

After disposing of the phone, I returned inside. The front door swung open to greet me, and I grabbed Ariana by the wrist and pulled her into me. Our cheeks pressed together. Sweat. The smell of her conditioner. Her chest was heaving. I cupped a hand around her ear and whispered, as faintly as possible, "Let's get ourselves to the greenhouse."

The only place on the property with clear walls.

She nodded. We pulled apart. "I'm scared, Patrick," she said loudly.

"It's okay. I know what they want now. At least what they want me to do next." I gave her the broad strokes of the phone conversation.

"And what about after this, Patrick? These people are *terrorizing* us. We have to call the cops."

"We can't call the cops. They'll know. They know everything."

She stormed toward the family room, with me at her heels. "So keep giving in and giving in?"

"We don't have a choice."

"There are *always* choices."

"And you're an expert on sound decision making?"

She wheeled on me. "I'm not the one who sold out my life to get fired off a shitty movie."

I blinked, stunned. Holding her hand low by her stomach, she beckoned with her fingers: *Come on.*

I caught my breath again. "Right. You're much more grounded. It took what? One crank call to get you to step out on our marriage?"

"It took a lot more than that."

"Because I was supposed to read your mind to know about all the resentment you were silently storing up?"

"No. You were supposed to be present in this marriage. It takes two people to be able to communicate."

"Nine days!" I shouted, so loud I caught us both off guard. Ariana started, took a half step away. Bitterness rode the back of my tongue. I couldn't stop myself. "I was gone *nine days.* That's less than two weeks. You couldn't wait *nine fucking days* to talk to me?"

"Nine days?" The color had returned to her face. "You'd been gone a *year.* You disappeared the minute an agent returned your phone call."

Her eyes welled. She turned and banged through the rear door. I shoved the heel of my hand across my cheek. I lowered my head, exhaled, counted silently backward from ten.

Then I followed.

When I pushed through the rasping door into the heat of the greenhouse, we grabbed for each other. She hugged me around my neck, squeezing hard enough to hurt, her forehead mashed to my jaw, my face bent toward hers, mossy humidity coating our lungs. We let go of each other a bit awkwardly, and then Ariana rotated a finger around the small enclosure. Lifting pots, crawling under shelves, running hands along posts, we searched. The translucent siding made the job easier. We finished and faced each other across the narrow aluminum staging table.

Our exchange inside, for the cameras and in spite of them, our clumsy embrace, the intruder's even stare, the feeling of horror when I'd discovered the first hidden device, the casually marked floor plans showing dozens more—the pressure from it all exploded in this first moment of relative privacy. I hammered a fist into the staging table, denting the aluminum, splitting the scabs on my knuckles. Two terra-cotta pots toppled off and shattered. "These assholes moved in to our house. Our *bedroom.* I've been *sleeping* on top of equipment they planted. What the *fuck* do they want from us?" I stared at the shards, waiting for the rage to recede. Nice work, Patrick. Sound strategy, responding to a grand master with a temper tantrum.

"They heard everything," Ariana was saying. "All the arguments. The petty stuff. What I told you Tuesday night over the dining table. Everything. Jesus, Patrick. *Jesus.* There's not an inch of our lives that's been just ours."

I drew in a deep breath. "We need to figure a way to get out of this."

Her lips were trembling. "What is *'this'*?"

"It's got nothing to do with an affair. Or a student. Or a pissed-off movie star. Whoever these guys are, they're experts."

"In what?"

"This."

Silence, broken by the gentle whir of the shutter fan. I wiped the back of my hand across my shirt, leaving a streak of crimson. Ariana looked at the lifted scabs and said, "Oh. *Oh.* That's how you . . ." She took a deep breath, nodded. "What else do I need to be clued in on here?"

I told her about everything from Jerry to Keith, Sally Richards and the boot print, and how I'd lied and told the caller I was standing on top of the sewer grate and he hadn't known the difference.

"So they're not watching everything all the time," she said.

"Right. We just don't know where the dead spots are. But they seem to be backing off the surveillance. Why else would they give us the location of the bugs in the house?"

"To set up something *else.*" She took a deep breath, shook her hands as if drying them. "What the hell's gonna be in that e-mail, Patrick?"

My stomach roiled. My lips felt dry, cracked. "I don't have a clue."

"What can we do? There's gotta be something we can do." She looked helplessly through the green siding at our house. Here we were, huddled, displaced. "If they know specifics about your trip to the police station, they probably have someone inside. Is Richards involved with this?" She'd dropped her voice instinctively to a whisper.

"It's not her," I said. Ariana regarded me skeptically, so I added, "I just know. Plus, why would she have told me about the boot print, which implicates the cops?"

"Okay. But even if it's *not* her, we can't go to her again or they'll find out."

"I doubt she can help us anyway. Whatever this is, it's well above the pay grade of a divisional detective."

"Fine. So let's go *above* her pay grade. How about the higher LAPD divisions?"

"No good. The make of boot could've been SWAT issue, so we can't trust downtown either."

"Then we need to get help from the FBI or whoever."

"These guys'll find out."

"Do we care if they *do* find out?" Ari asked. "I mean, what are they threatening us *with*?"

"I guess that would be another surprise," I said. "When it comes."

She shivered. "Should we risk it? To get help?"

"I think we should see what these guys want first. Or else it'll just be another futile conversation with cops or agents or whoever. We've already seen how that goes."

"Are you sure you don't want to go along with their directions just because you're scared of how they'll retaliate if you *don't*?" she asked.

"Of course I'm scared," I said. "I'm willing to believe they can do anything."

"That's the point," she said angrily. "That's what they've been trying to teach us. We don't *know* people big enough to help us. So what do *we* do?"

"First let's get the bugs out of the walls. At least the ones they're admitting are there. And let's do it quickly."

"Why quickly?"

"Because at midnight tomorrow, all the evidence goes down the sewer grate."

My arms cramped from holding the wand. Slowly, laboriously, I swept the circular head over the south wall of the living room. Though we'd checked every square inch of every surface, and though false positives abounded, the marked-up floor plan hadn't left out any bugs. At least any I could detect using the instrument they'd provided. Despite the endlessly swirling dust, we'd closed all the curtains and blinds, making the rooms as claustrophobic as the tiny greenhouse.

On the armchair in the corner sat our laundry basket, filled to the brim with a jumble of cables, mini-lenses, transmitters, mounting plates, assorted sleeves, and a catch-box for various optical fibers we'd dug out from behind our air-conditioning fan outside. Upstairs looked like a crack house—furniture slashed and upended, walls torn apart, paintings, mirrors, and books strewn on the floor. Pots and pans littered the kitchen, the cabinets stood ajar in the family room, and the contents of the drawers and medicine cabinet had been emptied into the powder-room sink. For hours we'd worked in dread-filled silence.

Dust and bits of plaster flecked the sweat on my arms. When I scanned down the inner doorframe, the green light glowed right on cue. Pulling the printout from my pocket, I checked the location against the final red circle, stepped down from the chair, and tapped the spot. Wearily, Ariana trudged forward and punched a hammer through the drywall.

I stepped over a nail-studded length of molding, set the wand down on a flap of turned-back carpet, and stretched my aching arms. Beside the torn carpet, I'd rested the photographs I'd found inside cabinets and drawers, the remaining pictures Ariana had printed up and playfully hidden six months back. Together they formed a visual CliffsNotes of our relationship. Smoking together outside a Bruins basketball game. Our first meal in the house, some moving boxes shoved together to form a makeshift table for take-out Vietnamese. Me grinning, holding up a check from Summit Pictures, the first dime I'd made as a writer. In the background the lopsided cake Ariana had baked for the occasion. The maudlin, tender things we did to celebrate ourselves, back before we discovered we could look foolish in front of each other. I stared at that cake, the candles still smoking. Whatever wish I'd made had been the wrong one. It was hard to believe, in light of the calamity of the past few days, that we'd actually thought we had problems before all this.

A length of runner cable wrapped around her fist, Ariana stepped back, fighting it from the hole like a fishing line. The embedded wire came lurchingly, carving a trench across the wall, past our framed wedding picture, which slipped from its nail to the floor, a crack forking the glass through our grinning faces. The crumbling channel zigged north through the ceiling, the cable eventually tearing free from the fan. She staggered a bit when the wire gave, standing stooped and openhanded for a breathless moment. Then she lowered her face into an upturned palm and finally broke the dour silence with a sob.

CHAPTER 21

"No one I like would call me at this hour."

"Jerry, listen, it's Patrick."

"As I said . . ."

I hunched against the pay phone outside Bel Air Foods, casting a glance over my shoulder at the empty street. The tinge of morning light stole some of the glow from the streetlamps. "This thing's taken a turn, Jerry. Our whole house was bugged."

"Ever think about adjusting your meds?"

"Can you—please, *please*—give us some guidance here?"

"Why the fuck are you calling *me*? You fishing for a restraining order, Davis? I told you the studio has zero interest in—"

"This has got nothing to do with the studio."

That stopped him. "Why not?"

"I'm telling you, come look at this stuff. You won't believe what we pulled out of the walls—lenses and shit that I didn't know existed. There was not a *trace* of the insertion. They must've run the wires behind the drywall arthroscopically or something. They hid a pinhole camera inside the speaker grille of my alarm clock, another one in the vent of a smoke detector."

He whistled, and then I heard him breathing. "Pinhole cameras?"

"That's the least of it. Listen, the house is supposedly clean now. But I don't trust it. I want it checked. They called, said I can't contact the cops."

"You must be in dire straits if you're calling *me*."

"I really am, Jerry." I could almost hear him thinking about that one. I prodded a little: "You've done surveillance, right?"

"Of course—you think Summit hired me for my temperament? I was an intercept analyst in the Corps. That's all anyone does anymore in Hollywood. Wiretapping. They barely even make movies these days."

"Look, I gather this is really advanced stuff. Do you have any contacts who can do it? Someone more current?"

"Fuck you 'more current,' you reverse-psychology prick. I'll admit—you've piqued my interest. I mean, if this stuff is what you described, I should take a look. Never hurts to see what new gadgets are in play."

"So you'll come?"

"*If*"—a pause—"you promise you'll *never* try to come near the lot again."

I blew out a deep breath of relief, leaned my forehead against the wall. "I promise. But listen, they might be watching the house."

"You tore your place apart, yeah? So how 'bout an early-morning visit from your contractor?"

An hour later the doorbell rang. I glanced past Jerry, dressed convincingly in jeans and a ripped long-sleeved T-shirt, to the white van at the curb. Magnetic signs on the door and side proclaimed SENDLENSKI BROS. CONTRACTORS. He hefted one of two giant toolboxes at me and barreled by, introducing himself brusquely to Ariana. Unsnapping the catches, he pulled out a remote, aimed it through the closed door, and clicked a button.

"Wideband high-power jammer in the van. Your cell phones, wireless Internet, any surveillance devices—they're all squelched."

I said, "Send*len*ski Brothers?"

"Who *couldn't* believe a name like that?" He tugged out a directional antenna and hooked it to what looked like a laptop with a shoe box–thick base. An electronic waterfall traversed the screen, a red stripe running down the center. "First things first. Let's see if there are any *other* devices still operating. You'll need to go about your business and stay out of my way. Now, listen, I have to turn *off* the jammer to pick up any signals. It's a good idea anyways, be-cause that thing takes out a four-block radius, so your neighbors are already dialing tech support." He fished an iPod nano, which he wore on a lanyard, from beneath his collar. A small contraption—a mini-speaker?—plugged the headphone jack. "Most high-end devices will only operate if there's noise to record. That's how they save juice. So guys started playing Van Halen when they swept rooms. Then the devices were upgraded to only transmit *speaking* tones. So . . ." Raising a finger to his lips, he aimed and clicked the remote again, turning off the jammer, then thumbed the iPod dial. A voice issued forth: *"Philosophy in the Boudoir, by the Marquis de Sade."*

Ariana caught my eye and mouthed, *Marquis de Sade? Really?*

While Jerry busied himself in the foyer, I settled on the couch and flipped through *Entertainment Weekly* but found myself rereading the same paragraph. In the kitchen Ariana emptied all the mugs out of the cabinet and then replaced them in what looked like the same order. She tore the lid from a box of mac & cheese and let the noodles patter on the countertop. No device hidden inside like a Cracker Jack prize. She lined up slices of bread by the sink. Crimp-searched the dry cleaning. Plucked a barrette from her hair and studied it. Her anxiety was infectious; I found myself eyeing our banal household clutter over the top of the magazine, wondering at each item's Trojan-horse potential. A ninja blowgun hidden in the potted philodendron?

Jerry made his way meticulously from room to room, the silence broken only by the drone of the audiobook from his iPod. De Sade's characters had plied an exhausting variety of orifices by the time Jerry whistled us over to the living-room coat closet, where he sat before a different, but equally bulky, laptop. My Nikes were set on the floor near the turned-back flap of carpet, Ariana's favorite raincoat spread out beside them.

He pointed at them. "I got something here. Embedded in the heel. See those hairline incisions? And stitched into the coat lining. Here."

From around his neck, the iPod cheerily proclaimed, *"I'm going to shoot the burning jism to my entrails' end."*

"So they're listening?" I asked. "Right now?"

"No." A glance to the laptop screen, a confusion of charts and amplitude waves. "These things are sending extremely short messages, once every five minutes. A low-power quick signal, hard to detect. Clearly not audio or visual."

"Shake it roughly! It's one of the finest pleasures you can imagine."

"Tracking devices," I said.

"Precisely. They're sending out position reports every so often, just like your cell phone does. In fact, the signal analyzer says it's transmitting over the data side of the T-Mobile network. Like a text message."

"That's the coat I wear the most," Ariana said. "They've been paying attention. Can you remove the tracker?"

Jerry said, "I wouldn't."

"Why?" she asked.

"Because," I said, "this is the first thing we know that they don't know we know."

She frowned at her jacket, as if mad that it had betrayed her. "Can you find out where the signal's sending to?"

"No," Jerry said. "I can grab the device's cellular ID number, but once it hits the destination gateway, it's gone."

"Raise your ass just a wee bit higher, my lover!"

I asked, "Would you mind turning that off?"

"Or up?" Ariana said.

"Sorry, old habit." Jerry clicked off the iPod. "They're less suspicious if they think they're eavesdropping on embarrassing stuff. Plus, it's a tedious job. You get bored. So, you know, stimulating mate-rial."

"Hey," I said, "it beats Tolstoy. Now, what do you mean you can't source the signal?"

"The destination gateway is connected to an Inter-net router, so from there it goes off into the soup—onion-routes and zips through an anonymous proxy in Azerbaijan or whatever. But that's the least of your problems." He tugged the laundry basket over and dug a hand into the tangle of gear, producing an envelope-thin component. "This uses the emissions of sensors from your burglar alarm and wireless router and such to power itself. No heat signature, no batteries to refresh."

"You're gonna have to dumb this down for me."

"This is not the cheap Sharper Image shit you get from Taiwan. This is the kind of no-serial-number, top-drawer gear that comes out of Haifa." He dropped the emitter into the basket again. "I did some joint training in Bucharest back in the day, when the Rus-sians were particularly attentive. We found stuff like this in our hotel-room walls." He grimaced. "You pissed off the wrong folks, Patrick."

Her back to the wall, Ariana slid slowly to the floor.

"Could it . . ." My throat was too dry to speak, so I swallowed and started over. "Could it be the cops?"

"This kind of gear wasn't paid for by a municipal purse. This is next-level shit."

"Agency stuff."

Jerry touched a finger to the tip of his nose.

"But the detectives lifted a boot print from the front yard," I said. "A cop make—Danner Acadia?"

His brow furrowed. "Danners aren't cop boots. A detective might think that, see it on a few SWAT wannabes wearing them to show off. But no, Danners are mostly used by Spec Ops guys. Or field agents."

"Oh," I said. "Swell."

"Why the hell would an agency or some kind of spy want to mess with us?" Ariana said. "We don't have much money. We're not influential. We've got nothing to do with politics."

Jerry started packing away his gear, neatly and lovingly. "There *is* your movie."

"What do you mean?" I asked.

"It pissed off a lot of folks. We had some back-and-forth with D.C. The CIA agents are hardly painted like American heroes."

"*What?* The CIA actually read the script?"

"Sure. We wanted official cooperation, the hardware, use of the seal, locations, all that. It can save millions. But it's just like dealing with the Pentagon—if it's a friendly script, they'll loan you a Black Hawk, open up facilities. But they won't give you shit for *Full Metal Jacket.* And let's face it, *They're Watching* puts the fuck on the Agency. Makes them look like the KGB or something."

"Oh, come on," I said. "That was just stupid movie fun. It didn't mean anything."

"Maybe it did to them. One man's fun is another man's jihad."

"It's a popcorn thriller, not some groundbreaking

commentary. And I'm just the *writer,* not a powerful studio head or something." I was sputtering. "Besides, the government's always corrupt in movies."

"Maybe they're sick of it."

"You really think it would provoke *this*?" I fanned a hand at the torn-up walls, ending with Ariana sitting on the floor, her face drawn and bloodless.

"You got a better explanation?"

Ariana broke the silence. "If it's some agency, we've got to go to the cops for help."

"Because *they've* shown such an inclination to believe us," I said.

"Look," Jerry said, "these guys have already demonstrated that they can monitor what goes on inside a police station. I mean, they didn't just know that you went to the West L.A. station; they knew which desk you went to. On the second floor."

Ariana asked, sharply, "How do you know that?"

I said, "I told him. On the phone."

We all regarded one another warily.

Ari said, "Sorry."

Jerry's face was tight. "As I was saying, you still can't rule out that they have a guy inside LAPD. Even if they don't, they've tapped into the internal surveillance cameras or something. They're watching you and the police, and they know how. You really want them finding out that you're starting a counteroffensive because you trotted back into a cop shop? You could be giving up what little you *do* know, your plans, your strategy."

Ariana coughed out a laugh. "Strategy?"

All business now, Jerry checked his watch, then

continued guiding his equipment back into the pristine foam-lined toolboxes. "The rest of the house is clean. Neither of your computers is sporting spyware or anything, but watch what you print. Printers, copiers, fax machines—everything's got a hard drive now, and people can get at 'em and know what you've been up to. Your cars are good, but check them now and again for a slap-and-track. Take this—it's a minijammer, knocks out any recording devices in a twenty-foot radius. They advertise fifty, but don't push your luck." He handed me a pack of Marlboro Lights and flipped up the lid to show the black button protruding through the fake cigarettes. "Use it to be safe when you talk in the house, in case they come back and install something else when you're gone. If neither of you smokes, stick it in a purse or a pocket—don't leave it lying around. Oh, and you might want to shit-can your cell phones. Or at least turn them off when you don't want your location known. Cell phones function more or less the same as the transmitters hidden in your shoes and jacket. If you need to use yours, turn it on, make a quick call, then shut it off. It takes a while to zero in on the location, so calls a few minutes long are more or less safe."

Ariana's elbows were locked, resting on her knees. Motionless. She said, "I'm assuming there's no point in changing the alarm or locks."

Even his smirk was exacting, as if he'd programmed it for precisely such occasions. "You can't *afford* technology that would keep these guys out."

"So . . . what? We just *move*?"

"Depends. Do you guys run from your problems?"

Ariana's eyes ticked over to me. If he hadn't been busy packing up, Jerry would have noticed how much was riding on the look between us. "No," I said to her. "We don't."

The phone rang.

Ariana scrambled to her feet. "No one calls us this time of morning. What if it's the cops?"

I glanced at my watch, barely registering that I was already a half hour late to start my commute. I said to Jerry, "Are the phones tapped?"

Another ring. The cordless was stuffed somewhere under the picture frames and cushions we'd stacked on the love seat.

Jerry snapped the catches on his toolbox and stood to go. "Only amateurs would tap you at a junction box and show draw on the line. They use electronic intercept these days. Undetectable."

I started digging through the stuff on the love seat, sourcing the ring. Squirming a hand between two cushions, I pulled out the phone. RESTRICTED CALLER. My thumb hovered over the "talk" button. "She's right. No one calls this early. It could be important."

Jerry shook his head. "I wouldn't risk it."

Another ring.

"Shit," I said. *"Shit."* I turned it on, listened a moment to the crackle of static. "Hello?"

Punch's hoarse voice said, "Patrick, man—"

I said, "I know, Chad. It's a bad time right now, though, a lot going on. I told you I'd have the papers graded by Friday."

More crackle while Punch contemplated my calling him "Chad." Finally he picked up the ruse. "Okay,

it'd really make my life easier if they were done earlier."

"I'll see what I can do." I hung up. Exhaled. Jerry
was already at the door. I said, "Hey, wait. Thank you
for this. If we didn't have your help, I honestly don't
know what we'd do."

Ariana said, "You have no idea—"

Jerry looked right at me, ignoring her. "This better
not come back on me with the studio."

"It won't," I said.

Ariana added, "Not from us."

He shifted his weight, those toolboxes straining at
the handles. "I'm done. Get it?"

He was the first one through all this who'd been
able to offer real insight. The only person I knew who
had remotely relevant expertise. I wanted to beg. I
wanted to plead. I wanted to bar the door and get him
to promise he'd be on the other end of an untapped
line when things got worse. Instead I just looked at
the torn-up carpet.

"Yeah," I said. "I got it." It took some effort, but I
lifted my gaze to meet his. "Thank you, Jerry."

He nodded and walked out.

CHAPTER 22

The throwaway cell phone looked an awful lot like the one I'd stomped to pieces and kicked down the gutter. Twenty-five dollars prepaid, AT&T, domestic only. I pulled it from the rack and rushed to the checkout counter.

Bill gave me the big grin. "How's Ariana?"

"Good." I eyed the old-fashioned clock above the stacked bags of charcoal at the front of the store. I'd double-parked by the electronic doors, and a petite blonde in a Hummer was laying on the horn. "Good, thanks."

"Would you like a bag?"

I found my gaze lingering on the other customers, the cheap security cameras pointing at the registers, the parked cars. "What? No, no, that's okay."

He dragged the phone across the bar-code scanner. I looked at the product ID that popped up on his little screen, then turned my head to peer through the automatic doors and all the way up the street. The gray shingles of our roof peeked into view above the Millers' cypress. My eyes jerked back to that product ID, lit up in dot-matrix green. The nearest throwaway cell phone to our house. So therefore the one I'd be most likely to buy? And the one they'd be most likely to monitor.

Because they thought of everything.

Bill had said something.

"Sorry?"

His smile lost a bit of its luster. "I said, I'd bet you guys are excited for that movie to come out."

The blonde honked again, and I hurried toward the door, spinning to face Bill apologetically. "Yeah. Listen, I don't think I need that phone after all."

I lurched off the jammed 101, dodging cars at the exit and running Reseda north toward campus. The brown bag sliding around the passenger seat held four pre-paid phones I'd grabbed at a gas station on Ventura. Punch's voice—for once not slurred—came at me through a fifth. "Next time you give me a fake name, it better not be Chad. I mean, *Chad*?"

"What do you want to be called?"

"Dimitri."

"Naturally."

"Why the nifty spy talk?" Punch asked.

"I'm under crazy surveillance."

"How crazy?"

"Cold War shit."

A silence.

He said, "Then we should do this in person."

"It may not be safe for you to be around me."

"I'm beginning to figure that out. But I'm a big boy. Can you get here now?"

"I'm already late for morning classes." I veered around a kid in a Beemer who flipped me off with both hands. Probably one of my students. "I'll see if I can duck out early for lunch, maybe. Any chance you can make it to this side of the hill?"

"Sure. Lemme just suspend what little of a life I have left to sit in hideous traffic so I can service your in-deep-shit ass."

"Fair enough. Then where do you want me to be?"

"I'll tell you what. I'll get to Santa Monica for you. It'll be my pro bono effort for the year. Parking structure at the end of the Promenade. Third level. Two o'clock. I would say come alone, but I figure you know that. Make sure you're not being tailed. And don't call me again from whatever phone you're using now."

"Aren't you the guy who told me not to worry about all this? Something about beakless woodpeckers?"

"That was before."

"Thanks for the reassurance."

But he'd already hung up.

The students—those who had waited for me—were restless, and rightly so. Bumbling into class at the half-hour mark, I was unprepared and exhausted, too distracted to think on my feet. Paeng Bugayong sat in the back, slumped over his writing tablet, his face sunk into his crossed arms so all I could make out was a band of face and a thatch of straight black bangs almost touching the tops of his eyes. A shy, harmless kid. I felt foolish—and guilty—for ever suspecting him. By the time I let the students out for lunch, they were more than ready to disappear.

In the crowded hall, Julianne materialized at my elbow. "You're not heading to the lounge?" she asked.

"No. I have to run."

"Walk you to your car?" She shouldered through a pack of students to keep pace. "Come on, I'm jonesing for the next episode. Plus, you owe me big time for covering your classes yesterday afternoon."

"I knew that would cost me more than a Starbucks." We pattered down the stairs. It took most of the way to my car to bring her up to speed. I left out Jerry's name and where he worked but gave her a rough overview of everything else. "You're a journalist," I said. "Where the hell does someone start looking into the CIA?"

"You mean if they're exacting revenge because of *They're Watching*?" Her face showed what she thought the likelihood of that was. It did seem a tough argument to make: that either an adjunct film teacher or his by-the-numbers script was important enough to capture the attention of the CIA. "I can pry into that for you, find out who their media contact is that deals with Hollywood. But if it *is* the CIA out to teach you a lesson, why would they be backing off?"

"What do you mean, backing off?"

"They showed you where all the surveillance devices were in your house and told you to remove them. If that's not letting you off the hook, I don't know what is." Her features had rearranged themselves to show impatience at my daftness.

I thought about what Ariana had said in the greenhouse, how everything so far had been merely the setup. "They're just getting ready for the next phase," I said. "Whatever's in that e-mail."

"So why would they give up the advantage of being able to monitor you?" She smoothed her red locks tight to her skull and flipped an elastic hair tie off her wrist and into place. With her hair back, she looked stunning and severe, a comic-book heroine trying to blend in as one of us. Her baggy black T-shirt undercut the effect, but not enough that a male student didn't slow his beat-to-crap Hyundai to gape at her. Of course she didn't notice; she was too focused on me. "They're indicating something else, I think. Establishing trust, even. It's a *dialogue*."

I thought about how the intruder had run from me, though he was big enough to have snapped me in two across a knee. The conflict hadn't turned physical, at least not yet, but we were adversaries, certainly. Weren't we?

"They didn't threaten you," she pressed. "Not explicitly."

"Just implicitly, about six different ways." I unlocked my car and threw my overstuffed briefcase into the passenger seat. "I gotta go. Don't mention this to anyone."

"Look"—she grabbed my arm—"I'm just saying, maybe you passed some test."

"How? What have I done that could constitute passing a test?"

"Say this *is* the CIA. Maybe they saw something in your script. Maybe they were impressed. And this is, I don't know . . . their way of recruiting you."

Even through the fear, I felt a flush of the old pride. "You think it was that good?"

"This is U.S. intelligence we're talking about," she said. "They don't exactly have high standards."

The idea took hold for a moment. Did I want to

believe it because it was less threatening or because it was flattering? I shook off the thought. "Nothing about this feels like a game. They've invaded our lives. The surveillance guy who checked out our house said these are top-level—"

"Of *course* Surveillance Guy doom-and-gloomed you. You said he was a government dickhead. Or *former* government dickhead. It's their *job* to tell us how scary the world is. It's in their DNA or something."

"This situation? I don't need anyone to tell me it's scary." I ducked into the car. The gas gauge was broken from one of my morning slugfests, the dial stuck on full. A glance at the odometer showed 211 miles since my last fill-up; I'd have just enough gas to make it to Punch without having to stop.

I started to pull out, but Julianne tapped on the window until I rolled it down. She leaned over, her milk-pale skin almost translucent in the blinding Valley sunlight. "Like I said before. Maybe they're not after the usual."

I touched the gas, easing back, the tires crackling over dead leaves. "That's exactly what I'm worried about."

Even though I was running behind, I circled the parking garage again, making sure I wasn't being followed. I called Ariana's cell phone, and she picked up on the first ring.

"You okay?"

"Yeah. I stayed home. Wanted to clean up a little. Not like I'd be able to concentrate on work anyway. Can you?"

"*Home?* Look—"

"I know. 'Be careful.' But it's not like they're planning on kicking down the door and shooting me, or they would've just done it already. This whole thing isn't exactly an efficient setup for that."

I stared at my real cell phone, turned off on the passenger seat. I wanted to give Ariana the number of the prepaid I was using, but her line wasn't secure, and now I was heading into the mouth of the parking structure. "Okay," I said. "Just—"

The reception cut out. Cursing, I zipped up three levels and slotted the Camry into an end space. I spotted Punch sitting on a flat bench near the elevator, reading a magazine. Hurrying over, I checked my shoes again, making sure my Kenneth Coles hadn't morphed into my GPS Nikes in the past thirty seconds.

I reached the bench and sat next to him, but facing the other direction. It was a good meet point—a lot of cars and foot traffic, plenty of ambient noise, a roof to protect us from Google Earth and its more ambitious brethren. But the question, put to me by the electronic voice, reverberated: *Do you have any question as to our capability to reach into your life and touch you where we want?* Was I foolish to be here? To be looking into this at all? But I had to. Blind submission was what they wanted, but it hardly guaranteed my safety, or Ariana's.

Punch kept his gaze on the magazine. "I was just calling to tell you I put out some feelers about Keith Conner and got back some really screwy signals."

"Like?"

"Like why the fuck am I asking around about Keith Conner and stop it. Look, this kind of search, it's improper and illegal. My cop contacts aren't allowed to just *run* people, especially not as favors for me. But the thing is, no one usually checks or notices. These improper searches got noticed, though. All of them. As in right fucking away. So my guys got chewed out, and I got burned. Someone's watching this shit, and it ain't some tea-sipping publicist for the studio. They're monitoring it from inside or above the department. Now, you want to tell me what the hell you got yourself into?"

I gave him more or less the version I'd laid out for Julianne. Punch's ruddy face got ruddier, accenting the broken capillaries across his meaty nose and cheeks. "Shit." He wiped his hands on his button-up. One shirttail was untucked. It was good he and Jerry never overlapped; he was Walter Matthau to Jerry's Jack Lemmon. "You're all over this. Investigating, figuring out the angles."

"It's like writing, I guess."

"Yeah, but you're good at this."

The elevator doors dinged open, and I felt a stab of apprehension. A mom emerged, tugging a squalling boy behind her. She scowled down at him. "That's why I *told* you to leave it in the car."

I waited for them to pass, then withdrew the mini-recorder from my pocket and handed it over. Punch took the unit from me, folded it into his *Maxim,* and clicked the button. That voice again: *"So . . . are you ready to get started?"*

"Electronic voice modulator," Punch said. "We see that shit all the time in crank calls."

"Any way to untangle it? Get a read on the voice, type of phone, anything?"

"No. I have a hotshot criminalist who wants in on a show I'm consulting for. To let him prove his worth, I let him play with some scrambled-voice threat to a producer, and he came up with jack shit." He tilted the magazine, letting the recorder plop back into my lap. "This whole thing is way too big for me and my IQ. Since your phone situation is compromised, don't call." He raised a sausage of a finger at me. "And don't send any e-mails either. Once you open that shit, even if you delete it, your hard drive holds the memory of it. Last thing I need is your Big Brothers tracking you right into my computer."

"So how do I contact you?"

"You don't. Too risky." He tugged at his jowls, taking in my expression. "You don't like it, put it in your fourth step and call your sponsor."

"I'm not in AA."

"Oh, right. That's supposed to be me." He stood, curling the magazine in a blocky fist, and offered a shrug before he walked off. "Good luck."

He meant it, but he also meant good-bye.

The lecture hall's emptiness seemed all the more glaring given the stadium seating. I stood in the doorway, peering in hopelessly. On the posted room schedule—3:00: PROFESSOR DAVIS, ELEMENTS OF SCREENWRITING. On the clock—3:47. My shirt and pants stuck to me; I'd sprinted from the parking lot to class. Dropping my briefcase, I sagged against the jamb to catch my breath.

As I retreated down the hall, I swore I was catching odd looks from students. The department assistant called out to me as I passed the main office. "Professor Davis? I have that student file you requested."

I'd all but forgotten about my underhanded request for Bugayong's file. Stepping inside, I noted the department chair chatting with a few professors at the mail cubbyholes. The assistant held the file across her desk and grinned pertly. Dr. Peterson paused from her conversation to regard me and the assistant, the proffered file floating between us.

I lowered my voice before I realized I had. "Thanks. But I got the matter straightened out." I nodded at Dr. Peterson a bit too solicitously and withdrew, leaving the folder in the assistant's hand. Moving back down the hall, I couldn't help but glance around nervously. A clique of students snickered at something as I passed.

I knocked on the door of the tiny room I shared in rotation with three other instructors so we'd have somewhere to hold office hours. But whoever had been there last had already cleared out. I shut the door behind me, thunked my briefcase down on its side, and sat at the narrow desk. There are few places as depressing as a shared office. Lipstick-stained coffee mug holding gnawed pencils. Several dated textbooks and a cheap wooden carving of the three wise monkeys on the otherwise empty bookshelf. A beige Dell from the turn of the century.

Poking a finger into the slit of my briefcase, I lifted it open. The sheaf of ungraded scripts stared back at me. I tugged them out, patted my pockets and behind my ears for a red pen, and finally located one in the bottom drawer, next to a partially eaten muffin. It would have to do. I got through a script and a half before I found myself drawing little circles across the page, like the ones that had marked off the surveillance devices on our floor plan.

The Dell took two solid minutes to fire up. Dial-up Internet took even longer. After chewing my cheek, stalling, I found myself on the Gmail page, typing in *patrickdavis081075* and my mother's maiden name for the password. My finger rested on the mouse, but I hesitated before clicking. An e-mail, they claimed, would arrive at four on Sunday, the day after tomorrow. So what was I so damn scared of now?

Deep breath. I tapped the mouse. The little hourglass trickled and trickled.

There it was. An e-mail account. *My* e-mail account. Waiting for me. With an empty in-box.

At the rap on the door, I jumped, almost knocking the keyboard off the desk. I hastily logged out just before Dr. Peterson stepped into the room. "Patrick, I've heard that things have been a bit uneven with you lately."

"Uneven?" I nudged the mouse over and tapped to clear the browser's history.

"Late for one class, another you never showed up for. An altercation with a student in the hall."

"Huh?"

"Some kind of shouting match? Professor Shahnazari overheard you cursing at a student."

"Right, that was—"

She raised her voice, talking over me. "Then I find

out you made a request to see a student file. Did anyone give you the impression that adjunct professors
were entitled to review confidential student documents?"

"No. It was a bad judgment call."

"We agree there." Her lips, etched with small ver-
tical wrinkles, compressed. "I hope you can pull it
together here in short order. And in the meantime,
you'd do well to remember, invasion of privacy is
something we don't take lightly."

"No," I agreed, "nor do I."

CHAPTER 23

Cleaned up, the house looked almost worse. I glanced around at the glaring holes in the walls, the misaligned flaps of carpet, the bags of trash. It looked more like itself now, just a badly damaged version. My Nikes were set out by the closet door, as if Ariana wanted to keep an eye on them, and beside her on the couch sat her raincoat, positioned over the slashed cushions like an invisible friend.

She'd taken up her hair in a ponytail and was wearing my ripped Celtics T-shirt from the '08 championship season. In her hand a Burgundy wineglass filled, no doubt, with Chianti; she loved cheaper reds, but the bowl-like glass made her feel more like she was drinking. She rolled her eyes at me and, pinching the phone between jaw and shoulder, made a mouth-flapping gesture with her free hand. "If he hasn't returned your call, don't text-message. It'll just seem desperate." A pause. "I'm sure he got the voice mail, Janice. You just left it yesterday. Give the guy the weekend."

I paused, taking in the surreal scene. In light of the ripped-apart house, the bugged raincoat, and the date we had with the curb drain in a few hours, it seemed bizarrely domestic.

"Look, I gotta go. Patrick just walked in. . . . I know, I know. You'll be fine." She hung up, tossed the phone into the cushions, and said, loudly. *"That'll* teach you guys to listen in." A weary half smile. "They probably committed hara-kiri in their surveillance vans. Speaking of . . ." She reached into her purse, withdrew the cigarette-pack jammer, and clicked the black button to knock out any surveillance devices that might have regenerated since Jerry's visit.

"You didn't say anything to Janice?"

"Please. Our problems *pale* in comparison to hers. Besides, I'm not sure how to slip *this* into casual conversation."

"You did a great job," I said. "With the house."

She blew a wisp of hair off her forehead. "Still looks like a ten-car pileup."

I handed her one of the throwaway phones. "I programmed the number of mine in here. I don't want to not be able to talk to you when we're apart."

Her face changed. My words hung there, so I replayed them, heard what they meant to her, to us. A few days ago, we were barely speaking.

I sat beside her. She offered her glass, and I took a sip. "It's pleasant," she said. "Being nice to each other for a change."

"We should have solicited techno-stalkers months ago."

"I was sitting here looking at our house. All the crap in it. Dunn-Edwards Shaved Ice paint. Cavetto molding. That stupid chandelier I picked up in Cambria. And I thought a week ago this all looked perfect. And it felt like shit living here. At least it's honest now. This mess. This is where we are."

A prim distance between us, we stared at the spray of wires where the plasma used to hang, sharing a glass of wine and waiting for midnight.

The black duffel tugged at my shoulder, bulging with the gear inside. We stood at the curb, Ariana clutching her jacket closed against a biting wind. Given the comforting yellow glow spilling around our curtains and blinds, it was easy to forget how torn up our house was inside. Apart from the occasional porch light, the neighboring houses and apartments were dark, which, along with an odd lapse in traffic, made the crowded neighborhood seem abandoned.

"Three minutes." Shuddering, she looked up from her cell-phone clock to peer at the mouth of the curb drain. "Hope it's wide enough."

As I stepped toward the gap, dead leaves crumbled underfoot against the metal grate, brown flecks spinning down into darkness. A mossy smell rose with the warm air. I guided the end of the bulging duffel through the curb drain. A snug fit, but a fit.

Ariana checked the time again. "Not yet." She looked across at the apartment balconies, then down the slope of Roscomare Road, her eyes tearing from the cold. "Wonder where they're watching us from."

A silver Porsche flew by, the engine's roar shattering the calm. We both recoiled, Ariana raising her arms as if to shield herself from a hail of drive-by bullets, me stepping back, almost losing my footing on the curb. The driver, annoyed beneath his baseball cap, had scowled at our overreaction; he wasn't going *that* fast. My head buzzed from the shot of adrenaline and the burn-out blend of sleeplessness and caffeine. Ari and I took our positions again. Placing a foot on the end of the bag, I waited for her signal.

How much our lives had changed in four days.

Moths battered the flickering streetlight. Crickets sawed.

"Okay," she said. "Heave-ho."

I shoved. The bag bunched at its midsection, then popped through. We waited to hear it hit, but instead there was a muffled thump. A soft landing. I looked down between my shoes through the metal grate, my eyes straining to discern the shape in the darkness.

What came into focus first were the whites of the eyes.

My skin was tingling everywhere—the back of my neck, up my ribs, the inside of my mouth. I blinked and the eyes were gone, the duffel with them. Just a muted sound against the moist, buried concrete—the faint heartbeat of footsteps padding away beneath the street.

Wearing sweats and a T-shirt, I stepped out of the bathroom, drying my wet hair with a towel. When I pulled it off my head, I noticed Ariana in the doorway of our bedroom with her nighttime cup of chamomile and the cigarette-box jammer.

"Sorry," she said. "I don't like being downstairs alone right now."

Unspoken rules had evolved with astonishing rapidity. We'd stopped changing in front of each other. When she was in a room with the door closed, I knocked. When I showered, she kept out of the bedroom.

"Then you shouldn't be downstairs alone," I said.

We sidestepped each other, giving wide berth, changing positions. I didn't continue down the hall, and she didn't climb into bed. Instead she leaned against the bureau, still filmed with drywall dust. We studied each other, my hands folding the towel, unfolding it, folding it again.

I cleared my throat. "Do you want me to stay upstairs tonight?"

She said, "I do."

I stopped folding the towel.

Her hand circled. She was trying for casual, but her eyes hadn't gotten the memo. "Do you *want* to stay?"

I said, "I do."

She walked over, turned back the comforter on my side. I sat on the mattress. She went around and slid in. Her clothes were still on. I got in, also fully dressed. She reached over and turned off the light. We sat with our backs against the curved headboard. I couldn't remember even touching the new bed before now. It was as comfortable as it looked.

"Do you really?" she asked. "Watch me cry some mornings through the window?"

"Yes."

Even in the dark, we were looking straight ahead instead of at each other.

"Because you want to know what? That I'm still

sorry?" Her voice was thin, vulnerable. "That I still care?"

We sat awhile longer.

"I want to come in to hold you," I said. "But I can never find the nerve."

I sensed her face rotate, slowly, toward mine. "How 'bout now?" she asked.

I lifted my arm. She slid down beside me, put her cheek on my chest. I stroked her hair. She was warm, soft. I thought of Don's hands. His goatee. I felt a compulsion to pull away, but I didn't. I considered the distance between what I wanted to do and what I thought I should do. A collision of alternate selves, a crossroads to alternate futures. My wife had cheated on me. And now I was holding her. We were together, right now. I was afraid of what that would look like—not to others but to myself. In my quieter moments. Driving to work. Sipping coffee between classes. Watching a clever movie scene about extracurricular fucking, Ari stiffening beside me, our sudden chagrin in the dark of a theater. That stiletto jab of paradigms past, of how it was supposed to be.

"I think I want to have a baby," Ariana said.

My lips were suddenly dry. "I've heard you have to have sex for that."

"Not right *now.*"

"I wasn't suggesting—"

"I mean, not a *baby* right now. Or even soon. But being threatened like this, I've been thinking about our life a lot. I'm sure you have, too. I've got stuff I like to do—the furniture, my plants. But I'm not gonna be content to turn into one of those women who drives her SUV up and down these hills, going to stupid appointments and Whole Foods. I mean, look at Martinique. That's where I'm headed."

"You're not—"

"I know, but you know what I mean." Her hand twitched, looking for something to do. "I want to have a baby, but at the same time I'm terrified that I want to have a baby for all the wrong reasons. Does any of this make sense?"

I made a soft noise of support. A flash of copper pipe gleamed where we'd torn through the drywall by the bathroom. Her head rose and fell with my breathing. We lay there awhile longer, as I worked my feelings into words.

"I don't want to keep doing what I've been doing," I said. "Or at least I don't want to feel the same way doing it."

"Yes. Exactly." She came up off my chest, excited. "So here we are. Now. Off balance from all this crap, but at least seeing clearly. Let's not upset that."

"What do you mean?"

"What if you *don't* check for that e-mail Sunday? What if we just stick our heads in the sand and pretend nothing's wrong?"

"And you think it'll go away?"

"Let's pretend it will. Let's pretend that everything's like it was before hidden cameras and Don Miller and screenplay deals. Just for tonight."

We lay together, fully dressed, in our bed. I held her until her breathing evened out, and then I lay there awake, listening to her sleep.

CHAPTER 24

Gmail's home page glowed back at me from my computer. The filled-in ID and password, my finger again poised above the mouse, Ariana over my shoulder, her breath scented of the strawberries she'd eaten in a cereal bowl with milk and sugar. The day, like yesterday, had passed in an excruciating crawl, Ariana and I on top of each other, slogging through mind-numbing work and household tasks, trying not to reference clocks and watches. The time in my menu bar showed 4:01 P.M.

As my finger lowered, Ariana said, *"Wait."* She pulled the mariposa—orange again—out from behind her ear and fiddled with it. "Listen, I know we were getting suspicious there for a while. Of each other. Now that we're getting clearer, I just wanted to ask you . . ."

"Go on."

"Is there something—*anything*—you want to tell me?"

"Like what?"

"Like what that e-mail's gonna hold?"

"As in me snorting blow off a stripper's thigh? No, there's nothing, Ari. I've been racking my brain, and

I can't think of a single thing." I clicked "Log In" brusquely, in protest of her question. Then it hit me to ask, "Is there something you want to tell *me*?"

She leaned forward. "What if it's me and Don?"

As the page loaded, I sat with that one, the weight of it low in my stomach. That was all I needed—my wife's one-night mess sent right to my desktop. A high-water mark of invasiveness. The thought brought to mind a snatch of my conversation with Punch— how e-mails, even once they're deleted, leave an evidence trail in the hard drive.

With dread, I stared at the loading page. It hadn't occurred to me that once I opened that e-mail, I couldn't control what it carried with it. Into my computer.

Before I could do anything, there it was, a single e-mail staring out at us from my in-box. The sender line, blank. Subject line, blank. For now, the unopened e-mail still resided safely on the server, not yet called up on my computer. I moved the cursor all the way to the side of the screen, in case it decided to double-click the e-mail by itself.

They'd visited this computer already, printed out those JPEGs of our floor plans. I checked the history function of Explorer to see which Web sites had been recently visited. It listed none I didn't recognize.

"Wait," Ariana asked. "Why aren't you opening the e-mail?"

I mimed someone listening, then gestured a question: *Where's the jammer?* In answer she tugged the fake pack of Marlboros from her pocket. She never let the thing out of her sight.

"I don't want to do this here," I said. "From my computer."

"Look," Ari said, still back a step, "if it *is* me and Don, we might as well face it together."

"No, I mean I shouldn't be retrieving data from them on my computer. Even if I erase it, the record of it stays in the hard drive somewhere. Or they could use an e-mail to piggyback in some virus that lets them read my computer remotely."

"Wouldn't they have just installed that when they were here?"

I was up now, whistling down the stairs, Ariana at my back. I said, "Jerry checked our computers for spyware, remember?"

Tugging on my shoes, I hurried for the garage. "Wait," she said. She pointed at my feet.

I looked down. I was wearing my bugged Nikes. Cursing, I kicked them off and stepped into my loafers. Given my white socks, not my best look, but I didn't want my stalkers to know I was heading to Kinko's.

Patrick Davis.

That's all the e-mail said, though my name had been turned into a hyperlink. Buried in a rented corner cubicle, I looked over my shoulder. The Kinko's guy was busy servicing a loud woman in louder clothing, and the other customers Xeroxed and stapled at the bank of copiers toward the front of the store.

Raising the hem of my shirt, I wiped the sweat from my forehead. Gritted my teeth. And clicked on my name.

A Web site popped up. As I took in the Internet

address—a lengthy series of numbers, far too many
to commit to memory—bold letters appeared:

THIS WEB SITE WILL ERASE
UPON COMPLETION OF ONE
VIEWING.

They faded into the black background, a ghostly
effect.

Digital photos flashed one after another, like a
PowerPoint presentation.

Ariana's greenhouse framed against our trees at
night.

Then, inside, the shot bathed in a green, otherworldly glow.

The row of pots on the middle shelf of the east-
facing wall. Her lavender mariposas, unpicked and
unworn these past months.

A familiar hand in a familiar latex glove, lifting
the end pot and saucer. Beneath them, on the soft wood,
a purple jewel case.

That disc hadn't been there three nights earlier
when Ariana and I had searched the greenhouse.

I was leaning forward at the monitor, my hands
tensed like talons. The discs, the devices, the phone
call—none of it had acclimated me to watching someone pry around in our possessions, in our lives. If
anything, my reaction was worse, trauma compounding trauma, sandpaper on raw skin.

The photo disappeared, replaced by a written
address: *2132 Aminta St., Van Nuys, CA 91406.* Desperately, I looked for a pen and some scrap paper—

none in my cubicle. I flew around the corner to the next desk, knocking over the plastic supply caddy and grabbing a pencil and Post-it from the spill. When I got back to my monitor, the typed address had been replaced by a Google Maps screen, the location marked smack in the shittiest part of Van Nuys. I managed to jot down the address, grabbing it from the location bubble, before that screen also blipped off.

The next featured four numbers, evenly spaced: *4 7 8 3.*

I wrote those down as well, an instant before they were replaced by a shot of a dingy apartment door. Flaking paint, cracking seams, and two rusty numbers nailed where a peephole should be: *11.* One of the nails had come loose, so the second *1* had sagged to a tilt.

And then, like a breath of icy air down my rigid spine, a message appeared, as bold as its type:

GO ALONE.

The browser window closed on its own, quitting out of the program. When I reopened it, it had no records stored of recent Web sites visited.

There was no evidence, no artifact that said this was anything more than an evil dream. All I had were an address and four mystery numbers written in my own hand.

CHAPTER 25

"That's *it*?" Ariana asked.

On the couch next to me, she turned over the purple DVD case as if it had a Blockbuster write-up on the back. The cover still sported a spot of moisture from the plant saucer.

"We must've missed something," I said, already fussing over the remote. We stared again at the plasma, remounted somewhat crookedly on our wall.

The picture flickered back on. Grainy black and white—probably a security camera. A basement, expansive enough that it wasn't residential. A dangling bulb putting out a throw of weak light, a set of stairs catching the shadows. A generator, a water heater, several unlabeled cardboard boxes, and a spread of blank concrete floor. On the second-to-bottom stair, what appeared to be a mound of cigarettes. A bank of fuse boxes, just in view on the far wall. Superimposed on the screen, the date and a running time stamp: *11/3/05, 14:06:31* and counting.

The footage ended.

"I don't get it," Ariana said. "Is there some coded meaning that we're missing?"

We watched the DVD through again. And again.

She bounced off the couch, exasperated. "How the hell are we supposed to figure out what that *is*?"

She watched with dread as I plucked the Post-it from the coffee table. That Van Nuys address.

I ejected the DVD, nestled it in its case, and slid it into my back pocket. Sitting on the floor in the foyer, I laced up my Nikes. I needed to wear them sometimes to not give away that I'd discovered the tracking device embedded in the heel. Might as well do it now while I was following orders.

Ariana stopped me at the door to the garage. "Maybe you just shouldn't. You don't know what's behind that door, Patrick." Her voice trembled with intensity. "You don't know how to handle this kind of thing. Are you sure you want to go poking a stick into this?"

"Look, I'm not Jason Bourne, but I know a little."

"You know what they say about a little knowledge." She started to cross her arms but thought better of it. "They could just be hoping that you're dumb enough to show up. What can they do if you don't?"

"You want to find out?"

She didn't answer.

I stepped down into the garage. "We've got to figure out what this is. And who's doing it to us."

"Think, Patrick. Right now? This moment? Nothing's *really* happened to us yet. Our house is safe. You could just come back in here with me."

At the side of my car, I paused to look at her. For an instant I thought about going back inside, making a cup of tea, and grading student scripts. What could they do if they built a maze and no rat showed up?

Was there more risk in scuttling along through their twists and turns or staying still and waiting for the walls to close in?

The keys poked the inside of my fist. "I'm sorry," I said. "I *have* to know."

She watched me from the doorway as I backed out. She was still standing there when the garage door shuddered down, wiping her from view.

Down in the bowl of the Valley, dusk seemed heavier, thickened with smog. Car fumes and sickly-sweet barbecue fragranced the still air. Crushed Michelob cans and fast-food wrappers lined the gutter. The apartment building was your typical Van Nuys disaster—crumbling stucco, deteriorating concrete walkways, a bent security gate. Air conditioners hung from windows, dripping condensation. The Vacancy sign flapping from the rain gutter was hardly enticing.

I'd been standing across the street for several minutes, steeling myself for whatever waited behind the door to Apartment 11 and hoping that the acid at the back of my throat would dissipate. What was I stalling for? If they were monitoring the tracking device in my Nikes, they already knew I'd shown up to the party.

The hum of an engine sent me, finally, into motion. A patrol car creeping up the block, each cop looking out his respective window, scanning the sidewalks and buildings. Turning away, I shouldered against a parked van and pretended to talk into my cell phone to bury my face. The sedan neared, tires crackling over asphalt, static-laced bursts from the scanner. I caught a glimpse of mirrored sunglasses, a muscular forearm resting on the open windowsill, and then the car coasted past aloofly. I exhaled the held breath burning my lungs. I felt like I was doing something illicit. Was I?

I jogged across the street and confronted the security gate. A waffled metal door, housed in a frame that blocked the entrance to the courtyard. To my left, a speaker unit with a keypad. The instructions for dialing up to the apartments were soggy from rainwater, illegible beneath the cracked casing. A directory, under intact cover, paired owner names with apartments, but 11 and a number of others were blank. The yellowed form looked as if it hadn't been updated in years. Shrugging, I tried to call up to number 11, but a disconnected signal bleated from the speaker.

I nodded to myself.

Then I dug the Post-it from my pocket and smoothed it next to the keypad. I punched in those four numbers I'd written beneath the address—*4783*—and thumbed the pound symbol. A grating buzz released the gate, and with a stab of exhilaration I walked through.

Maybe not *Enemy of the State*. Maybe I was living out *The Game*.

Apartment 11 was at the back of the courtyard on the second floor. My unease mounted as I ascended the stairs. Ariana was right—this was foolhardy. I could be strolling into my own murder.

The floating walkway serviced four apartments, each in worse shape than the last. I reached number 11. Those rusting numerals, loosely nailed to the door.

No peephole. With its cracks and curling paint, the ancient door looked even worse than in the picture. The knob hung loose. A new dead bolt, the sole upgrade, had been installed high on the door, compensating for the old-fashioned keyhole assembly.

I took out the DVD in its purple case, regarded it, tapped it against my thigh. Sucked in a breath, blew it out hard. Then I pushed the doorbell. Broken. Given the condition of the complex, I wasn't surprised. I pressed my ear to the wood, dry paint poking the side of my face. More nothing.

I raised my hand but couldn't bring myself to knock. I don't know what stopped me. Dread, maybe. Or perhaps an early warning system, some heightened awareness my cells were registering even if my mind was not. I rethought my decision to wear the GPS Nikes. Did they rule out a retreat? I lowered my fist. Released a silent breath. Was that a muffled creak I heard from inside or merely the floor groaning beneath my own weight? Slowly, cautiously, I crouched to look through the old-fashioned assembly.

Filling the keyhole, squirming to take in my nearing face, was an eye peering back at me.

I yelped and leaped back as the door flew open, and then a stocky man in a tank top charged, shoving me into the railing.

"Who are you?" he yelled. "Why are you doing this to me?"

He pounced again, pushing me into the floor, as if unsure what to do with me. I flung him away and we squared off, but it quickly became clear neither of us wanted to fight.

His breathing was ragged, more agitated than angry. At five foot nine, he was a few inches shorter than me, but thicker. Massy arms bulged from his worn undershirt. His curly hair, mussed high and paired with a receding hairline, added a comedic note to his otherwise tough-guy appearance.

He pointed to the purple jewel case, lying cracked where I'd dropped it on his doorstep. "Why are you leaving those?"

My mouth goldfished. "I . . . I'm not. Someone's been delivering discs to *my* house. Surveillance footage of me. They got that DVD to me, along with your address."

Keeping his eyes on me, he picked up the case and flipped it open. Then he glanced down, quickly, at the disc. "These are the kind of DVDs you use, too?"

"No. Mine are different. . . ." It took me a moment to register the "too." I said slowly, "They send you footage, recorded onto your own discs."

"Yes. Through my mail slot. Under my windshield wiper. In my microwave." He wiped his mouth with the back of his hand, then swiped his thumb twice across the inside of his wrist, his movements quick, jittery. "Little movies of me walking to the park. Shopping for groceries. That kind of shit."

"Did they call you? On a cell phone?"

"No. Never talked to anyone. But my service got shut off—bills. And I don't have a landline."

"Do you have the DVDs?"

The thumb moved across his wrist again, a nervous tic. "No. I threw them out. Why would I keep them?"

"How long have they been doing it?"

"Two months."

"Two *months*? Christ, it started five days ago for me, and I'm already . . ." Dread overtook me, and I paused to breathe.

"Why me?" He tapped his chest with a fist. "Why film *me*? Filling up my fucking truck with gas?"

"They got me taking a leak. Have you talked to the cops?"

"I don't like cops. Besides, what are they gonna say?"

"How were you contacted?" I asked.

"I wasn't. Just the discs showing up. I don't know why . . ."

"Why they're doing this to us."

His expression shifted. We were comrades all of a sudden, patients with the same affliction. "Why they *chose* us," he said.

I thought of that two-word directive at the end of the e-mail. *GO ALONE,* not *COME ALONE.* A mission, not a summons. We'd been put in touch to figure something out. Our gazes moved in concert to the DVD in his hands.

He rushed inside the apartment, me at his heels. The dense reek of mold overwhelmed me two steps in, less a smell than an impression on my pores. I blinked into the drawn-curtain dimness to see him fumbling the disc into a player beneath a hefty TV. Dirty clothes and grocery bags were strewn across the patchy carpet, as well as a few discs in purple cases marked with TV-show names. No chairs, no couches, no table by the run of counter that passed for a kitchenette. The only items that couldn't be swept up were a twin mattress thrown in the corner, topped with a twisted fuss of sheets, and the TV denting a metal trunk.

He shoved himself up and took a few steps back, standing shoulder to shoulder with me, facing the screen, his knee jackhammering.

The picture came up. Basement, stairs, concrete floor.

"It's nothing," I said. "It's—"

He let out a creaking gasp. He fell to his knees. Crawling forward, he paused the image and put his face right up against the screen, scrutinizing something in the bottom-right corner. Then he sat back on his heels and swayed a little. It wasn't until a gut-wrenching moan filled the room that I realized he was crying. He lowered his face to the dank carpet and sobbed. I stood a few feet behind him, mystified, completely at a loss.

He rocked and cried some more.

"Are you . . . ?" I asked. "Can I . . . ?"

Pulling himself to his feet, he fell into me, squeezing me hard. A tinge of soured sweat. "Thank you, thank you, God bless you."

I raised an arm awkwardly from my side as if to pat his back, but my hand just hovered there. "I don't know what I did. I don't know what that is."

"Please," he said, stepping away. He looked around,

as if only now realizing he had nowhere for me to sit. "I'm sorry, I can't remember the last time I had someone . . ." He seemed disoriented.

"It's fine." I sat on the floor.

He followed suit. His hands moved in circular gestures, but he couldn't manage to speak. A square of yellow light from the window fell across him, filtered through thick, dusty curtains. A water stain in the far corner darkened the carpet, climbed the wall.

"I was a custodian," he finally said. "At a high school outside Pittsburgh. The water heater gave out, and we were tight, you know, budget cuts." His thumb skimmed across the inside of his wrist again, as if smoothing the skin. "A guy on the school board was in on some low-income housing deal, they were tearing down a complex, whatever. So he got a big water heater from there." He gestured at the screen, the water heater. "They delivered it for me to install. An older unit. I said I didn't like the looks of it. They told me it wasn't a beauty pageant, that it had been tested and met whatever qualifications. So I put it in. The thing is . . . the thing is, they'd prepped it for delivery. Drained it, I mean, and wired the pressure-relief valve so the leftover water wouldn't drip out during transport." He fell silent.

"What happened?" I asked.

"I drank back then. Not anymore. But I may have had a few nips that morning. The morning I installed it, I mean. Just to get going. Third of November."

I glanced over at the date stamp on the screen: *11/3/05.* My skin, tingling with anticipation.

"Through that wall's a basement room. Shop class."

He pointed, his hand shaking, and there on the inside of his wrist was a thin white ridge of scar tissue. His other hand lay in his lap, exposing a matching razor-blade remembrance. "When the wall blew apart, one kid got killed. Another got her face mostly burned off. That she lived . . . well, in some ways that's even worse." Again he thumbed the line of one of the scars, rocking a little. "During the investigation someone found the flask in my locker. There were liability issues, you know. And they said I forgot to remove the wire, so the pressure-relief valve couldn't open. Steam built up." His voice thickened. "They never found any part of the wire in the whaddayacallit."

I managed to say, "Debris."

"Right. No piece of anything big enough." He broke off. "I knew I never would've forgotten. But as the whole thing went on, the questions, I wasn't positive. Then I wasn't sure at all. I'd installed security cameras down there a few months before, and I asked to see footage, so I could know. I *needed* to know."

"Why have security footage in a basement?"

"Kids were sneaking down there smoking, having sex. They found a few condoms. So the principal pulled me aside at the beginning of the year, told me to put in a surveillance cam. I don't know who reviewed the tapes or anything, but kids got pulled out of class and spoken to, and then they stopped going down there. But when I asked about the footage after the explosion, all I got was, 'We would never *spy* on members of the student body.' I even went to the basement with the investigators, but the camera had been removed. So this footage, *this footage*"—he jabbed a finger at the TV—"never existed." His face broke, and he bowed his head but didn't make a noise. "A cop buddy of mine told me later that illegal monitoring like that's a real big deal. If they recorded students having sex, they could've been busted on kiddie-porn charges, even. So they hung me out. What they didn't take from me, I found a way to throw away myself."

I did my best to keep my eyes from those slash lines on his wrists. Instead I looked at *my* hands, scuffed up with scabs and scar tissue of my own. Regret, and the marks it leaves on us. There I was, punching a dashboard over a shitty run of luck and my wife's transgression. It seemed so insignificant compared to the dead kid and the faceless girl riding his conscience, driving him to the razor's edge.

"I been dead, mostly. Moving around in a haze, city to city. Can't hold down jobs too long. Can't look people in the eye. But look at that. *Look* at that." The paused screen again, the time stamp, that water heater—his eyes glistened taking it all in. "No wire on that water heater. No wire in the whole picture. It's the most beautiful goddamned thing I ever seen in my life." He shook his head, drew in a quavering breath, then refocused on me. "Listen, maybe we can figure out some overlap between us that explains why we were chosen."

"Some way to trace the puppet strings back to whoever's holding them."

"I'm a little . . . I'm not so good right now. A lot to take in, you know? Will you come back so we can do that? Coupla days, maybe?"

"Yes. Of course."

"Don't forget. I'd like to know. I'd like to thank them."

We found our feet and shuffled, dazed in the half-light, to the door. "They didn't . . ." I licked my dry lips. "They didn't give you anything for me." I couldn't bring myself to phrase it like a question.

"No," he said. "I'm sorry." His eyes moved across my face, seeming to read my disappointment. I could feel empathy coming off him in waves, how badly he wanted to reciprocate, to do for me something like what had been done for him. He offered his hand. "We never . . . I'm Doug Beeman."

"Patrick Davis."

We shook, and he clutched my forearm. "You changed my life. For the first time, I feel like . . ." He bobbed his head slightly. "You changed my life. I'm so appreciative you did this for me."

I thought of what the voice had told me: *This is nothing like what you imagine.* I'd taken it, wrongly, as a warning. I said quietly, "I didn't do anything."

"Yes," he said, stepping back and drawing the door closed. "You were the instrument."

CHAPTER 26

My head still thrumming from my encounter with Beeman, I stepped from the garage into our quiet downstairs. After dispatching with the shrieking alarm, I could hear the shower running on the second floor, the rush of the water pipes the sole sound of life. With the lights off down here, the house felt desolate.

I clicked on the kitchen overheads and noticed that the caller ID screen on the kitchen telephone showed a missed call. I checked the message, my back going rigid when I heard my lawyer's voice, asking me to call him. On a Sunday?

I reached him at the home number he'd left.

"Hello, Patrick. I got a call from opposing counsel today. The studio is hinting at a willingness to resolve all issues quickly and quietly if you'd agree that the entire matter be made confidential as a stipulation of the settlement. They indicated that the terms would be favorable to us, though they were unwilling, yet, to spell out the specifics. I was told we can expect paperwork early this week."

My mouth moved, but no sound was being produced.

"Did they mention *why* they had the sudden change of heart?" I asked after my tape-delay pause.

"They didn't. I agree—it seems odd in view of the signals they were sending. We'll wait and see what they spell out for us, but judging from the tenor of the conversation, I'm feeling cautiously optimistic."

I found myself checking the clock, a habit I'd grown accustomed to, given the heft of even a narrow slice of my attorney's billable hour.

As if reading my mind, he said, "You've been having a bit of trouble keeping my evergreen retainer . . . well, evergreen. After this push to untangle matters next week, would you like someone from Billing to call so you can work out a payment plan?"

I mumbled a half apology and an affirmative, then hung up. But even considering my sheepishness, the news—combined with the exhilaration from my experience with Beeman—left our house feeling a little less desolate.

It seemed a hell of a coincidence to get home from Beeman's to this good news. Were my omnipotent stalkers scripting this plot thread of my life, too? The whole intrigue with the DVDs seemed to be conducted on a tit-for-tat basis; I follow their instructions, and obstacles in my life fall away. Even the thought of that seven-figure lawsuit dissolving made me weak with relief. If they could do that, what *else* might they do for me?

The thrill, I realized, was the same one that came with the anticipation before a movie deal. All-play-and-less-work Hollywood, get rich in the snap of a studio head's fingers, take a shortcut to page one of *Variety* and a Bel Air mansion.

Heading upstairs to bring Ariana the news of the

past few hours, I couldn't help but wonder if my life was, at long last, finally coming back together.

"This guy, Beeman, was being held *hostage* by this stuff." I put my hand on the small of Ariana's back, guiding her over the rush of rainwater in the gutter. We passed Bel Air Foods, strolling down the hill, the air dense with humidity, the rain so faint it only came visible passing through the streetlights' glow. Cars shot by, gleaming with beads of water. "And to walk in there, and just . . . just liberate him."

I blew out a breath, which steamed and dissipated. I couldn't remember the last time I'd felt so alive. Instead of *The Game,* it seemed I'd found myself inside *Pay It Forward.*

"I mean, if this is the *first* e-mail," I said, "what the hell is the next one gonna be?"

Ariana stuffed her hands in the pockets of her parka; she refused to wear the coat with the bug stitched into the lining. "Aren't you cold?"

"What? No."

"Why would CIA agents care about helping a guy like Doug Beeman?" she asked.

"I can't think of any reason they would."

"Which means it's probably not them. Which is good." A frown. "Or bad." She chewed her worn thumbnail. "So, seeing as how these guys were *stalking* you before, what's with the new charity angle?"

"I have a theory."

"I feared as much."

She tugged me off course, and we splashed through a puddle together. Ahead, crowding its too-small lot, loomed the McMansion she and I liked to marvel at, with its solemn portico and gables and Tudorbethan mock battlements. Beyond the stucco facade, cheap vinyl siding composed the non-street-facing walls. Neighborhood rumor had it that the hodgepodge construction was built by a film distributor, and the design gave every indication it was a Hollywood-inspired fantasy. Thrown up like a peacock's tail, part enticement, part aggression. All that money, and still not enough. Cheaper the farther you wade in. I recalled the first time I walked behind a set on the lot at Summit, how those great Norman Rockwell exteriors gave way to scaffolding and two-by-fours, and how it felt like catching Santa Claus, beardless and undershirted, in the department-store locker room.

Ariana said flatly, "They need more pillars," and I laughed. Across the way, the Myerses sat in the warm glow of a dated chandelier, talking over glasses of wine. Bernie raised a hand in greeting, and we waved back. It had been months since Ariana and I had gone for an evening stroll, and I realized how much I missed it. Out in the open, breathing crisp air—for once not on top of each other, smothered by our disappointments or pinned down by a hidden lens. And later we were going to pick up an order of pho from our favorite Vietnamese place and we were going to sit on the couch and eat and talk, the coming evening as familiar and safe as an old sweatshirt.

I reached for her hand.

It seemed a little unnatural, but we both held on. "Your theory . . ." she prompted.

"I think the assault on us, our house, was to show

me what they were capable of. How else would I believe that they could know all this? I mean, about some water heater that blew up in Pittsburgh and a hidden security tape?"

"And it also ensured you'd do what they wanted."

"That, too. It was a setup so I'd be forced to be their errand boy. I mean, if someone just contacted me randomly, said, 'Take this package to an apartment in a shady part of town'?"

"But why do they need *you*?" Ari asked. "Why didn't they just send him the DVD anonymously, say, in a Netflix envelope?"

"Clearly they didn't need me."

"So then the question is . . . ?" Her hand spun in the air.

"Why did they *choose* me?"

One of her eyebrows lifted. "You're special." She said it flatly, but I knew it was a question. A challenge.

"No, not *special*," I said. "But maybe at the end of this . . ." I paused, not wanting to admit it, but she nodded me on. "Maybe I'll get a DVD that absolves *me*."

"Of what?"

"I don't know. But maybe I'll get something that does for me what that recording did for Doug Beeman. Jars me out of my—"

I caught myself.

"Like footage that shows Keith Conner banging his own damn chin?" she said. "Maybe they got that to the studio and that's why the studio's pushing for a quick confidential agreement?"

"The thought certainly occurred to me. And maybe they have something *else* that could help us, too."

"Like what?"

"I don't know." I realized that I sounded excited, and I made an effort to tone down my demeanor.

"Look, whatever this is, someone wants to fit you into their agenda," she said.

"Or someone wants to make use of me to help other people."

Her hand stiffened in mine. We walked a few more steps, and then I let go. "What?" I said. "How do you know that's not it?"

Ariana said, "Because it's what you want to believe."

My laugh had a bitter edge. "What I want is to get back at the assholes who invaded our lives. But right now playing along on the surface is the only way I can get more information. And the more we know, the closer we'll be to finding out what the hell is going on."

"Don't you teach about hubris?"

"I teach that a character has to impact the plot. He has to determine his own destiny. He can't merely react to external forces."

"So it's all about out-tricking the tricksters?" She gave me that same skeptical stare. "Tonight wasn't something more to you?"

The old frustration pricked my cheeks. "Of course it was. It's the first meaningful thing I've done in I don't know how long."

"It's not *meaningful*. For Doug Beeman it is, but for you it's fake. You didn't *do* anything but add water and stir."

"I sure as hell impacted his life."

"But you didn't *earn* it," she said.

"So what? No matter how I got manipulated there and no matter how fucking scary it was going in, freeing him from his guilt—how is that not a good thing? And if the studio caught a signal that they should back off me, that's positive, too. Why are you being so cynical?"

"Because, Patrick, one of us has to be. I mean, the way you're throwing yourself into this. You've been blocked at the keyboard for what? Half a year? And losing your interest for months before that. And now you're approaching this . . . *adventure* like it's your chance to write again."

I said swiftly, angrily, "You can't compare writing to this."

"You think this is *better* than writing?"

"No," I said, "I mean the opposite."

"You didn't see your face when you said it."

I kept my mouth shut. Despite how horrible the past week had been, was some small part of me relieved that these guys had given me something to do? Beeman's focus on me had been as absolute as that of the men behind the DVDs. When was the last time I'd been at the center of *anyone's* attention?

The elementary-school teacher from the cul-de-sac sauntered by with her down vest and twin rottweilers, and we had to pause to smile and exchange pleasantries. A young couple across the street were in their family room, hanging a hefty painting. The husband bending under the frame, his pregnant wife, one hand pressed to the small of her back, directing him with her other. A little more to the left. Left. Now right.

I used to have that life. And it was enough for me, until my script sold, until Keith Conner and Don Miller strolled into the picture and hit me smack in the blind spot. I couldn't find my way back, and every time I thought I glimpsed the route, I got derailed. What I had was more than anyone could ask for, but I couldn't figure out how to inhabit it again.

The high from Beeman's place deserted me, leaving me drained. The redemption I'd witnessed literally before my eyes had been so intense that everything else seemed bleached by the afterglow. I visualized the crappy shared office at Northridge, the unpaid legal bills and Ari crying on the arm of the couch, the braying neighbors, my unfinished scripts, the staff room with the broken coffeemaker, how-are-you chat with Bill the checkout grocer. It all seemed to pale in comparison with the dreams I'd grown up dreaming, lying on my back on the Little League grass, the New England air biting my cheeks, letting me know, minute to minute, that I was alive. Aliens and cowboys. Astronauts and outfielders. Hell, maybe I'd be a screenwriter one day, get my movie poster on the side of a bus.

I thought about what Ari had told me about the world closing in on her in a hurry, about how her life didn't have a lot of what she hoped it would. The term "soul mates" got thrown around at our wedding, and here we'd found ourselves, for better or for worse, aligned in perspective even when we weren't. My visit to Doug Beeman had cut through all that stagnation, right to the pulsing heart of what mattered. I didn't want to have to defend how it had made me feel.

The rotties were straining on their leashes, so we said good-bye to our neighbor, who gave us a wink and a smile. "Happy Valentine's Day, you two."

We'd both forgotten. As she and the dogs padded away, our frozen grins faded and we regarded each other, wary under the strain of where we'd left off. Our breath was visible, mingling.

"I guess . . ." It was going to be hard to say. "I guess I can't remember the last time I felt significant."

"If it's meaning you're looking for, don't you think you'd do better to find that in your own life?" Her tone wasn't judgmental or harsh; it was the hurt in it that made me drop my gaze.

"I didn't choose this," I said.

"Neither of us did. And we're not gonna get out of it if we don't keep our heads clear and our eyes open."

Worms lay helpless and limp, pale squiggles on the wet pavement. We circled back toward home, leaning into the incline, our heads down. By the time we passed Don and Martinique's, we were a full stride apart.

The bags, lettered in Vietnamese, sat on my passenger seat, emitting the rich scent of ginger and cardamom. The heat of the food fogged the windshield, and I had to crack a window to let in the night air. Though Ariana and I had been polite back at the house, our squabble had taken some of the shine off our newfound rapport, and I'd offered to pick up the food myself as an olive branch.

At the stoplight the *click-click-click* of my turn

signal seemed to echo my mounting restlessness. I glanced across three lanes and up the street in the opposite direction of where I was headed. Glossed with rain, the Kinko's sign peeked out from behind a church billboard. A half block away. In fact, it was along the other route I occasionally took home, so it wouldn't even qualify as a detour. I was wearing boots rather than my Nikes, so my stalkers didn't necessarily know where I was right now. My eyes ticked to my rearview, then back up the street. The Roman lettering of the billboard proclaimed EVERY MAN'S WORK SHALL BE MADE MANIFEST, a riff from Corinthians that I took as a sign.

The weather had kept a lot of thin-blooded Angelenos off the streets, so I reversed about ten yards, pulled across the empty lanes, and turned right. I couldn't help but wonder at myself—had this been my real motive in offering to come down the hill alone? Tapping the steering wheel, I pounded out my growing agitation. Slowing as I passed the strip mall, I peered at the dark interior with a blend of relief and disappointment. Closed. That was that.

The windshield wipers worked double-time, trying to clear my view. I was a few blocks from home when, seized by an impulse, I U-turned back down the hill and trolled Ventura, wired with agitation. Finally I found a late-night Internet café.

A few minutes later, snugged to a rented computer amid the sharp scent of coffee and the banter of two MySpacers comparing piercings, I logged in to the Gmail account. As the page loaded, I had to concentrate to slow down my breathing.

Nothing from them, just a pop-up window for Viagra on the cheap and uppercase spam from Barrister Felix Mgbada, urgently requesting my help in setting straight his wealthy relative's affairs in Nigeria. I blew out a breath and cocked back in the rickety chair. I was just about to shut down the computer when another e-mail chimed into the in-box. No subject. They knew I was logged in.

My palms were slick. I clicked on the e-mail. A single word.

Tomorrow.

CHAPTER 27

Awakened by the sound of the running shower, I took a moment to get my bearings. Upstairs. In our bed. Ariana getting ready.

New e-mail coming. Today.

I hadn't done laundry all week, so the only suitable clean thing on a hanger was a trendy, faded salmon button-up that I'd bought overpriced at a Melrose boutique for some screening my agent had invited me to the week after she'd sold my script. Back then I was neither that cool nor did I have the money to afford it. And now I was less cool and more broke, so I would've felt sheepish wearing it if my apprehension about the coming e-mail hadn't drowned out competing emotions.

In my office, nauseous with stress, I booted up and logged in. Even if I wasn't going to open an e-mail from my computer, I could at least see if there was anything waiting in my in-box. But there wasn't. I hit "refresh" to check for new mail. And then again. I jotted down a few sentences for my morning lecture before my attention pulled back to the screen. Still nothing.

The shower stopped, and I felt a flare of unease. Hoping the student scripts might be more distracting,

I pulled one from the growing stack. I read through it, retaining next to nothing. I tried the next one, too, but just couldn't find it interesting. Worse, I couldn't see the point of it anymore. Words on a page. How was I supposed to find interest in a fabricated plot when a real-life one was a single e-mail away?

My hand reached for the mouse. Came back to my pad. Went to the mouse again. Refresh. Nothing new. Tapping my pen against the notepad, I refocused on my lecture, trying yet again to care about character arcs.

Ariana poked her head into my office. "Bathroom's all yours."

I quickly closed out of my browser screen. "Great. Thanks."

"Want to have breakfast with me? I mean, we *are* sleeping in the same room now, so I figure we're at least intimate enough to try sharing a Pop-Tart."

I smiled. "I'm ready. I'll be right down."

"Whatcha doing?"

I glanced at the mostly blank notepad. "Just finishing up some work."

"Are you having an affair?" Navigating the hall, Julianne placed a hand on the neck of a student and steered him out of our way.

I was slightly winded, having just run upstairs from the computer lab, where I'd logged in to my Gmail account so I could watch my empty in-box for the fifteen minutes before class. I could feel the blood in my cheeks. "No," I said. "Why?"

She tilted her head back, appraising me. "You're positively glowing."

"A lot of excitement lately."

I started to peel off, but Julianne pulled me aside, out of the Monday crush, and lowered her voice. "I looked into that media contact. Even found a few producers who've gone through the process with her."

It took me a moment to figure out who she was talking about: the person at the CIA who read movie scripts to see which were worthy of agency cooperation. "Right," I said. "Thanks for doing that, but—"

"Not all the producers got their scripts approved, but to a one they vouched for her. I got her on the phone, said I was doing an article on the approval process—blah, blah, blah. Mentioned your script, and she had *less* than no reaction. She said it didn't circulate past her staff. She also said—like most scripts she assesses—it didn't paint a picture of the Agency that made them want to help with the movie. But there was no fire to it. So my guess? Unless she's Oscar-worthy, no one at the CIA gives a shit about *They're Watching* any more than you'd expect them to. I doubt they're behind whatever you're dealing with."

"Yeah." I pictured Doug Beeman on that dank carpet, face to the screen, sobbing with relief. "I think I figured that out already."

She glanced at the clock, swore under her breath, and began to backpedal up the hall. "So I guess that leaves you wide open again."

SHE NEEDS YOUR HELP.

The message, standing out against the black of the screen, made my gut twist. The tiny office in the department felt even more cramped than usual. The air gusting from the vent overhead smelled like freezer-burned ice cubes, and the scent of stale coffee lingered from whoever had taken office hours here last period.

As the bold letters faded away on-screen, I checked my Canon camcorder, which I had pointed at the old Dell monitor. No green dot—the damn thing wasn't recording.

I knocked the camera with the heel of my hand, but already the slideshow had moved on.

A photo of a well-kept prefab house, taken at night, stars in the windows from the camera's flash. Just visible inside, the silhouette of a woman sitting on a couch and watching TV, her curly hair piled high. Two chairs pinned down the little strip of grass in the front, and a lawn gnome kept mischievous lookout.

My eyes jumped frantically from my camcorder to the monitor and back again. After testing the Canon this morning, I'd left it briefly unattended at a few points—in the car when I stopped to get coffee, in the faculty lounge when I'd gone down to the computer lab. They must have disabled the recording function. To stop me from doing this.

Dropping the camera on the desk, I searched out a pencil, finding a broken one in the coffee mug. My other hand rooted in my briefcase, yanking free the notepad and spilling scripts onto the floor. All the while I kept one eye on the monitor, fearful of missing something. Cracked pencil poised over pad, waiting to write. That hazy outline of the woman on the couch. *She?* Who the hell was *she*?

A new picture showed our house from the front. Standard shot, like a Realtor's photo.

A knocking on the office door.

"Just a minute!" I shouted, a bit too loudly.

"Patrick? This isn't your slot. My office hours started five minutes ago."

The next photo showed the fake rock by the driveway, where we used to hide the spare house key, a flash illuminating the night scene.

My heartbeat pounded. "Right, sorry about that. I'll clear out in a minute."

And now a car key laid on the grass of our front lawn beside the fake rock. The plug on the rock had been pulled out and the key angled toward the hole. I squinted at the plastic key head, made out the Honda insignia.

Her voice, more polite to mask the rising tenseness: "I'd appreciate it. You know our time in there is limited as is."

I did. But I had only a ten-minute window between afternoon lectures, not time enough to leave the floor to hit the computer lab, and my colleague hadn't shown up for her office hours. Or so I'd thought.

The next shot showed my Red Sox cap lying on our bed, as stark as Exhibit A in a crime-scene photo. The air-conditioning froze the sweat on the back of my neck. In the picture, our bedroom walls weren't torn up, so it had been taken before Thursday night. I dug in my pocket for my cell phone and thumbed it on, the spinning Sanyo graphics taking their time.

"I'm just packing up. Gimme a sec." Navigating its menu, I held the phone up next to the monitor so I could take in the cell-phone screen and computer monitor at a glance. Furiously punching at the tiny buttons, I finally called up the camera function on the phone and hit "record."

On the computer a QuickTime video lurched into action. A driver's view through a windshield, the lens carefully positioned so not a sliver of dashboard or hood crept into the frame. The rumble of an engine. A low view—a car, not a truck or SUV, leaving a familiar parking area. Northridge Faculty Lot B2. The footage played on fast-forward, the car zipping through streetlights, turning corners, other vehicles speeding by.

My eyes jerked back and forth from the real screen to the view of it through my cell phone's camera, as I made sure the Sanyo was picking up the footage.

A frustrated thump at the door—a little more than a knock this time. I could hear her keys jangling in her fist. "Patrick, this is getting a bit rude. Don't you have class now anyway?"

"Yes. Sorry. Literally give me two minutes."

My phone beeped twice, and the camera shut off— the memory was limited, so it recorded only in ten-second chunks.

About two blocks from campus, the driver pulled in to a dead-end alley between a Chinese restaurant and a video store. Parked tight in front of a Dumpster, facing away, was an old Honda Civic. The screen went black, and when it came back on, the driver was no longer in his car—he'd edited out his exit from the vehicle so I wouldn't catch even a glimpse of the door.

A handheld approach to the Honda, the screen tilting back and forth. Not wanting to take my eyes from the monitor, I struggled with my phone, punching buttons by feel and memory, trying to call up another ten-second recording session. A quick glance-over showed me to have succeeded in getting myself into a cell-phone game of Tetris.

With frustration, I dropped the phone into my lap. The rapping on the door intensified.

The view pushed in tight on the Honda. Closer. When I realized what it was zooming in on, a chill spread through my insides.

The trunk lock.

A wave of light-headedness, static specking my vision.

Another set of messages appeared and faded. Forgetting to breathe, I read them numbly.

6PM. NO SOONER. NO LATER.
GO ALONE.
TELL NO ONE.
FOLLOW ALL INSTRUCTIONS.
OR SHE DIES.

The screen went blank. The browser quit of its own volition. Sagging back in the chair, I stared vacantly at the sad little office. Out in the hall, high heels clicked angrily away, and then only my ragged breathing remained to interrupt the silence.

CHAPTER 28

"I know some of you are starting to feel impatient. I will get to your scripts this week."

"That's what you said *last* week," someone called out from the back of the lecture hall.

I riffled my pad, staring at my notes. Aside from the three sentences I'd jotted down this morning, the page was empty. I kept picturing those ghost letters, rising and fading against the black screen: *FOLLOW ALL INSTRUCTIONS. OR SHE DIES.*

Did I know the woman on the couch? Or was she merely a stranger I was supposed to help, like Doug Beeman? Was she locked in the trunk of that Honda? Alive? And if so, if they wanted me to help her, why did I have to wait until six o'clock? Dread had returned, blacker and more certain than before, wiping out any foolish excitement that might have tinged my encounter with Beeman. Their runaway plot had veered across the line, finally, into life-or-death terrain.

The clock in the back of the lecture hall showed 4:17. Class let out in thirteen minutes—I'd have just enough time to race home, grab the key and my Red Sox hat, and get back to that alley. Though dozens of countermeasures ran through my head, I couldn't seriously consider them. My choices would determine whether that woman survived.

One of the students cleared her throat. Loudly.

"Okay," I said, regrouping. "So dialogue . . . dialogue should be succinct and . . . uh, compelling. . . ." I was just considering how poorly I was exemplifying this principle when I scanned the class and caught sight of Diondre in the back. I detected a hint of disappointment in his face. I forced my head into the lecture again, trying to hold it together, and had just started to get my focus when I heard the classroom door open and close.

Sally stood to the side, her back to the wall, her holstered sidearm poking conspicuously from the bottom of her rumpled coat. I did a double take, but she offered only an amiable smile. I'd lost the cadence of my thoughts again. The mostly blank page offered no help. I checked the clock. An hour and thirty-five minutes to showtime.

"You know what?" I said to the class. "Why don't we call it early today?"

I grabbed my notes and started for the door. As I approached, Sally took in my faded salmon button-up. "Nice shirt," she said. "They make it for men?"

Valentine lingered beyond the door. I couldn't wait for the last of the students to shuffle out, so I pulled him and Sally aside in the hall. "What's wrong?"

"Somewhere we can talk?" she asked.

"I don't have my office right now. Maybe the faculty lounge."

"Coupla teachers," Valentine said. Something

hummed in his shirt pocket, and he pulled out a Palm Treo and silenced it.

"You went in there?" I glanced around nervously. Dr. Peterson was passing through the intersecting hall at that moment, of course, discussing something with a student. "It *really* looks bad for me to be questioned by cops at work right now."

"We're not questioning you," Sally said. "Just wanted to check in. And here we thought you'd be flattered by all this attention."

Peterson didn't slow down or stop talking, but her eyes tracked us until she passed out of view. My watch read 4:28. I needed the key before I could get to whatever—or whoever—was locked in the trunk of that Honda. If I didn't get moving, soon, I wouldn't make it there by 6:00.

My shirt felt damp. I resisted the urge to run my sleeve across my forehead. "Okay," I said. "Thank you. Thank you for checking in."

Sally said, "We didn't make a scene in the faculty room. Though I must say, one of your colleagues was rather solicitous."

"Julianne."

"Yes. Attractive woman."

Valentine sucked his teeth. "She's *straight,* Richards."

"Thanks for pointing that out. I won't abscond with her to Vermont now." Sally hitched her belt, rattling the gear. "When you comment that Jessica Biel is hot, do I point out that she doesn't go for aging black guys with jelly-doughnut guts?"

Valentine scowled. "I have a jelly-doughnut gut?"

"Wait five years." She took in his expression of strained amusement. "That's right. And there's more where that came from."

I snuck another peek at my watch, and when I looked up, Sally was studying me with those flat eyes. "Late for something?"

"No." I felt like vomiting. "No."

"Yeah," Valentine said. "We got it the first time."

"Went to your house this morning," Sally said. "All the curtains are drawn. Your wife barely opened the door enough to poke her head through. Like there's something in there she didn't want us to see. Is there something in there you don't want us to see?"

Only torn-up walls, peeled-back carpet, dismantled outlets—the kind of mess a paranoid schizophrenic with a toolbox might make if left unattended. "No," I said. "We're just a little sensitive to being watched right now. You can hardly blame her. Why were you at the house?"

"Your neighbor called."

"Don *Miller*?"

"The very one. He said you were acting weird."

"That's a news flash?"

"A lot of banging from your house. The closed blinds. And maybe you shoved something down into the sewer a couple nights ago."

"Like a body?" I said.

She waited patiently as I did my best to feign amusement, then said, "I came by to make sure I didn't mislead you in our last conversation. 'Look around' means look around. It doesn't mean go Falcon and the Snowman and get your ass shot off."

My half grin felt frozen on my face. *TELL NO ONE,* they'd warned, *OR SHE DIES.* But for a moment I almost caved. Spilled about the e-mail and the key and the Honda's trunk. Wouldn't the police have a better chance at saving that woman than I would? All I had to do was open my mouth and make the right words. But before I could, a cell phone bleated out the Barney theme song.

Sally sighed, her considerable weight settling. "The kid likes it. One in an avalanche of humiliating parental concessions." She stepped away to take the call.

Valentine pouched his lips, looked down the hall with unfocused eyes. He took a step closer, like he shouldn't be telling me something but wanted to anyway. "Listen, man. One thing I learned in my time on the force is, shit leads to more shit. I can't tell you how many guys we've put away for taking one wrong step at a time." He smoothed his mustache, and in his brown eyes I saw the weariness of experience, the wisdom he'd rather not have accrued.

Sally doubled back briskly. "We got a 211 in Westwood. We gotta move." She turned her focus to me. "If you're into something, we can help, *now.* If you keep us out, when things go south, we won't be able to help. Because by then you'll be part of the problem. Now: Is there anything you want to tell us?"

My mouth had gone dry. I took a breath. I said, "No."

"Let's go." Sally jerked her head at Valentine, and they hurried up the hall. She paused to look back at me. "Be careful," she said, "wherever you're rushing off to."

CHAPTER 29

Through the strobe flicker of passing vehicles, I could make out the Honda in the alley across the street. I'd rushed home to retrieve the key and my Red Sox hat, and made it back with two minutes to spare. The whole ride I talked myself into and out of detouring to a police station, but the image of that woman sitting on her couch kept my foot on the gas and my hands steady on the wheel. She was no more than a hazy silhouette in a photo that I'd barely glimpsed, but the thought of her vanishing, of feeling terror or pain because of a gamble I took, was unbearable.

Now that I was here, confronting that locked trunk, my convictions seemed less clear. Removing the paper from my pocket, I unfolded it and read my scrawled handwriting.

I received an anonymous e-mail telling me to come to this car, or a woman would die. The key to this car was hidden in a fake rock in my front yard. I don't know what's in the trunk. I don't know where this will lead. If something bad happens, please contact Detective Sally Richards of the West L.A. station.

Of course, if I did get caught in some transgression, any idiot would still think I was guilty and that I'd just written the note for insurance. But it was better than nothing.

Two minutes left. My spine felt stuck to the seat. The digital clock—one of the few things on the dashboard I hadn't smashed—stared back at me unwaveringly. The final minute seemed to last forever, and yet I felt I had no time left at all. They'd made me responsible. If she died, it would be as though I'd murdered her myself. But was it worth potentially risking my life for a woman I didn't even know?

FOLLOW ALL INSTRUCTIONS. OR SHE DIES.

The clock ticked to the hour.

I got out, my breath echoing in my hollow chest. I jogged across the street, paused at the mouth of the alley to collect myself. But there wouldn't be time for that.

I reached the Civic. Relatively clean, specked with dirt, moderate wear on the tires—it was ordinary in every way. Except it had no license plates. I pressed my ear to the trunk but could hear nothing inside.

There was no one deeper in the alley or at my back, closing in on me. Just the whir of passing traffic, oblivious people on their oblivious way. I fought the key into the lock. The pop of the release vibrated up my arm. I took a deep breath, then let go, stepping back quickly as the trunk yawned open.

A duffel bag. *My* duffel bag, the same one I'd kicked into the sewer. It was stuffed full, blocky imprints shoving out its sides.

I leaned over, hands on my knees, and finally exhaled. The zipper came reluctantly, and after a nerve-grinding pause I threw it open.

Dumbfounded, I stared down, breathing the rich scent of money. Stack after stack of ten-dollar bills. And lying on top of them a map with a route traced in familiar red marker.

In person, $27,242 seems like a lot more than it is. When it's composed of ten-dollar bills banded in packs of fifty, it seems like half a million. Pulled over in my car in the far reaches of a nearby grocery-store parking lot, duffel in my lap, I'd counted. The bundles kept coming and coming, uniform save the one made up of disparate bills. If the movies weren't lying, tens were untraceable, or at least harder to trace than hundreds or twenties. The ramifications of that were almost as troubling as the rest of it.

The Honda had proven as inscrutable as the altered voice on the phone. No registration or anything else in the glove box, nothing hidden under the floor mats—even the skinny Vehicle Identification Number plate had been unscrewed from the dash.

I couldn't stop staring at the map. The red line started at the freeway entrance nearest the alley, snaked east along the 10 for a good hundred and fifty miles, and finally dead-ended in Indio, a broke desert town east of Palm Springs. A small square of paper with an address—produced, no doubt, by my printer—was taped beside the terminus. Beneath it was typed *9:30 p.m.* If I didn't hit traffic, I'd get there by then. That was the point—just enough time to react.

A truck throttled by in the parking lot, and I quickly

zipped the bag back up. For a moment I sat with my hands on the steering wheel. Then I called Ariana from my crappy prepaid phone. The matching one I'd gotten her went straight to automated voice mail, so I dialed her office line. It was likely monitored, but I had no other way to get hold of her.

"I'm not going to be home," I said carefully. "Until late."

"Oh?" she said. I could hear the whine of the lathe in the background. Someone shouted something at her, and she answered tersely, "Gimme a sec here." Then back to me: "What's this about?"

Had she forgotten that we could speak openly only on the prepaid phones?

I said, "I just . . . have to take care of some stuff."

"Just when we're getting on track, it's back to this? Another double feature after work? Anything to avoid being home?"

Was she acting right now because we weren't on a secure line? And if so, how could I signal that there actually was a problem?

"It's not like that," I said lamely.

"Have a nice night, Patrick." She hung up. Hard.

I stared at the phone, unsure what to do next.

A few seconds later, it vibrated in my hand, and I clicked on. I could tell from the scratchy connection that she'd called back from the Batphone. "Hi, babe," she said.

I exhaled with relief, reminding myself that I should never underestimate my wife's acuity.

"What's up?" she asked.

I told her.

"Jesus," she said. "This could be anything. Ransom money. A laundering operation. A drug deal. For all you know, you could be delivering payment to a hit man for your own murder."

"I need to be driving"—I checked the clock—"five minutes ago. There's no time."

Someone shouted in the background, and then I heard her footsteps and it got a little quieter. "What are you gonna do?"

I lowered the visor, looked at that picture of us from the college formal. The color in our smooth cheeks. All the time in the world in front of us. Nothing to worry about but morning classes and whether we had enough money for import beer. "If something happened to that woman because I didn't go, I don't think I could live with myself."

"I know," she said quietly. Her voice wavered, only a beat, but I caught it. The screech of machinery filled the pause. "Look, I . . ."

I reached up to the photograph, touched her smiling face. "I know," I said. "Me, too."

Halfway there, on a stretch of highway, I almost ran out of gas. On occasion I still forgot that the damn fuel gauge was broken on full, but the odometer caught my eye, telling me the tank was due, and I eked it out to the next exit. My mouth had cottoned up, so I ran into the mart to buy a pack of gum. Outside again, pumping gas, I stared at my reflection in the side mirror. It stared back skeptically, figuring me for a fool.

The housing tracts in Indio felt like Legoland—all the same pieces configured differently. Five or six house designs, alternating minutely in color or size, the streets and cul-de-sacs laid down along the same few templates. I got lost, and then lost from where I was lost, driving through the oppressive repetition, concern rising to panic once the clock passed 9:15. I prayed that my Nikes with the embedded tracking device were alerting them that I was almost there.

Finally, through a miracle, I reached the proper housing loop, prefabs thrown around a dirt circle of road. At the end, angled off by itself in a manner to suggest privacy or loneliness, was the house from the photo.

I parked a good ways up the road and climbed out, the duffel bag straining at my shoulder, BoSox cap sitting protectively low over my eyes. It was 9:28, and my breath was coming hard. I'd forgotten how damn cold the desert got in winter. Cold enough to freeze the sweat across your back.

Crunching over dead leaves, I approached. I couldn't see the interior through the drawn blinds, but a bluish flicker from the TV played along the seams. Despite the time, the other houses were as still as midnight, their windows black. An early-to-bed community of workers getting in their sleep before the early desert sun.

I didn't have time to detour to peer in the window or inspect the area. Whatever was waiting for me in there—a bound woman, a crew of cigar-chomping kidnappers, a DVD holding another mystifying piece of the puzzle—I would meet it. Before I could lose my nerve, I stepped up on the two wooden stairs, pulled back the screen door, and knocked softly.

Rustling inside. The shuffle of footsteps. The door creaked open.

The woman. I recognized her from the heap of curly dark hair, shot through with gray. She was foreign. I wasn't sure how I knew, but something in her features and manner spoke of Eastern Europe. Her eyelids were pouched, flecked with skin tags, and rimmed red with exhaustion or crying. She seemed to personify a type—the doleful eyes, the homely features, the nose crooked just so. An inch or two over five feet. Her irises were striking, crystal blue and nearly translucent. She looked to be sixty, but I guessed she was younger and just worn down.

She said, "You're here," in a thick accent I couldn't place.

"You're okay," I stammered.

We looked at each other. I swung the duffel down off my shoulder, held it by my side. The small living room behind her seemed to be empty. She said, "Come in."

I stepped into the house.

"Please," she said. "Shoes off." Her accent turned "off" into "uff."

I complied, setting my Nikes on a hand towel laid to the side of the door. The humble place had been maintained with a lot of pride. A wicker bookshelf held dustless porcelain cats and snow globes from various American cities. The counters in the little kitchen area gleamed. Through an open door to a tiny bathroom, I saw a candle flickering in a wall sconce. Even the couch looked brand new. Oddly, a plate holding three or four banana peels sat on a side table, the bottom ones brown.

She gestured, and I sat on the couch. After setting a bowl of cashews and a dish of tangerines on the coffee table in front of me, she took up on an armchair, displacing her knitting. We stared at each other awkwardly.

"I receive e-mail," she said. "I was told man would come with Red Sock hat. That I must see him." For some reason she was speaking in a hushed voice, which I inadvertently mimicked.

"Did you get any DVDs?"

"DVD?" She frowned. "Like movie? No. I don't understand. Why do you come?"

I glanced around, bracing myself for a bomb, a violent son, a SWAT-team entry. On the microwave, three more bunches of bananas. To the right of the cashews, a school photo of a young girl, maybe six, with a bright, forced smile. Frizzy brown hair, both front teeth missing, dressed in a smock checked like an Italian tablecloth. One pigtail had slid lower than the other, and a purple spot stained the front of the smock; whoever had dressed her up so carefully for picture day would not be pleased. Something in that grin—the eagerness to participate, to please—made her seem so damn vulnerable. Stuck to the frame was a Chiquita sticker—what was with the bananas? I forced my eyes back to the woman. She wore a plain gold wedding band, but somehow I knew that her husband had died. Her sadness was palpable, as was her kindness, conveyed in the small smile she'd shown me when she'd set down the bowl of nuts. I would have done anything to avoid upsetting her.

"I was told that you could be in danger," I said.

She gasped, hand to her chunky necklace. "Danger? Someone threaten me?"

"I . . . I think so. I was told to come see you. Or you'd die."

"But who would want to kill me?" It came out "keel me." "Are you come to harm me?"

"No, I—*no.* No, I wouldn't hurt you at all."

Though she was distressed, still she kept her voice quiet. "I am Hungarian grandmother. I am waitress at crappy diner. Who do I threaten? What do I do to hurt anyone?"

I leaned forward as if to rise, practically crouching over the cushions. What was I going to do? Enfold her in a comforting hug? "I'm sorry to upset you. I . . . look, I'm here, and we'll figure this out together and fix it, whatever it is. I came to help."

She balled a Kleenex and pressed it to her trembling lips. "To help what?"

"I don't know. I was just told . . ." I struggled to figure out the connection, the angle in, the nudge of the dial that would bring the picture into focus. "My name's Patrick Davis. I'm a teacher. What's your name, ma'am?"

"Elisabeta."

"Are you . . ." Grasping at straws, I pointed at the picture. "Is that your daughter?"

"Granddaughter." She couldn't say it without a smile lightening her face. But quickly the haggardness returned. "My son, he is in the prison ten year for he sell the"—she acted out shooting up in her arm, making a *pccht-pccht* sound as if she were shooing a cat. A shiny manicure made her nails surprisingly beautiful—that quiet dignity showing through again, a pride that felt oddly like humility. "His wife, she go back to Debrecen." She waved a hand at the photograph. "So I get her. My little jewel."

I got it finally, the hushed voice. "She's sleeping."

"Yes."

"Why . . . ?" I asked, looking around. "Why are there so many bananas?"

"She is not well. She take many pill, one type so she can urinate off extra fluid. Low potassium, they say from this. So the banana—it is game we play. If she get her potassium from banana, one less pill to take." She shook a frail fist. " 'We beat it for one pill today.' "

My pulse quickened. *SHE NEEDS YOUR HELP.* But how?

"What happened to her?" I asked.

"She have the surgery back when she is three. Last month I notice her shoes no fit again. The swelling . . ." Her hand circled. "I do not want to believe. Then she have the breathing"—she mimed shortness of breath—"again on the playground. And yes, it is the heart valve again. She needs new. But it is hundred of thousand of dollar. I cannot afford. I am waitress. I already spend second mortgage on this house for first surgery. It will give out. This *valve*"—she spit out the word. "Tomorrow or next week or next month, it will give out."

The duffel sat a few inches to my side, nudged up against my shoe. What good was twenty-seven grand in the face of that kind of money?

My amped-up drive here had left me more emo-

tional than usual; seesawing between dread and relief, fear and concern, I could hardly find my bearings.
The girl peered up at me from the picture, and I recognized now that she had her grandmother's curly hair.
The desperate conversations they must have had right
here in this room. How do you explain to a six-year-
old that her heart might give out? I swallowed, felt
the tightness in my throat. "I can't imagine."

"Except I see in your face," she said, "that you
can." She plucked at the loose skin of her neck. "A
friend of mine back home"—a wave to cross the
Atlantic—"lost his wife to Lou Gehrig. A cousin of
my cousin lost her daughter and two grandson in
plane crash five year back. On anniversary this year,
my cousin ask her, 'How do you handle this?' And
she say, 'Everyone has a story.' And it is true. Before
we go, everyone has sad story to tell. But this child,
this child . . ." She rose abruptly, crossed to one of
the closed doors at the end of the room, and set her
hand on the knob. "You come see this beautiful child.
I will wake her. You come see and tell me how I am
to explain her this is *her* story."

"No, please. Please don't disturb her. Let her sleep."

Elisabeta came back and sank into her armchair.
"And now someone want to kill me. And for what?
Who will take care of her? She will be left alone
to die."

"Don't you have . . . is there health insurance?"

"We are nearing lifetime maximum, they call it. I
meet with—what do they call it?—finance committee
at hospital. They are willing to make charitable dona-
tion for operating room, surgery. But even between

their generosity and what is left on insurance, I am still left with more than I can . . ." She shook her head. "What do I do?"

My voice shook with excitement. "How much is left?"

"More than you can imagine."

I leaned forward, put my hand on the table, upsetting the bowl of nuts. "How much *exactly*?"

She got up and went into the kitchen. A drawer opened, jangling with flatware. Then another. She thumbed through a sheaf of menus and flyers, finally returning with a paper. She fluffed it out like a royal decree. "Twenty-seven *thousand* two hundred forty-two dollar." Her mouth tugged down in the beginning of a sob, but she caught it, transformed her expression to contempt for the figure.

"No one's threatening you. I misunderstood." My throat closed, and I had to stop talking. A sheen rose in my eyes. I lowered my head, said a silent prayer of gratitude. I walked over to her and set the duffel on the floor at her feet.

She stared at me, shocked.

I said, "This is for you."

I stepped into my Nikes and left, careful to ease the screen door shut so as not to wake the girl.

CHAPTER 30

I was up again, pacing around Ariana, who listened, glazed, from the patio chair. Her knees were drawn up to her chest, her sweatshirt pulled over them, the parka flaring out to either side. It wasn't raining, but moisture flecked the air. Two in the morning and counting, and my heart rate showed no signs of slowing down. "The fear, then the relief—even fucking gratitude. And then it starts all over again. It's like a drug. I can't take it. I don't *care* that it worked out this time—"

"We don't even know *that*," Ariana said.

"What do you mean?"

"Delivering cash to a woman in Indio? What if it was a scam?"

"How? It wasn't our money. I was just playing Santa Claus."

"I'm not saying *you* were the target." She watched her words sink in. "What happens if someone shows up at that woman's door and asks a favor of her? A favor to be repaid?"

"I'm the one who gave her the money."

"But it wasn't your money. She doesn't owe *you*."

Nausea crept into my stomach, an ice-water trickle.

I sank slowly into the chair opposite Ari. I could tell from her face that she felt bad. Her hand rooted in her purse and produced a roll of Tums. That purse was like the stomach of Jaws—she was always pulling out a pair of sunglasses, a new shade of lipstick, a waffle iron.

Chewing a tablet, Ariana double-checked the cigarette-box jammer and pushed forward—"If there are no strings attached to that cash, why wouldn't they just give it to her themselves? For all you know, that money puts her in danger."

"I think she'd take that risk," I said quietly. "So her granddaughter wouldn't die."

"But she didn't get to make that decision."

"Because I made it for her." I pressed the heels of my hands to my eyes, my groan turning to something like a growl. "But what the hell was I supposed to do? Go to the cops? Thinking it might kill that woman?"

"Not then. But now. Why not *now*?"

"They'll find out. Given what these guys have shown us so far, do we really want to see how they retaliate when they're pissed off? Plus, are you forgetting that a seven-figure lawsuit might be hanging in the balance, pending my cooperation?"

"So you keep doing this?" she asked. "Following orders blindly from an all-powerful boss you don't even know? Waiting around like some clown in a Beckett play? For how long?"

"Until we get the settlement agreement from the studio. Until I figure out an angle into this. Into *them*."

"And in the meantime? These aren't your lives to tamper with."

"It's not that easy, Ari."

"There are probably thousands of kids in this country with that girl's heart condition," she said. "Millions of people with millions of problems. What makes her life any different from anyone else's?"

"Because I can save hers." I could feel the knots up the back of my neck. Ari lifted her eyebrows, and I held up my hands, half in apology, half to slow myself. "I know it sounds like this is some kind of God complex—"

"Not even, Patrick. It's a God complex by proxy."

"But these people are hostages, even if they don't know it. That girl was entrusted to me, like Beeman. She's been *made* my problem, my responsibility. When I've been given a bag of money to save her life, how can I not leave it for her?"

"You don't show up to begin with, that's how. What's that line from *WarGames*?"

I cast out a sullen sigh. " 'The only winning move is not to play.' "

She nodded solemnly. "Look, we both agree we need to break through on this thing. And to do that, you can play *your* game all you want. Just don't play theirs."

I stared over the sagging fence at Don and Martinique's dark bedroom window, the curtain at rest. A bedroom like ours, a house like ours. Our quiet little neighborhood, all of us with a story to tell. And yet the scale of what I was confronting, the danger, had gone suddenly out of whack. How had I come unhinged from this ordinary life?

"You're right." I lifted my hands, let them slap to

my thighs. "As long as I keep taking the bait, they have me trapped. I'll stop. No more checking e-mail. No more following their instructions. Whatever that brings on, it brings on."

"I'll be here for it." She leaned over and kissed me on the cheek. "It's the only good choice left. You have to call their bluff."

She rose and headed inside, her head bowed.

I sat for a few moments with the crickets, looking out to where the yard lost itself in darkness. I mumbled to the shadows, "What if they're not bluffing?"

I lay beside my wife in the quiet dark of the bedroom. She'd fallen asleep maybe an hour ago, leaving me to study the ceiling. Finally I got up, went into my office, and unplugged my cell phone from its charger. On the built-in camera, I watched the ten seconds I'd managed to capture of the QuickTime video from them.

View through a windshield. Car driving. The recording stopped well before the alley and the Honda.

I downloaded the clip into my computer and enlarged it to fill the screen. A passing semi with daytime running lights swept through the field of vision, playing tricks with the light across the windshield. A dab of silver at the bottom of the glass caught my eye. I backed up the recording, froze the image. Not much more than a smudge at the base of the windshield. Leaning forward, I squinted at the finger-long reflection thrown up from the top of the dash.

The metal plate stamped with the Vehicle Identification Number.

It was blurred and faint, but perhaps the clarity could be brought up with the right tools. My first concrete lead. I ran a thumb across the tiny image, savoring it.

My cell phone emitted an Asian chime. Slowly, I turned and regarded it lying there next to the keyboard. Picked it up. A text-message alert, sender unknown.

A cold sweat crept over my body. My thumb moved before I could stop it.

E-MAIL TOMORROW, 7 PM.

A MATTER OF LIFE AND DEATH.

THIS TIME IT'S SOMEONE YOU KNOW.

CHAPTER 31

I sat in my car in the parking lot, watching students drift in to class. The phone rang and rang, and finally he picked up. "Hallo."

"Dad?"

"Stop the presses." And then, shouting over the receiver to my mom: "It's Patrick. *Pat*rick!" Then back: "Your mother's in the car." My dad, from Lynn, Massachusetts, had the harsh Boston accent I'd never acquired growing up in watered-down Newton. *Mothah's in the cah.* "Still goin' through it with Ari?"

"Yeah, but we're figuring it out." Hearing his voice made me realize how much I missed them, how sad it was that it took this for me to pick up the phone. "I'm sorry I haven't been great at keeping in touch these past couple months."

"That's okay, Paddy. You've had a rough go. You get a real job yet?"

"Yeah. Teaching again. No more writing."

"Listen, your mother and I were just heading into town. Everything okay?"

"I just wanted to know how you both are. Health-wise or whatever else. If there's anything you need, I mean, I can hop on a plane, no matter what I'm in the middle of."

"What'd you join one of those cults out there?"

"I'm just saying. I hope you know that."

"Everything's fine here. We got a ways to go, you know."

"I know, Pa."

"We're not in the grave yet."

"I didn't mean—"

Car honking in the background.

"Listen, your mother just discovered the horn. Do me a favor, Patrick. Call her this week. You don't just have to call when you're feeling okay. We're your parents."

He signed off, and I sat there a moment, reliving the chill that had passed through me when the threatening text message had chimed into existence on my cell phone last night. Not surprisingly, it had vanished into thin air within seconds of my reading it. All this autodeleting left me wondering if I was making up this whole intrigue myself. But the knot in my throat said it was far too real.

A passing student waved, and it took effort to lift my hand and wave back. My car might as well have been a submarine for how detached I felt from the world beyond the glass.

THIS TIME IT'S SOMEONE YOU KNOW.

I clicked through the saved numbers in my cell phone. All those names, more bases than I could cover even if I knew what to ask. Not to mention all

the names *not* in there. It could be anyone from Julianne to Punch to Bill at Bel Air Foods. Someone I'd
graded, someone I'd roomed with in college, someone who'd loaned me a cup of sugar. Someone I loved.

I flipped the phone shut and set it on the cracked
dash. "The only way to beat them," I told it, "is not to
play."

I found Marcello alone in the editing bay, fussing
over the digital sound console. On the attached computer monitor, a guy in a Speedo was paused mid-
bounce at the end of a diving board. When Marcello
released the diver with a click of the mouse, the *bwang*
of the board was out of sync.

"Take a look at something for me?" I asked.

He froze the diver as he hit the water, and leaned
over my cell phone. I played the ten-second clip.

"Cinema verité," Marcello said when it was done.
"I think the car is a metaphor for the journey of life."

"I can't pause it on the cell, but look right here." I
played the clip over again. "There's a little reflection
on the windshield when the truck passes. You see it?
I think it's the VIN. Is there some way to download it
into Final Cut Pro and bring up the resolution?"

"Could take some time. The focus part, I mean."
A note of annoyance. "Patrick, what *is* all this?" He
crossed his arms impatiently as I figured out how to
phrase what I wanted to say.

"They're sending me glimpses into people's lives.
Their problems."

"Like what they were doing to you?"

"Yes. Sort of. It's complicated."

He was scowling.

I said, "What?"

"There's no damn privacy anymore. It's like we all got used to it. Or we gave it away, bit by bit. Wiretapping laws. Citizen enemy combatants. Homeland Security looking up your nose. Not to mention all this reality shit. *Girls Gone Wild*. Crying politicians on YouTube. Spouses trash-talking on *Dr. Phil*. You can't even die in war anymore without every schmuck with a flat-screen watching the infrared footage. There's no . . ." His jaw shifted; his lips twitched, searching out some suitable term. ". . . *propriety*." He heaved out an agitated breath. "You used to have to be famous to be famous. But now? It's *all* real. It's *all* fake. What's the goddamned fascination with monitoring everything, putting an eye up to every peephole?"

"I guess . . ." I stopped, studied my loafers.

"Yeah?"

"I guess people want the comfort of knowing that things can be bad everywhere. That it's not just them. That no one's got the magic answers."

His empathetic gaze made me feel naked. "When I was growing up, I thought the movies were magic. And then I got around them." He gave a wistful chuckle, his hand rasping over his beard. "Guys in rooms. Guys on sets. Guys at computer monitors. That's it. There's a loss there. I suppose everyone feels it. When you catch up to whatever you're chasing and get a close-up, warts and all. Then what do you do?" He made a popping sound with his lips, turned back to the console brusquely, and resumed adjusting the mix on the student film. The footage reversed, the diver unsplashing from the pool, the water vacuuming itself back into a flat sheet. How easily all that chaos was undone.

"Marcello." My voice was a bit hoarse. "This has turned into a lot more than voyeurism."

"I know." He didn't look over. "Gimme the phone. I'm done ranting."

I set it down next to him on the desk. "You sure?"

"I think so. I was gonna throw in something about Britney Spears and her lack of underwear, but I sort of lost the thread."

A few students started to trickle in, and I had to whisper. "No one can know you're doing this. It could put you at risk. You okay with that?"

He waved me off. "Don't you have a class you're late for?"

Though no light shone in Doug Beeman's apartment, I knocked again on the peeling front door. And again there was no response. No eye hiding behind that old-fashioned keyhole this time, only blackness. Resting my forehead against the jamb, I stood helplessly, the neighborhood sounds and smells washing over me. The pump of a tricked-out car stereo. The scent of spicy cooking, maybe Indian. A static-fuzzed Lakers game coming through economy walls.

I was impatient for answers. Absent those, I was desperate for contact, eager to mull over the bits and pieces of what had happened, to rub them to a high polish. On my way to Doug Beeman's, I'd detoured by the alley near campus and had not been surprised to find the Honda Civic gone. Once I'd cleared the cash from the trunk, they'd cleared the car from the alley. And now silence at Beeman's door, darkness at the curtains. As I turned away, I realized just how much that concerned me.

Ariana's words were there like an echo in my head, warning of all the consequences I hadn't considered. I wished I'd found something here to assuage her concerns. I'd come back tomorrow first thing to make sure Beeman was all right; I'd already decided to go to Indio after morning classes to check on Elisabeta.

I turned away from the door. The complex—and the surrounding streets—were alive with life and movement, music and engines, the crack of beer cans opening, the giggle of children, a woman yelling into a telephone. So many people. How many were on the verge of catastrophe? An aneurysm, a lurking blood clot, a heart valve a beat away from giving out? How many of these apartments had a gas leak, a compromised roof, lethal mold growing beneath the drywall?

Which name in my address book faced a similar deadline?

At the intersection my discomfort revved into high gear. Knee bouncing, fingernails strumming, squirming in my seat like a kid before recess. The clock on my dashboard read 6:53 P.M. Seven minutes until their next e-mail hit my in-box. It occurred to me yet again that though it was Tuesday and the workday over, I had yet to hear from my lawyer with the studio's terms for the legal resolution. Were *they* waiting to see if I played good little soldier? I was still a rat in their box—push the lever, get a pellet.

The red light was taking forever. I rolled down my

window, tapped my foot, hummed along to the Top 40 tune I was pretending to listen to. But no matter how hard I tried to ignore it, it remained at the edge of my peripheral vision, rising into view from behind the church billboard. Finally I looked over at that Kinko's sign, beckoning like neon to a drunk. In the foreground rose that redoubtable lettering—*WITHOUT WOOD, A FIRE GOES OUT*—and for the first time in a long time, I felt like the universe was talking to me, even if it was telling me something I didn't want to hear. It was easy enough to heed the Word; I was in the left-turn lane, Kinko's was across three lanes of traffic and up the street the opposite way. Not a temptation at all.

The only way to beat them is not to play.

Forcing my gaze ahead, waiting for the light, I listened to the *click-click-click* of my turn signal.

Hotel Angeleno, a cylindrical white rise a stone's throw off the 405 where Brentwood meets Bel Air. The crisp photo, perfectly framing the seventeen stories, looked like an advertising shot. The place was a Holiday Inn that had gotten a face lift a few years back, but it didn't take much to qualify as a landmark in Los Angeles.

Hunched over a computer in my corner cubicle at Kinko's, I took in the image, holding my cell-phone camera at the ready. My thumb pressed "record," and the Sanyo camera whirred into action. I'd acquainted my thumb with the cell-phone buttons so I could record however long, back-to-back in ten-second chunks, without moving my eyes from the monitor.

The picture on-screen faded, replaced by a close-up of a hotel-room number: *1407.*

Next was a service door, sturdy and metal, the edge of a Dumpster peeking into view. The parking-lot lines and concrete exterior showed it still to be the hotel.

The next slide put a charge into my chest: my silver key chain, placed on our kitchen counter. A daytime shot, but there was no way to tell when it had been taken.

The close-up photo that followed showed one key angled free and clear of the others. Sturdy, brass. Not one of my own.

Numbly, I reached into my pocket. Lifted my key chain, flat on my palm, up before my eyes. There it was like a Christmas present, hidden in the jumble. A new key. Riding along with me all this time.

The PowerPoint presentation had moved on. Inside my Camry now, the angle from the passenger seat; the photographer must have been sitting. My glove box had been laid open and a hotel key card set on top of my tin of Altoids.

A message appeared and faded:

2AM. TONIGHT. COME ALONE.
DO NOT GET SPOTTED.

Followed by another:

YOU NEED TO SEE HIM.

Him. *Him?*

My Sanyo stopped recording a moment before the

top browser window closed, leaving me to stare at the e-mail with the hyperlink they'd sent to my Gmail account. My fingers ached from being clenched around the phone. I released my fist and watched the pink creep slowly back into my skin.

I clicked "reply" on the e-mail, and to my surprise an address appeared. A long string of seemingly random numbers, ending with *gmail.com.*

The digital clock on the desktop said I was late for dinner, a walk with Ariana, my life. I thought of my briefcase, bulging with unread student scripts. Our walls, torn down in spots to the studs and pipes. The house I had to get in order, with all that implied. I owed the people in my life more than this. Except the one whose neck was on the line.

I typed, *I won't do this anymore. Not without knowing who you are and why you're doing this to me,* and sent it off before the second thoughts gnashing at my heels could overtake me.

I sat and stared at the screen, wondering what the hell I had just done.

A comic pop sounded from the computer speakers, breaking through my black thoughts. An instant message had flashed up on the screen in its cheery little AOL cartoon bubble.

TONIGHT YOU WILL
UNDERSTAND EVERYTHING.

I hadn't even logged in to an IM program, but there it was.

Grinding my teeth, I stared at the smug little sentence. I was sick of being manipulated, toyed with, led down the gallows path one blindfolded step at a time. Something inside me had shifted, whether because of Ari's persistent reasoning or the ominous silence I'd just encountered at Beeman's front door. But my resolve had been chipped away, one assumption at a time, leaving me far from convinced that the course I'd been taking was the right one.

Breathing hard, summoning courage, I stared at the screen.

My fingers hammered the keyboard, asking the question I was afraid to know the answer to: *What if I say no?*

I rocked back in the chair. Across the store, the cash register jangled and copy machines whirred and clicked like futuristic life-forms. The air conditioner blew cool air down my collar.

Another popping sound, another message. This time it could just as easily have been my own thought bubble; the words seemed to look right through the windows of my eyes and read my mind.

THEN YOU WILL NEVER KNOW.

CHAPTER 32

Midnight.

I wasn't going to that hotel room.

Ariana asleep beside me, I lay and watched the clock. She'd taken an Ambien to help her doze off, but I was fairly certain that no sleeping pill would get me down tonight. Whatever this thing was, I had it by the tail or it had me by the neck. When I didn't show up, would they come after me, renewed? If they *didn't,* could I stand never knowing? Could I go back to student papers and faculty-room joking and neighborhood walks? I would have to. As Ari had said, I was tampering with other people's lives. And if I kept following instructions, when would it end? By noshowing, I was taking my fate into my own hands. And if they reacted with wrath, I would be ready for them. If the lawsuit returned, I was no worse off than I'd been two days ago. In the quiet dark, I began listing the precautions I'd start taking at first light.

12:27 A.M. *12:28* A.M.

I wasn't going to that hotel room.

TONIGHT YOU WILL UNDERSTAND EVERYTHING.

Who was waiting in Room 1407? A face from the past, a wronged friend, a man in a dark suit, legs crossed, silenced pistol in his lap? Or a stranger with a gift, nothing more to me than I was to Doug Beeman? How long would the person wait before figuring out that I wasn't coming through that door?

12:48 A.M. *12:49* A.M.

I wasn't going to that hotel room.

I pictured Doug Beeman on his knees, his face up against the TV, how he'd sat back on his heels and swayed and how I hadn't known he'd been weeping until I heard the sobs choke out of him. The school photo on Elisabeta's table, the missing-teeth grin. Those heaps of banana peels. The despair, thick as a scent in that cramped living room. The duffel of cash that I prayed would lift that despair as the DVD had lifted Beeman's, that might just buy a wink of light at the end of the tunnel.

1:06 A.M. *1:07* A.M.

I wasn't going to that hotel room.

Snippets of text floated in the darkness.

SOMEONE YOU KNOW. A MATTER OF LIFE AND DEATH.

What was I going to do? Lie here miserably un-asleep until I was awakened by a ringing phone? Or would the death notice come later? A day, a week, three months. Could I live like that, waiting, knowing I could have prevented whatever was coming?

1:17 A.M. *1:18* A.M.

The only way to beat them is not to play.

I wasn't going to that hotel room.

1:23 A.M.

I kissed Ari on the sleep-warm neck. Regarded her sleeping face. Lips fat and luscious, popped open just slightly, giving off the faintest whistle.

Whispered, "I'm sorry."

Slid from bed, guilty, miserable, and racked with fear.

It wasn't that I had to go.

It was that I couldn't *not*.

Having parked at the curb up Sepulveda beyond eyeshot of the valets, having retrieved the key card from my glove box and snugged it in my back pocket, having pocketed my Sanyo *and* the prepaid cell phone to cover any recording or calling contingency, having waited for a break in traffic and threaded through the rear parking lot in my jeans and black T-shirt, I stood at the base of Hotel Angeleno, key in hand, confronting the service door from the photo.

Crinkling in my pocket was the note I'd jotted hastily under the dome light of my car:

I received an anonymous message telling me to come to Room 1407, and that it was a matter of life and death. I don't know who's in the room. I don't know where this will lead. If something bad happens, please contact Detective Sally Richards of the West L.A. station.

Past the concrete freeway wall to my left, invisible cars swooped by, rushing smooth and soporific, an endless wave. The cylindrical building loomed overhead, a cool green glow uplighting the penthouse soffit.

A car approached from the curving drive, a valet closing my brief time window, but before the headlights swept into view, I zippered the key into the lock and twisted. A satisfying clunk. I slipped inside, breathed the heated air, and tried to shake the tingling from my fingertips.

Immediately I heard a squeak of a wheel, but before I could move, a worker turned the corner, pushing a room-service cart. In the frozen instant before our eyes met, I put a hand up on the door nearest me and noted with great relief that it led to the stairwell. Hoping he wouldn't catch a glimpse of my face, I swiveled quickly and stepped through.

"Excuse me, sir—?" The closing door severed his voice.

I huffed my way up, the tapping of my Nikes coming back at me off the hard walls. The fourteenth floor was blissfully quiet. Ariana would've liked the L.A.-hip deco—sleek, slate, stone, earth. Dark wood trimmings, amber glows from wall sconces, silent carpet underfoot. A clock showed 1:58. Passing the elevator, I felt a jolt of panic as a woman dressed for the gym stepped from her room, but, busy on her cell phone, she didn't bother with eye contact.

The key card ready at my side like a stiletto, I counted down the room numbers. Reaching 1407, I jammed it home. The little sensor gave me a green light, and I turned the hefty handle and shoved the door open a few inches.

Darkness.

A few inches more. A bottleneck hall by the front bathroom, only a sliver of bedroom visible from the doorway. The curtains had been thrown back, floor-to-ceiling glass doors letting out onto a cramped balcony.

"Hello?" My voice, strained and thick, was completely foreign to me.

Barely cutting the black of the room, the glow of the distant city lay in faded puddles on the floor. The hum of freeway traffic blended with the rush of blood in my ears as I inched forward. The door shut itself firmly behind me, cutting what little light the hall had afforded.

Somehow I sensed an emptiness in the room. Was I supposed to wait for someone here? Would it be another phone call leading to another wild-goose chase?

A faded smell—sweet, spicy, a trace of ash. My body tense, I stepped even with the threshold to the main room. The comforter had been dimpled where someone had sat on it. And lying next to the indentation, a slender object, about four feet long.

Scanning the room, I took an exploratory half step forward and picked up the object by the rubber grip. The metal head swung up on the graphite shaft, glinting in the city lights. A golf driver. *My* golf driver. The one I'd hurled after the intruder as he'd hopped our rear fence. The etching on the face of the head was dark with something, probably dirt; I had left it out there in the leaves, after all. But the stuff didn't act like dirt.

It was sliding slowly down the titanium face.

I dropped the driver abruptly on the bed. That smell in the air resolved, the faintest whiff of smoke. Clove cigarettes.

YOU NEED TO SEE HIM.

My chest heaving, I took another half step to my side to steady myself, and my foot struck something with a bit of give.

It was attached to a dark mass sprawled to my left beside the bed. I sucked in a breath, amplified to a screech inside my head, and blinked down through the darkness at the body splayed grotesquely on its back, the death curl of the white hands, the dent at the forehead, the black tendrils of blood worming into the hair, the ear, pooling in the eye socket. The famous brow. Those perfect white teeth. And my nemesis, that well-defined jaw.

*TONIGHT YOU WILL UNDERSTAND
EVERYTHING.*

Horror knotted at the back of my throat, blocking off air, making my gorge lurch. I knew even before I heard the pounding footsteps coming up the hall. Stepping away from the bed to the middle of the room, facing that glorious smog-diffused cityscape, I tugged the woefully inadequate insurance note from my pocket and put my arms up over my head a split second before the door smashed in and the powerful beams of police flashlights hit me.

CHAPTER 33

I didn't kill him. I didn't kill him. It sounded like my voice, saying it over and over, but I wasn't sure whether it was in my head or coming out of my mouth until one of the cops said, "Yeah, we got that part."

Patrolmen, huddled in twos and threes, alternately fielded phone calls and mumbled into their radios. They peered at me not with animosity but with a sort of bemused wonder, awed by the scope of what they'd stumbled into. I heard them from the end of a tunnel, their words strained through the humming in my ears. I'd gone into shock, I think, but I'd thought that when you were in shock you weren't supposed to be so fucking terrified.

I'd been frisked roughly and moved to a room up the hall, a match of 1407. They'd seized my note asking them to contact Sally Richards, though I didn't know whether they had tried to reach her. Hotel Angeleno fell within her and Valentine's jurisdiction, so that gave me my only glimmer of hope.

I sat on the corner of the bed. Looking down, I realized I wasn't wearing handcuffs, though I had a vague memory of being cuffed at some point earlier when they'd wiped my hands with a forensic swab. It seemed they weren't sure what to do with me yet.

One of the female cops asked, "Want us to call your wife?"

"No. Yes. No." I pictured Ari waking up, finding me gone. It would take her about two seconds to put together that I'd gone to the hotel, though I'd promised her I wouldn't. "Yes. Tell her I'm okay. Not injured or dead, I mean." That drew some odd looks. "They led me here. They put a bug on me. Give me a pen. Here. Here. I'll show you."

One of the cops withdrew a pen from his breast pocket, clicked it, and handed it to me. Another said, "Watch him."

Using the tip of the pen, I dug into the heel of my Nike, right where the thin incisions were. The pen bowed and almost snapped, but I managed to fight out a chunk of rubber. "They bugged me. Right here. They were keeping track of—" I bent the sole back, digging my fingers into the gash.

Nothing inside the tiny cavity.

My breath left. I wilted.

One of the cops snickered. The others looked like they felt sorry for me. My shoe slipped from my hands, hit the floor. My sock had a hole at the toe. My voice, little more than a whisper: "Never mind." With a shaking hand, I raised the pen. I couldn't even look up, but I felt the cop take it back.

There was a brisk knock at the door, and then Sally entered, Valentine at her heels. She frowned at me brusquely, then asked the nearest cop, "Look at that color. He gonna pass out? You sure? Good. Leave us alone." A low murmur from the cop, and then Sally snorted and said, "Yeah, I think we can handle him."

Her wry tone—something familiar, at last—brought me back a step from the edge. The cops shuffled out, and Valentine took a post by the slider to block me in case I decided to go for the balcony. Sally dragged a chair over from the sturdy hotel desk, flipped it around with a twist of her thick wrist, and sat facing me.

"You were found with an unauthorized hotel security key in a room that isn't yours over the dead body of your declared enemy and plaintiff with a murder weapon containing your prints. What do you have to say?"

The room smelled of dust and Windex. Just beyond my right foot was the space corresponding to where Keith Conner's body lay, stiffening, four or five rooms up the hall. My throat was so dry I wasn't sure I'd be able to speak. "I'm an idiot?"

A curt nod. "That's a start." She checked her watch. "We have about twenty minutes before RHD rolls in and takes over—"

"*What?* How the hell am I supposed to trust Robbery-Homicide?"

"That's not exactly your—"

"If they take over, I'm finished. They've got me from *every angle* here. No one else will believe anything I say." I'd come off the bed, and she gestured sternly for me to sit back down. I said, "Why can't you keep the case?"

Her thin eyebrows lifted a few millimeters. "Do you have any idea what this thing looks like? The press has already caught wind of Keith Conner's demise, and comparisons are being drawn to River Phoenix and—I shit you not—James Dean. The DA called me twice on my drive over here. That's the DA *herself.* This is a dead movie star. Valentine and I haven't worked a movie-star murder since . . . well, that'd be, uh, *never.* You bet your ass this thing is going upstairs, and upstairs from there. So if you have something you want us to hear, you'd better talk fast."

I did. Though my thoughts were scattered and my voice quavered, I forced myself to pull it together and lay out for them everything that had transpired. Valentine stayed with his arms crossed, expressionless, the only sounds the occasional *thwick* of him sucking his teeth, Sally's pen scratching at her pad, and helicopters chopping the night sky, circling like hawks, their beams livening the curtains at intervals.

Sally looked at me blankly once I'd finished. "You're serious."

It didn't seem like a question, but I said, "If I could make something like that up, I'd still be a screenwriter."

She said, "The cops were tipped by an anonymous call, made from a courtesy hotel phone. A man claimed to have spied someone matching your description forcing Keith Conner into Room 1407."

"*That*'s the killer. For a frame-up to work, he had to plan the time of death for right before I got there. Keith had just been killed when I—"

She held up her hand. Stop. I waited, desperate and hopeful, trying to read her face. She looked back, mad at herself, or maybe me.

"You have to believe me," I said. "Because no one else will."

She chewed her cheek for what seemed a very long time. "With innocent suspects, the more you sweat 'em, the angrier they get. It's a great rule. Half the time."

A chill moved through me. Had I been angry? Angry enough?

"The other half?" I asked.

"They *don't* get angrier."

Valentine said, "That is a problem."

"Isn't it?" Sally cracked her knuckles by squeezing her fist, as close to worked up as I'd seen her. "I don't like generalizations. I put stock in global warming and the Second Amendment. I think war is sometimes the answer. I believe in Yoda, Gandalf, and Jesus. I like veal and porn—not in that order and not together. It's a complicated damn world, and I think this thing stinks to high heaven. So I'm gonna do something alarming. I'm gonna take you seriously."

I blew out a shaky breath.

She pointed a finger at my chest. "But for us to be able to have a *chance* to help you, here's what you have to say—"

The door banged open, and a tall, lean man in a suit ambled in.

Sally kept her eyes locked on mine, even as she said, "You're five minutes early."

"Kent Gable, RHD."

"I'm Sally Richards. This is Detective Valentine. He'll give you his first name if he's feeling social."

"My partner's up the hall in 1407," Gable said.

"Thanks for holding down the fort. We got it from here."

Sally kept staring at me expectantly. A loaded look, as if it could convey what she'd been about to tell me. Valentine's gaze was on me, too. My brain lurched through possibilities.

"We set up a cordon outside, but the area's thick with media." Gable swiped a hand across his clean-shaven jaw and finally looked at me directly. "Why isn't this man in cuffs?"

I placed my hands on my knees. "I'll cooperate fully with Detective Richards and Detective Valentine. But only with them. Anyone else, I'll lawyer up." I didn't sound confident, not at all, but it was the best guess I could muster about the move Sally needed me to make.

Valentine's nostrils quivered ever so slightly, and Sally exhaled with quiet relief, a vein standing out in her forehead. She blinked once, long, then turned to face Gable, who was staring at me, slack-jawed. "We've had some interaction with the suspect over the past week," she said. "He had a note requesting us should he wind up in troub—"

Gable said crisply, "I know about the note, sweet-heart—"

Valentine made a pained face.

"—but I don't think that means the suspect writes his own ticket."

A standoff. All of us staring at one another, the three of them standing, me seated on the bed like a schoolboy watching grown-ups argue. Totally at their mercy.

Valentine cleared his throat. His mustache twitched. "You know whose ass is on the line with this one? Even more than ours? The DA's. You might know from the newspapers that her office's performance on celebrity trials hasn't exactly been stellar, not even with you boys taking point on those investigations. Now, if we have the key suspect in the Keith Conner murder talking, my guess is the DA's gonna want that suspect to keep talking instead of getting busy building a legal dream team."

The Barney theme song chimed out. Sally palmed her cell phone. "Speak of the devil." She offered Gable a sugary smile. "Excuse me a minute, *dear heart.*" She walked past him and out the door, and he followed, a fresh urgency in his step.

Valentine walked over and crouched before me, his mouth set in a sour curl. Behind him, early-morning light seeped around the curtain, edging his notchless rise of hair with copper. "I worked a lot of years with a lot of cops. And lemme tell you, that woman has the best gut instinct on the force. Don't underestimate her. Her and I, we play this front. That I don't like her, I'm a bigot, whatever. Works well for us, gives us some angles. But lemme tell you: That's out the window now, along with everything else. I know how you feel right now. The fear. I can see it in your eyes, smell it out your pores. But you still can't know, not yet, how bad this is. Sally and I, we don't have to play no good-cop/bad-cop. *If* we get a chance, you tell us everything you know and we will do what we can to save your life. That's the only play here. The *only* play. You got it?"

I said, "I got it."

The door handle jangled, and Valentine and I looked tensely to see which detective would reenter.

Sally leaned in, one hand riding the lever. "Better get the handcuffs on. We need 'em for the cameras."

Light-headed, I stood. Static dotted my vision, then cleared. Valentine cinched metal around my wrists and steered me forward. My feet felt dead, like blocks of wood.

Sally took a deep breath, and I could see, beneath her unflappable facade, that she was rattled. As I approached, those flat eyes appraised me. "Ready for your close-up, Mr. DeMille?"

CHAPTER 34

"Let's start putting this thing together," Sally said.

After being assailed by news crews and camera flashes, I'd had the relative calm of the sedan ride to try to settle down and focus. The helicopters tracked us, compounding my headache until the bulletproof door of the station sucked closed behind us, silencing the thumping. I never thought I'd be relieved to be taken into custody. I was now backstage in a tiny office overlooking the interrogation room, on the cop side of the two-way mirror. It was private, unoccupied, and—aside from the various recording decks and closed-circuit units—as sparse as my shared Northridge office. Swivel chair, cup of coffee, TV on a mount—a casual, just-friends approach to keep the information flowing. The view into the interrogation room with its foreboding wooden chair, sporting rings for handcuffs, was a reminder of where I would wind up the minute I stopped being useful.

Pay It Forward was a distant memory; I'd wound up playing the wrong role in *Body Heat*.

Sally clicked on a digital camera and swung it from its usual angle through the two-way so it pointed at the three of us, sitting like colleagues spitballing a case.

I was still winded from being hustled upstairs, past the too-long stares of the other cops. "Has someone reached Ari?"

"We believe so," Valentine said.

"Where is she? What'd they tell her? Is she all right?"

"I don't know," Sally said, "and you have other concerns at the moment."

"I need to know that my wife is—"

"You don't have that luxury," she said sharply. "The captain of Robbery-Homicide is bending the chief's ear *as we speak,* and unless we find a crack in this case and turn it into a fissure, Detective Sweetheart will be back to arrest your skinny ass and throw it in Men's Central. So fucking focus."

Valentine caught me numbly staring at the news crawl beneath the live helicopter footage of Hotel Angeleno, and he reached up and slapped the muted TV, which clicked over to a soap. "Where were you at nine P.M. on February fifteenth?" he asked.

I closed my eyes, fought for clarity. Monday, two days ago . . . "Driving out to Indio to meet Elisabeta. Why?"

"Do you have anyone who can corroborate that?"

"Of course not. They told me not to . . ." Dread formed a lump in my throat to match the one in my gut. "Why? What happened?"

"We responded to a vandalism report at Keith Conner's house. Someone spray-painted '*LIAR*' across his fence, then scaled the gates and left a dead rat on the windshield of one of his cars. A security camera picked up some footage of the intruder on the grounds, in the shadows. The guy was about your build, but his face was obscured because he was wearing—"

I said quietly, "A Red Sox cap."

"Right. It's not our jurisdiction, but we got pulled in because—"

"Conner assumed it was me. Of course. I'd gone to see him a few days before."

"Not a friendly visit, we heard." Valentine flipped through his notepad. "Left a bad taste in Conner's mouth. He filed a complaint the morning before the break-in at his house."

"So he and I did exactly the dance they hoped we would. Me charging over there, him documenting my erratic, aggressive behavior."

"Yeah, and his counsel advised him to start a paper trail."

"*That's* why you came to see me at work. To follow up on the complaint."

Sally said, "Given your and Conner's grudge, we had to do some prying, see if you were keeping both oars in the water. At first we considered that Conner had invented your visit just to smear you, but then we found a paparazzi guy who confirmed you were there. Pictures, even."

Joe Vente.

"And afterward we spoke to the head of security at Summit, your boy Jerry Donovan, who told us how you were trying to get Keith Conner's address. The bartender at the Formosa has you drinking the brown stuff at breakfast time."

"Great," I said. "Unstable, drinking, obsessive." I drew in a breath. "Here's what's gonna come out next. The murder weapon? It belongs to me. It'll be the same club I threw at the intruder in my backyard. Also, I've been having problems at school—missing classes, conflicts with students. I have a paranoid view of government agents, as evidenced by my screenplay. I even tore my house apart in a delusional fit, looking for imaginary planted bugs."

"Your wife can confirm that they were there," Sally said. "The bugs."

"Right," I said, "an unbiased witness."

"After we filled Jerry Donovan in about the break-in at Conner's, he told us about the surveillance equipment he inspected at your place and about the transmitters he found in some of your clothes. So there's one independent confirmation."

Jerry must've really thought I'd posed a threat to Conner if he'd come clean about his clandestine visit to our house. I said, "But for all he knows, I could've planted all that stuff myself as part of some elaborate cover story."

"Okay . . ." Sally's cheeks were flushed. "If you clubbed Keith Conner to death, why was there no spatter on your hands or clothes?"

"That's angle-dependent, and two out of four expert witnesses will get the math right. Or wrong. Plus, did the crime-scene guys check the U-pipe under the hotel-room sink?"

Sally and Valentine looked at each other. "Yes," she said slowly. "Traces of blood."

"Which will prove to be Keith's. Which shows I washed off what spatter there was after killing him."

"Which side are you arguing here?" Valentine asked.

"I'm arguing the facts. I've got no copies of the discs or e-mails, and the Web sites have vanished, leaving me with only ten-second cell-phone-recorded bursts of secondary footage I could've generated myself. Then I steal out of bed late at night, having lied to my wife, to break in to Hotel Angeleno. I even ducked past a staff member, making sure to look conspicuously furtive."

"You build a convincing case," Valentine said.

"I'm the perfect fall guy. Angry, discontented. All they had to do was push the blinking buttons and I charged right down that road."

A news flash cut in over the soap opera, a picture of Keith Conner with the dates bookending his life, then footage of me being led from the hotel, anguish written across my gray features, my teeth bared like a chimpanzee simulating a human grin. I didn't remember anything of that walk but flashbulbs and photographers shouting my name to draw my focus. My name, my face, out over the morning airwaves. The East Coast was already reading about the whole sordid affair. My parents, over their Maxwell House. I was now one of those creepy, unhinged assassins, men with vacant stares and odd fixations and grievances lovingly nursed to bloody fruition. It hit me powerfully, devastatingly, that nothing in my life could ever get back to normal again.

But Valentine gave me scant room for self-pity. "Since you have all the answers, why don't you tell us why anyone would bother to frame *you*."

"This isn't about me. It was about killing Keith."

"Or having you go down," Valentine said.

"There are easier ways to take down someone like me than killing a movie star."

"Yes," Sally said, "but maybe none this nasty."

Valentine said to me, "Explain."

My head was lowered, but I could feel them studying me. Through the muddle of my terror, I'd forced myself to work out at least this. "They wanted Conner dead, so they looked around for someone with a good motive. They didn't have to look far. He and I had a well-publicized dispute, not to mention the outstanding lawsuit and battery charge."

Anyway, I figured the lawsuit was still outstanding; to my knowledge, my attorney had never received the settlement offer from the studio. Had a resolution *ever* been close, or was that just another way I'd been strung along? Was the legal back-and-forth even related to all this? Given the barrel I was currently staring down, I didn't want to sidetrack Sally and Valentine for something so vague, at least unless my lawyer could wrangle some concrete information out of the studio.

Valentine broke me from my thoughts. "If this whole thing wasn't about you, why go to these lengths? Why have you jump through all these hoops?"

"Think about it," I said. "Does *any* case anywhere in the world get the kind of attention that a Hollywood murder trial does? Every footprint, every timeline, every scrap of expert testimony is laid bare for public consumption. And with a star as the *victim*? This is going to be the most closely scrutinized case since the one that invented the genre. Every base has to be covered. Even *then* you guys usually can't get a conviction."

"So you're saying they needed more than a fall guy," Sally said. "They needed a fall guy they could *operate,* who they could steer into the ideal frame-up." She chewed the cap of her pen. "Robbery-Homicide's been known to get tunnel vision when they lock on to a suspect. The guys framing you knew if they could make the case look like an open-and-shut, that would prevent a thorough investigation."

I said, "So the question is, what would a thorough investigation lead to?"

"Someone else with motive. Who else has motive to kill Keith Conner?"

"Movie critics," Valentine said. He weathered Sally's look. "What's it always come down to? Money. Sex. Revenge." A nod in my direction. "Your spat with him involved all three."

That tripped a memory. I snapped my fingers, excited. "That paparazzi guy, Vente, told me that Keith got some club girl pregnant and that there's a pending paternity suit. If Keith winds up dead, his money might go to that woman and the baby."

Sally flipped the page in her notebook, kept scribbling.

"A guy like Keith," Valentine said, "there's gotta be more stuff like that."

"Yes," I said. "Plenty. Someone's got to look into his business dealings, if he owed the wrong people money, fucked the wrong wife, whatever. Whoever did this is still out there. You have to make sure the DA doesn't treat this as a closed case. You've got to help me."

Sally and Valentine just looked at me, their faces tense and, I feared, helpless.

A door slammed somewhere in the building. A muffled shout grew louder—"I know he's here"—and then Ariana lunged into the interrogation room through the looking glass, flinging her arm as if she'd just twisted free of someone's grasp. "Where is he? *Where?*"

Two beat cops followed her in, the scene unfolding as if the two-way mirror were a big-screen TV. Ari's sudden appearance in this context was disorienting; the whole thing felt somehow removed in time and space, a vision of Christmas present.

Her face was flushed, her fists clenched. She got the table between her and the cops, and they squared off over the surface. "I want to see him. I want to see that he's okay."

Reality slammed me, and I heard myself shouting, "Ari! *Ari!* I'm right here."

Soundproofed.

I scrambled to my feet, but Sally placed a surprisingly powerful hand on my shoulder. *"No,"* she said. "Not until we get separate statements."

We stood there an instant, watching my wife despair, me and two cops. I grabbed for the intercom. "I'm not gonna let her—"

Valentine had my arm twisted back across itself so hard I let out a grunt. "We haven't filed on you *yet*, but if you push it, we will. You want to keep chatting or take out a third mortgage to cover a bail bond?" He set me firmly back into my chair. "You will listen to what you're told."

Inside the interrogation room, Ariana's shoulders curled forward and then she shuddered, and I realized she was on the verge of weeping. The resolve had drained out of her. One of the cops circled the table and took her by the arm. "Ma'am, you'll come with me now."

The other cop was casting nervous glances at the mirror, at us. Ari, of course, picked up on it immediately. "Patrick? He's there? He's back *there*?"

She moved toward the mirror, the cop letting her arm slide through his grasp. "Patrick, why are you back there? Are you okay?"

She leaned forward, putting her face to the two-way, trying to peer through. She was looking right at us.

Sally made a noise in her throat, and Valentine said, "Christ."

I pressed my hand to the glass, touching Ariana, the outline of her palm. There was nothing else I could do.

The cop took her again by the arm, and she let him lead her out.

My face burned, and I bit down on my lip and willed my breath to freeze in my chest. All the time we'd wasted on our petty problems, and here I was, reduced to observing my wife through an interrogation mirror, she unable to see me, I unable to talk to her. The symbolism, oppressive enough for a student script. My voice came gruff and uneven. "You've got to keep me out of jail."

Sally said, "Then you'd better give us something."

"I don't have anything. They have me dead in the water."

"We've got no time for you to feel sorry for yourself. The men behind that size-eleven-and-a-half Danner boot bet on you being nothing more than a second-rate screenwriter. You lapped up what they laid down. If you want to save yourself, you're gonna have to come up with your own material."

Valentine: "Is there anyone besides your wife who can corroborate that they—whoever *they* are—exist?"

I tapped my head with the flat of my hand, prodding myself. "Elisabeta got an e-mail claiming that someone wearing a Red Sox hat would pay her a visit, but an e-mail's pretty thin. Wait, though. Doug Beeman. They recorded him also. He got DVDs, too."

"It could be argued that *you* recorded him."

"He'd been getting them for months. We could compare our schedules to prove I couldn't have made them. Plus, he still has the footage from that high-school basement."

"Give us an address."

I jotted it down.

"Your job is to get your head clear, go over the last nine days inch by inch, and think of *anything* else we can use. And you'd better do it fast." Sally ripped the address off the pad. "In the meantime we'll see Beeman."

"He'll confirm my story."

"You'd better hope so," Valentine said, and they walked out.

I sat for a long while, shuddering, gazing at the oblivious rectangle of the muted TV up on the mount. Color and movement. Shapes. The soap gave way to a commercial about a new razor with five blades, which to my dulled brain seemed like four too many. Squeezing my eyes shut, I tried to relive everything that had happened, starting with my stepping out onto the porch in my boxers that cold Tuesday morning, but my thoughts kept crashing off course. Prison. My marriage. What was left of my reputation.

I crossed to the door. A uniformed cop slumped against the wall just outside, flipping through a magazine. Not surprising. His eyes flicked up and held on me. I took a step out into the hall. He came off the wall. I retreated a step. He leaned back against the wall.

I said, "Okay," closed the door, and returned feebly to my chair.

Elisabeta was on the television.

Yes, that was her, sitting on a white couch, legs crossed, curtains billowing behind her.

For a moment my brain couldn't catch up to what I was seeing. Had reporters somehow uncovered her link to me? Already?

But no, there was advertising script across the screen. I stood, took a few halting steps forward, and went on tiptoe to raise the volume.

Elisabeta was saying, "—high-fiber drink mix that keeps me regular *and* decreases the risk of heart disease."

No accent. It was startling, bewildering, as if I'd

tuned in to an interview to find Antonio Banderas speaking in a Jamaican patois.

Now she was walking over a grassy rise, a canary yellow sweater draped across her shoulders, smiling. A purring voice-over said, "Fiberestore. For a healthy digestive system. And a healthy life."

A smiling close-up. That face, the slightly crooked nose, those Everywoman features—if she could benefit from increased fiber intake, so could you.

My lungs burned; I'd forgotten to breathe.

Elisabeta. In a TV commercial. Sounding as if she hailed from Columbus, Ohio.

An actress. Hired to play a part.

Which meant that Doug Beeman, my last good hope, was probably no longer my last good hope. I pictured Sally and Valentine, speeding toward that apartment this very minute. A fool's errand.

Dazed, I backed away from the screen and sat, nicking the edge of the seat and landing on the floor, the chair toppling over behind me. Still, I couldn't tear my eyes from the TV, though it had long returned to the soap opera.

The door opened briskly, and Kent Gable entered with a small entourage of suited men. Slacks, holsters bulging beneath jackets, badges gleaming on belts. Robbery-Homicide Division, right down to the assured lockstep of the loafers. Gable cocked his head to look down at me. Beneath my hands, the cheap floor tiles were as cool as death, as cool as the chill that had crawled into my bones.

"Sorry, Davis," he said. "Honeymoon's over."

CHAPTER 35

"Why . . . ?" I cleared my throat and tried again. "Why'd the DA have a change of heart?"

Pulling onto the freeway, Gable threw a folder over the seat back in answer.

It struck me in the chest. Since my wrists were cuffed, I had to move my hands together to flip through the pages. They looked like printed e-mails.

His partner, a wide Hispanic guy who hadn't offered a name, said, "We went to search your place—looks like you already tossed it for us." He didn't bother to turn around. The skin on the back of his head was visible through his shaved hair. "And after, after we paid a visit to your work. That shared little office with the Dell computer? What did you think, that we wouldn't check *all* your computers?"

The top e-mail, sent from peepstracker8@hotmail. com to my work e-mail address, read, *Received your inquiry. This what your looking for? Let us know if theres other informations you require.* The printed attachment showed a blueprint of what looked to be a mansion. I checked the time stamp—dated six months ago.

Dread turned my voice hoarse. "What's this, now?"

"Keep reading," Gable said. "It gets better."

A reply e-mail, ostensibly from me: *Can you follow people, get schedule information?*

I glanced back at the blueprint. The mansion looked familiar, all right. Clear down to the Olympic pool and eight-car garage.

Flipping forward again: *We dont do that. Documents only. Sorry buddy. Leave cash at drop point.*

The next several e-mails were thwarted attempts, apparently by me, to secure an unmarked handgun from various not-quite-unsavory-enough sources. The final page was an online booking for Hotel Angeleno that I'd evidently made under a fake name.

Gable's eyes watched me steadily from the rearview. I was frozen with disbelief. My mouth was open, wavering but not forming words. Sally and Valentine, the only ones who believed me, were off running down a dead lead. And now there was even more to deny, the evidence so overwhelming. The first thought to cut through the panic haze was that maybe I *had* lost it. Was this what it felt like inside a psychotic break?

Cars zipped by on either side of us, people coming back from their lunch breaks. A petite brunette smoked and chatted on her cell phone, one pedicured foot up on the dash next to the wheel. Mexicans sold flowers at the off-ramp. Lou Reed's colored girls doo-doo-doo-doo-dooed from someone's radio.

"You really think that deleting something off your computer gets rid of it for good?" Gable's partner snickered. "That shit's never gone. Our guy had it pulled off there in minutes."

I said slowly, "But my computer at home was clean?"

"So far." Gable's eyebrows drew together. "What's that get you? We have you dead on the Dell."

I shook my head, looked out the window again, the sun warming my face. I was cold and hungry and more scared than I thought it was possible to get. But they'd just shown me the first chink in the armor, giving me a new kind of resolve. If I were to have a prayer at staying out of jail, I had to retrace every minute of the past nine days and find any other chinks. As quickly as they stitched together the case against me, I had to unravel it. And I had to do it in the twenty minutes before we hit downtown and I vanished into Men's Central.

A tattooed giant in an orange jumpsuit, his cuffs cinched to a belly chain, all but blotted out the end of the corridor. He had a guard on either side of him, and I wondered if there was enough room for us to pass. Gable tightened his grip on my forearm and kept me moving forward. As we neared, the prisoner made a head lunge at me, and I stumbled back. I could hear the echo of his chuckles even after we'd turned the corner.

We passed into the booking area—a few desks, the mug-shot camera and backdrop, metal benches bolted to the concrete floor. A bunch of bored deputies ate Taco Bell over paperwork. A tiny TV showed that picture of me in a blazer that my agent had insisted I take for the trade announcement after the script sale. I looked like any other asshole readying himself for a golden ascent.

A jowly deputy looked up. "The Keith Conner guy. Can we get those fingerprints?"

"Mine are in the system already," I said.

"Good. Then they'll match nicely. It's procedure."

My heart still hadn't slowed from the scare in the corridor. I nodded, and he printed me expertly while Gable and his partner bullshitted with the others about some of Keith's cop movies and where they missed the mark. The deputy's thick hands manipulated my fingers this way and that. He didn't talk to me. He didn't make eye contact. I might as well have been inanimate. My few possessions were in a plastic tub, but at least I was still in my own clothes. Right now, still having my own clothes seemed like the greatest comfort imaginable.

When he was done, I said, "I'd like to make a phone call." Blank stares. "I get one call, right?"

The deputy pointed to a pay phone mounted on the wall.

I said, "I'm calling my attorney. Can I have a private line, please?"

Gable's partner said, "Want us to send for a psychic, too, so you can commune with Johnnie Cochran?"

Through scattered laughter Gable led me around the corner into an interview room split by a Plexiglas shield with a pass-through box for documents. No lawyer beyond the window, of course, just an old-fashioned black phone on my side of the pitted wooden ledge.

"You have a criminal attorney lined up already?" Gable said. "How 'bout that. You planned ahead."

"No, I'm calling my civil lawyer for a referral. But our conversation's still privileged."

"You have five minutes." He left me alone.

His footsteps ticked away, and then conversation resumed down the hall.

I picked up the phone, punched "0." When the jail operator picked up, I asked to be transferred to the West L.A. station. After a few seconds, the station desk officer picked up.

"Hello, this is Patrick Davis. I need to speak to Detective Sally Richards immediately. Any way you can put me through to her cell phone?"

"I— Huh? Wait a minute, Patrick *Davis* Patrick Davis? Didn't we just have you?"

"Yes, ma'am."

"Where you callin' from, son?"

"Men's Central."

"I see. Hold yourself. I'll see what I can do."

I waited through the static-cracked silence. Not all the ink had wiped off, navy blue filming the swirls of my fingertips. I touched the Plexi, leaving faint streaks.

Sally answered, "*Pat*rick?"

"Yes, I—"

"We're off the case. I can't talk to you, not like this. You know the pay phones there are monitored."

"I told them I was calling my lawyer so they'd put me on a line in the interview room. So we're good."

"Oh." A note of surprise.

"Are you at Beeman's?"

"No, we left. No one was home. We'll go back in a few—"

"Forget it. Listen—Elisabeta? She's an actress. She's in a Fiberestore commercial, the older woman sitting on a white couch. Find her. She was a hire, so you can bet Beeman was, too."

"Wait a minute. They hired *actors*—"

"To manipulate me. Yes. I don't have much time, so I'm gonna talk fast. Gable pulled some incriminating documents off my computer at work."

"I heard about them," Sally said.

"I think they were installed like a virus when I opened the e-mails."

"Why do you think that?"

"Because I was careful not to open any of their e-mails at home, and according to Gable the forensics guys didn't get anything off my own computer."

"Which is where the guys framing you would most logically want to have the stuff found."

"Right. They knew *when* I logged in to retrieve e-mails, but I don't think they knew where I was logging in from."

"Okay . . . so?"

"I also opened e-mails at Kinko's and an Internet café"—I gave her both locations—"so will you check those and see if any documents about Conner were installed on the computers I used there?"

"What would that give us?"

"Some of those fabricated documents—the e-mails—are time-stamped and backdated. If any like them were installed on those computers, they're gonna show times and dates when I wasn't there renting computer time."

Sally sounded excited, or at least her version of it.

"Kinko's and Internet joints keep time logs for usage. Even have sign-in codes to track users. You pay with a credit card?"

"Yes."

"Better still."

I could hear her pen scribbling. She said, "Even if this does pan out, I'll need anything else you got to reapproach the DA."

"I went through everything, inch by inch, like you said, and came up with another piece you can use. The night of February fifteenth. Nine P.M.?"

"When Keith's house was vandalized. Yes."

"I was driving out to Elisabeta's. Indio. They sent me that far to make sure I was well out of the picture. But my gas gauge is broken."

"And?"

"It looks like I have a full tank, even when I don't. They probably checked it to make sure I wouldn't have to stop for gas, so no one could alibi me."

"But you did. Stop for gas."

"Yes. Check my credit-card records to find which gas station I used."

"You could've sent someone else to gas up there with your card. Not all stations have security cameras outside at the pumps."

"I went into the mart to buy a pack of gum. They always have surveillance inside. I bet you'll be able to pull footage of me there at about the same time that someone else in a Red Sox hat was leaving a dead rat on Keith's windshield. That gives you a second suspect and supports me on the frame argument. Might even be enough to keep me out of jail while they shore up probable cause."

"Maybe you're *not* just a second-rate screenwriter."

"Yeah, I'm a second-rate suspect, too." A banging on the metal door. I lowered my voice. "He's coming back in, so one more thing. They didn't book me. I don't think I've actually been arrested."

Gable shoved the door open. "Chat time's over, Davis. Time to move."

Sally said, "What do you mean? They printed you and read you your rights?"

I eyed Gable. "Just the former."

A brief silence. "So they probably *asked* if they could print you, making it consensual even though you thought you didn't have a choice."

"Exactly."

"You can be held for questioning—for a reasonable time—without being arrested."

Gable said, "Did I just talk to you?"

"Yes," I said to him, "I'm wrapping it up."

"If they haven't booked you yet," Sally said, "then the DA's skittish about charging you."

I asked, *"Why?"*

"It's a weird fucking case, to say the least, and she has—*had*—me and Valentine pressing an alternate scenario. Her office can't afford another embarrassment, which means moving slow and right. You can be charged whenever—she's not gonna want to jump in on day one unless she's positive everything is lined out and she's got the case together. They waited a *year* to charge Robert Blake, and look how that turned out."

"Get off the phone," Gable said.

I fisted the receiver. "But the latest stuff—"

"I know," Sally said. "I'm not gonna lie to you. The e-mails, fabricated or not, are damning. The DA's deciding whether to charge you right now, and her moving the case to Robbery-Homicide is a pretty good indication of which way she's leaning."

Gable blew out a sigh and started toward me.

I said, "Listen, Frank, I gotta go. Can you—"

"Call the DA with the new leads you gave me? If they yield, yes. Evidence like that could be the deciding factor—push her to play it conservatively and hold off on the arrest."

I thought of the hulking inmate in the hall, how he'd lunged at me. If things went badly, by tonight I'd be sharing a cage with men like him. "How long will it take you?"

"Give us two hours, then force their hand."

I did my best to keep desperation from my voice. "How am I even supposed to know how to . . . ?"

Sally said, "They'll have to formally charge you or let you go."

I said, "But I don't want to push it if—" Gable was staring at me, so I stopped.

"It's your only play," she said. "Two hours. By then either we'll have gotten something to the DA or your leads are a bust."

Gable reached for the phone impatiently, but I turned away. My hand was squeezing the receiver so tightly that my fingers ached. "How will I know which?"

"You won't."

Gable put his thumb down on the telephone base, severing the connection.

An hour and fifty-seven minutes in the hard wooden chair of the interrogation room left me sore, my lower back cramped. Working in shifts, Gable and his partner had hammered me on every aspect of my life, and I'd answered honestly and consistently, all the while tamping down my panic and racking my brain for how to play it when the time came. Up until now, Gable had been careful to phrase everything as a question—"Step into this room for me?" As long as I complied, there was no need to arrest me, and I didn't let on that I was aware of my options. Until now.

Gable paced in front of me, his watch flashing again into view. I'd bought Sally and Valentine their two hours to look for conflicting evidence and talk to the DA. It was time to force the issue and see whether I wound up free or in a cell.

"Am I under arrest?"

Gable stopped. Grimaced. Then, carefully: "I never said that."

"Pretty heavily implied."

"At the crime scene, you said you were willing to go with Detectives Richards and Valentine to cooperate. You gave your full consent to go to the station with them. All we did was transfer you. We asked you to come with us. We asked if we could print you. We asked if you wouldn't mind answering a few questions."

"So," I said, "I'm free to go?"

"Not quite. We're allowed to hold you for—"

"A reasonable time to question me. Right. I've been in custody now for about sixteen hours. You detain me much longer without charges, that might piss off a jury if we get there."

"*When* we get there."

"You're out of reasons to prolong my detention. I've answered all your questions. You've had time to search my house and my office, so it's not like you need to hold me to prevent me from destroying evidence. You know where to find me if you decide to take me back into custody. I'm not a flight risk. My face is on every news channel, so even if I *wasn't* in dire financial straits, I couldn't exactly throw on a pair of Groucho glasses and hop a flight to Rio."

Gable had stopped pacing, his surprise giving way to irritation.

I continued, "So please tell the DA I'm done cooperating. She needs to pull the trigger and arrest me now—or let me try to get back to my life."

Gable crouched so his head was lower than mine. He worked his lip. "You've known. You've been planning this. The whole time." He glared at me with equal parts hatred and amusement. "That was your lawyer on the phone, was it?"

I didn't answer.

"Good lawyer," he said.

"The best."

"I need to make a phone call of my own. I'll be back to you shortly with an answer. One way or another."

The door closed, leaving me with the throbbing in my back and my doleful reflection in the two-way mirror. To say I looked like hell would be an under-statement. My face was pale and puffy, dark crescents holding up my eyes. My hair was thoroughly mussed; I'd been tugging at it anxiously. My joints ached. Leaning over, I ground the heels of my hands into my eye sockets.

I might never go home again.

Did California have lethal injection or the electric chair?

How the hell did I wind up here?

A creak to my right and Gable loomed in the doorway. Desperate, I tried to read his face. It was tight and filled with disdain.

He turned, walking off, flinging the door open in a burst of temper. It smashed against the outside wall and wobbled back, giving off a tuning-fork vibration.

I sat in my chair, watching that door wobble. I rose. I walked out. Gable was nowhere to be seen. The plastic tub holding my possessions had been placed on the floor outside the jamb, the throwaway cell phone right there on top, for anyone to see. I looked for my Sanyo before remembering that Sally had taken it to review the bits of recorded footage. My knees cracked as I crouched to pick up the tub. The elevators were in view at the end of the hall. My breath echoing in my skull, I walked toward them, braced for someone to seize me, condemn me—the inverse of a last-minute pardon.

But I got there. Once the doors slid closed behind me, I leaned weakly against the elevator wall, plastic tub under my arm. The ride down to the main floor took an eternity. When the doors opened, no one was there waiting to grab me. I trudged across the lobby, through the solid front doors, and out into the dusk. A polluted breeze blew up from the street, but the air felt as fresh as spring in my lungs. I dumped the disposable cell in the trash.

I had some trouble keeping my balance down the wide steps. I walked over to the street and sat heavily on the curb, my feet in the gutter, buses and cars blowing by. A brittle leaf fluttered against the asphalt like a dying bird. I watched it, then watched it some more.

"Get up." There she was above me, backlit. I was surprised and also somehow not. "We've got work to do." Sally offered a hand, and after a moment I took it. I got halfway to my feet when my knees went out, and I lowered myself back onto the curb.

"I think I need a minute," I said.

CHAPTER 36

"Two things did it," Sally told me as we barreled along the 101. "The gas station had digital security footage of you at the counter, which the clerk e-mailed right over. That alibied you for the break-in at Conner's and got a second suspect into the mix. Enough to give the DA pause."

Valentine was still off trying to run down Elisabeta, so I rode in the front of the sedan, which made me feel vaguely human again. I dialed Ariana for the fifth time, but all her numbers remained busy. Sally had given me my Sanyo cell phone back, after declaring the recorded clips on it useless. When I'd turned it on, it had been jammed with excited condolences from virtually everyone who had the number, too many to listen to right now, given my state of mind.

"*And,*" Sally continued, "the computer you rented at Kinko's—a Compaq. It had a bunch of time-stamped documents implanted in various places, showing the planning of the crime, your obsession with Conner, stuff going back a year. Beyond the question of why you would leave that stuff on a rented computer, it's impossible that you created those documents."

"Because the time stamps didn't match the dates I rented the computer?"

"Even better." She let slip a pleased smile. "The serial number on the Compaq shows it to have shipped as part of a bulk buy on December fifteenth. Which means the computer didn't yet exist when you were supposedly generating incriminating documents on it. Looks like you outthought them on one front— they were counting on you to check your e-mail at home or at the office."

"Me: one. Bad guys: ninety-seven."

"Hey," she said, "it's a start."

I resumed calling our house, Ariana's cell phone, her work. Busy or off the hook. Full mailbox. No answer.

A blinking icon on my cell phone caught my eye. A text message. Another threatening communication? Nervously, I thumbed it onto the screen, relaxing when I saw that it was from Marcello:

I FIGURE U MIGHT NEED THIS RITE ABOUT NOW.

The accompanying photograph was a freeze-frame from the footage I'd recorded onto my phone. It showed the windshield reflection of the Vehicle Identification Number, blown up and clarified. Closing my eyes, I gave private thanks for Marcello's postproduction skills.

Sally said, "What?"

I held out the phone so she could see the image. "This is the VIN of the car from the second e-mail.

Where the guy filmed through the windshield to show me the route to that Honda in the alley."

She unclipped the radio and called in the VIN, asking the desk officer to look into it. She gave a few uh-huhs, then an "Oh, really?" When she signed off, she said, "That club girl? She had a miscarriage. So the paternity suit's a dead end. At least *that* paternity suit. As for the VIN, that should be easy. We'll get word back on the car soon."

"Thank you," I said. "For taking me seriously. All of it. I know you're out on a limb."

The tires thrummed over the freeway exit. "Let's be clear about something. I like you, Patrick. But we're not friends. Someone got murdered. He may have been an asshole, but he was killed in my jurisdiction, and that angers me. Deeply. I want to know who killed him and why—even if it's you—and there is no condition more motivating to me than curiosity. Plus, call me old-fashioned, but the thought of an innocent person behind bars makes me chafe. Justice, truth, and all that crap. So I appreciate your thanks, but you should know I didn't do any of it for you."

We drove in silence. I looked out my window for a time before trying Ariana again. And again. The home phone was still busy—had she taken it off the hook? Between attempts my cell rang. I checked caller ID eagerly, but it was the Northridge film department. Probably not calling to offer me a raise. Frustrated, I threw my phone onto the dash. It rattled against the windshield. I took a few deep breaths, staring at my lap. At first I hadn't noticed we'd stopped moving.

We were parked outside a familiar run-down Van Nuys apartment complex. Sally climbed out, but I just sat there, taking in the bent security gate and the courtyard beyond. VACANCY, written on rusted metal, swaying from the gutter. APARTMENTS FOR RENT.

All the signs had been there, and yet I'd read none of them.

Sally knocked the hood impatiently, and I climbed out, regarding the building with awe. It was familiar, and yet altered in my mind, given what had transpired. The directory box, with its blank renter spot for Apartment 11. I thought about how I'd tried to call up to the apartment anyway, but the line had been out of service. How pleased I'd been with myself when I'd figured out to punch in the entry code. So pleased I hadn't lingered on the fact that I was heading to an apartment with no renter and a disconnected call-up line.

We stopped before the locked front gate. Sally waited expectantly until I realized why. Reaching out a trembling finger, I pressed the four numbers. The gate buzzed, and Sally tugged it open, giving me an after-you wave.

Up the stairs, down the floating hall to Beeman's apartment. That old-fashioned keyhole where I'd seen Beeman's eye peering out at me.

"I reached the manager by phone," Sally said. "He claims the place hasn't been rented in months. Water damage—I guess the owner's waiting to pay for mold remediation. The manager's not on site to let us in. And I can't get a warrant. It's not my case, you know. Shame." Sally put her hands on the railing, looked out across the courtyard below, humming to herself. Something classical. I watched the back of her head.

Then I turned and kicked in the door.

The brittle wood gave easily. Stooped, I stood in the doorway. Empty. No mattress, no dirty clothes, no big-screen TV partnered with a convenient DVD player. Just the moist reek of mold, dust motes swirling in a shaft of light, that water stain bleeding through the wall.

It felt like entering a dream world. I paused a few steps in.

There he'd sat, back on his heels before the TV, swaying, clutching himself.

An actor.

That beaten-down humility I'd identified with so strongly. A man I'd taken for vulnerable, frustrated, damaged.

Paid to play me for a fool.

He'd embodied my hopes and fears. He'd known how desperate I'd been to redeem him, to redeem myself. Even in light of everything else, that betrayal was blinding, humiliating.

Sally was saying something. I blinked hard, my ears ringing, an echo chamber of my thoughts. "What?"

"I said, we find Doug Beeman, we clear you."

An electronic chirp issued somewhere in the apartment, and Sally's hand went to her hip. We looked at each other. Sally tilted her head toward the bathroom. We inched over, our steps silent on the worn-through carpet. The door gave silently to the pressure of her knuckles.

The bathroom was empty, but behind the toilet

bowl, to the side, visible only once we'd inched past the chipped counter, was a cell phone. It had probably fallen from a pants pocket onto the wraparound shag rug as someone sat.

Another chirp.

As Sally exhaled, I crouched and flipped it open. The screen saver featured a *Sin City* shot of Jessica Alba and the owner's name, keyed in purple: MIKEY PERALTA. Doug Beeman's real name, on the cell phone he'd claimed not to have?

Clicking the speaker button, I hit "play."

"Message from"—and then a prerecorded wheezy voice with a strong New York accent—"Roman LaRusso." Then, "Mikey, it's Roman. The deodorant people rang me in a panic when you missed your call time this morning. I figured you were just hungover, but then I heard you might have been in an accident? Are you all right? Can you make it to the set tomorrow? Call me. C'mon, I'm worried."

Twenty minutes later we were at Valley Presbyterian Hospital, standing over Mikey Peralta's body, the cardiac monitor going strong, peaks and gullies to shame a tech stock. One of his eyelids was closed, smooth as ivory, the other at half mast, revealing the wine-red sclera beneath. His forehead was dented on the right side, a bloodless divot the size of a fist. The teal hospital gown stretched across the compact rise of his chest, and his arms lay limp, his hands curled unnaturally inward. Dark puffy hair, blown back from that receding hairline, framed his chalky face against the pillow.

Brain-dead.

The ICU nurse was talking to Sally behind me. "—filed an accident report. Hit-and-run, yeah. I guess no one saw anything, and he was pretty much gorked on arrival."

I was still struggling to overcome my shock. As Sally had stepped in and out, taking phone calls and gathering information, I'd stared blankly at the supine body. It was impossible not to think of him as Doug Beeman.

Stepping forward, I lifted his hand. Dead weight. Turned it over. The insides of his wrists were perfectly smooth. The razor-blade scars had been nothing more than makeup and special effects.

I set his arm gently back in place. The smell of whiskey tinged the air around him.

Valentine arrived, and he and Sally conferred in hushed voices. "RHD ain't gonna like him here one bit."

"Look, we've got bigger concerns," Sally said. "Obviously they're snipping off the loose ends here, covering their tracks. Once they know Patrick's out—"

"Come on. They're not gonna want to Jack Ruby him. That'll only make it obvious there *is* a frame and open up more—"

I turned, and they went silent. "Elisabeta's next," I said. "Did you find her?"

Valentine said, "I couldn't run her down. The Fiberestore commercial's two years old. The name on the contract says Deborah B. Vance, but the Social doesn't line up and there are no last-knowns. Actresses are a pain in the ass. They reinvent themselves every five minutes, always working under different names, moving, ducking taxes. Their credit history's a mess, so their financials look like spaghetti. I called SAG and AFTRA, but they've got no one paying union dues under that name. I could keep digging, but"—a pointed look at Sally—"this isn't our case, and you can bet RHD is already all over every move we—"

From outside we heard, "Officer, you can't just keep piling into the patient's room—" and then a booming voice, "It's not 'Officer.' It's *'Captain.'*"

Valentine looked at Sally, mouthed, *Fuck.*

The door opened, and the captain entered with his assistant. The captain's eyes, the same coffee color as his skin, swept the room. Of middling height, his bulk softened with middle age, he would have been unimpressive if not for the sense of authority emanating from him like a radioactive glow. A vein throbbed in his neck, but aside from that, his rage seemed to be restrained. "You brought the lead suspect along to investigate the death of a person of interest in his own case?" He forked two fingers at me. "For all you know, he was the hit-and-run driver."

"That's not possible, sir."

"No? And why is that, Detective Richards?"

"Because I've been with him since the time of his release."

"You picked him up downtown?" Each syllable enunciated.

Peralta's monitor kept emitting those soothing beeps.

"I did, Captain."

A deep breath, nostrils flaring. "A word, Detectives." The stare hitched on me a moment, the first direct acknowledgment of my presence. "You, wait in the hall."

We all snapped to. As I parked myself in a reception chair, Sally and Valentine followed the captain into an empty patient room, the assistant standing post outside, expressionless. The door clicked neatly, and then there was an absolute silence. No baritone thundering, no foghorn blare of displeasure, just a chilling graveyard quiet.

My phone hummed, and, praying it was Ari, I scrambled for it. But the number on the caller ID screen was my parents'. I took a hard breath, returned the phone to my pocket. Not the best time for explanations.

The captain exited, his assistant falling into step beside him, and they breezed by me, nearly stepping on my shoes. Valentine came out a moment later, a sheen of sweat on his forehead. He paused before me but kept his gaze straight ahead. "Four boys, Davis. That's a lotta bills. The case is with RHD and only with RHD. I'm sorry, man, but I'm not gonna fall on my sword for you."

I pointed at Mikey Peralta's room. "They killed him."

"That boy's got two DUIs on record. So a car accident? Not exactly a shocker."

"They knew that. That's why they chose him."

"That, too, huh?" He smoothed his mustache with a thumb and forefinger. "This thing is too big for you. The cops, the conspirators, the press—everyone is watching you. If you get in a speck of trouble—and I do mean a speck—you're fucked. And we won't be able to help you. My advice is you go home, get quiet, and let this thing shake itself out."

He kept on to the elevators. I studied the tips of my shoes, all too aware of Sally's presence behind the shut door across the way. My sole remaining ally? I almost didn't want to go in and find out.

But I did. No one had bothered to turn on the overheads, but an X-ray light box cast a pale glow. Sally was sitting on a gurney, her broad shoulders bowed. The creases of her shirt at the stomach were dark. "I'm done," she said.

Dread filled me. "As in fired?"

She waved me off. "Please. I'm a broad detective and a dyke, so I can't be fired. Single mother, too. Shit, talk about job security." Her voice held no hint of levity. "But I'm off this case. As in I will need to keep my captain advised of my location at all times." She wiped her mouth. "The VIN number you gave me traced to a Hertz rental. The credit card securing the vehicle was paid by a limited-liability company called Ridgeline, Inc. The desk officer glanced into the company, said it's like a Russian nesting doll. A shell within a shell within a shell. There might've been another shell in there—I kinda lost track when my cell phone cut out."

"Why are you handing this off to me? What am I supposed to—?"

But she continued, undeterred. "Unless that body one room over is the biggest coincidence since Martha Stewart's stock trade, these guys are covering their tracks. They probably want you living, since a dead fall guy makes everyone cry conspiracy, which—" She flared her hands. "But clearly you're in their crosshairs, and they're waiting and watching."

"Can I get protection?"

"*Protection?* Patrick, you're the lead suspect."

"You and Valentine are the only cops who believe me. And he's walking. There could be a leak somewhere else in the department—in RHD, even. I've got no one else who can help me. No one else I can trust. Don't hang me out."

"*I don't have a choice.*" Her head was tilted, the bulge of her cheek blotched with red. She'd stiffened her hand to punctuate the point, and it floated, four fingers aimed at nothing. Steady beeping from the next room was audible, and I realized with a chill that it was the cardiac monitor hooked up to Mikey Peralta.

"Will you . . . ?" I needed another moment to find my composure. My voice, after her outburst, sounded faint. "Will you hand off the conflicting evidence to Robbery-Homicide?"

"Of course I will. But, Patrick, every case has edges that won't align, and given the preponderance of evidence, they're eager to move in one direction and entrench. If they're batting .900 against you, that's about .400 better than they usually get."

"But there's *hard evidence*—"

"All evidence is not created equal." She was growing angry again. "And you have to understand: Pieces of evidence are building blocks, nothing more. The same ones can be shoved together to form different arguments. *Counter*arguments. The gas station's security tape gets you off the hook for the Conner break-in, but you might have hired someone else to do it to give you the alibi. You see? There are sides. The lines have been drawn. It's not corrupt. It's not political. It's not an agenda. It's how the system works. That's why it's a system."

My voice rose, matching hers. "So all Robbery-Homicide's gonna do is sit back and piece together what they already have?"

She looked at me like I was an idiot. "Of course not. They're gonna be working day and night to shore up the case against you so they can come arrest you. For good this time."

"What . . . what do I do, then? Go home and wait to get arrested?"

Her hands lifted from her knees, then fell. "I wouldn't."

The hospital air tasted bitter, medicinal, or maybe it was just me. Sally slid off the gurney, headed past me.

I said, "I have to find my wife. Can I get a ride to my car?"

She paused with her back to me, her large shoulders shifting. "Not from me."

The door closed behind her. The perpetual beep of the monitor came through the wall. I stayed in the semidarkness, listening to a dead man's heart beat.

CHAPTER 37

Seeing my dinged-up Camry from the backseat of the cab, I breathed a sigh of relief. Since I hadn't been formally arrested, my car hadn't been impounded. Media stragglers hung on outside Hotel Angeleno, but fortunately I'd parked up the street last night, which was now beyond the fray.

As I pulled the remaining bills from my repossessed wallet, the well-mannered Punjabi taxi driver pointed and asked, in beautiful English, "Did you hear what happened here last night?"

I nodded and slid out, ducking quickly into my car, anonymous in the thickening dusk. I kept the radio off. My hands, bloodless against the steering wheel, looked skeletal. The streets were dark and wet. Bugs pinged around streetlight orbs. Coming up the hill, I heard the thrumming of helicopters, the bass track of Los Angeles. My Sanyo was at my ear, and my father was saying, "Give the word, we'll be on a plane."

"I didn't do this, Dad." My mouth was dry. "I need you to know that."

"Of course we know that."

"I told him not to go to that city."

"Ma, not now," I said, though she was in the background, crying, and couldn't hear me.

"Didn't I tell him?"

"Right," my dad answered her, "because you foresaw *this*."

I came around the bend and saw the news choppers circling, bright beams laid down on our front yard. I was shocked. Though I'd registered the noise, I hadn't put together that our house was the draw. *I* was now the sordid news beat, the pinned frog under laboratory lights. Cars and vans lined both curbs, and news crews swarmed along the sidewalks. A guy in a baseball cap was peeking into our mailbox. Ari's white pickup was slant-parked five feet from the curb, as if abandoned for a flood or an alien invasion.

I'd dropped the phone but could still make out my mom's tinny voice: "Whatever you need, Patrick. Whatever you need."

I hit the brakes to reverse out of there, but it was too late. They rushed me, and I caught a full frontal view of the floodwater that had forced Ari to ditch her truck. Bulbs popping, knuckles tapping, voices shouting. I nosed the car toward the driveway, nudging aside hips and legs, before the need to flee overtook me and I gave up.

Grabbing my cell, I shoved my door out into hands and elbows. A camera cracked against the window. I stood, but the swell pushed me back into the car—*Give him space give him space!*—and then I rose again, pressing forward. Lenses and foundation-tan faces and bundled microphones slanted in on me. *What are you feeling right Does your wife know Is it true that Keith Tell us in your own words Are you—*

They moved as a floating mass around me, tripping over the curb, banging into each other. When I stepped onto our property it was like crossing a magic line. Most of them stayed back, straining against an invisible fence, though a few followed me. I was too shell-shocked to protest. The helicopter spotlight glowed around me, blazing white, though I was certainly imagining the heat. Churning air blew specks of dirt into my eyes. Our porch was scattered with yellow DHL boxes, *SAME DAY SERVICE* written in screaming red across the sides. As I fumbled out my keys, a few names jumped out at me from the air-bills—*Larry King Live, 20/20, Barbara Walters.*

I jabbed the key at the lock, but then the door gave way on its own, Ariana shouting, "I told you, off the porch or I'll call the cops aga—"

She froze, and we stared at each other across the threshold, dumbstruck, her strained face flickering beneath a cascade of camera flashes that matched the crescendo of my heartbeat. *How 'bout a homecoming hug Are you upset with your Can we get a moment between What you must be feeling—*

Ari grabbed my hand and tugged me inside, and the door flew shut, and I was home.

She said, "Dead bolt," and I complied. She wouldn't let go of my hand. We walked together to the couch and sat next to each other, almost calmly. On the muted plasma, Fox News showed the angle from the sky, the angle I'd just been on the receiving end of. I watched myself, a puzzled dot emerging from the crush of the crowd and working its way clumsily up the front walk.

The doorbell chimed, and Ariana's sweaty hand tightened around mine. The home phone rang. Then Ari's cell phone. Then mine. The home phone. The home phone. Someone knocked politely on the front door. Ari's cell phone. Mine again.

The cushions had been tugged off the couch or clumsily replaced, no doubt by the cops when they'd searched the house. Papers and bills lay scattered on the carpet. The kitchen cupboards stood open, the drawers pulled out and upended. She'd been through hell, and it was my fault.

By my shoe was one of the many bills from my lawyer, reviewed and tossed aside by the cops. I'd require a criminal attorney now on top of that, which meant, barring a miracle, we'd have to sell the house.

What had I done to us?

Ariana said, "I woke up. And you were gone."

"I didn't want you to be scared."

"How'd that work out?"

"Not good."

She started to say something, then swore sharply, rooted through her purse, turned on the jammer, and threw it on the cushion between us. It sat there, silent and innocuous-looking, withstanding her glare. She took a moment to steady her breathing. "The bed was still warm. And I had to sit with it. Knowing you'd gone to the hotel."

"I couldn't resist," I said. "I had to go."

"I knew in my gut it was bad. I thought you'd get killed. I almost called the cops. But then they called me. I thought—" She shoved a fist against her mouth until her ragged breathing evened out. "Well, let's just say I'd never have thought that hearing you got arrested would be a relief."

The phones bleated out their reveille again, and when the home line paused to catch its breath, Ari rose and swatted the receiver off the wall mount. She came back and took up my hand again, and we sat, staring ahead at nothing. "They went through everything. My fucking Tampax carton. They emptied the trash. I came into the bedroom, a cop was reading my journal. He didn't apologize. He just turned the page."

My mouth was dry. I said, "You knew. And I didn't listen."

"There's plenty I haven't listened to."

I looked down at the legal bill at the tip of my sneaker, my face hot, burning. "What I've done to us . . . if I could take it back—"

"I forgive you."

"You shouldn't."

"But I do."

I blinked, felt wet on my cheeks. "Just like that?"

Her grip was so firm that my fingers hurt. The helicopters beat at the night air overhead. She said, "It's gotta start somewhere."

Every action seemed freighted with considerations. Changing channels on the TV. Walking past a gap in the curtains. Deleting cell-phone messages. My Sanyo, at capacity, held twenty-seven. Julianne, supportive. A neighbor, crying. A friend from high school, his excitement hidden beneath a veneer of concern. My civil attorney, confirming that he'd never received the studio's settlement offer and *now,* understandably, could get not a peep out of them; there did remain, however, the issue of his depleted retainer. My department chair, Dr. Peterson, bemoaning "a full day of missed lectures. I understand there are extenuating circumstances, but unfortunately we still have students we are responsible for. I need to see you. I'll expect you tomorrow morning at ten."

Her brusque hang-up punctuated my dismay. I'd be there, even if it killed me. Especially in the midst of everything I was up against, I had a desperate need to hold on to something normal. All I had was an adjunct faculty position, but I realized now what that job meant to me. It's what had gotten me up all those mornings when I'd wanted to curl up in defeat, and I owed it back more than I'd yet repaid. Plus, it was grounding. A desk and a function. The last piece of my identity as I used to know it. If I lost that now, who would I be?

I turned off my cell phone and set it on my desk in the place my computer used to occupy before the cops had seized it. The media had thinned out a bit once the photographers grabbed the homecoming shots and the reporters did their stand-up reports, but quite a few unmarked vans remained, idling hopefully at the curbs, and the news copters maintained their tireless loops. The clock showed 3:11 A.M. I was a kind of exhausted I hadn't known was possible.

I'd used Ariana's laptop earlier to look up Ridgeline, Inc., and had found nothing worthwhile. Shell within a shell. Rolling up the window shade, I stared across the rooftops, wondered who was staring back at me. Who the hell had done this to me? Were they out there gloating? Were they planning their next move or just waiting for LAPD to swing back and roll me up?

I walked down the hall. Ariana was lying under the covers, balled in the fetal position, the fake Marlboros on the nightstand. Someone was shouting outside, and a dog barked, but then it was quiet except for the white noise of the helicopters.

"When I tried to write," I said, "my characters were always levelheaded. They thought on their feet. Grace under pressure. It's such bullshit. It's not like that at all. I was so fucking scared."

She said, "You did okay. You got yourself out."

"For now." I got into bed—our new bed—and stroked her head. "I mean, murder? Prison? We live in a death-penalty state. Jesus, the fact that's even *relevant* . . ."

"If we sit in this, we won't make it. It's too bleak. So let's make each other a promise. The last time we were up against it, after Don, the movie, we shut down. We drifted." Her dark eyes shone. "Whatever happens now, we stay in it together. And we fight like hell. If we go down, we go down swinging."

Gratitude welled in my chest. My wife, reiterating the vows we'd made to each other on a cloth-draped altar, when everything was simple and the road ahead clear. I didn't realize back then, standing on weak knees as the priest droned on, what those vows meant. I didn't realize that they mattered most when they were hardest to uphold.

"No matter what"—my voice was low, hoarse with emotion—"we stay in it together."

Her arm tightened over my chest, and that sense of protectiveness rose in me again, even stronger.

"They weren't expecting me to get out of jail," I said. "I should get us each a gun."

"You know how to fire a gun?" Her head rustled against me as she looked up. "Me neither. And I doubt a firearm license would clear for the Davis family anytime soon. Plus, I don't think we want an unregistered gun floating around, not this week."

"They're still out there," I said. "And no one's looking for them. But you can bet they're watching us."

"Yes," she said. "But so is everyone else." Beyond our dark ceiling, a helicopter carved an arc, the whirring rising to a whine and then fading. "That makes us safe, at least for tonight. No one's gonna sneak in here past the klieg lights and threaten us. There are advantages to being watched. Everything that's thrown at us, we have to figure out how to use to our advantage. That's the only way out of this."

"Play the hand you're dealt."

"Detective Richards told you as much," she said. "There are questions we need to answer before a jury writes your name in the blank space with permanent ink."

"Who wanted Keith Conner dead. Who stood to benefit from his death. Who's standing behind a left-handed guy wearing size-eleven-and-a-half Danner boots with a pebble stuck in the tread."

"Tomorrow I'll look into criminal lawyers."

"And I'll keep digging," I said. "If I get something tangible, Sally and Valentine will have to listen."

"Or we'll find someone who will."

I slid down next to her. Moonlight, even through the cinched blinds, bathed our sheets in a pale glow. Ariana lay on her stomach, facing me as I was facing her. The line where her skin met the mattress perfectly halved her face. My hand was out, palm flat, before my cheek. Hers beside mine. We stared at each other, two parts of a whole. I could feel her breath on my face. I took her in. Right here, in front of me. The nearest beating heart this night and nearly every other for the past eleven years. Those dark curls, climbing the pillow she'd shoved up against the headboard. Etched at the edge of her eye, premonitions of crow's-feet. I'd watched them creep into existence these past few years, and I owned them as much as she did, owned the hurt and laughter and life that had gone into them. I wanted to be with her to see them deepen, and now I could no longer take for granted that I'd get to. She blinked long, and then again, and her eyes stayed shut.

I cleared my throat. "In good times and in bad."

She put her hand over mine, mumbled, "For better or worse."

I thought, *Until we are parted by death.*

Sometime around daybreak the helicopters left.

CHAPTER 38

After a few hours of stone-dead slumber, I jolted up, puffy-faced, the recollection of the prior day raging in my skull along with a headache I could practically hear. Transmitters and hidden lenses had haunted my sleep, and the first thought to chisel through my stirring panic was of Ariana's raincoat.

I crept downstairs. Seven A.M., and golden morning light fell through the break in the living-room curtains. Faint as it was, it made me squint. A harsh world out there, waiting.

The coat was hanging in the front closet, and I sat on the foyer floor and draped it across my lap. Deep breath. My fingers pinched the seam. Metal beneath. The tracking device remained, sewn into the fabric. I wasn't sure how long I sat there, rolling the bulge between finger and thumb, appreciating its existence, but I was startled to hear Ariana behind me.

"I already checked that it was there," she said, "after the cops left."

"Whoever's behind this removed the one from my Nikes but kept yours in," I said. "Which means they don't know that we were aware they bugged our clothing."

She held the jammer loosely at her side. "Why remove the one from your shoe and leave mine in?"

"I was supposed to be arrested, in which case the cops would've put my clothes and stuff through a security scanner. And they'd have been hard-pressed to explain why I planted a tracking device on myself."

"So what do we do with this?" She pointed at her jacket.

"Don't wear it. It's not raining, so even if they are still monitoring it, it won't seem suspicious that you left it behind. If you go out or into work, keep your cell phone off—remember, they can track that, too. Have Martin or one of the carpenters meet you in the parking lot and walk you from your car."

"I'm not going in today," she said. "It's a madhouse even there, and besides, I need to start calling lawyers."

"Whenever you're home, keep the alarm on."

"Patrick," she said, "I know how to be careful."

She went into the kitchen, surveyed the mess on the floor where the cops had dumped the drawers and the trash bin, then gave a shrug, plucked a pan from the heap, and set it on the burner. I took the jammer, went up to my office, and stared at the blank desk. My thoughts were scattered, but I figured I had to start with Keith. Getting information about a movie star's private life was hard enough, even without a murder complicating matters. I needed people who knew how he spent his days and with whom, people who might not mind talking to the lead suspect in his murder. The list was short. In fact, it was two names.

Using the throwaway cell phone I'd given Ariana,

I tried to dial, but the thing wouldn't work. After a few more attempts, I realized that the jammer was knocking out the signal. So I returned the jammer to Ari and went out into the backyard, which I figured more likely to be clear of surveillance devices. I made an anonymous call to my former agency and had a kid in the mail room get me the number of the production office for *The Deep End*. When I called over, giving a fake name, the assistant was short with me, weary from fielding calls about Keith's murder. She refused to give me any contact information for Trista Koan. Keith had mentioned that Trista had flown in for the production, which meant corporate housing, hotels, or a sublet, which in turn meant no easy trace. Predictably, I couldn't turn up a listing on her by calling information. And I didn't know where she was from.

Back in my office, I rifled through my drawers and finally came up with an ivory card bearing the name of the second person on my list. I found Ariana's laptop in the bedroom and Googled him. Endless photo credits—he was real, not an invention like Doug Beeman and Elisabeta.

Back outside to dial. The phone rang, and finally he picked up.

"Joe Vente."

"Patrick Davis."

"Patrick. Don't you think it's a little late to sell out Keith Conner?"

"I need to see you."

"That shouldn't be hard."

"Why not?"

"I'm camped out in front of your house."

I hung up, walked back inside, and peeked through the living-room window. Shadows in drivers' seats, but I couldn't make out faces. My car and Ari's remained floating off the curb; I'd have to move hers into the garage before I left for my meeting at school. From the kitchen Ariana called out, "Poached eggs?"

"I don't think I can eat."

"Me neither. But going through the motions seems like a good idea."

I pointedly didn't say anything, and a moment later I heard a click—her turning on the jammer. After sixteen years her ability to read my mind was staggering. I called out, "I'll be right back. I'm going to see Keith's paparazzi stalker. He's right outside."

She said, "Play the hand you're dealt."

When I stepped onto the porch, a few car doors opened and slammed, and then a couple of guys jogged toward me toting cameras and trailing wires. A female reporter ripped the paper makeup collar from around her neck and charged, wobbly on her high heels. I felt tentative, exposed in the sunlight, but I had the world to face and everything to prove, and I wasn't going to prove it holed up in my house with the curtains drawn. On blind faith I walked to the end of the walk, and sure enough a van materialized and the door rolled open. I stepped in, and we pulled out and away. Joe hunched forward, smoking, humming along with Led Zeppelin on a crackly stereo and tapping the wheel. His shiny scalp was visible through thinning yellow hair, and he was growing the back out into a ponytail that hadn't quite gotten there.

The van was equipped for a stakeout—cooler, sleeping bag, hot plate, camera with giant zoom lens, swivel chairs, stacks of magazines and newspapers with porn mixed in.

He drove around the block, pulled over, then climbed back to sit opposite me. The carpeted interior held the fragrance of incense. "You're a hot ticket."

"I want to talk to you about Keith."

"Lemme guess: You didn't do it."

"No," I said. "I didn't."

"Why are you bothering with a scumbag like me?"

"I need to know what Keith was up to in the days before he was killed. I figure nobody followed him as closely as you."

"You got that right. I know every fucking coffeehouse and production office and midnight booty call. Hell, I know every dry cleaner his *clothes* visited." His cell phone piped out an old-fashioned ring, and he snapped it open. "Joe Vente." He chewed a chapped lip. "Britney or Jamie Lynn? What's she wearing? How many frames they have left to bowl?" He checked his watch, rolled his eyes for my benefit. "Not worth the drive. Call me next time right when they get there." The phone disappeared back into a pocket, and he bared his teeth at me. "Another day in paradise."

"Did Keith ever overlap with a company called Ridgeline, Inc.?" I asked.

"Never heard of it."

"Do you know his life coach?"

"Life coach?" He snorted. "You mean that hot blond bitch? Course I do."

"Can you get me an address?"

"I can get you whatever you want."

I waited. Waited some more. Finally asked, "In return for what?"

"Photos of you and a rundown of exactly what happened in that hotel room. And I want it for tomorrow's headlines."

"Not gonna happen. Not for tomorrow. But I can promise you an exclusive as this thing unfolds."

" 'As it unfolds'? My business is all about *tomorrow*. No one's gonna pay my quote as it unfolds. As it unfolds, *everyone* gets it. It becomes a court and press-release game, not an inside sneak peek. The more it drags on, the more it favors Big News."

"Big News?"

"You know, legitimate—and I use the word with great reverence—news outlets. Not opportunistic camera whores like me. You need to understand that you're a perishable commodity. There's a limited window for Patrick Davis in His Own Words. Look at your front yard. There were, what, fifty of us there last night? Eight this morning? By next month it'll be the lone sharks sipping from brown paper bags and hoping to catch you sunbathing nude so they can make page four of *The Enquirer,* because pages one, two, and three will be filled with bullshit leaks from RHD and squalid details of the investigation."

"I don't even have a lawyer yet. I can't go on record. I can't talk about anything to do with this case."

"Then why are you coming to me about Conner's schedule?"

"I can offer you a long-term play. And it's a good one."

"I'm not a long-term thinker."

I leaned over and rolled the door open. When I turned, the giant zoom lens covered his face, the clicking a continuous whir. I held up the film I'd stripped from his camera, then tossed it past him into the messy interior. "If you change your personality, give me a ring."

CHAPTER 39

Pulling in to the faculty lot, I felt enormous relief. Finally something recognizable. Some part of a routine preserved from the time before I entered Room 1407. I was human here, again.

I checked my rearview to make sure the news-van tails hadn't reappeared, then parked and headed for Manzanita Hall. At the edge of the quad, a few guys sat on a bench, spitting sunflower shells, and it was only once I passed behind them unnoticed that I registered the camera straps around their necks. Like most of the other paparazzi I'd seen, they weren't the sweaty pigs of the movies, but attractive young men in trendy shirts and slick North Face jackets, their designer gloves cupping lenses. They looked like you or me. Chagrined, I noted a few more camped out on the front steps of Manzanita, along with a news crew. My soft leather briefcase, full of student papers, felt suddenly like a prop. A few heads swiveled my way.

I hurried around behind the building, startling an Asian student, who took one look at my face and gave me a wide berth. The back door was locked. I could hear approaching footsteps from around the corner, so I banged on the window. A face appeared inside.

Diondre.

For a frozen moment, we regarded each other. His trademark do-rag was off, his hair made up in corn-rows. Down the length of the building, a cluster of photographers spilled into view. One spotted me, and they surged forward. I gesticulated behind me help-lessly, then at the door.

Finally Diondre got it, reached over, and pushed down the door handle.

I slid inside, yanking the door shut after me. It locked just as the paparazzi swarmed into sight. Diondre tugged down the window shade.

Though I was shaking, he gave me the carefree grin. "Guess I was wrong about Paeng Smoke-a-Bong. Couldn't be a student stalker. No-o-o—you had to have *bigger* plans."

I managed a weak smile and nodded at the door. "You just saved my ass."

"Did you do it? Kill Conner?"

After everything, it was refreshing to have such a straightforward conversation. "No," I said.

"I hear that." He clasped my hand, grabbing it around the thumb, and we parted ways. That was all he needed to hear. That's what I loved so much about students—they could distill the complexities down to simple questions. And answers.

A few steps away, Diondre paused. "I know it ain't the most glamorous job in the world, teaching. But I'm glad you're doing it."

I looked down, my face warm. I couldn't manage to get the right words together, so I said, "Thank you, Diondre. I'm glad, too."

He half nodded and walked away.

I took the stairs up and slunk through the halls, my name audible in the whispers that followed me.

The department assistant's hands were folded on her blank desk. "She's waiting for you."

When I entered, Dr. Peterson looked up from some papers. "Patrick. Please, sit down."

I did, mustering a faint grin that felt hard and rigid on my face.

She said, "The department has been inundated with press inquiries. It's been something of a spectacle."

I waited, my dread mounting.

She said, "We received numerous complaints even before the unfortunate events of . . . of—"

I said, "Keith Conner's murder."

She flushed. "Not just about the missed classes, but I guess your grading on their scripts has been delayed?" She nodded at my briefcase, which sat on my knees, a beacon of my incompetence. "Are they done now?"

"No," I said. "I . . . I'd like the chance to make it up to them." She started to say something, but I held up my hand. "Please," I said. "I'm sorry for the impact that this has had on the department, but just because I'm a suspect doesn't mean . . . I don't know how long the investigation will last. Months, maybe. Life has to go on, even if . . ." I was crumbling. I hated the sound of my voice, but I couldn't stop. "Our financial situation—I really need to earn a living. I know there's some damage control I'll have to—"

Mercifully, she cut off my rambling. " 'Damage control'? I don't believe you have any idea what kind of a disruption this represents for this college."

"I'll work double-time. I won't miss another class."

"What do you think? You can defend yourself against potential murder charges and somehow *improve* your attendance record?"

I didn't know what I had thought. In light of everything I had before me, it certainly sounded stupid now. I said hopelessly, "Maybe I could take a leave of absence."

"Funny, it seems that's what you've *been* doing." She rearranged the papers on her desk. She jotted a note. "Our feeling is that this isn't a tenable situation."

Through the gap in my briefcase, I could see those student papers staring out at me. For two weeks I'd kept those kids on hold. Some of them, like Diondre, could scarcely afford tuition, and yet I'd spent all this time scrambling to defend myself against one threat after another. I took a deep breath, tried to pull myself together.

She continued, "We've kept documentation. It's quite cut and dried. I hope you won't consider . . ."

I could hardly muster the energy to lift my head. "What?"

"Legal . . . ?"

"No. Oh, no. Of course not. You took a gamble on me, and I blew it." I rose to offer my hand across her desk, and she came up to a crouch above her chair, her hand cool in mine. I said, "Thank you for the opportunity."

She did her best to disguise her relief. "I'm sorry for all your trouble, Patrick. I really am. And I'm sorry to come on like a hard-ass when you're dealing with . . ."

I set the papers at the edge of her desk, gave them a tap with a knuckle. "Find someone good for my students."

Walking out, I was overtaken by a profound sadness. It sank in just how much I loved my job, but that wasn't what hit me the hardest. The grief I felt came from how infrequently I'd paused to appreciate being here, as with so many other aspects of my life I'd failed to recognize and savor.

From the outer office, I peeked out into the hall, checking that it was empty. Feeling like a fugitive, I hurried through the corridors. In the faculty lounge, Marcello reclined on the fuzzy plaid couch, pretending to grade, and Julianne was fussing irritably over the coffeemaker. Like old times.

From the doorway I said, "I'll miss you guys."

They both looked up, and then their expressions changed.

"Really?" Julianne rushed over and embraced me tightly.

"Yeah. I just relinquished the last of the student papers."

"Goddamn it, Patrick. This sucks." Her breath smelled of cinnamon gum.

Marcello offered his hand. I said, "C'mon," and hugged him.

Julianne was hovering. "How's Ariana? What can I do? There's gotta be *something* I can do."

"Honestly?"

"No, I was just being polite."

"I need a couple of addresses for people. A commercial actress and one of the producers from that documentary Keith was gonna do."

"Industry folks?" she said. "That shouldn't be hard."

"The cops had no luck with the former, and I'm having trouble with the latter."

She said, "Neither of you has a degree in investigative journalism from Columbia."

Marcello said, "Neither do you."

Julianne shrugged. "Columbia, Chico State, whatever."

Sitting, I jotted down, *Elisabeta, aka Deborah B. Vance* and *Trista Koan—The Deep End.*

Julianne took up the slip of paper and said, "If I can't get a bead on them myself, I still have good contacts at the papers."

"I should go," I said. "I've got . . . you know, a lot I have to figure out. Thank you. For the whole thing. The job. Getting me back on my feet. It was a good time for me."

Beyond the lounge, doors opened and closed, the buzz of students growing louder.

"I should go," I said again. But I was still sitting there.

"What's wrong?" Marcello asked.

I took a deep breath.

He followed my gaze to the door. "Scared?"

"Little bit."

"Wanna go out like a man?"

I said, "Yeah."

Marcello cleared his throat. "A NEW BEGIN-NING . . ."

I got to my feet.

"A MAN ALONE . . ."

I walked to the door.

"AND NOW HE WILL LEARN THAT NOTH-ING WILL EVER BE THE SAME."

The hall was alive with motion and noise. When I stepped out, the nearby students froze. The reaction rippled outward, faces turning in wave after wave, hands and mouths pausing midmotion, until the corridor was so silent I could hear the squeak of a sneaker against tile, a BlackBerry chiming in someone's pocket, a single cough. As I stepped forward, the nearest clique parted, drawing back and gaping anew.

My voice sounded gruff, preternaturally low. "'Scuse me . . .'scuse me."

The kids farthest away were up on tiptoes. A professor leaned out the door of her classroom. A few students snapped pictures of me with their cell phones.

I forged my way through. A conversation burst from the opening elevator doors, gratingly loud in the strained silence, and then two girls stepped out, took stock of the scene, and ducked giggling behind their hands. I passed them stoically, dead man walking.

The elevator had gone, leaving me to confront blank metal doors. I pushed the button, pushed it again. Glanced nervously across the sea of faces. Way down the hall, Diondre stood on a chair he'd pulled from a classroom. I raised a hand in silent farewell, and he smiled sadly and tapped his chest with a fist.

Mercifully, the elevator arrived, and I vanished into it.

CHAPTER 40

Muted by a coating of dust, the crime-scene tape fluttered across the door. The knob hung a little crooked, broken from the forced entry, and it came off in my hand. I pushed the door open, ducked under the tape, and stepped into the lonely little prefab house I still thought of as Elisabeta's.

The emptiness was startling. Most of the furniture had been cleared out. No bowl of cashews, no banana peels, no porcelain cats and wicker bookshelf. The coffee table stood on end. How clean the place had been. I'd taken it as a reflection of Elisabeta's quiet dignity, never guessing that the furniture had no dust because it had probably just been rented. Another misassumption I'd been primed to make.

I'd been hustled like a rube in a Chicago pool hall.

I crouched, my face burning, fingertips set down on the threadbare carpet for balance. It wasn't embarrassment, but shame. Shame at my transparency, at how common my hopes and needs must have seemed to this cast of players. At how common they had proven me to be.

With noble indignation, Elisabeta had crossed this very floor to her granddaughter's bedroom. I pictured her, that grave face taut with grief, that hand resting on the knob of the closed door. *You come see this beautiful child. I will wake her. You come see and tell me how I am to explain her this is* her *story.*

And me, the concerned fool: *No, please. Please don't disturb her. Let her sleep.*

I followed Elisabeta's path, opened the door.

A coat closet.

Two wire hangers and a trash bin into which Elisabeta's snow globes had been dumped. They lay cracked and dribbling, price tags still affixed to the bottoms. Props. Beneath them the school photo of the little girl with the frizzy brown hair. The frame had cracked. I raised it, sweeping off the pebbles of broken glass. The picture was thin and came out easily. Not a photograph, but a color copy.

It had come packaged with the frame.

A chill crept along my scalp, down the back of my neck. I dropped the frame into the trash again.

When I stepped back outside, the wind whipped up clouds of dust and snapped my pants at my shins. I walked the front of the house, finally finding what I'd been hoping for: a hole in the hard dirt of a flower bed where a rental sign had been staked. Driving slowly around the housing loop, I called the numbers on various signs hammered into front lawns until I tracked down the right Realtor who also represented Elisabeta's house. When I told her I was interested in the property but curious about the crime-scene tape, she'd been only too eager to reiterate what she'd already told the cops and, from the sound of it, everyone else: It had been a one-month rental paid by money order, the transaction conducted by mail. She'd never seen a soul, and no one had even bothered to come back to collect the balance on the security deposit. Of course, she'd never *imagined* . . .

Nothing linked that house to me except my word and my memory, both of which were of questionable merit.

Elisabeta was my only breathing connection to the men who had killed Keith and framed me. She alone could corroborate my story, or at least a key part of it, which would go a long way toward clearing my name. She was also at grave risk. Valentine had been unable to locate her, and I doubted that Robbery-Homicide was knocking themselves out to do better.

I thought about jail, about prison, the movies I'd seen and the horror stories I'd heard. That tattooed inmate I'd passed in the corridor at the Parker Center, how the metal chains seemed barely to contain his muscles, how I'd flinched away, a pebble before a crashing wave. What could a man like that, unbound, do to a man like me?

If I couldn't find Elisabeta myself, she'd wind up like Doug Beeman.

And, chances were, so would I.

I vaulted over our rear fence, one foot on the greenhouse roof, and then down onto the overturned terracotta pot and the soft mulch of the ground. A reversal of the leap the intruder had made when I'd discovered him on the back lawn. I'd left my car up the street behind our house so I could come and go unmolested by the media stragglers out front. Since I didn't carry a key for the back door, I circled toward the garage. When I yanked open the side gate, I nearly collided with someone crouched by the trash cans. He and I both let out startled yells. He fell over himself running away, and only then did I see the camera swinging at his side.

Leaning against the house, I caught my breath in the grainy dusk.

Ariana was sitting cross-legged on a spot of cleared kitchen floor, notes fanned in a half circle around her. We hugged for a long time, my face bent to the top of her head, her hands gripping and regripping my back as if she were taking my measure. I breathed her in, thinking how for six weeks I could have done this whenever I wanted and yet for six weeks I hadn't done it once.

I followed her to her workstation—she was always most productive spread out on the floor—and we sat. The ubiquitous fake cigarette pack sat beside her laptop, and a sturdy Ethernet cord trailed to the modem she'd moved into the kitchen; wireless Internet couldn't work with the jammer on. She clicked through a few e-mails. "I was on the phone with lawyers all day," she said. "Referrals and referrals from referrals."

"And?"

"Referrals from referrals from referrals. Okay, I'll stop. The bottom line is that to get anyone worth having, we're gonna need at least a hundred grand for a retainer in case the arrest happens. Which, based on courthouse scuttlebutt that most of them were too happy to impart, seems to be more of a *when* than an *if*." She watched this news sink in, her face matching what I was feeling. She continued, "I was on with the bank, and we can max out the home-equity line, which with our income—"

I said quietly, "I got fired."

She blinked. Then blinked again.

"I don't know what to do but keep apologizing," I said.

I braced for anger or resentment, but she just said, "Maybe I can sell my share of the business. I've had buyers sniffing around in the past."

I was speechless, humbled. "I don't want you to do that."

"Then we'll have to sell the house."

When our down payment was sitting in escrow, Ariana and I used to drive up here and park across the street just to look at the place. The trips felt charged and vaguely illicit, like sneaking out at night to loiter beneath the window of your high-school sweetheart. When we'd moved in, with Ari's eye, my back, and our sweat, we'd dressed it up, planing out the cottage-cheese ceilings, switching the brass hinges for brushed nickel, replacing rust carpet with slate tile. I watched her eyes moving around our walls, our art, the countertops and cabinets, and I knew she was taking stock of the same sentiments.

"No," she said. "I won't sell this house. I'll go in tomorrow and see what I can figure out. Maybe a loan against the business. I don't . . . I don't know."

For a moment I was too moved to respond. "I don't want you to—" I caught myself, rephrased. "Do *you* think it's safe for you to go in to work?"

"Who knows what's safe anymore? Certainly not

you prying around. But we no longer have any options."

I said, "You do."

Her mouth opened a little.

I said, "This is hell. And it's going to get worse from here. It makes me sick to think about you having to . . . Maybe we should think about putting you on a flight—"

"You're my *husband.*"

"I haven't been much good on that front lately."

She was angry, indignant. "And, if you want to keep score, I've been a shitty wife in a few obvious ways. But either the vows mean something or they don't. This is a wake-up call, Patrick. For both of us."

I reached for her hand. She squeezed once, impatiently, and let go. I said, "No matter how many years it takes, I will figure out some way to make this up to you."

She managed a faint smile. "Let's just worry about making sure we *have* those years." She shoved a fall of hair out of her eyes, then looked at the notes around her, as if needing to take refuge in details. "Julianne called. She said she looked into the names you gave her, to no avail. I guess between the cops, the agents, and the press, everything around *The Deep End* went into information lockdown, so there's nothing on Trista Koan. And Julianne had no more luck than Detective Valentine finding out about Elisabeta—or Deborah Vance or whoever. She was very apologetic, Julianne. She's desperate to be helpful. Did you check out that prefab house in Indio?"

I told her what I'd learned—or hadn't learned—on

the trip. "What was so amazing is the level of detail that woman saw to. I mean, the accent, the banana peels. Her performance was amazing."

"Where would you find people to play those roles? I mean, how would you even *locate* talent like that? Let alone talent willing to work a con?"

As usual, she'd jumped into my stream of thought. "Exactly. *Exactly.* You'd need an agent. A sleazy agent willing to plug his clients in to cons."

"Would an agent *do* that?" she asked.

"Not any I've heard of. So I'd imagine if you found one willing to play ball, you'd probably stick with him."

She got it immediately. "Doug Beeman's agent," she said. "That message. On Beeman's cell phone. Asking him why he missed his call time on the set for the shaving-cream commercial."

"Deodorant," I said. "But yes. Roman LaRusso."

Already she was typing. "And what was Doug Beeman's real name?"

"Mikey Peralta."

She paired them, and the search engine threw back its results. Sure enough, a Web site. The LaRusso Agency, in an average neighborhood that the site announced as "Beverly Hills–adjacent." Head shots of various clients formed a row, the photos spinning like slot-machine reels, replacing themselves. From the looks of it, LaRusso repped character actors. Barrel-chested Italian, cigar wedged between stubby fingers. Scowly black woman, curling red nails pronounced against a yellow muumuu. Mikey Peralta, grinning his offset grin. We watched with held breath as the little square head shots flipped and flipped, replenishing themselves. All those cheekbones, all those dimples, all that promise. The precious slideshow seemed an inadvertent commentary on Hollywood itself—dreamers and wannabes tethered to a gambling machine, their faces replaceable, interchangeable. And, as Mikey Peralta had learned, expendable.

I tensed with excitement and pointed. There she was. Her photo flashed up only for a few seconds, but there was no mistaking those doleful eyes, that profound nose.

Ariana said, "That's *exactly* how I pictured her."

The deck of photos shuffled Elisabeta back into obscurity.

I sat in the dark of the living room, peering out at the street. The front lawn gleamed with sprinkler water. I couldn't make out any vans or photographers or telescopes in the apartment windows across the street. They were still there, hidden in the night, but for a moment I could pretend that everything was as it had always been. I had come down to sit in the armchair and sip a cup of tea, to think about a lesson plan or what I wanted to write next, my wife upstairs in a plumeria bubble bath, on the phone with her mom or reviewing sketches, and I would go up, soon, and make love to her, and then we'd slumber, her arm thrown across my chest, cool beneath the lackluster heating vent, and I'd awaken, find her in the kitchen with bacon on the griddle and a lavender mariposa in her hair.

But then Gable and his compatriots came crashing

through the fantasy. I pictured them laboring even at this late hour in the detective bullpen, charts and timelines and photographs spread on desks and pinned to walls, piecing together a story that had already mostly been written. Or maybe they were already speeding up Roscomare with renewed determination and a signed warrant. Those headlights there, touching the artless block of boxwood framing the steps of the apartment across. But no, just a 4Runner, slowing to rubberneck, gaping college faces at the window, taking in The House.

My tea had gone cold. I dumped it in the kitchen sink, walked past the spilled trash, and trudged upstairs. A car backfired, and I actually left the floor; I'd been braced for RHD to kick down the front door. How would we live, waiting, knowing that that moment could come at any time, and probably the instant we let down our guard?

The TV was on, Ariana curled in bed, watching a candlelight vigil taking place in Hollywood. Teddy bears and photo montages. A weepy teenager held up a fan picture of Keith as a young boy. Even as a child, he was astonishing to look at. Perfect features, pug nose, that well-proportioned jaw. His hair was sandy blond, lighter than it had become. He held the end of a garden hose and wore a bathing suit and cowboy six-shooters in double hip holsters, and his smile was pure delight.

The news cut away to the Conners' house in Kansas. Keith's father, a fireplug of a man, had a rough-hewn, almost ugly face. I remembered he was a sheet-metal worker. His wife, a stocky woman, had the pretty cheekbones and singer's mouth that Keith had inherited. The sisters also took after their mother—small-town pretty dressed up with new money. Mom was crying silently, comforted by the daughters.

Mr. Conner was saying, "—bought us this house right here after his first deal. Put both the girls through college. Most generous soul I've ever known. Cared about the world around him. And he knew what he was doing up there on the screen. Got his mother's looks, lucky for him." A tearful smile from his wife, and he caught her eye and looked away quickly, and then the creases in his wind-chapped face deepened and his bottom lip rose, clamping over the top, trying to hold it still. "He was a good kid."

Ariana turned off the TV. Her face was heavy.

I asked, "What?"

She said, "He was real."

CHAPTER 41

There was no receptionist, just a desk with a bell. When I rang, a familiar wheezy voice called, "Just a minute," through the open office door. I sat on the lop-sided couch. The trades on the glass table dated from November and the sole *Us Weekly* had been used to mop up a coffee spill. An antique sash window, warped with dry rot, looked out five feet to a brick wall, but a glimpse of billboard was visible in the sliver of sky above. I knew the one; I'd seen it go from Johnny Depp to Jude Law to Heath Ledger and now to Keith Conner. I was weary of this town. My life here had traced a brief arc from obsolete to defunct, and from where I was, even the big time didn't seem so big anymore.

Finally the voice called out again, rescuing me from the waiting room. The office looked to be a movie set from the fifties. Crooked venetians, stacks of files rising architecturally from every surface, an artichoke of cigarette butts blooming in a porcelain ashtray, all suffused with a yellowed light that seemed dated in its own right.

Crammed behind a chipped desk, visible through a flight path between piles of paperwork, Roman

LaRusso was overweight, but his face was fatter than he was, blown Ted Kennedy wide at the cheeks so the bulges tugged his earlobes forward. He was immersed, it seemed, in work and didn't favor me with even a cursory glance through the delicate rectangular reading glasses screwed into either side of his jiggling lion's mane. It wasn't a disgusting face, not at all. It was improbable, magical, something to behold.

I said, "I'm interested in Deborah B. Vance."

"I no longer represent her."

"I think you do. I think you hired her out for a con job."

He made a big show of reading something on his desk, frowning down over the glasses and breathing ponderously through his nose, which gave off a faint whistle. Then he put away his glasses in a case the size of a nail buffer and finally looked up. "Admirably direct. Who are you?"

"The lead suspect in the Keith Conner murder."

"Uh . . ." He didn't get further than that.

"You specialize in commercials?"

"And features," he said quickly, by habit. "Did you see *Last Man on Uptar*?"

"No."

"Oh. Well, a client was one of the aliens."

Eight-by-tens graced the walls, a few I recognized from the Web site, along with midgets, an albino, and a woman missing both arms.

He followed my gaze. "I don't like the pretty ones. I represent talent with *character*. Actors with disabilities, too. It's sort of a niche. But it means more to me. Don't think I don't know what it's like to be stared at." He put his knuckles on the blotter and tugged to pull in his chair, but it didn't budge. "I give my clients a place in the sun. Everyone wants to fit in. Have a piece of that sunshine."

"Is that what you did for Deborah Vance?"

"Deborah Vance, if that's what you're calling her, didn't need anybody to look after her."

"What's that mean?"

"She's a hustler, that one. Ran lonely-hearts scams. Chat-room stuff. She'd e-mail pictures to men, they'd wire her money to set up a condo in Hawaii for assignations, that sort of thing."

"Her?"

"She didn't send pictures of herself. Thus the death threats."

"Death threats?" It was becoming clear not just why they'd chosen Deborah Vance but how they planned to cover their tracks when they erased her from the picture.

"Nothing to be taken seriously," he continued. "Men don't like being embarrassed, that's all. Especially when their good intentions are preyed on."

"Tell me about it."

"So she went to ground, switched off names, that kind of stuff. We lost touch. Her and me had a good run on commercials a few years back. They were booking a lot of ethnics. I got her a Fiberestore and two Imodiums." He smirked. "No business like show business, right? But I never got involved in her scams."

"Then how do you know about them?"

He hesitated too long, saw that I'd noticed. "We used to talk."

"Why's she still on your home page?"

"I haven't updated that thing in ages."

"Yeah, I noticed a picture of a client who's deceased."

He looked down sharply, his features sliding on their cushioning. A drawer rattled open, and then he mopped at his neck with a handkerchief. "The cops said Mikey had an accident."

"They came to see you?"

"No. I read . . ."

"They know about Peralta and Deborah Vance but haven't figured out you as the connection. You should tell them you sent her to the same guys you sent him to."

His considerable weight settled, and he tugged miserably at his ruddy face. "I get these side jobs sometimes. It's legitimate work. Mall openings. Dinner theater. Kids' parties or whatever. People want to rent certain types sometimes." Sorrow had worked its way into his voice. "I couldn't have known. . . . It was just a hit-and-run. Mikey drank some. The papers *said* it was a hit-and-run."

"No," I said. "Mikey Peralta was killed because of this job."

LaRusso's face shifted; he'd known but had managed to keep it from himself at the same time. "You don't know that."

"I'm on the inside of this thing. I do know."

He balled the handkerchief in a fist. "Did you really kill Keith Conner?"

"You think I'd be here trying to save your client if I had?" I said. "Make no mistake: They will kill Deborah Vance next. And then they'll probably come after you."

"I don't . . . I don't know anything about the guy. Everything over the phone. Money orders. I never even saw a face. Jesus, you really think . . . ?" His eyes were leaking from the edges, and the tears were confused about which way to go.

"She has to be warned."

"Like I told the guy, all she gives out anymore is an e-mail. *I* don't even have a better way to reach her." He couldn't hold my stare, and finally he gazed up. He flipped through some papers, tipping a stack of folders onto the barely visible floor and came up with a leather planner. His hands were trembling. "She hasn't been answering her phone."

"Then give me an address," I said. "And get yourself out of town."

She opened the door and laughed at me. It wasn't to mock me, I didn't think, but to underscore the absurdity of our meeting again, here, in a ground-floor apartment in Culver City. Her affect and bearing— her very posture—were completely different from Elisabeta's. Even that cackle had a different timbre; it was somehow accentless. She looked well, as she had in the Fiberestore commercial—less puffy and worn. I wondered how much makeup it took to turn someone into a haggard Hungarian.

The fuzzy red bathrobe hanging to her knees made her look like Blinky from Pac-Man. Stepping back, she waved me in with a dramatic sweep of her arm. The cramped apartment gave off a humid floral scent, and I could hear a bath running. Pinching the lapels over her bare chest, she scurried back and turned off the faucet, then returned. "Well," she said.

I tried to get a read on whether she knew that I was a suspect in Keith's murder, but she seemed too blasé about my appearance. No, it seemed I was still just a guy she'd scammed.

"You're in danger," I said.

"I've had people after me before."

"Not like this."

"How would you know?"

I still couldn't get used to the perfect English, how effortlessly her mouth shaped the words. I glanced around. Antique furniture, broken down but hanging on. A Victrola with a dent in the horn. Noir movie one-sheets covered the walls, and vintage travel posters: CUBA, LAND OF ROMANCE! Since moving to L.A., I'd been in a variation of this place countless times. All that style at garage-sale prices, all those fantasies projected onto the walls, the cloche hats, the deco coasters, the metal cigarette cases from another time, not your time—if only you'd lived then, things would've been different, you would've glided seamlessly into all that smoke and glamour. I thought of my own Fritz Lang movie print, bought with such pride at a schlock shop on Hollywood Boulevard the week I'd graduated college. I'd thought it was my initiation into the club, but I was just another kid trying too hard, buying a leather jacket two months after they'd gone out of fashion. If they don't let you walk the walk, doggone it, you can still lease a PT Cruiser.

"If I found you," I said, "they will, too."

"Roman gave you my address, I'm sure, because it's clear that you're harmless."

"You want to stake your life on Roman's backbone?"

"Roman would never hurt me," she said. "He's part pimp, sure, but part daddy, too. No one else connected to this knows my name or this address."

"What *is* your name?"

"This week? Does it matter?"

It did matter. Paired with an address, a real name—and, I hoped, a real rap sheet—it seemed concrete enough for me to try to reenlist Sally. But I'd have to let it go for now. "Can I call you Deborah?"

"Honey," she said, in a perfect Marlene Dietrich, "you can call me whatever you want."

"Does a company called Ridgeline, Inc., ring a bell?"

"Ridgeline? No."

"You never met whoever hired you," I said. "Phone calls and money orders."

"That's right."

"You must have thought . . ."

"What?"

We were still standing, a few feet inside the closed front door. I noticed her nails, that beautiful manicure that had seemed so out of place on a penniless waitress. "That I was an idiot."

"Oh, no," she said. "Not at all. You were so goddamned sweet it about killed me." Humiliation coursed through me like a fever; I couldn't meet her eyes. "That's why most cons work," she said in consolation. "Everyone wants to believe they're more important than they are."

The pity was worse somehow. And worse even than that, her empathy. I wanted to be nothing like her, and yet of course we shared the same broken promise, the same stymied dreams; she had reached right through the looking glass and tapped me down the primrose path.

"How did you even . . . ?"

"I was e-mailed a script. Well, more like a treatment. It had all the basics—sob story, sick kid, stingy health-insurance company. I filled in the rest. My background is mostly Russian, but how standard is that? Plus, with my luck you'd have had some bubby from the old country and known something about it. But I'm also Hungarian, I guess, and who the hell knows anything about Hungary? So you know how it works—it's like writing, I'd imagine. Those telling details. Budapest is too obvious, so I picked Debrecen, the second-largest city. They'd provided the affliction—the heart thing. But the bananas were my own touch. I figured you'd ask, you know? Sometimes you lead someone in from an angle, they don't see the obvious."

Despite her nod to our colleagueship, I doubted I'd ever had her talent or professionalism. I could no more contain my bitterness than she could her pride. "You're a gifted actress," I said. "You'll go far in this town."

"Too late for that. But I make a living."

"The cash . . . ?"

"A few hours after you left, I delivered the duffel bag to the trunk of a parked car on a quiet street."

"A white Honda Civic."

"How'd you know?"

I shook my head, not wanting to get off track. "They told you about me."

"Little bit. No more than last time."

"Wait a minute," I said. *Last time?*"

"There was another guy." Now with the accent. "He come also to help poor Elisabeta and granddaughter with terrible illness."

I stared at her, dumbfounded. "Do you . . . Who? Who was he?"

As quickly as she'd transformed into the world-weary waitress, she'd morphed back again. "I don't remember his name. But he gave me his card. He was big on his business card. I have it here somewhere. . . ." She crossed to an apothecary cabinet with more tiny drawers than I could count and started searching them.

I said, "You don't understand what this whole thing is, do you?"

But she didn't break focus. "Hang on, I know I kept it."

After a few more moments watching her open and close drawers, I said, "Mind if I use your bathroom?"

"Not at all. The damn thing's here somewhere. . . ."

The bathroom window looked across a narrow strip of quartz and succulents to a matching window in the neighboring complex. The waiting bathwater thickened the air, misted the mirror. After closing the door behind me, I eased open the medicine cabinet, praying it wouldn't squeak. No prescription bottles inside, but I found a few in one of the drawers. The neat type read, *Dina Orloff.*

"Got it!" she called out triumphantly, mimicking my own sentiment. I gently pressed the drawer closed and turned to go, reaching for the knob. The doorbell shrilled in the tiny condo. I froze, the knob twisted in my hand. The button lock popped open into my palm.

Through the door I could hear her mutter something. Then a few padded footsteps.

The door opened with a jangle, and then there were two muffled percussions. A thump of body hitting carpet. Then the door closing, at least two sets of footsteps moving. Dragging.

My stomach clutched, and I fought not to gasp, not to start, not to do anything but breathe and rotate that doorknob slowly and silently back to its resting position.

If they'd followed me, then her death was my fault. And, obviously, they'd know I was here. If that were the case, I wouldn't live long enough for the guilt to seep in.

Barely audible—"Let's move, let's *move.*"

The bedroom door banged open.

They were searching.

Holding my panic at bay, I crept across the bathroom and started turning the crank to open the casement window. The pane made a soft pop as it broke the seal and began to swing outward.

Now I heard the closet shutters one room over, raked back on their rails.

A drop of sweat ran down my forehead and stung my eye. I rotated the crank as quickly as I could, but the window seemed to move in slow motion.

That same voice: "Check the bathroom."

I tried to swallow, but my throat clicked dryly, wanting to gag.

Approaching footsteps. The window lazily rotated outward, wide enough for my foot, my calf, my thigh. Judging from the creak of the floorboards, the guy was right outside the bathroom door now.

I slithered through, the gap still tight enough to mash my nose against the pane. My sneakers grinding the rocks outside, I flattened to the wall, just out of sight of the window.

The bathroom door shoved open, banging the wall behind. Footsteps.

The sidewalk was no more than twenty yards away, but a single step on the rocks would broadcast my position. My head was craned to the side, taking in a thin sliver of bathroom floor. I breathed, prayed, willed my muscles still. If he came to the window and peered through the gap, I was dead.

When the next step creaked the floorboards, I saw the toe of a black boot come into view. Through my terror it hit me that I was probably looking at a size-eleven-and-a-half Danner with a pebble jammed in the tread.

If they *had* followed me here, he'd probably think to check outside. But that boot remained, still. What was he looking at?

Held breath burned in my lungs. Every muscle taut. My unblinking eyes stung. He was maybe four feet away; I could probably reach through the window opening and tap him in the chest. The faintest sound would buy me a face-to-face. My hand curled into a fist. I forced myself to plan an attack in case a face appeared in that narrow window gap. Eyes and throat. Then a wind sprint.

The boot withdrew silently, and I heard a hand stir the water, no doubt parting the bath bubbles. Then the steps moved away, and it took a few wild and disbelieving moments for it to sink in that he'd gone.

In the main room, they mumbled, conferred. The front door opened and shut, and then there was a moment of silence.

But no relief.

I remained in full view from the street; depending on which way they exited the building, they'd spot me. A gate creaked open around the corner, jarring me into action. I stepped back through the window into the bathroom and plastered myself against the far wall. Waited. And listened for footsteps across the quartz. But none came.

Sometime after, the held breath burst from my lungs and my whole body shuddered and slid down the wall. I clutched my knees.

I sat there for ten minutes, or maybe thirty. Breathing. Then I stood, my muscles stiff and creaking.

She lay about five feet from the front door. No sign of damage, save a neat hole in the fabric above her ribs and a crimson halo beneath her head; one of the shots must have entered her open mouth. The bathrobe had come open, and thrown on her bare chest was a note composed of clipped magazine letters: *LyINg bITcH*.

Lonely-hearts scams and death threats and chickens coming home to roost. Another solid cover for a murder that was nothing more than a cold efficiency.

The more I tried to press forward, the more everything spiraled out of control. I had landed, now, in a whole different order of trouble. I was the lead suspect in Keith Conner's murder. I had set the cops on the trail of this woman; from their perspective she was a centerpiece in my paranoid delusion. I couldn't be here, at the scene of her murder. I needed to be across town with newfound submissiveness and an airtight alibi. I needed to flee. But I couldn't stop looking at her.

Sprawled on the floor, vulnerable and hopeless, she was Elisabeta again. And again I would have done anything to help her. Beside her, I took a knee, tugged the bathrobe up over an exposed breast. I didn't know what else I could do for her.

A single drawer in the apothecary cabinet remained half open. I stared over at it for a time before rising.

The drawer itself was no bigger than a business card, and sure enough it held a single ivory rectangle of sturdy paper stock. I withdrew it, read the name, and bit down on my lip to hold my shock in check. It couldn't be. And yet it made perfect sense.

Moving swiftly, I grabbed a paper towel and used it to wipe the bathroom doorknob and surfaces, and then I stepped back out through that window. I tiptoed through the cacti and veered out onto the street, glancing around and blinking against a bright day that seemed an impossible contrast to what I had just witnessed. My heart had yet to slow. I tossed the paper towel down a storm drain.

A half block away, I pulled out that card and double-checked the name, just to make sure I hadn't dreamed it.

Joe Vente.

CHAPTER 42

He sat in the back of his van in a freestanding swivel chair with stuffing leaking at the seams, facing me and blinking over the business card I'd just handed him, along with an explanation of how I'd gotten it. He'd met me at a park off Sepulveda, and I'd only left my vehicle to step into his. I was badly rattled and doing my best not to show it. No matter how hard I tried, I couldn't shake the image of that sprawled corpse, those striking blue eyes reduced to glass.

"I don't . . . I don't believe this," Joe said. "You met with her, too? The sick kid? The duffel bag of cash?"

"Yes. And the same people who directed me there set me up at Hotel Angeleno."

"*That's* where that whole thing was leading? Keith's murder?" He smacked both palms down on the top of his head, a childlike gesture of agitation. "Why us?"

"Think about it."

"I *can't* think right now."

"We both had grudges against Keith Conner. We

both have ongoing lawsuits with him. Paparazzo and movie star? It's obvious you two can't stand each other any more than he and I could."

"So we were both prospective fall guys for the murder?" Joe whistled, ran his hands through his stringy hair. "Jesus, I dodged a bullet."

And I'd walked right into one. He could continue snapping invasive photos, a free man, while I scrambled for my life against a ticking clock. The fact that Joe Vente had proven more circumspect than I—*that* was a bitter pill to swallow.

"What?" Joe was studying me. "You never seen a body before?"

I followed his gaze. A muscle in my forearm was quivering. I reached over, squeezed until it ached. When I let go, my arm was still. "When did you see Elisabeta?"

"A few months ago. I'd been getting these DVDs. Footage of me sneaking around, spying on celebrities. Footage of me getting footage. It was weird as shit, like some French film or something."

The overlap with Doug Beeman's story left me wondering if this was merely another wrinkle in the scam, another ruse within the ruse. Could I know what was real and what was fabricated anymore? I no longer trusted myself, the world. My eyes drifted around the cluttered van, searching out clues that could point to duplicity, gauging the distance to the door handle. But I reminded myself that I'd checked Joe out online, that he was real, or at least as real as anyone got in Los Angeles. Sally and Valentine had interviewed him, too, confirmed his existence. *Some* of my instincts had to be right; I couldn't stay this worked up and remain functional.

He was saying, "At first I thought it was a rival, one of the guys I beat out for a payday. I mean, makes sense, right? Then, when it got creepier, I figured some rich star had hired someone for revenge. Some celeb, maybe I took a picture of his kid at soccer practice, someone I caught on the can in a public restroom or something."

I tried for casual, covering my jitters. "Who'd you catch in a public restroom?"

He told me.

I whistled. "Crouching Tiger, indeed."

"Then I got an e-mail like you got, but without the 'She needs your help or she'll die' note. Just an MPEG of a car trunk in an alley. It was under my skin, the whole thing. I had to know what the fuck it was about. I found the duffel. I followed the map, delivered it to Elisabeta. Figured out her story, you know, the grand-kid. I floated outta there—it was like heroin. A few days later, I get this call, right? And they lead me to a blue-print that shows where they've hidden surveillance crap in my house. Like *all over* my house. I freaked the fuck out. Pulled all that shit out of the walls and dumped it into some trash can they specified, along with all the DVDs and other shit. That was it for me. They sent me more e-mails, but I couldn't do it anymore."

I stared at him, spellbound. Joe Vente had served as their rough draft. They'd learned what had worked and what hadn't. Then they'd honed their strategy, switching the order of events, adding implicit threats, building a more effective ruse.

"So they just left you alone?" I almost couldn't believe it.

"I stopped playing the game. What the fuck were they gonna do?"

I had no answer, only an echo of regret through the hollow of my chest. "You're smarter than I was," I said. "You had more restraint."

"Smarter?" He snickered. "Restraint?"

"What then?"

He rummaged in a bag, came up with what looked like a recording device, a thin receiver rising from the center of a clear, inverted dome the size of a small umbrella. "You see this? It's a parabolic microphone. You aim and click, and it collects and focuses sound waves. I can pick up a whisper at a hundred yards. I can also hook up a device that reads vibrations off glass. Living rooms, vehicles on the freeway, doctors' offices, the whole nine. What I'm saying is, I know this world. I have it wired." He sat back in the chair, crossed his arms.

I said, "I'm not following."

"I got out*gamed*," he said angrily. "*I* did. It fucked with my head. I lost track of which way was up. It wasn't about smarts or restraint. I didn't have the stomach for it. Not for this end of the equation anyway. I'm a hypocrite and a parasite, but at least I don't fucking lie to myself. So I shriveled up. Leave me alone if I leave you alone. And it worked. Not that it doesn't haunt me every fucking day, who got the better of me, where it was leading."

"At least now you know," I said, "what was at the end of the trail."

"The electric chair." He'd meant it as a joke, but he read my expression and said, "Look, I'm just fucking around. You'll get off."

"How? You gonna corroborate my story for me?"

He laughed. "Let's just say that when it comes to the cops, my word probably counts for less than yours. I'd hurt you more than I'd help you. Besides, I've got no evidence. Nothing concrete."

"Neither of us does."

"Yeah, you're out of witnesses. They keep dying." He finally put two and two together, and a ripple of fear moved across his face, left it changed. "That's why you came to find me. To warn me."

"Yes."

"You think they'll really . . . ?"

"I think I wouldn't want to take the chance."

"Jesus, I—" He looked around the van, as if the walls were closing in. His panic sweat clinched for me that he wasn't in on the scam. "Okay," he said. "Okay. I've gotten lost before when the heat's turned up." He stuck a thumb in the upholstery, widened the tear. "You didn't have to come find me. Thanks for the warning."

I said, "Trista Koan. I need an address."

He nodded, one pronounced dip of his head, a man used to dealing. "I'll get one for you. Gimme an hour. What's your cell?" I gave him the number of the throwaway I'd reclaimed from Ariana. He had me repeat it twice and didn't write it down. "What else?" His eyes were light green and surprisingly pretty set in that coarse face.

Those two muffled percussions echoed in my head,

making me flinch. The toe of that black boot, barely in view at the edge of the door. Joe was looking at me funny.

I cleared my throat. "I'd like you to call in the location of Elisabeta's body. Anonymously. I can't have anything to do with it."

"Like you said, this broad ran cons and had death threats against her. The cops're gonna connect the dots to draw the wrong picture or to lead back to you. Either way, they'll be all over you once she turns up dead. So why report it?"

"What, just leave her body there?"

"Not like *she* cares."

"She's got family, I'm sure."

"So what? She'll still have family in a week when the neighbors complain about the smell, but at least you'll buy yourself a few more days to dig around without the cops up your ass. She *fucked* with us. It's not like she deserves better."

I said, "Her family does. Make the call for me."

"It's *your* jail sentence."

"Anything else you can give me on Keith Conner?"

"I can give you everything on Keith Conner," he said. "But that's my currency, man. What do I get?"

"You say you want to know who fucked with you. Well, this could be your chance. I'm not even asking you to share the risk."

He was back at his fingernails again, but he noticed and set his hands down in his lap. "From what I've learned, movie stars don't do shit. Meetings, lots of meetings. Business managers, agents, the Coffee

Bean on Sunset. And fucking lunches. You just sort of hang in and hope for some break in the routine, something weird. One day, about two weeks ago, I noticed something like that. Another car following him, keeping an eye. Not one of the regulars. We all know each other. And no one trolls in a Mercury Sable with tinted windows. I call the license plate in to my hook at LAPD, and guess what? The number doesn't exist."

He'd lowered his voice, and I found myself leaning toward him. The smell of the van—peanuts, coffee, spent breath—was making me claustrophobic, but the hook was set and I was going nowhere.

Joe continued, "Now I'm curious. So when it peels out, I follow it. I lose it at a light but find it parked two blocks up at the Starbright Plaza, one of those crappy strip malls on Riverside by the studios. You know, stores downstairs, offices up? I go kick the tires. It's got a Hertz sticker on the windshield."

Hertz again. Just like the car Sally traced the VIN back to.

He continued, "So someone had switched the plates. I check the mall directory, walk around, but there's a ton of offices and nothing looks suspicious. I stake the car out for a few hours, then get bored and leave."

"Starbright Plaza?"

"Starbright Plaza. That's the best I got for you."

I pulled open the door, drew in a deep breath of fresh air, and stepped down onto the street toward my car. I'd gotten the key into my lock when I heard the van behind me, sputtering.

"Hey," Joe's gruff voice called out. "If you live, I still want that exclusive."

When I turned around, he was already chugging off.

CHAPTER 43

A bland-as-hell two-story sprawl, brown wood and beige stucco, named Starbright Plaza. The inadvertent irony was common around these parts, in the slices of neighborhood around Warner Bros., Universal, and Disney. A-List Tires and Rims. Blockbuster Orchard Supply. Red Carpet Motel with FREE cable in every room!

The parking lot was jammed, so I valeted in front of the café at the far end of the complex. None of the patrons took note of me, though I assessed their faces with skittish defiance, searching for signs of recognition. Amazing how self-centered a good dose of fear can make you.

The valet handed me a slip featuring a glossy ad with Keith Conner's scowl:

This June, Be Afraid.

This June, There's Nowhere Left to Hide.

This June . . . THEY'RE WATCHING.

Another driver tapped the horn politely; I'd zoned out there a few feet off the curb. I stepped through the mist of the outdoor air conditioner onto the sidewalk and took in the shops and offices, feeling some of the frustration Joe must have felt: How do you search a massive strip mall for something suspicious?

Two workers carried a picture window out of a glass shop, like extras in a Laurel and Hardy sketch. Figuring that the other downstairs businesses, which ranged from a dry cleaner to a Hallmark, were equally innocuous, I walked to the stairwell. A FedEx delivery guy tapping at an electronic clipboard whistled down, not even bothering to glance up as I skipped aside at the landing.

The upstairs hallway, shaped in a wide V, hosted an endless row of doors and windows. Quite a few were open as I strolled by, uncertain of what I was looking for. Cubicles and wall charts, young guys on phones working baoding balls, selling penny stocks and exercise equipment in three no-hassle payments. I passed a fly-by-night insurance shop, then a straight-to-video operation with proudly displayed movie posters featuring giant insects wreaking havoc on metropolises. A few of the offices had been hastily cleared out, clipped cables poking from the ceilings and walls, jumbles of telemarketing phones mounded in corners. Others, with closed blinds and un-marked doors, were as silent as a surgeon's waiting room. Clearly the rentals had a considerable turnover rate.

Ducking the occasional shitty security camera, I kept walking, noting business names and glancing at faces, wondering what the hell I was doing here. Finally I ran out of room, reaching the far stairwell. I was just starting down when the brass placard drilled into the last office door caught my attention:

Do not leave any packages without
signature. Do not leave any packages
with neighboring businesses.

A FedEx tag had been left compliantly around the knob. Except for its number, 1138, the door itself was blank, like many others.

I plucked the tag free, stared down at the sloppily penned business name: *Ridgeline, Inc.*

My face tingled with excitement. And fear. Careful what you look for—you just might find it. In this instance the likely operating base for the men who'd sent me those e-mails, who'd framed me for murder, who'd killed three people and counting.

The orange-and-blue tag indicated a second delivery attempt for a package sent from a FedEx center in Alexandria, Virginia. Just inside the Beltway, the city was rife with influence peddlers and power brokers. The package's origin struck me as ominous.

The blinds of the office window were imperfectly closed. I went up on tiptoe to get an angle through the slats. The front room was as plain as could be. Computer, copier, paper shredder. There were no plants, no paintings, no Sears family portrait taped to the monitor. Not even a second chair for a visitor to sit in. A windowless door led back, I assumed, to a hall and more rooms.

I jogged downstairs and through the dingy alley behind the complex to check out the rear of 1138. A rickety fire escape rose to a thick metal door. The dead bolt was shiny, and traces of sawdust on the landing said it had been recently installed.

I huffed back around and confronted that front door again, in case it had decided to unlock itself. It hadn't.

Now what?

I thought about that FedEx driver, shouldering past me on the stairwell.

I dialed the 1-800 number on the tag, keyed in the tracking code, and waited through a xylophone rendition of "Arthur's Theme." When the customer-service rep picked up, I said, "I'm calling from Ridgeline. I just missed a drop-off, and I think your driver's still in the area. Will you please have him swing back around?"

I walked a ways up the outdoor corridor, not wanting to hang around 1138 in case someone with Danner boots reported back to work. Twenty minutes passed in a crawl. My rising anxiety and discouragement had just reached a tipping point when I saw the big white box of the FedEx truck making its way through traffic. Positioning myself at the office door, I touched the tip of one of my keys to the dead-bolt lock and waited for what seemed an eternity. Finally I heard footsteps coming up the stairs, and I pivoted, key in view, as he approached.

"Oh," I said, "you just caught me locking up."

"Missed you the last few times." He handed me a thin express envelope and the electronic clipboard. "You guys are tricky."

I scrawled *J. Edgar Hoover* illegibly and handed the clipboard back. "Yeah," I said, "we kind of are."

I had to force myself not to sprint downstairs and across to the valet. Waiting for my car, I glanced nervously along the length of the building toward the

Ridgeline office. Only then did I see the silver security camera mounted on top of the overhang right above 1138, out of sight from the corridor itself. It didn't match the others.

And it was pointing at me.

On the FedEx label, under *Contents*, was written, *Insurance.*

Sitting at our kitchen table in the quiet of the house, I tore open the envelope. A piece of corrugated cardboard, folded once and taped to protect its contents. A Post-it read, *Going dark. Do not contact.* I broke the tape with a thumb. Inside lay a computer disc. I took a deep breath. Rubbed my eyes. Frisbeed the cardboard into the heap of trash on the floor.

Insurance? For whom? Against what?

"Going dark" implied it was sent from an inside operative of sorts. A spy?

I took the disc upstairs to my office and, feverish with anticipation, slotted it into Ariana's laptop.

Blank.

I swore, banging the desk with the heel of my hand so hard that the laptop jumped. Couldn't one damn clue pan out? After all I'd risked to get it. The security footage of me left behind for the crew at Ridgeline. The wrath that could bring down on us.

Ariana was at work, looking into our financial options. Worried, I tried her as I had several times earlier, and again got voice mail all around. She was keeping her cell phone turned off, as we'd agreed, so she couldn't be tracked by its signal. I'd taken back and was using—right now—the disposable cell phone I'd gotten for her to carry so we could be in touch through-out the day. Smart.

In Ari's address book downstairs, I found her assistant's cell number and waited as it rang, my knee hammering up and down. A wash of relief when she answered.

"Patrick? You okay? What's going on?"

"Why aren't you guys picking up?"

"We're still getting bullshit calls about . . . you know, so it's easier to just let everything go to voice mail."

"Where is she?"

"At another meeting—she hasn't stopped scrambling all day. I can't reach her because she's keeping her cell phone off for some reason."

"Okay, I just wanted to know that she's . . ."

"No shit, huh? But don't worry. She's being super careful. She took, like, our two *biggest* delivery guys with her."

That made me feel incrementally better.

"When she checks in, can you have her call me at home?" I asked.

"Sure, but the meeting should be wrapping up, and she said she's heading home after, so you'll probably talk to her before I do."

I hung up, pressed the phone to my closed mouth. Given that it was the middle of the day, the drawn curtains were oppressive, confining. I'd sneaked in over the back fence again, and it struck me that I hadn't been in my own front yard since getting home from jail. Bracing myself, I stepped out onto the porch. Who could have imagined that something so simple would feel like a bold act? A few shouts, and then a throng appeared at the end of the walk, calling questions, snapping pictures. Closing my eyes, I tilted my face to the sun. But I couldn't relax out there, exposed. In the pressure of darkness behind my eyelids, I relived Elisabeta's bathroom window shoving against me as I'd tried to slither through to safety.

Back in the kitchen, I pounded a glass of water and rooted around for food, adding torn boxes and moldy bread to the trash heap on the floor. Chewing a stale energy bar, I returned to my office and stared some more at the blank disc on the screen. Maybe a hidden document? But the memory showed as zero. It seemed unlikely that data could have been embedded in a way that took up no memory, but with these guys anything was possible. I hid the disc in the middle of my blank DVDs impaled on the spindle and dropped the FedEx packaging into a desk drawer.

The phone rang. I snatched it up. "Ari?"

"I'm under a rock." Joe Vente. "Memorize this number." He rattled it off. "I'm bedded down. Safe. No one has this number, so if they come kill me, I'll be really pissed off at you."

"I won't breathe a word."

"I called in the body of Elisabeta or whoever the fuck she is. Get ready for the shit to hit."

"I will."

"Oh, and now I've earned that exclusive twice over."

"Does that mean . . . ?"

"You bet your ass. I found her."

CHAPTER 44

I caught Trista outside the Santa Monica bungalow, dumping an armload of empty Dasani bottles in the recycle bin. I said, "Bottled water? Isn't that environmentally irresponsible?"

She turned, shielding her eyes against the setting sun, and gave a sad grin when she recognized me. Which quickly turned coy. "Your shirt's made of cotton," she said, "which requires a hundred and ten pounds of nitrogen fertilizer per acre to grow. Your car there"—a flick of her lovely head—"if you upgraded to a hybrid, you'd pick up about a dozen miles to the gallon, which would keep ten tons of carbon dioxide out of the air a year." As I approached, she leaned toward me, blond hair drifting, and eyed my trousers. "That a cell phone in your pocket, big boy? It's got a capacitor strip made of tantalum, extracted from coltan, eighty percent of which is torn out of streambeds in eastern Congo where gorillas live. Or used to."

I said, "Uncle."

"We're all hypocrites. We all do damage. Just by living. And yes, by drinking bottled water, too." She paused. "You're smiling at me. You're not gonna get flirty and patronizing?"

"No. It's just been a long couple days, and you're a breath of fresh air."

"You like me."

"But not like that."

"No? Then why?"

"Because you think differently than I do."

"It's good to see you, Patrick."

"I didn't kill him."

"I know that."

"How?"

"Your anger's all on the surface. It's really just hurt you don't want to acknowledge. Come inside."

Moving boxes littered the tile floor—evidently the production company had wasted little time in dismissing her from the movie once it was no longer necessary for her to look after Keith. I glanced around the bungalow. A choice location, four blocks from the ocean, eight hundred square feet that probably rented for a couple grand. A slab of floating counter barely accommodated a kitchen sink, a microwave, and a coffeepot. Aside from a tiny bathroom next to the closet, the place was one room.

Whale posters adorned the walls. She caught me looking and said, "I know, it's the decor of a sixth-grade girl. I can't help it, though. They're so magnificent. It kills me." She swiped a bottle of Bombay Sapphire off the floor and refilled her glass, adding a splash of tonic. "Apologies. You probably think I'm . . ."

I said, "No, please. You can trust a woman who drinks gin."

"I'd offer you some, but I'm running low and I'm

gonna need it to get through this." She placed her nightstand lamp into a metal trash bin along with a handful of socks and then looked around, over-whelmed.

"I'm moving back to Boulder," she said. "It'll be fine. I'll get going on another project and . . . and . . ." Her back was to me, and her hand rose to her face and then her shoulders bunched, and I realized she was crying, or trying not to. She made a high-pitched gasp, and when she turned, her face was red, but she looked otherwise normal, if a touch pissed off.

She took a slug from the glass, sat on the bed, pat-ted the spot next to her. I went. Glossy photos of beached and autopsied whales had spilled across the comforter. They were crime-scene graphic, impossi-ble to ignore. I felt a sense of despair at seeing those magnificent animals reduced to driftwood. A help-lessness that turned to revulsion at the back of my throat.

She picked one picture up and gazed at it almost fondly, as if it were a remembrance from some other life. "It's all fucked up, Patrick. You know that. The dream is never the dream. It's a bunch of compro-mises and, if you're lucky, a few decent people now and then." She rested her head on my shoulder, and I could smell the gin.

She wiped her nose with her sleeve, sat back upright. "It was my job to baby-sit him. Keep him from dying in a drunken car crash, from fucking a seventeen-year-old, whatever. Keep him alive and out of jail and we get our movie. How hard can that be?"

"Pretty hard."

"I know you hated him." Her words were slurred, ever so slightly.

I said, "Maybe he wasn't so bad."

"No," she said. "No, he wasn't. He was kind of a dumb Labrador, but he tuned in enough that we could get him on board. Stars, movies, opportunism—Christ, it sounds so cynical." She looked down at one of the eight-by-tens—blubber and pink meat. "But I actually believe in this shit."

"And Keith?"

"He was a movie star. So who the fuck knows? He got used for all kinds of agendas." The irony sat with us. She said, "They get bored, you know. Look for hobbies, for causes. But he didn't have to pick this one. He didn't have to pick anything. But he did. Remember when the gray whales were washing up in the San Francisco Bay?"

"No, sorry."

"Right at the foot of the Golden Gate. I took him up there. You know, in the field with marine biologists. Get your shoes dirty. They love that shit. He was all excited, bought a new Patagonia windbreaker. When everyone finally left, I couldn't find him. He was back by the water, his hand on the whale. He had one tear going down his cheek. You know, the Keep America Beautiful crying-Indian tear? Like that. But no one was looking. He wiped it—he was all fine, sure, no problem. But I forgave him a lot for that tear." She stood abruptly. "I gotta finish packing. I'll walk you out."

But she just stood there, glaring at those sagging posters. "What the hell am I doing?" she said. "I don't know anything about movies. Or financing. I'm just a bleeding-heart idiot with half a master's degree who loves whales." She looked around the cramped bungalow as if these four walls held all her shortcomings and disappointments. When she snapped out of it, she caught me watching her and flushed at the glimpse she'd given up. "I *said* I have to finish packing."

"Listen, just give me a minute. Please. You were with Keith a lot at the end—"

"You have to remind me?"

"Can I ask you a couple questions?"

"Like?"

"Did he ever mention a company called Ridge-line?"

"Ridgeline? No, never heard of it."

"Did he ever go to the Starbright Plaza? A strip mall with office buildings off Riverside in Studio City?"

"He *never* went to the Valley." She sank back onto the bed. "Is that all?"

"I've got limited time, Trista. I'm the lead suspect. I have to figure out who framed me, and I have to do it before the cops come and put me in jail. Because once that happens, no one will be left to figure it out."

"What am *I* supposed to do about it? Haven't I helped you enough already?"

"What does that mean?"

"I got him and Summit to drop the lawsuit against you. At least they were *going to.*"

I gaped in disbelief. "That was *you*?"

"Yes, that was me. After you vandalized Keith's house—"

"That *wasn't* me."

"Whatever—I convinced him that all this legal mess was a distraction and a pain in the ass for him, and I practically wrote the cue cards so he could convince the studio they didn't need a stink hanging around *They're Watching* when the movie was riding such good buzz. I know you didn't hit him anyway—like I said, you're too harmless—and if the truth *were* to come out, he'd lose all credibility to be a caring environmental spokesperson for us." She flicked at a chipped nail, then stared at me from beneath her curled eyelashes, an incredible package of style and substance. "Now, is there anything else or can I get back to my solitude and misery?"

I struggled to regain my mental footing. "Can you tell me *anything* Keith did or anyone he met with that seemed out of the ordinary?"

"Out of the ordinary? For all the excitement at his fingertips, he was one of the dullest, most predictable people I've ever been around. It was all stupid childish shit—clubs and bars and midnight limo rides with underwear models. There were a lot of pranks and drunkenness, sure, but nothing serious. I doubt he ever *met* anyone interesting enough to want to kill him. And that includes you."

Assuming that her last words were a dismissal, I got up quietly. She was right; it was difficult to imagine Keith doing *anything* serious enough to elicit the attention of people with top-shelf intelligence gear at their disposal. He breezed around from one thing to the next. Parties, movies, projects. He'd fallen into Trista's cause like anything else, then worked himself up into a state of conviction over it.

I paused in the doorway and turned back to face her. "I lost my job, too," I said. "Teaching. I never realized how much it meant to me until it was gone. And you know what's funny? It was always just a backup job to me, a consolation prize, but it feels worse losing it than it did getting booted off my own movie." I realized I was rambling, and I cut myself off. "I guess what I'm trying to say is, I'm really sorry you got fired from something that meant that much to you."

"Fired?" she said. "I didn't get *fired*. The whole production shut down." She sank into herself, her shoulders bowing. "The first day of shooting was gonna be Monday. Three days away. So fucking close."

The wind blew through my shirt, but my skin had already gone taut. "The financing fell apart?"

"Of course," she said. "Environmental documentaries can't get a real release unless there's an Al Gore or a Keith Conner driving them."

My mouth was suddenly dry. My gaze pulled back to those glossy photos on Trista's bed. Beached whales. Exploded eardrums. Ruptured brains.

Sonar.

Keith had talked about high-intensity sonar wreaking havoc with whales, blowing out their organs, giving them emboli, driving them onto shores.

All those bits and pieces, sliding into alignment.

I felt a quickening of the blood, a predatory thrill at breaking through to the heart of the matter.

She was talking. "If anything goes wrong—a recession, a Senate vote, a new development—the environment is always first to suffer." A wry chuckle. "Well, I guess Keith was the first this time."

I heard myself ask, "You can't find another star and get funding again?"

"It won't matter." She tucked a fall of hair back behind an ear. "We had a limited window to make this thing happen. The money's gone."

I pictured him the last time I'd seen him alive, reclining on that teak deck chair, smoking his cloves and trying on earnestness. *It's a race against time, man.*

What had Jerry said? *The idiot's doing some bullshit environmental documentary next. Mickelson tried to get him to wait until he had another hit under his belt, but it had to be* now.

"What window?" My voice sounded far away.

At my tone she glanced up. "Excuse me?"

"You said you had a limited window to make the movie happen. Some big rush. Why?"

"Because we needed it to hit theaters before the Senate vote."

My heartbeat, a vibration in my ears. "Wait a minute," I said weakly. "Senate?"

"Yeah. The proposal to lower limits on the decibel levels of naval sonar. To protect the whales. It's calendared for October. Which means we needed to be in production, like, *now*." She frowned, checked her empty glass. "Why are you being so weird?"

"If *The Deep End* comes out before October, saving the whales from sonar becomes a popular cause.

Certain senators who vote a certain way wind up with egg on their face. It's an election year."

"That *is* how the game is played," she said. "What are you, fresh out of Cub Scouts?"

"They'd feel pressure to vote to impose limits on sonar."

"Yes, Patrick. That was the hope."

"Unless the movie doesn't get made."

"Right."

"And the only thing that can shut down a production once you get a green light is . . ."

She set down her glass. "Oh, come *on,* Patrick."

". . . the death of the star."

For the first time, her face held fear. She got it. I'd found a new ally, someone already in the battle on a different front. A resource.

But her gaze ticked to the rear door, then back to me, and I realized with crushing chagrin that she was afraid not because she believed me and saw what I— what *we* were up against but because she was afraid of *me.* In my eagerness I'd made a mistake in rushing in, in not debriefing her. She had a limited vantage into the whole sordid mess, and so, given my wild claims, she could only think I was as paranoid and unhinged as I'd been billed in the media.

I held up a hand, desperate, pressured, trying to circumvent the argument she'd started with herself. "You said you knew I wasn't a killer."

"I want you to leave now."

"It's not as crazy as it sounds. Please, just let me lay out for you what—" I took a step in from the doorway, and she lunged to her feet, breathing hard. For a loaded moment, we faced each other across the room, terror coming off her like a heat signature.

Showing her my palms, I backed away and closed the door quietly behind me.

CHAPTER 45

"All this time I've been asking the wrong question." I was so agitated I was nearly shouting into the phone. "I was asking myself who stands to benefit from Keith Conner's death."

"Okay . . ." Julianne said. I'd reached her at the office, and she'd been appropriately oblique as I'd filled her in on my talk with Trista. "And the *right* question would be?"

Accelerating up the hill, I veered into the opposing lane to dodge a cable-repair van. "Who stands to benefit from the *movie's* being killed."

"I'm with a student right now, so maybe you could . . ."

"Talk. Sure."

But of course she didn't let me. "Did the ingenue have any answers? To that question?"

"Trista? No. But the list is obvious. Any advocates of that sonar system. Select senators. The Department of Defense. NSA. Defense contractors."

"Well, that narrows it down nicely. But given her role, can't she specify—"

"She thinks I'm fucking crazy—"

"Mm-hmm."

"—threw me out."

"Which leaves . . . ?"

"Can *you* look into the naval sonar and this Senate proposal?"

"I thought that might be where you were—"

"I mean specifics," I said. "Names, programs, how the funding works. Whoever this is, they're obviously powerful. I mean, if this is the Department of Defense or NSA? Think of their resources. The gear, the reach. People everywhere. Clearly they flipped someone in LAPD. How do you go up against a monolith like that?"

"You don't," she said. "And let's not get dramatic. Something like this? It's not a sanctioned deal across, you know, a whole . . ."

"Agency?"

"Exactly. You have to figure out which corrupt piece of the whole is relevant to your . . . situation."

"Can you help me with this? Or is it too far out of your field?"

A sigh. "*The Wash Post.* And *The Journal.* Former classmates, you know. Investigative. Plus, I'm no slouch."

I wasn't sure whether her choppy sentences and inverted answers were any more veiled than normal speech, but I was too grateful to take issue. I gave her the Studio City address for Ridgeline, Inc., and asked her to dig up whatever she could on them and how they might hook into all this. She uh-huhed a few times and signed off without uttering my name. I pounded the steering wheel in triumph. Finally, traction.

I debated trying Ariana once more—I'd run through her numbers yet again before calling Julianne—but I was almost home. On our block, news vans waited at the curb, so I pulled a sharp right and parked behind our back fence. The minute I climbed over, I knew there was a problem. Setting one foot on the greenhouse roof, I looked down through the pane to see the shelves yanked off the walls, the pots shattered, the tulips loose in scatterings of dirt. My foot slid out from under me, and I hit the slope, hard, and was deposited on my back in the dirt.

From this angle the greenhouse looked worse. Everything had been not just broken but overturned.

Searched.

It was past four o'clock. Ariana could well have been here when they'd come. I rolled my aching head toward the house.

The back door had been left ajar.

I was on my feet instantly, running. The house looked no more ransacked than I'd left it; we'd never put it back together all the way after the cops had gotten through with it. The living room—also empty. Our framed wedding picture, leaning against the wall, peered back at me, the crack zigging the glass across our beaming faces. Calling Ari's name, I ran upstairs. She wasn't in the bedroom. I flew into my office, yanked open the desk drawer.

The FedEx envelope I'd stolen from Ridgeline was gone.

The spindle of blank DVDs remained on the shelf. I ran over, tore off the cap, and dumped the discs on the floor. All matching. They'd taken the CD, too.

I fumbled the phone out of my pocket and called Ariana. Voice mail and voice mail. Running downstairs, I threw open the door to the garage—no white pickup. That was good. Maybe she hadn't made it home yet. Maybe she'd just gotten hung up at the meeting and—

Panic rose, sweeping away the fantasy. She should've been home a half hour ago. I ripped through Ariana's address book, called her assistant.

"Patrick, what? As far as I know, her meeting wrapped up a while ag—"

Hanging up, I jogged out into the street. A few photographers had resumed their stakeouts. They half emerged from their cars and vans, puzzled and amused.

"Hi, listen, did you see . . . Did you see anyone breaking into this house? Leaving this house? My wife?"

They were snapping pictures of me.

"You've been camped out here how long? How long?" Nothing. My temper rose, broke like a wave. "Did you fucking *see* anything?"

I spun around. The neighbors in the apartments across the street were at their sliding doors, a face or two on every floor. Next door, Martinique shivered on her doorstep, Don draping an arm across her shoulders. "Were you home?" I shouted to them. "Have you been home? Have you seen Ari? Did she—"

Don turned, steering his wife inside.

I wheeled back. Cameras covering faces, clicking.

"I don't know, I don't fucking know where she is," I pleaded with them. Two snickered, and the third nodded apologetically, backing away.

Through the open front door, I heard the telephone ring.

Thank God.

I ran inside, snatched it up. "Ari?"

"I had hoped that the last time we spoke would be our last."

That electronic voice, stiffening the hair at the back of my neck.

"But you're a bit more resilient than we'd anticipated."

I couldn't breathe.

"We can't kill you. Too suspicious." A measured silence. *"But,"* he said, *"your wife . . ."*

My mouth was open, but no sound was coming out.

"You're a pretty troubled guy. Maybe you'd hurt her, too."

"No," I managed. "Listen—"

"The disc."

"No, I . . . *no.* I don't have it. I don't have any disc."

"Bring us the CD. Or we will send your wife's heart to you in a FedEx package not unlike the one you stole from us."

I put a hand on the kitchen counter to keep from collapsing. "I swear to God, someone took it from me."

"Drive to Keith Conner's house. Enter through the service gate. The code is 1509. Park within two feet of the cactus planter next to the guesthouse. Stay seated. Keep your windows rolled up. Do not change position when we approach. If you talk to the cops, she dies. If you fail to deliver the disc, she dies. If you're not here at five o'clock sharp, she dies."

"No, *wait*! Listen, I can't—"

He'd hung up.

My thoughts spun without orientation. If that was Ridgeline, clearly *they* hadn't broken in and reclaimed the disc. Then who had? The cops, for evidence? Dirty cops, for blackmail? NSA, the Defense Department, a senator's henchmen? Where was I in this thing? Clearly the CD wasn't blank as I'd thought, so what the hell did it have hidden on it?

Five o'clock—that was in thirty-seven minutes. Barely enough time to drive over, let alone figure anything out.

How could I track down a disc if I had no idea who had it?

Thirty-six minutes.

I grabbed the phone to call Detective Gable to see if he'd seized it. But the time. Even if he had, there was no way I could resolve anything with him and get over to Keith's in the next thirty-five minutes. I smashed the receiver against the base, hitting, missing, crushing my knuckles.

Was she okay? Had they hurt her? Yet?

I pulled at my hair, shoved tears off my cheeks.

A disc! I could pass off one of *my* unused blank CDs. I'd tell them I tried to copy it and everything had autoerased, just like with the DVDs. A flawed plan, sure, but it was something, and maybe it would buy me a few more minutes to figure out where Ariana was and make another play. I ran upstairs, grabbed a generic CD from one of my drawers, and rammed it into Ari's laptop to double-check that it was in fact blank.

Thirty-three minutes.

Downstairs again, running, halfway to the fence, sweating through my shirt. I stopped abruptly in the middle of our lawn. Then I came back and grabbed the biggest blade from the block on the kitchen counter.

Navigating a hairpin turn, I gripped the steering wheel hard and did my best not to slide in the driver's seat. If the butcher knife tucked beneath the back of my thigh shifted, it would open up my leg. The blade was angled in, the handle sticking out toward the console, within easy reach. The acrid smell of burning rubber leaked in through the dashboard vents. I resisted the urge to flatten the gas pedal again; I couldn't risk getting pulled over, not given the deadline.

I flew up the narrow street, my hands slick on the wheel, my heart pumping so much fear and adrenaline through me that I couldn't catch my breath. I checked the clock, checked the road, checked the clock again. When I was only a few blocks away, I pulled the car to the curb, tires screeching. I shoved open my door just in time. As I retched into the gutter, a gardener watched me from behind a throttling lawn mower, his face unreadable.

I rocked back into place, wiped my mouth, and continued more slowly up the steep grade. I turned down the service road as directed, and within seconds the stone wall came into sight, then the iron gates that matched the familiar ones in front. I hopped out and punched in the code. The gates shuddered and sucked inward. Hemmed in by jacaranda, the paved drive led straight back along the rear of the property. At last the guest quarters came into view. White stucco walls, low-pitched clay-tile roof, elevated porch—the guesthouse was bigger than most regular houses on our street.

I pulled up beside the cactus planter at the base of the stairs, tight to the building. Setting my hands on the steering wheel, I did my best to breathe. There were no signs of life. Way across the property, barely visible through a netting of branches, the main house sat dark and silent. Sweat stung my eyes. The stairs just outside the driver's-side window were steep enough that I couldn't see up onto the porch. I couldn't see much of anything but the risers. I supposed that was the point.

I waited. And listened.

Finally I heard the creak of a door opening above. A footstep. Then another. Then a man's boot set down on the uppermost step in my range of vision. The right foot followed. His knees came visible, then his thighs, then waist. He was wearing scuffed worker jeans, a nondescript black belt, maybe a gray T-shirt.

I slid my right hand down to the hilt of the butcher knife and squeezed it so hard that my palm tingled. Warmth leaked into my mouth; I'd bitten my cheek.

He stopped on the bottom step, a foot from my window, the line of my car roof severing him at the midsection. I wanted to duck down so I could see his face, but I'd been warned not to. He was too close anyway.

His knuckle rose, tapped the glass once.

I pushed the button with my left hand. The window started to whir down. The knife blade felt cool hidden beneath my thigh. I picked out a spot on his chest, just below his ribs. But first I had to find out what I needed to know.

His other hand came swiftly into view and popped something fist-sized in through the open gap of the still-lowering window. Hitting my lap, it was surprisingly heavy.

I looked down.

A hand grenade.

I choked on my breath. I reached to grab it.

Before my splayed fingers could get there, it detonated.

CHAPTER 46

My eyelids were made of concrete. They lifted slightly, then clanked shut against the burn of the overhead lights. My ribs ached. My ears rang. My right cheek and the edge of my lips felt like they were missing skin. I went to raise a hand to my throbbing head, but for some reason it couldn't get there.

It was a slow process, but I finally pried my eyes open. The fluorescents seemed to bleach my surroundings, but after a few more blinks I realized that the room was plenty bright in its own right—white tile, white walls, large mirror doubling the glare. Empty, aside from a chair pushed into the far corner. For a moment I entertained the notion that I was in a divine waiting room, but then, through a sliver of open door across from me, I spotted the LAPD poster tacked up behind a desk.

An interrogation room.

I'd wound up in custody?

I was lying on a metal bench, a handcuff connecting my right wrist to a security bar bolted to the wall. I'd been too groggy to figure out that's why I couldn't raise my arm.

The thought of Ariana jerked me to a sitting position, and my head nearly exploded. My right arm was pins and needles. I tugged up my T-shirt and held it with my chin. The skin on my chest was raw. Standing, I tried to stretch far enough from the bench to look in the two-way mirror and assess the damage to my face, but the cuff kept me inches shy of the mark.

My throat was too dry to allow words through, but I rasped for help. No one came.

I took stock of the room. Thick metal door with a dead bolt just out of reach on the same wall to which I was shackled. The white noise wasn't only in my head; the air conditioner was working double-time, recycling room-temperature air. In the adjoining room, a clock by the LAPD poster showed seven o'clock—A.M.? P.M.?—and a clear plastic tub next to an overstuffed in-box held my wallet, keys, and disposable phone. One of my pockets was inside out.

A scalding thought cut through the haze—*She's dead*—but my mind recoiled, fled toward other possibilities.

They could've released her. Or maybe the cops had rescued her when they found me. I was desperate to believe anything.

I was able to move four paces parallel with the wall, the cuff sliding along the rail until it caught. I could reach nothing. Swallowing a few times finally got my voice working. I stared at the two-way mirror. "Where am I?" Hoarser than Brando.

An unseen door opened and closed, and a moment later a detective entered from the adjoining room, badge hanging around his neck. He was so broad that I almost missed his colleague slipping in behind him.

The big guy ran a hand over his blond, grown-out flattop and gave a businesslike wave at the mirror. "Okay, we got him, thanks. You recording?" His wide face, big-featured and handsome, fixed on me. He looked quintessentially American, a Norman Rockwell football player. "I'm Lieutenant DeWitt, and this is Lieutenant Verrone."

Lieutenants. I'd been upgraded.

Verrone had a cigarettes-and-booze complexion— tinged yellow, rugged and sickly all at once—and he looked like he could fit in DeWitt's pant leg. His mustache turned the corners of his mouth, aiming at a handlebar but cut short, no doubt, in keeping with department regs.

"My wife," I croaked.

"What about her?" DeWitt asked.

Verrone dropped into the chair in the far corner. His button-up shirt pulled tight against his torso, revealing a surprisingly sinewy build. He only looked insubstantial next to DeWitt.

"Is she okay?" I said.

"I don't know," DeWitt answered carefully. "Did you hurt her?"

"No, I—*no*." There was a ring of shiny red skin at my wrist. My head wasn't back online yet; everything seemed so uncivilized, so bewildering. "You . . . you didn't see her?"

DeWitt squatted in the middle of the white tile, facing me. Such a big guy and yet his movements were precise, graceful. "Why should we see your wife?"

From his chair, Verrone continued to stare at me. Not a glower per se, but dispassionate eye contact, menacing only in its reptilian endurance. Since sitting, he hadn't broken eye contact or moved any part of his body, at least not that I could gather from the glances I'd allocated myself.

I shook my head to clear it, but that only compounded the pain. "How am I . . . ?" The rest couldn't make it from brain to mouth.

DeWitt obliged the obvious question anyway. "Stun grenade, military issue. You add the overpressure of being in a car, you're looking at a pressure wave of thirty thousand pounds per square inch. You're lucky you're not more seriously injured."

Had it been my attacker's plan to knock me out all along? Or had he spotted the butcher knife at my side and decided to drop the grenade? They'd let me live. Which meant they still had use for me. Clearly they'd realized that the blank CD I'd brought was a sham. Maybe they thought I could still lead them to the real one. Hope flared in my chest; if that were the case, they'd keep Ari alive to ensure my cooperation.

If you talk to the cops, she dies.

Shivering off the remembered threat, I did my best to focus. I had to get out of here without revealing anything, and make myself available to Ariana's kidnappers. No step of which would be easy. First thing would be to get myself to a lower-security building. Like a hospital. "Am I . . . Can I see a doctor?"

"Medics cleared you at the scene. You were conscious—remember?"

"I don't."

"We brought you here, then you dozed off."

"Where's here?"

"Parker Center."

LAPD headquarters. Great.

"I should be at a hospital. I was *unconscious*. I don't remember anything."

DeWitt cocked an eyebrow at Verrone. "We'd better re-Mirandize him, then."

"Nah, we got him on tape. And he signed." Verrone's mouth had barely moved, and for a moment I wondered if he'd spoken at all. He remained eerily still.

I tried to stand, but the cuff jerked me back onto the bench. "You can't arrest me. I can't . . . be in jail right now."

DeWitt said, "I'm afraid it's a little late for that."

"Can I talk to Detective Richards?"

"She's no longer involved with this case."

"Where's Gable?"

DeWitt said, more firmly, "We're above Gable."

"*Sixth* floor," Verrone said.

My brain revved and revved but couldn't find traction. With Ariana's life on the line, was I finally out of plays?

"A neighbor called in the blast a few hours ago." DeWitt eyeballed my handcuff, unconsciously jostling the dive watch on his own right wrist. "Keith Conner's house, you know?" He whistled. "So we got on our horse. Then you, there. Look at it from our perspective. I gotta be a hard-ass here and get some answers out of you."

I could feel Verrone's impassive face pointed at me,

those steady eyes posing some unspoken challenge. I realized he scared me.

"I don't know that I have any answers," I said.

"Who assaulted you?" DeWitt asked.

"I didn't see. And I don't know names."

"But they didn't kill you. Which means you must have something they want."

"No, they don't *want* me dead. I'm the fall guy for Keith Conner's murder. If I die, it looks suspicious."

"And this doesn't?"

"Sure it does. It makes *me* look suspicious. That's why I'm the one under arrest."

"Listen closely, assfuck," Verrone said. This time there was little uncertainty that he was talking. There was also little uncertainty about who would be playing bad cop. A crime-scene bag appeared from inside his jacket. The butcher knife. Swaying. "We want an explanation for this. And we want an explanation for what you were doing at Keith fucking Conner's house."

I said, "Assfuck?"

"You know how to boil a frog, Davis?"

"I know the story," I said. "You can't throw it in hot water or it'll just hop out. So you put it in a pot of cold water on a stove, then you turn up the temperature, a degree at a time. It's so gradual, the frog doesn't notice. It sits there until it's cooked. And just in case I haven't noticed—to coin a phrase—how *fucked* I am"—I gestured to my cramped surroundings, my cuff rattling—"this is where you tell me I'm the frog."

I could have sworn DeWitt looked mildly amused.

Verrone stood up swiftly, the chair rolling back. After his perfect stillness, the gesture was intimidating. DeWitt rose and turned to face him. Verrone studied me, his jaw corded with muscle. He pointed at my face. "You get *one* of those for free."

DeWitt walked over and breathed down on me. "This is the end of the road. You can't wriggle off this time. The pieces are lined up from the DA to the chief to the investigative file. You've gotta come clean. Why were you at Keith's?"

Even when I bowed my head, that broad shadow pressed in on me. I could feel the heat off his body. The CD was out there somewhere. Ariana was out there somewhere, too, terrified. I was behind bars, powerless to help her. And if I talked, they'd kill her.

I said, "I want to see a lawyer."

DeWitt sighed. Took a step back.

Verrone said, "Wow. He wants to play it *that* way." He turned to leave, disgusted. "I'm gonna take a leak." He walked out.

Me and DeWitt, alone. I glanced nervously at the two-way mirror, but it just looked back at me.

I said, "You have to give me access to counsel."

"Sure." DeWitt took another step back. His big, pleasant face looked disappointed, as if he'd caught me in the backseat with his girlfriend. "Sure thing. Lemme just tell the chief."

Leaving the door partially ajar, he walked out, moved a stack of crisp manila folders, and sat on the edge of the desk. The desk didn't sound too happy about it. His fist encompassed the phone. "Yeah, Chief? I'm in Interrogation Five with Davis. He wants to lawyer up. . . . Yes, I stopped asking him questions immediately. . . . I know, I know." He made a clicking sound. "Bad traffic now? He'll have to wait while his lawyer drives over. But the holding tank's filled with those Familia bangers that Metro just rolled up." Those soft blue eyes swiveled to take me in. "Look, he's a white-collar guy. I don't think he'd want to mix with—" He nodded. And again. "Okay. I know. I can't inform him how much we can help him if he's just willing to have a conversation with us. . . . What? . . . No, I don't think he's aware that you think Detective Gable is incompetent and shortsighted. . . . Right, the whole forest-for-the-trees thing. If Davis would walk us through this mess, we might be able to get somewhere, but he feels we're past that point. It's a shame, since I get the vibe that he's a decent guy who's in over his head. But he's not giving us any options. . . . Okay. . . . Okay." He hung up.

"Nice performance," I said.

He sat down at the desk, ruffled through some files. I stared at him through the sliver of open door, but he didn't look up.

"I *can't* talk to you," I said.

He turned and called to someone out of sight. "Murray, we're gonna need a transfer form on Davis."

I said, "My wife . . . My wife could be in . . ."

He looked through the slender gap in the door. "I'm sorry, were you talking to me?"

"Come on."

"You're willing to continue talking to me about the events of earlier today, even in the absence of counsel?"

I looked over at the two-way so they could get it on tape. "Yes."

He came back inside, crossed his arms.

I said, "I can't tell you anything helpful." He started out again. "Hang on, just *wait* a second. I'm not dicking you around. My wife is in danger."

"Tell us whatever you know, and we will get on it. If your wife is at risk, we can protect her."

"You don't understand. They want . . ."

"What do they want?"

"They think I have something."

"What do you have? We can't help you if you don't let us."

"They will kill my wife. Do you understand? They will kill her if I tell you *anything*."

"No one has to find out what you tell us." Frustrated at my silence, he tried a different tack. "Who is 'they'?"

"I don't know."

His blue eyes glowed with intensity. "Where is your wife?"

"They *have* her."

"Okay," he said calmingly. "Okay. First things first. You can't tell us anything without putting your wife at risk. So we're gonna locate her ourselves."

"You won't find her."

"Finding people is what we do. And *when* we find her, then you'll come clean?" His gaze was level, unblinking. "I want your word."

"Okay," I said. "*If* you find her. And I talk to her, to know she's okay."

He looked up at the two-way and nodded briskly, a call to action. "I'm going to have you wait here. Do you have to use the restroom?"

"No. Just keep her safe."

"Don't go anywhere." A soft smile. He closed the door behind him.

I stretched out on the bench and tried to slow the pounding in my head. I must have drifted off, because when the door opened again, the wall clock over Verrone's shoulder showed 8:15.

DeWitt was sitting behind the desk in the other room, the phone wedged into the shelf of his deltoid, his head tipped forward into a hand. Stressed.

Verrone grabbed the chair from the corner, dragged it over so he was sitting right across from me. I shoved myself up, rubbing my eyes. "What? Did you find her?"

In the other room, DeWitt leaned back in his chair, hoisting his feet onto the desk. He was holding eight-by-ten photos, but I could see only the backs of them. He raged into the phone, "I know that, but we need to get a shrink here *now.*" Verrone shot him a look, and DeWitt raised a hand apologetically and quieted.

Verrone turned back to me. His whole demeanor had shifted. He leaned forward, as if to take my hand. His lips pursed, and a line appeared between his eyes—a line of empathy, concern. My fear skyrocketed.

"What?" I said. "Tell me."

"A hiker found your wife—"

"No." My voice was thick, unrecognizable. *"No."*

"—in a gully in Fryman Canyon."

I stared at him without sensation, without thought. I said, "No."

"I'm sorry," Verrone said. "She's dead."

CHAPTER 47

The crime-scene photo, a close-up of Ariana's face, quivered in my hand. I couldn't handle the sight, and yet I couldn't look away either. Her eyes were closed, her skin an unnatural gray. Her dark curls straggled across dead weeds. I'd refused to believe it, and so Verrone had produced proof. My wife, dead in a gully.

My voice was tiny, far away. "How."

Verrone shook his head.

"How."

"Stabbed in the neck." He licked his lips uncomfortably. "You're a suspect, obviously, but I'm willing to give you the benefit of the doubt until the time of death and evidence come in." He tugged at the photograph, and finally I let it go. "My wife was . . . uh, I lost her to a drunk driver. There's never . . ." Leaning back, he picked at the leg of his jeans, his mustache twitching. "There's never anything anyone can say." He looked at me directly and tilted his head in a show of respect. "I'm sorry."

I could barely comprehend his words. "But we were just starting . . ." I was choking on my own breath. "To get it right again."

I couldn't get any further. I turned to the wall. My

fists were against my face, and I was trying to com-
press my chest, my body, trying to harden myself
into an insensate rock. If I didn't crack, if I didn't
sob, it wouldn't be true. But then I did. Which meant
it was.

I tilted forward, one wrist cuffed ridiculously
behind me. His hand was warm on my shoulder.
"Breathe," he was saying. "Just one breath. Then another. That's all you have to do right now."

"I'll find them. I'll fucking find them. You gotta
get me out of here."

"We will. We'll figure this out."

But I already knew how that evidence would come
back: The electronic voice had broadcast the plan.
*You're a pretty troubled guy. Maybe you'd hurt her,
too.*

"It was all because of a CD I took from them,"
I said. "A fucking CD cost her life. Why did I think
I could . . . ?"

"We can use that to get to them. Do you know
what's on it?"

"No, I have no idea."

"Do you still have it?"

Tears fell, tapping the floor and Verrone's boots. I
blinked hard, blinked again, trying to see through the
warped veil, trying to determine if what I was seeing
was real.

The little cursive logo by Verrone's laces.

Danner.

I stopped breathing.

Through the doorway, DeWitt was still on the
phone, his enormous boots, no doubt size eleven and

a half, propped up on the desk. My eyes went to the white pebble wedged in the tread of the heel. Then to that Timex on his right wrist. My left-handed intruder, in front of me all this time.

My shock registered almost like panic, and it was all I could do to keep from shouting out. And then I came through it and landed in a nest of cold rage.

I sucked air until my heart stopped hiccupping and the tingling in my face diminished. I did my best to order my thoughts, to reconstruct how everything must have gone down. These men had kidnapped Ariana and dropped a stun grenade in my lap. When they'd found only a replacement CD in my car, they'd hauled me here—wherever *here* was—to get me to tell them where the real one was or whom I'd given it to. And once they figured out I wouldn't talk because I was worried that might put Ariana at further risk, they'd disposed of her as they'd planned all along. When they stabbed her in the neck, they had me locked in this room. Which made *them* the only people who could ever alibi me.

Had they plucked a few hairs from my unconscious head and planted them on Ariana's body? Who had punched the blade through her throat? Who had held her down?

Verrone was leaning forward, his cheek close to mine. His hand stayed on my shoulder, rubbing in tight little circles. Concerned friend, fellow widower. "Do you still have this CD?" he asked again.

It was all I could do not to turn my head and rip a hole in his face with my teeth.

"You said you'd talk to us," he prodded gently.

"You've got nothing left to lose now anyway. Let's nail these fuckers."

His dialogue was right out of central casting. As my eyes darted frantically around, I realized that the interrogation room itself seemed like a stage set. It felt legitimate because it looked like every TV and movie police station I'd ever seen. The big two-way mirror, the white lights, the desk crowded with case files— they were running a movie on me. Which meant, with my life on the line, I had to play my role without letting on that I'd figured out I was inside a script.

Verrone tilted closer. "Now, do you still have that CD?"

I tamped down my rage, worked up the lie. "Yes," I said.

"Where is it?"

I looked up at him. I could smell lunch on his breath. I could feel the pulse beating at my temple. I was having trouble keeping fury from my face, but he couldn't know that it was anything more than grief or shock.

I had to get free. Which meant I had to get both of them to leave.

I struggled to come up with dialogue to fit the scenario. "There's an alley by campus where I work," I said. "Where the guys who killed my wife parked a Honda with a duffel of cash in the trunk. You have that location from the investigation report?"

"Yes."

Another lie—I'd never given the cops the precise location.

"The northern wall is brick," I said. "About midway down the alley, ten or so feet from the ground, there's a loose brick. The CD is hidden behind it."

He rose swiftly. "I'll get it."

"It's a long alley. And you have to use a chair or something, which'll slow you down. You might want me to go with you to show you where."

He hesitated. "No way the chief'll let us take you out into the field. Especially in light of the news you just received."

"Okay, but it could take a long time. You'd better find it fast so we can use it to snare the motherfuckers who killed my wife."

We were close, my gaze unwavering. He bunched his mouth, that almost handlebar mustache bristling as he assessed my face. His eyes were murky brown, as unyielding as flint. Did he know I knew?

He rose. "Okay," he said to the two-way mirror, addressing whoever was listening behind it. "I'll take DeWitt, too, so we can get this done quicker." He looked over at me. "Hang in there. A shrink's on the way. If there's anything you need, we'll see to it when we get back."

He walked out, closed the door. A moment later I heard another door open and close.

I pressed my ear to the wall. Traffic sounds. Distant, but not six stories away. Overhead, the air conditioner cycled room-temperature air, contributing nothing but white noise to keep me from hearing outside sounds.

I'd read once that a broken elephant can be leashed with a string tied to a stake in the ground; it *believes* it is trapped and never dares to challenge the perception.

I tugged at my handcuff, testing the bar. The bolts securing it to the wall were substantial, impressive. Crouching on the metal bench, I gripped the bar, squatted, and gracelessly managed to get both feet against the wall on either side of my hands. Leaning back, I shoved until the pressure sustained me above the bench in a strained float. My legs ached, the edge of the bench biting into my hamstrings, and then the bar ripped from the wall with a tired thud, and I flew back, landing hard on the floor. The wind left me in a grunt, my breath screeching, my shoulder blades on fire.

No approaching footsteps. No one barging in from the adjoining room.

I slid my handcuff off the curved end of the security bar and stood. The bolts had gone into the plaster and one wooden stud, but there was no metal or concrete beneath the wall as there should have been. Holding the bar, I approached the giant mirror. So much color on my face. A purple mottling across my right cheek. One eyelid blue and blown wide. The edge of my mouth cracked and red. A bruise on the side of my neck. I leaned closer to the mirror, noting the dark dot at the center of that bruise. A needle mark. How long had they kept me drugged?

I recalled how DeWitt and Verrone had made sure to address their colleagues in the observation room there, behind the two-way mirror: *Okay, we got him, thanks. You recording?* A nice touch, to leave me believing I was being watched.

I swung the security bar at the mirror. The bar

bounced back hard, as I'd expected, and glass rained down around me, winking in the light.

Beneath the mirror was not an observation room but solid wall. The clinging shards broke my reflection into fragments.

A string and a stake in the ground. A security bar and a mirror.

The door to the adjoining room was closed but unlocked. Bracing myself, wielding the bar, I stepped out into darkness and fumbled for a light switch. I clicked on the overheads and dropped the bar in disbelief.

I knew this place.

Aside from the desk, the poster, and the clock—the sliver of room visible from the bench to which I'd been chained—the room had been largely emptied.

The last time I was here, from outside peering in, I'd spied DeWitt's desk. Now it had been moved across the floor to put it in view from the interrogation room. The venetian blinds were closed. To the left of the doorway was nothing but a few discarded computer cords, a capsized paper shredder, and a large copier shoved into the corner.

Torn from a key ring, a glossy valet parking slip lay on the floor:

This June, Be Afraid.
This June, There's Nowhere Left to Hide.
This June . . . THEY'RE WATCHING.

I trudged to the desk. There were my things, neatly collected in the plastic tub. With trembling fingers I pocketed them. Then I dug through the mess around the in-boxes. One of the crisp manila folders fell to the floor, spilling its contents. I stared down at the fan of blank paper. Then I riffled through the other files, my consternation growing as I realized that *all* the folders on the desk were filled with nothing more than blank copy paper. The top drawer held stacks of unused pads and manila folders. But beneath them I found a handcuff key. With great relief I freed my wrist.

The file drawer held a revolver. I stared down at it like it was a coiled snake.

I was numb, overloaded, moving on autopilot. It was almost as though I was directing myself from outside my body. When I turned away from the drawer, the gun was shoved in my waistband.

Stumbling across the room, I opened the hatch on the paper shredder and tugged out a clear plastic bag filled with crosscut scraps. It was probably useless, but I wanted to leave with *something.* As the front door swung open under my unsteady hand, that brass placard flashed into view:

DO NOT LEAVE ANY PACKAGES WITHOUT
SIGNATURE. DO NOT LEAVE ANY PACKAGES
WITH NEIGHBORING BUSINESSES.

I staggered out onto the second-floor hallway of the Starbright Plaza.

Nighttime. It seemed impossible, but all was normal in the real world. Down the unlit hallway, I could hear people working late, voices on phones, selling, selling, selling. Flatware clinked in the café below. In the parking lot, streetlights dropped glistening mercury onto the roofs of sleek cars. A not-quite-rain left everything dusted with dew.

Halfway down the stairs, clutching the bag of shredded paper, I stopped. Jerry's warning from last week played in my head: *Printers, copiers, fax machines— everything's got a hard drive now, and people can get at 'em and know what you've been up to.*

I ran back up. When they'd cleared out the place, they'd left the unwieldy copier behind. A beat-up Sharp, some years old. Nothing in the tray, nothing facedown against the glass. I swung open the plastic front and peered among the mechanical insides. There it was, an innocuous-looking beige rectangle. With a straightened paper clip, I poked the release hole and extracted the hard drive. Then I jotted down the copier's model number and fled.

What was waiting for me? Had the arrest warrant for Ariana's murder already been issued? How else had the world changed since that stun grenade had gone off in my lap?

Clearly DeWitt and Verrone and whoever else Ridgeline comprised had planned to hold me long enough to get the CD back and ensure an airtight frame for Ariana's murder. Then they'd turn me loose to whatever remained of my life, and I'd be snatched up by primed Robbery-Homicide detectives and put away for killing Keith and my wife.

No car. My wallet, empty. I'd sent them to that alley in Northridge because it was a good forty-minute drive before they'd arrive and be reminded that there was no brick wall. That left me time to drive home and get cash, a checkbook, and the list of defense attorneys Ariana had compiled for me, then disappear before the real cops closed in on me. I could regroup in a Motel 6. Watch the news, build a case to clear my name, get a lawyer, negotiate turning myself in. The revolver handle pressed into my stomach, cold and reassuring. Maybe there would be other options, too.

With the copier hard drive in my pocket, the bag of shredded documents in hand, I stumbled off the bottom stair onto ground level and out in front of a dry cleaner, the lights out, plastic-wrapped shirts shimmering on the carousel like dormant ghosts. As I hustled past the glass shop next door, the sight inside brought me up short. Lined on wooden racks and hung on the walls were endless mirrors. No doubt the one I'd shattered upstairs had been bought right here, a simple prop carried upstairs by Laurel and Hardy, the workers I'd spotted during my last visit. Ariana's words returned to me yet again, my eyes stinging at the thought of her: *A misinterpretation, a white handkerchief, and a few well-placed nudges.* How easily they'd knocked me off course, a tap at a time, until the world in my head no longer matched the world outside. My palm was flat against the cool window, my quick breath fogging the glass. Fragmented reflections stared back at me, bruise-faced and stupefied.

Shaken, I staggered on my way, cutting behind the valet stand into the café. The patrons regarded me with polite unease, and the waiters made eye contact with one another. I could only imagine what I looked like.

The place was emptying out for the night. The bartender was putting the well bottles to bed. And yet the clock upstairs had shown eight-thirty when I'd left.

"What time is it?" I asked a silver-haired gentle-man in a booth.

A glance at his weighty watch. "Eleven-fifteen."

They'd kept me unconscious for hours longer than I'd been led to believe. Had they needed the extra time to put the final touches on the fake interrogation room? To find an opening to transport my unconscious body from the rear alley, up the fire-escape stairs, and through that metal back door with the shiny new dead bolt? Or to drag Ariana to Fryman Canyon? Maybe they'd killed her before I'd even regained consciousness.

Whatever that disc held, it couldn't be worth the price I'd paid for taking it.

My head still felt thick from whatever drugs had been shot into me. I realized I was still standing there, interrupting the couple's dinner. I searched for words, for more grounding: "What . . . what *day* is it?"

The man's wife rested a hand nervously on his forearm, but he offered me a consoling grin. "Thursday."

"Good," I muttered, backing up, nearly colliding with a busboy. "That's what it's supposed to be."

I ducked from their stares into the bathroom, dumped the throwaway cell phone into the trash, and cleaned up as best I could. Flashing on Ari's gray face, I came apart a little and had to clamp down. I had to hold it together long enough to get out of there.

Walking out, I grabbed a twenty someone had left on a table as a tip. The coatrack by the door had a black windbreaker, which I lifted and pulled on as I approached the valet stand, tucking the bag of shredded paper under my arm. The hood, protection against the wet breeze, obscured my fucked-up face.

The valet hopped up off his director's chair. I gestured at a BMW four spots over and said, "That's me right there." I pointed the twenty at him. "I can get it myself."

He tossed me the keys.

CHAPTER 48

I screeched up behind our back fence, leaving the Beemer a few feet off the curb. But I didn't hear the tires, didn't feel the fence biting me in the stomach, didn't smell the mulch beneath our sumacs. Suspended in grief, I'd come unmoored from my senses. There were a thousand impressions of her and nothing else.

It's bizarre what sticks in your brain. Ariana sitting on the kitchen floor, digging in a bottom cabinet, a carton of eggs waiting on the counter. Home from a night run, she wore a sports bra and had a sheen of dried sweat across her forehead, four pots pulled into her lap and twice as many spread on the floor around her. Her heel poked through a hole in her sock. She looked up, biting her lip, playing embarrassed, as if I'd caught her at something. Behind her hair band, a thick lock had bunched unevenly, and the light halved her face in shadow. She said, "What?" but I just shook my head and took in the sight of her. They talk about it like it's all jukebox slow dances and sweaty lovemaking and princess-cut diamonds. But sometimes it's just your wife sitting frog style on the kitchen floor after a workout, looking for an omelet pan.

Dazed, I floated through the side gate, keys in hand, heading for the front of our house. The dark sedan creeping into view ahead brought me crashing back into my body. The bag of crosscut documents slapped the concrete at my feet. It couldn't be the real cops yet—it seemed unlikely that they'd have found out about Ariana's body already. It had to be DeWitt and Verrone, coming to take their interrogation to another level.

The driver eased into the darkness beyond our mailbox and killed the engine. The first thing to hit was fear, compounded by everything that had come before. But then, cutting through my paralysis, came something else. Rage.

I headed for the car, my hand diving beneath my shirt, seizing the handle of the revolver. Just as I was about to pull and aim, the door cracked, the interior light illuminating Detective Gable. I jerked to a halt.

"You have one job right now," he said, climbing out. "And that is to stay reachable. Where the hell have you been all—"

We were close enough now that he caught sight of my face. Should I run? But my will had evaporated. Deflated, I wobbled a bit on my feet. My shirt was still bunched up, and I tugged the hem weakly, pulling it smooth over the gun.

"Jesus, what happened to you?"

"Did you break in and take a disc from my office? Because you have no idea what you did."

"Yeah, I broke in without a warrant and stole shit just to jeopardize my top case." He had the game face on, but my aggression had caught him off guard.

"You here to arrest me?"

He stiffened against the anger in my voice. "People involved with you keep dying."

"Arrest me if you're going to, but don't you fuck with me," I said. "Not right now. Not over this. There are limits. Basic human decency."

"I saw the body. Doesn't look like you showed *her* any decency." He stepped forward, and I shoved him, hard, against the sedan. His shoulder blades clapped loudly against the door, and when he ricocheted back to his feet, his hand had come up with his pistol. He pointed it at the street between us. He was as calm as I'd ever seen him. "Watch yourself."

"*Say it.* Just you fucking say it. Say I killed my wife."

"Your *wife*?" He looked astonished. "I'm here because Deborah Vance turned up dead."

Deborah Vance? The name was from a different lifetime. And yet it was only twelve hours ago I'd asked Joe Vente to tip the cops to check her apartment.

I became aware of the half dozen photographers who had crept like mice from the shadows. In light of the drawn gun, they kept their distance, but flashes strobed the uncertain standoff.

"You pointed Detectives Richards and Valentine to that woman," Gable said. "She played the Hungarian grandmother, was it? To get the mythical duffel bag of cash you found in the trunk of the mythical Honda? I want the *real* story." His breath misted. "And I'll need your alibi."

"I don't have a fucking alibi."

"I haven't told you when she was killed." He looked troubled, unsure of himself.

"You think I care about Keith Conner or Deborah Vance? My wife is dead. And you're running around like this other shit matters. That's all you guys do. You don't save anyone. You're historians—you come in after the fact and write reports and point your fucking fingers."

I took a step to the side, the paparazzi behind me now. Gable's gun hadn't moved. The tip remained perfectly still. "They killed my wife," I said. "They took her and they killed her." Saying it out loud gave it more force. I fought my voice steady. "They tried to hold me in a . . . a fake jail—"

"A *fake jail*?"

I clutched for a response. The false interrogation room was so audacious and mind-boggling that the mention of it sounded outlandish spilling from my mouth.

Gable couldn't decide between amused and irate. "And let me guess. If we go to find it, the space'll be cleared out."

A bar, a mirror, and a poster. DeWitt and Verrone were probably removing even those at this very moment, leaving the Ridgeline office as blank as a wiped chalkboard. "Yeah," I said. "That's exactly what'll happen. And then you'll find Ariana's body in a gully in Fryman Canyon, with evidence showing I killed her. And you idiots won't believe me because I don't have a single concrete thing to prove that her killers exist, except for this."

Fisting my shirt, I tugged it up, revealing the revolver stuffed in my waistband. But Gable wasn't looking at me. He was looking at our garage door.

It was wobbling open.

My hands fell to my sides, my shirt dropping just before he glanced back at me.

Footsteps sounded on the concrete floor of our garage. Gable's gun finally moved, inching over toward the house.

Ariana stepped into view.

At first I didn't believe. And then I was drifting toward her in a daze, stumbling over the curb, finally meeting her in the garage next to her truck. I clutched her shoulders, felt her flesh and bone in my grip.

"You were dead," I said.

"Your face—"

"You were gone, and they had you, and you were dead."

"No," she said. "*You* were gone." She was tilting my head this way and that, appraising the damage. "My meeting was delayed, and I stopped after to pick up more prepaid cell phones, since you'd taken the last one. There was no one here when I got home."

"So this whole time, you . . . you . . . ?" Was I sobbing or laughing wildly?

Gable stood in our driveway, backlit by the sparkling flashes, though the photographers themselves blended into the dark, a murmuring chorus. The firm line of his shoulders had taken on a droop, and in the grainy darkness he looked like a figure torn from a noir movie.

He called out, "We should just have you committed and save us all a lot of aggravation."

I was gripping Ariana—her hips, her arms—testing the realness of her. She had a hand against my unbruised cheek and a look of bewildered concern. "What happened to you? Who did this?"

Gable, chafing at being ignored: "You think you can just fuck with us this way? Play games with the investigation? I saw what you did to that woman, the bullet through her mouth. And when I nail your ass to my trophy wall, we'll see how well this insanity routine holds up." He turned toward his car, then spun on his heel, incensed. "Next time I come back, I'm not just gonna ask questions."

Ari's eyes didn't leave mine. She reached over to the wall, hit the glowing button, and the garage door tilted down. Detective Gable stood his ground as the lowering door cut off his glare, his chest, and finally his spotless loafers.

The doors were locked and bolted, the burglar alarm set. The day's bouts of street theater had left the paparazzi reinvigorated, sipping coffee from Thermoses, patrolling the block, and comparing lenses beyond the curb. A news helicopter had returned to circle our roof, waiting for another meltdown. The bag of shredded documents sat on the kitchen counter, beside the hard drive I'd tugged from Ridgeline's copier. The revolver rested at arm's length on the coffee table. Gable and RHD were using all resources to shore up the case against me; they didn't even have to waste manpower keeping surveillance on me, since the press was doing the job for them. The men from Ridgeline—DeWitt and Verrone and whoever else—were out there somewhere in the night, plotting. And Ari and I were sitting on the couch, facing each other, our bent legs intertwined.

I ran my fingertips across her mouth, her neck, each living part of her. I held my knuckles before her trembling lips and felt the rush of her breath. I marveled at her coloring, pressed on her skin and watched pink fill in the white, as if this evidence of her moving blood could wipe from my memory the image of her face against the weeds, the shade of her flesh Photoshopped to an unliving gray.

Leaning forward, she kissed me, tentatively. A nervous whisper—"Still remember how to have sex?" Her mouth was at my ear, her hair brushing my bruised cheek.

"I think so," I said. "You?"

She pulled away, rolling her lips as if still assessing the feel of my mouth. "I don't know."

She rose and walked up the stairs. A moment later I picked up the revolver and followed.

We met in a collection of present-tense flashes, a bedroom mosaic. The sheets, shoved back under her impatient heel. The feather-soft grasp of her hand. Her mouth, wet and exploratory against my collarbone. I insisted on seeing every part of her—the mole at the curve of her hip, the arch of her foot, the V of fine blond hair on her nape beneath the weight of her curls.

After, or in between, we lay exhausted, interwoven, tracing drops of sweat across each other's skin.

We hadn't been naked in front of each other in months, and it was all the excitement of the new with the comfort of the familiar. The tendon at the back of her knee was firm and fragile against my lips. The revolver remained beside the jammer on the nightstand, poking into view, never forgotten, but our bedroom had become a sanctuary of sorts, keeping the night and the terrors it held at bay. A trail of clothes led from door to bed. The UCLA hoodie she'd bought at the Student Union and cut thumbholes in the sleeves for the cold early mornings I'd walk her back to her dorm. The Morro Bay T-shirt we'd gotten when we'd gone up to feed the squirrels and stayed in a flea-bitten place we'd renamed The Horsefly Inn. Pulled inside out, her varnish-stained jeans. And dropped into the nest of a fallen pillow on the floor, her wedding set. If ever a string of objects charted a relationship.

My ear was flat against the back of her thigh, and I could hear the hum of her voice through her flesh. "I missed you," she said.

I soaked in the warmth of her skin. I said, "I feel like I found you again."

CHAPTER 49

Burned adrenaline kept me up almost to daylight, before my vigilance finally gave out beneath the weight of so many sleepless nights. I slumbered—dreamless, solid, untroubled—as I hadn't since my teenage years. When I awakened, the revolver was missing from the nightstand, but I heard Ariana's familiar footsteps moving around in the kitchen. By the time I finally hauled myself out of bed, popped four Advil, and slumped downstairs, it was nearly two o'clock.

The gun and jammer resting beside her, she sat cross-legged on the family-room carpet, facing away, scrutinizing a mound of shredded paper she'd dumped from the bag I'd stolen from Ridgeline. No scrap was bigger than a thumbnail. As I neared, I saw that she'd made a few preliminary piles, organized by color. Her biggest collection, with maybe ten pieces, was dwarfed by the unsorted heap, but she seemed characteristically undaunted.

"We're pretty much fucked on white," she said as I walked up behind her. "There seems to be slightly less gray. Sparse pink, but I think it's a take-out menu. And a few of these harder ones. Weird." She held a white-silver square over her head, and I took it, bent it between thumb and forefinger. It bowed, regained its shape.

"Magazine cover?" I ventured.

"No writing on the few I've found." She leaned back into my legs and looked up at me. A mariposa tucked behind her ear.

Lavender.

"You haven't—" I stopped.

She raised a hand self-consciously to the flower. "You noticed? That I'd stopped wearing this color?"

"Of course."

She didn't smile, but she looked pleased. She went back to sorting through the mound of scraps.

"Is there any hope of piecing something together out of all that?" I asked.

"Probably not. But it's one of two leads you took from there. They pulled out all the stops to get that missing CD—maybe something here'll lead us to it. Are you going back to Starbright Plaza? To ask about the lease or whatever?"

"I'm not leaving you. You just died."

"Patrick, we're not gonna get out of this if we hole up here. What are we gonna do? Hold each other until Robbery-Homicide kicks down the door?"

I didn't want to confess that after the grueling past twenty-four hours, that was pretty much my plan. The notion of being apart from her right now was excruciating. "There's no point in my going to Starbright Plaza," I said. "We both know how that'll end up. They'll have covered all their bases. If I try to get the cops to check it out, I'll only wind up looking more delusional. Besides, I already took anything useful out of there." I glanced at the hard drive, still on the counter. "Which reminds me, I need to call around and see which shops have that model of Sharp copier."

"There are two at the Kinko's down the hill," she said. "The one on Ventura. You might be familiar with it."

I stared at her, slack-jawed. "You are a whirlwind of competence."

"Yeah, well, I didn't have to sleep off a stun grenade like some people." The phone rang. "That'd be Julianne. She's been calling all day."

"Why didn't you wake me?"

"I tried. But like I said, you were inanimate."

I grabbed the phone.

"Hey." Julianne's voice was rushed, intense. "I need to get those papers you're handing off to the professor taking over your classes. It's urgent."

I started to respond, then caught myself. She already knew that I'd handed those papers over to the department chair on the day before yesterday. So what was she signaling to me?

"Okay," I said carefully. "I would drop them off now, but I—"

"I'm afraid that wouldn't work anyway. I have to go to Marcello's nephew's birthday party in Coldwater Canyon Park at three."

Marcello was an only child. No nephew, no party. Julianne was trying to set a meeting with me?

"Okay," she said. "I'll call you tomorrow, and we'll pick a time then."

Before I could figure out how to tell Julianne that I didn't want to leave the house, she clicked off.

Ariana asked, "What's up?"

"She wants me to meet her at Coldwater Canyon Park." I checked my watch. "Right now. She's been looking into the Ridgeline-sonar connection for me."

"So you're going?"

I hedged.

"Patrick"—the stern tone now—"I know you don't want to leave, and I can't stand the thought of being away from you either right now, but if we're gonna have a shot at saving ourselves, we've got to go on the offensive. We have too much to handle right now. We need to split up and get it done." A nod to the mound of scraps. "I've got plenty of work ahead of me. Sorting this. Hiring you a lawyer. I'll stay here. I have the burglar alarm. And this." She patted the revolver.

"I thought you didn't know how to shoot a gun."

She took in my battered face. "I'll learn."

Hearing her say it gutted me.

I said, "They have guns, too, which they *already* know how to use. Plus, they know how to bypass the alarm system."

"Right. But they can't bypass *this*." She beckoned me into the living room and threw open the curtains. The paparazzi and reporters at the curb stumbled into motion. She waved at the flurry of lenses, then tugged the curtains shut. "Now. What's the deal with Julianne?"

"Sounds like she has something," I admitted.

"What are you hoping for?"

"Something undeniable. If I can get my hands on

concrete evidence, I bet I can get Sally Richards back into it with me."

"She told you pretty clearly she's done."

"But there's no condition," I quoted, "more motivating to her than curiosity."

"Pot, I'd like you to meet kettle."

"I just need to give her a good enough excuse."

"Your car's still at Keith Conner's, right? You need to take the pickup?" Her expression was fierce, uncompromising.

She was right. We had to attack this on two fronts.

I took a deep breath. "I can't take the pickup," I said. "The paparazzi will be all over me the minute I leave the driveway. I need to drive something more . . . anonymous."

"So borrow my license plates."

"And do what? Screw them onto the stolen BMW?" I laughed, then saw she was serious. "I'm sure the lawyer we haven't hired will be thrilled."

She pointed. "Now, go."

I pocketed the copier's hard drive, headed to the garage, and unscrewed her license plates. Then I came back in, took two of the new prepaid cell phones, and programmed each number into the other so she and I would have a way to talk on a secure line. Hers I left on the counter. Taking a deep breath, I walked over, kissed the top of her head, and started for the rear door.

Without looking up from her sorting, she said, "They're back there, too. The stalkerazzi. Surround-sound protection."

"Can you create a diversion out front? Get them running to you?"

"Okay," she said. "I'll flash them. It'll bring back my sorority days."

"You weren't in a sorority."

"Yeah, but I always feel like I missed out." She stood, dusted paper squares from her hands, and in the gold morning light I could see that her fingers were trembling. Her tone, I realized, was less breezy than defiant; she was as fearful as I was of whatever was hurtling toward us. She caught me looking, shoved her hands into her pockets.

She drew in a breath, held it. "Last night was the beginning for us, not the end," she said. "So you be goddamned careful."

The playground, on a green plot perched off intersecting canyon roads, had all the earmarks of Beverly Hills. Restaurant-packaged picnic lunches with sparkling French lemonade. Upmarket climbing apparatuses polished to a high gleam. The lone TV star with windshield-size sunglasses and a street-cred Yankees beanie, tailing a toddler and mustering up the occasional blip of feigned interest. Beautiful second wives tending newborns, the babies resembling their ugly fathers who hovered away from the sand and the concrete turtles, aggressively uninvolved, dressed in Rodeo Drive silk, reeking of cologne, poking at iPhones or yammering into earpieces, their hairlines moving one way, their waistlines another. The mothers bunched and chatted, but the husbands stood apart, lords of their own fiefdoms, their sagging eyes betraying more buyer's remorse than could penetrate the nip-and-tuck surface tension of their wives' frozen expressions of contentedness.

Julianne had chosen the park, I guessed, because everyone was famous here, or at least they all fancied themselves so. Introductions were gauche—either they knew who you were or you weren't worth knowing. Patrick Davis, in his newfound infamy and Red Sox cap, might pass unscrutinized here.

Julianne was lingering over by the swings like a spinster aunt left out at the family reunion. I parked my appropriated car, the Beemer with conveniently tinted windows, and started to get out, but my hand froze on the door handle. Gripped by a spasm of justified paranoia, I looked up the street at all the vehicles and passersby, then stayed put. I dialed.

"Where are you?" she asked after I explained.

"I'm at your nine o'clock. Turn, turn. Here."

"The Beemer?"

"That's me."

"Nice rims, Coolio. Care to fill me in?"

"It'd take too long. I owe you a big catch-up at the end of this, if I'm still standing."

"You'll owe me more than that. I spoke with my hook at *The Wash Post*. One of his colleagues has specialized in uncovering all this stuff since Clinton signed the rendition directive in '95."

"Wait a minute. All *what* stuff?"

"Ridgeline is based in Bahrain." She paused, reading my silence. "I know. Given that 'Ridgeline' doesn't exactly have an Arabic ring, I'm assuming the company is Western, but they wanted to set up as a nonreporting entity for maximum secrecy. They specialize in international executive protection."

The car interior was suddenly too warm. I tugged at my shirt, fanning it. "What's a corporation like that doing in a strip mall in Studio City?"

"Ridgeline's bodyguard business is a front for a shadow operation. Any money they're paid is untraceable once it hits Bahrain, so no one can untangle how much they get for doing what. Plus, they're hidden behind a mess of holding companies and shell corps. But once you cut through the veils, it becomes clear that Ridgeline was formed mainly to service one client: Festman Gruber."

Julianne paced around the swings, taking up her burgundy hair in the back with a restless hand. A family unloaded from a Porsche Cayenne in front of me, the youngest girl fiddling with a fake plastic cell phone. Her older sister snatched it away. "It's not a *toy*."

I said weakly, "I'm not familiar with Festman Gruber."

"Oh, they're just a seventy-billion-dollar global defense and technology company. And yes, that's a *b*. These are the kinds of guys you outsource a war to. I'm guessing they're the only type of operation, aside from one of our agencies or someone else's, that could make the moves against you that've been made. This rings all the right bells."

"Or the wrong ones."

"Whatever."

"What do they specialize in?"

"Surveillance equipment, obviously. And also—"

"Sonar."

She stopped pacing. Beside her, a just-deserted swing bucked on its chains. "Bingo."

I could see her mouth shaping the word, her voice transmitting on a half-second delay. It struck me as ridiculous that I was reduced to hiding here in a car thirty yards away rather than talking to her face-to-face.

Her hand went to her back pocket, and then she was thumbing through her notepad. "Festman's based in Alexandria."

I thought of that package I'd stolen containing the CD, sent from a FedEx center in Alexandria. And the affixed note: *Going dark. Do not contact.*

"Going dark"? A Ridgeline operative, inside Festman Gruber? Why would they have a spy inside the company that employed them? The motive, I realized, was written right on that FedEx slip: *Insurance.*

Abruptly it all made sense. Ridgeline was a cutout group hired under legit cover to do Festman Gruber's dirty work—killing Keith, which killed the movie that threatened Festman's financial interests. Ridgeline's main job was to frame me for Keith's murder so all fingers pointed at me and not at Festman Gruber. But once I'd squirmed out of the arrest, Ridgeline had wanted a little insurance of their own, some leverage in case things went south and Festman hung them out. They'd managed to infiltrate Festman or bribe someone inside to FedEx them whatever dirty secrets were hidden on that seemingly blank CD. *That's* why Ridgeline was desperate to recover the CD—to hold on to their leverage and to keep Festman from discovering the betrayal.

If Ridgeline still hadn't recovered the disc—and assuming Festman Gruber didn't know about it yet—then who the hell had broken in to our house and taken it?

Julianne was still talking. I said, "I'm sorry, what?"

"I said, Festman's based in Alexandria. But they have a satellite office here in Long Beach. Obviously they have operations on both coasts."

"Why obviously?"

"Uh, *sonar*?"

"Right, the ocean."

"Both of them. They conduct biannual RIMPAC— Rim of the Pacific—exercises, and a lot of the tech development's housed out here, too. But they've got reach everywhere."

"What's that mean?"

"It seems their critics have a higher-than-normal mortality rate. An outspoken environmental activist had a hiking accident two summers ago in Alaska, fell off a cliff. An investigative journalist in Chicago committed questionable suicide. That kind of stuff. Festman was under some pretty intense scrutiny a few years back."

"So they couldn't have another mysterious death on the books. Like, say, that of a celebrity starring in a documentary about the damages caused by their sonar system."

"Thus the need for Patrick Davis, fall guy. I mean, given how things went down, who the hell would connect Keith Conner's murder with a fucking naval-technology company? But if there's not you at the scene wielding your own bloody golf club—"

"I wasn't *wielding* it."

"Whatever. Without you there panting over the body, then maybe people start raising questions, fitting Keith into a pattern of murders that have proven convenient for Festman." She blew out a long breath, puffing her cheeks. "I think it's safe to say Ridgeline and Festman have enjoyed a fruitful relationship for a while now."

The thought of that FedEx package brought me some solace. That fruitful relationship was growing strained, Ridgeline taking countermeasures against their employer. As fearsome as my enemies were, at least now I knew where the cracks in the alliance were. The CD, wherever it was, was the holy grail for all of us.

I turned over the engine and pulled slowly out.

"I trust this is useful?" Julianne said with mock humility.

"You're amazing."

In the rearview I could see her standing in the bright light of the sandbox, phone to her ear, a hand shielding her eyes. I turned the corner, and she was gone, except for the voice in my ear.

"Take care of yourself," it said. "You're heading into uncharted waters."

CHAPTER 50

"I'm sorry, sir, you can't do that."

I was crouched in front of the copier, having swung open the panel and removed the hard drive. Even with my back turned, there was no way to insert the Ridgeline hard drive into the vacant slot without his noticing. I shoved the Kinko's hard drive down the front of my jeans before turning around, holding the other in clear view. "Oh, sorry. It just jammed up. I was checking—"

"The hard drive?" The Kinko's cashier, a highschool kid with a thatch of curly blond hair and gauged earrings, chewed listlessly on what smelled like Black Jack gum. "You can't do that. Give it to me." He swiped the Ridgeline hard drive from my hand. I almost grabbed for it, but then he leaned over and plugged it in to the copier. "Listen, if you mess with the equipment—" He did a double take, and his expression changed.

Sally and Valentine had been in here checking the computer-rental logs and probably flashing my picture. Or maybe he recognized me from the news. My bad bruises probably compounded his unease. I raised a hand awkwardly to my cheek.

He backed to the counter. "Sorry," he said. "Take your time." He pretended to bury himself in his reading, a dog-eared trade paperback of *Y: The Last Man,* but his eyes flicked at me over the tops of the pages.

I quickly key-tapped my way into the copier's memory and clicked the button to print out everything on it. My fingers drummed the counter as the machine spit out one piece of warm paper after another. Looking over my shoulder to make sure the kid wasn't calling the cops, I was too distracted to read anything. It came to about thirty pages. I paid with a spill of crumpled bills and rushed out to the car.

A cold sweat hit when I thought of Ariana at home, unprotected. I made it only a few blocks before I had to pull over and call her on the prepaid cell phone. My heart pounded until she picked up.

"You still alive?" I asked.

"No," she said. "Oh, wait. Yeah, sorry. I am."

"Paparazzi still surrounding the house?"

"Our inadvertent guardian angels? Yes, they're here. Noses to the glass."

"You call me if they leave."

"They leave, we're throwing a party."

I hung up and took a deep breath, the stack of copies heavy in my lap. Rain clouds threatened above, giving dusk a head start, and I had to click on the dome light to see the top sheet clearly.

A surveillance photo of me standing at our front window looking out at the street, the pane blurring my face. The voyeuristic view and my smudged features gave the copied photo an otherworldly feel, which sent a chill burrowing beneath my scalp.

Keith as well was tracked in a number of pictures, the time stamps indicating they were taken in the days before his death. A handwritten log, presumably derived from a wiretap, listed various numbers he'd called from home and cell phone. The next few surveillance photos followed an older gentleman in a suit, stepping out of a limo beneath a glass-and-steel building with a slick logo in the lobby window—the letter *N* on a tilt within a circle. He wore a silver goatee, and his bearing suggested justified confidence. Beneath was a copy of a cell-phone bill under the name Gordon Kazakov, with various numbers underlined. Another enemy of the board? Other grainy photos followed, featuring various men and women. Someone at a base camp in the snow—the environmental activist who'd "fallen" off a cliff? There were answers here to questions I hadn't even known to ask.

I kept flipping through. Airline tickets, hotel bills, more phone records, a bank ledger with transactions circled. Check stubs and wire confirmations. Matched to certain payments were names: *Mikey Peralta, Deborah Vance, Keith Conner.* And, sure enough, *Patrick Davis.* It read like a menu of prices—the cost to stalk, to frame, to kill.

The next page held copies of four money orders for $9,990—each just below the $10,000 bank-reporting threshold. Scrawled at the top of each one was *#1117.*

What the hell was that? Some kind of internal code? An account number? And why were these payments set apart and given prominence?

With growing astonishment I turned to the last page. A photo showed Keith sprawled dead on the floor of that hotel room. The forehead divot, the pool of ink in the eye socket, the perverted angle of the neck—it brought back the horrid epiphany of that moment with a force that made me forget to breathe. I examined the photo more closely. The wink of the flash was visible in the glass of a framed watercolor on the wall, and the time stamp showed 1:53.

Five minutes before I'd been spotted by the room-service waiter on the ground floor.

Not only could I not have been in the room at that time, but I couldn't have shot the photograph; I'd had no camera, and certainly no film when I'd been taken into custody.

My hands shook with excitement.

My name—cleared. The dots—connected.

Before DeWitt and Verrone had emptied out the office in preparation for my captivity, they'd copied these key incriminating documents, probably so all the members of Ridgeline's team could keep a packet to inoculate themselves against future threats. They'd documented their transactions with Festman Gruber all the way to the bank-account numbers on either end of each wire. If they went down, they could take Festman down, too. Mutually assured destruction. But I wasn't part of that equation. I was out of the circle, and now I had my thumb on the detonator.

I reached Sally Richards on her cell phone. There were voices in the background, what sounded like a get-together, so I said, "Give me ten seconds to talk."

She said, "Go."

"I have definitive proof clearing me of Keith's murder. I have hard evidence of the conspiracy. Like you said—justice, truth, and all that crap. Here's our shot. I can serve it to you and Valentine on a silver platter. Meet me for five minutes."

I held my breath, listened to that background noise—a radio playing, someone's joke going over big, the jangle of a dog collar. The last crescent of sun dipped behind a bank of clouds, and the sky downshifted three shades of gray. She hadn't hung up, but she hadn't replied either.

"Come on," I said. "Show me that motivating curiosity."

Silence. My hopes were dissipating along with the daylight.

Finally she exhaled across the receiver. "I've got a place."

Mulholland Drive rides the ridge of the Santa Monicas, overlooking the world. To the north the Valley stretches out like a sequined tarp, flat and unforgiving, a hothouse of trapped air and bad associations—porn, meth, movie studios. The Los Angeles Basin, cooler in all regards and eager to point that out, dips south, pushing west until ever-pricier real estate terminates in a throw of sand and the polluted Pacific. A glamorous road befitting a glamorous city, temptation and danger at every turn. It lures you to take in the view but never stops twisting. You fix on the pretty lights until you plummet to your death—L.A. in a nutshell.

Finally I turned off on a compacted dirt road, a cloud of red-brown dust rising to escort my car to the secured yellow gate. NO PARKING AFTER DUSK. Outside the gate I slotted the Beemer next to the familiar Crown Vic, grabbed the sheaf of copies, and hoofed it up to the old Nike missile control facility. A quarter mile up the dirt trail, the place waited, a Cold War relic as cracked and desiccated as Kissinger's accent.

The scattered buildings, trimmed in fallen barbed wire, had the feel of abandoned playground equipment. Rusted, forlorn, municipal. They didn't look like much, perhaps because the power of the place was never here. It was buried in missile silos in the tranquil surrounding hills.

My shoes crunched rock. The air was heavy and smelled of rain. A path wound around to the hexagonal observation tower. Following, I entered the overhang. Steep metal steps zigged and zagged with cold military precision. Educational signage sealed the structure's fate—it was now a musty museum, a gutted time capsule, a temple to an obsolete paranoia.

Khrushchev's prediction shouted from a plaque bolted to the base of the tower: WE WILL BURY YOU. Breathing in metal and dirt, I could picture the clean-shaven soldiers who had manned this facility around the clock, smoking their Lucky Strikes, eyes on the horizon, waiting for a shift change or the world to end.

The stairs—all treads, no risers—seemed to ascend into darkness. The view up filled me with dread. I didn't want to be here. I wanted to be home with my wife, the door locked behind us. But I made my way up, the structure rigid against the night wind. Air whistled past the railings, through the mesh-steel steps, but the tower itself didn't creak or groan. It was built in a time when they knew how to build things.

By the time I reached the top, I was slightly winded. Sally was standing near the edge, leaning on a sturdy pay telescope, looking out at the panoramic darkness. Her flat eyes took note of me. "They say on a clear day you can see Catalina."

Pacing tight circles, his dark face shiny with sweat, Valentine could have been on bomber lookout himself. "I told you, Richards, I don't like this Deep Throat shit."

I asked, "Did Robbery-Homicide seize a CD from my house yesterday?"

"No," Sally said. "At least not officially." She grew uneasy under Valentine's outraged glare. "I've been keeping tabs on the case," she told him. "Word in the halls, that's it."

"You're flirting with dismissal here, Richards." He threw up his hands and started for the stairs. "I'm not going down this path with you."

"We're here," she said. "We see what he has. That's all."

I said, "I have a copied photograph of Keith Conner's corpse taken five minutes before I entered the room."

Sally's mouth tensed, but Valentine continued as if I weren't there. "This is *way* too hot a potato for us. The captain was clear as fuck what would happen to our asses if we went sniffing. I got four boys to take care of, so yes, thank you, keeping my job and pension would be a nice way to go into next week."

I held out the picture of Keith's body, and Sally shoved herself skeptically off the telescope and walked over. After taking a defiant pause to eye my bruised face, she squinted down at the page. For a moment her expression was unchanged, but then she swallowed sharply and color crept into her cheeks. "Even if the time stamp is doctored," she said, "you didn't have a camera." She couldn't lift her eyes from the picture. Her hand reached for the railing, groping the air, and then she caught it and leaned a sturdy hip into the structure, as if grounding herself. "What else?"

I fanned through a few surveillance shots of Keith. "These were taken by a company named Ridgeline. Two of their men kidnapped me."

Sally's eyebrows lifted a few centimeters.

I held up a hand. "I know. I'll explain. But first let me lay out motive. Keith was making a documentary that condemned naval sonar for killing whales."

"*The Deep End,*" Sally said. "Dolphins, too, I've heard."

"There's a vote coming up in the Senate to lower the decibel levels of naval sonar. Keith's documentary was timed to influence that decision. A company named Festman Gruber is a huge contractor specializing in sonar equipment. I'm guessing they've got a lot to lose if that Senate vote doesn't swing their way."

Valentine pleaded with Sally, "Can we please call this before we catch crazy?"

"So they knocked off Keith and framed you?" Sally's lips were pursed in a faint, worried smile. "What do you have to back up that elaborate theory?"

"I have banking, wire, and phone records tying Ridgeline to Festman Gruber. I have the names of murder victims written next to specific payments."

I flipped through the documents to show them off,

Sally frowning down at them, biting her lip. Despite himself, Valentine crowded in, peering over her shoulder.

"And," I said, "I have these weird withdrawals they made."

"Weird how?" Valentine said.

"There's some code attached to them. Right here." I turned the page, pointed at the money orders with *#1117* written across the top.

Valentine looked down and almost absentmindedly snapped open the thumb break on his holster. His hand jittered once above the pistol grip, a seesaw of indecision. Then, with a single fluid motion, he lifted the Glock from the leather and shot Sally in the chest.

CHAPTER 51

A plume of blood erupted from Sally's shirt. She took a thundering step back, her weight cocked above a bent leg, and then collapsed. Valentine and I stared on in horror as she shuddered and gasped, and then he lifted the barrel weakly and aimed it at me.

The muzzle sparked again, and I felt the air move by my head, but I was already leaping for the stairs, the documents crumpling around my fist. I landed halfway down the top flight, my shoulder ringing off a rail, my momentum carrying my body up over my head. I hit the landing on a roll and half scrambled, half fell down the switchback, putting all that metal between me and Valentine. Skidding to a painful halt, mesh steel digging into my back, I could hear Valentine up there.

"Oh, Jesus. You're hurt. Why'd you have to go and do this, Richards? You *had to* push it. I tried to talk you off it, but there you went. Wouldn't let it go. You're hurt, Christ, you're hurt. You left me no choice. You left me *no* choice."

A moist gurgling. Liquid tapping metal.

A low moan, which I realized wasn't Sally but Valentine. It rose to an almost feminine scream, accompanied by a violent series of blows—him banging his fist against the deck?

He was sobbing. "I couldn't go down for this. I go away, who's gonna take care of my boys?"

But she wasn't saying anything back.

"I'm sorry," he wept. "I'm sorry. C'mon, open your eyes, Richards. Open your eyes. Gimme a pulse now. Oh, Jesus, I'm sorry."

I folded the documents and shoved them into my pocket, wincing at the crinkling. The wind kicked up a bit more, drowning out the shrill serenade of the crickets.

As I edged down another flight, Valentine seemed to perceive my movement and return to his senses. I heard the chirp of his radio, and then he bellowed, "Officer down! I have an officer down on the observation tower of the Nike facility off dirt Mulholland. Send backup and medical *now*!" His voice wavered, and I realized that even my own mind-numbing shock didn't compare to his. He panted for a moment, catching his breath, then continued, "The perpetrator, Patrick Davis, wrestled away my gun and shot her. I have my partner's weapon and am in pursuit. Over."

Dispatch came back in a burst of concerned static, and the volume eased down, and then it was him and me, breathing in the silence.

Valentine's shoes moved slowly across the platform, then onto the stairs. Two flights below, enveloped in a kind of calm terror, I shadowed his steps, quiet and steady. The thought of that picture on Sally's desk, her holding her toddler, threw me into a moment of denial. It didn't seem possible for me to have witnessed what I'd just witnessed.

He was coming a little faster, the shadows from his legs flickering through the gaps between steps. I sped up. Another flight and I would run out of room. Then it would be a dash in the dark with a loaded gun behind me.

I reached the bottom, and he was still coming strong, shoes clanging. For a suspended moment, I looked ahead at the path that would leave me vulnerable to a bullet in the back.

The options were clear: run and get shot or turn and counterattack.

On heavy legs I ducked back under the stairs. The dirt sloped up hard beneath the first flight. I pressed myself into the darkness beneath the landing, my body starting to register the pain from my tumble. My breath was firing, and I fought to tamp it quietly back into my chest.

My sneaker lost purchase on the angle, and I nearly went down, broadcasting my position, but my hand flew up through the gap where a riser would be and hooked a stair tread, stabilizing me.

Valentine's footsteps quickened, then slowed as soon as his shoes drew into view on the next flight up. He was bracing for an ambush. The toe of his loafer gleamed with blood, so dark it looked black, and the cuff of his slacks was smeared. As he descended, I let go of the step, withdrawing my hand carefully. The treads carved him into horizontal slivers—shoe and ankle, thigh and waist, chest and neck—but when he eased his weight down onto the landing above me,

I caught a clear view of the Glock he held firmly before him with both hands on the grip.

He slowed some more. The wind was up and would have covered the sound of my doubling back. But had he spotted me? Or guessed?

His next step carried him out of view, directly overhead, the landing blocking him from sight. I realized I was holding my breath, and I couldn't now exhale. My lungs burned. His shoe padded down onto metal. And then again. Through the gap I saw the gun come into view first, and I nearly gave in to panic and bolted. But it wasn't pointed down at me; it was drifting five feet above the stairs. His hands slid into view, his wrists, his forearms. He was aiming up the path, breathing hard. His loafer set down on the top step, no more than six inches from my eyes. I could smell the bitter tint of blood on the soles. His other foot touched down on the second tread, seemingly in slow motion.

My hands floated in front of my face, half raised, quaking in the darkness. I watched his heel drop flat, a millimeter at a time. For an awful instant, I froze up. But then everything inside me broke free in a burst of terrified fury. Reaching through the steps, I seized his ankles and ripped them toward me as hard as I could.

He bellowed, tumbling violently, and then his torso struck metal with a clang and a gunshot exploded, amplified off the surrounding metal. He lurched down a few more steps on his face and chest before rolling over and jerking to a halt, his hand dangling into view off the side. He grumbled something unintelligible, and then the night gave over to the crickets and an odd sucking sound that came at uneven intervals.

I stayed crouched, frozen, waiting for who knew what, until I saw the dark drops working their way through the steel mesh of the bottom stair and tapping the dirt below. I crept out.

He'd wound up in a leaned-back sitting position at the base of the stairs. His eyes rolled to and fro, straining, the whites pronounced in the dull moonlight, but as I tentatively approached, they tracked over and fixed on me. He had a tiny hole in his side at the base of his ribs, the tear in the white shirt no bigger than a penny. The surrounding fabric had darkened, the blotch the size of a Frisbee. His right hand, bent unnaturally, clutched the Glock. His finger remained threaded through the trigger guard. His chest lurched, and his lung gave off that sucking sound, fluttering the torn cloth at the edge of the bullet hole.

The right lapel of his sport jacket was flung back, a band of moonlight falling through the crisscross stairs to illuminate the revealed badge at his belt, with that all-too-familiar number.

LAPD 1117.

His hand firmed around the Glock, and I tensed, but he couldn't seem to lift his arm from his side to aim it at me. The ledge of his brow lowered with exertion. He jerked his head, and one of his legs stiffened, and the gun fired down into the dirt. And again. And again. The reports rolled off across the hills, across the blanketing trees and hidden missile silos. The recoil from the next shot knocked the gun from his hand. He looked down at it helplessly, tears mixing with his sweat.

The next sucking sound from his lung was fainter. His legs twitched, and then the fabric no longer fluttered at the edges of the hole in his shirt. His stare stayed fixed on me, every bit as alive as it had been moments before.

I had sunk to one knee before him, as if in fearful worship of the act I'd just committed. Through the roar of my thoughts, I could feel nothing.

Bolted to the wall to Valentine's left, Khrushchev's words addressed the bloody aftermath: WE WILL BURY YOU.

A loud hum sounded, breaking my trance, and I jerked back, tripping over my heels. Cautiously, I rose. It came again, vibrating Valentine's shirt pocket.

I approached his body with trepidation; my nerves were sandpapered raw. Keeping my head pulled back, I reached over and tugged a Palm Treo from his pocket.

A text message read:

YOUR CASH AT USUAL DROP POINT.

WE'RE MOVING IN NOW.

THIS MESSAGE CHAIN WILL ERASE IN 17 SECONDS.

16.

15.

Moving in *where*?

A chill crept across my bruised shoulders. The message was a reply. Furiously, I clicked back to the original note Valentine had sent:

HE'LL BE OUT OF HOUSE AT 8:00.
MULTIPLE UNITS WILL RESPOND TO A FAKE
BREAK-IN CALL TWO DOORS UP TO DRAW
PAPARAZZI AWAY.
SHE WILL BE ALONE.

CHAPTER 52

Stunned, I stared at the glowing screen, words disintegrating into letters, my brain lurching to comprehend and shield myself at the same time. The message vanished, a crumpling sound announcing the auto-erase, but the letters seemed to remain, floating in the darkness. They became words again, their meaning shattering my paralysis.

I caught up to myself ten feet down the dirt path, sprinting, dialing my wife on a dead man's phone. The Glock was shoved in the back of my jeans, the documents crammed in my pocket, digging into my thigh. The sole reception bar blinked out every time I pressed "send." By the time I hit the dirt road, the screen showed a satellite dish rotating haplessly—nothing.

Without slowing, I dug out the throwaway phone, held it in my other hand, glanced from one screen to the next. No signal from either, not up here in the hills at the fringe of the Topanga State Park.

The cell-phone clock read 7:56 P.M. Four minutes and they'd be clear to breach our house.

The ground was a confusion of ruts and mounds, and I stumbled in the dark, going down and skinning my palms, the phone and Treo skidding from my grip. I groped, found the throwaway, and after a few seconds of searching gave up on the Treo—the incriminating message had autotrashed anyway, and the reception was just as crappy. Clutching the phone, I kept sprinting, holding the damn lit screen in front of my face as I hurtled forward in the blackness, letting my legs figure out the terrain on their own.

SHE WILL BE ALONE.

No signal. No signal. No signal.

A light rain had opened up, softening the ground that kept duplicating itself beneath my feet, a potholed treadmill. The same hillside kept whistling by. Wheezing, drenched in sweat, I was stuck in a horror-movie loop.

Finally the yellow gate cut the dark, and I flew through, clipping the post with a shoulder, the collision spinning me in a half circle and depositing me on the hood of the BMW. I leaped into the car, peeling out, heading toward home, toward cell-phone coverage, the crappy throwaway clenched in my wet hand so I could steer the curves and watch the signal.

At last it gave me a bar. It wavered but came back, and the call went through. It rang and rang, and finally—

"Ari!"

"Patrick?"

"They're coming for you! Get the hell out of the house!"

But she couldn't hear me now. "I just got out of the

shower. I moved the pickup around back for you to use from now on, so get rid of the stolen car before you come back here. But listen—you're not gonna *believe* what I taped together." Sirens wailed faintly in the background. "Hang on. This is weird."

Her breathing shifted as she hustled down the stairs, the noise of the sirens growing louder.

I was shouting, as if volume, not reception, were the problem. "They called in a diversion up the street so the paparazzi will follow and leave our house open. Grab the gun and get out of there. Go to the cops. Ari? *Ari!*"

Oblivious to my yelling, she continued, "All these cop cars passed our house, but they're not coming here. Looks like they're up at the Weetmans. I wonder if Mike got framed for killing a movie star, too."

The signal cut out. I looked down at the phone in disbelief. A horn blared; I'd drifted into the wrong lane. Screeching over, I veered off the road, kicking up a plume of dirt, then overcompensated again, wobbling back across the center lane and narrowly missing a Maserati. I righted the BMW, skidding around a rain-slick turn and leaving the clutch of the hillside.

Two bars. Now three.

I dialed.

She picked up. "Hi. Lost you. I was saying—"

"Get out of the house. *Right* now. Run up the street to the cops."

The piercing scream of our alarm. "Shit, Patrick, someone's—"

Thundering footsteps. The phone dropping. Ariana's yell was severed abruptly, and an instant later the alarm shut off.

The Beemer scraped along the hillside, sending a pattering of rocks across the roof and reminding me I was driving. Sweat stung my eyes. I was screaming into the phone, but I didn't know what I was saying.

Some muffled directions: "Have her finish getting dressed. We don't want to drag her around half naked. You, stop resisting or we'll break an arm. Move it."

And then a rustle as the phone was plucked from the floor. A calm voice. Verrone's. "We're done playing now." The calm tenor brought back the memory of his jaundiced complexion, that droopy mustache.

"Don't hurt her."

"We need that disc."

"I don't have it. I swear to fucking God, if I had it I would've given it to you."

"You told us you had it. You just sent us to the wrong hiding place."

It took a moment for me to realize that the sirens were now not on the other end of the phone but approaching me. Coming around the bend, I saw six police cars and an ambulance heading at me, lights flashing, sirens screeching. Instinctively, I shrank away from my window, but they blasted by, heading for Valentine and Richards. I had to shout over the high-pitched wailing. "You *kidnapped* me! I would have said anything to get away!"

"You have two hours to find it."

The dropping of that ultimatum, a tank in my path, brought the horror of my situation home to roost. I'd scrambled and forged ahead, despite a false imprisonment and a real one, despite being set up and shot at, despite a concussion grenade dropped in my lap, and still it hadn't been enough. The helplessness I'd been fighting to hold at bay and the rage at having my life seized from my own control flooded in, overwhelming me. A hundred and twenty minutes from now, my wife would no longer be alive.

I yelled, *"How am I supposed to fucking find something when I don't know where it is?"*

"Then you're useless to us. Which means we can shoot her now." Over the phone: "Go ahead."

"Wait! Okay, okay. I have it." I cringed, listening, breathless. But no gunshot followed. "I . . . I . . ." I was falling into terror, grasping at anything, trying to formulate a story, any story that would buy us time. Did I dare to reveal the only cards I held—those incriminating documents I'd retrieved from their copy machine? Right off the bat, in a state of panic, with no guiding strategy? Where did that leave me to go? There had to be something else. It seemed I hadn't spoken in hours, though the delay was probably no more than a few seconds. "I put the disc in our safe-deposit box," I blurted. "I can't get it until the bank opens in the morning."

"You have until nine o'clock."

"Richards is dead," I said. "Valentine is dead." A cold silence as Verrone reassessed the chessboard. But I didn't wait for his next move; I pushed forward while he was off balance. "I'm *wanted* now. I need some time to get clear and figure out who to send in to grab the disc from the safe-deposit box in the morning." Still no response. I added, "A couple extra hours even."

Stop talking—you're negotiating with yourself.

He pulled the phone away again as he spoke to DeWitt or whoever else. "Take her out back, watch her closely over the fence. Paparazzi should be up the street chasing their tails, but keep an eye out just in case. Listen, sweetheart, if anyone's out there, we're all friends heading out for a drive. That's the better of the two ways to do this. If you struggle or scream, we'll shoot whoever we see and drag you anyway. . . . What? Yes, get it, it'll look more normal. Now, go."

Get *what*?

Look more normal?

What the hell did that mean?

Verrone had come back to me. "Fine. You have until noon tomorrow. And you'd better stay away from the cops. You're useless to us in custody. Call your wife's cell-phone number—her *real* cell phone, not that disposable crap you've been playing around with. We'll have it patched through to an untraceable line, so don't bother playing Maxwell Smart. If that phone doesn't ring by noon with good news, we will put a bullet in the base of her skull. And yes, this time it's real."

The phone cut out.

My brain vacillated between high-rev panic and complete blank-out. I remember passing another convoy of police cars. I remember telling myself to slow down, since I couldn't risk getting pulled over, but I also remember not obeying. I remember screeching over the curb, scattering the paparazzi, and leaving the Beemer sunk in our wet front lawn, car door open in the slanting rain, dinging.

And then I was inside the quiet of our entry, dripping. On the floor by the living-room window, a broken teacup. The prepaid cell phone. And a lavender mariposa.

I crouched over the fallen flower, my heart thundering. Instinct brought it to my nose—the smell of her. Across the room, Ariana and I gazed out from our fallen wedding photo. The symbolism was obtrusive, sure, but it cut me to ribbons nonetheless. The arty black-and-white, our stiff formality, and the fragmented glass imbued the image with a haunted, bygone feel. A past age, dated conventions, ghosts of happier days. Looking at her soft-focus face, I made a silent vow: *I promise.*

The thought of her, trapped between DeWitt and Verrone in the back of some van, nearly brought me to my knees. But I couldn't give in to fear, not now. How much time did I have before the cops found Valentine and Richards and came here?

I tried to collect my frayed thoughts. Was there anything in the house I had to take with me before I fled? When I'd first reached Ari, she'd been excited about something she'd figured out: *You're not gonna believe what I taped together.* Had they found whatever she'd come up with, or was it still here?

I ran into the family room. Aside from a few scraps, they'd gathered up and taken the mounds of shredded documents.

Taped together, she'd said. Taped.

I rushed into the kitchen. The mess on the floor remained from when the cops had tossed the house— trash dumped, drawers emptied. I couldn't spot any Scotch tape in the mound, and I doubted that Ari would've rooted through in search of it. Which left my office.

I bolted upstairs. Sure enough, on my desk was a plastic tape dispenser and beside it a round piece of paper composed of taped-together bits.

A *disc*?

I snatched it up. It was made of the white-silver squares she'd noted in the confetti jumble, those scraps that had stood out as firmer than the others. I bent the CD. Stiff but flexible. I'd seen discs like this before, hip-hop promotional singles slipped into *Vanity Fair* or the occasional DVD in *Variety* before awards season.

They'd destroyed this CD along with other documents before clearing out the Ridgeline office. The Frankenstein disc was beyond salvaging, but I didn't have to put it into a computer to realize that a CD like this, with a pliable, thinner design, had certain advantages for an operation like theirs. Easier to shred.

And easier to hide.

Rain tattooed the roof, a drumroll score to my quickening thoughts.

I closed my eyes, pictured opening that FedEx envelope addressed to Ridgeline. That blank CD, wrapped protectively in corrugated cardboard.

What if that disc really had been nothing more than what it appeared—a blank CD? If someone like me intercepted the package, I'd think it contained nothing more than that useless disc. But the intended recipient would see the blank CD as a symbol, a key showing what was *really* being shipped in the same package.

I ran down to the kitchen and dug through the trash. There it was, beneath a half loaf of moldy bread and a PowerBar box. The corrugated cardboard that I'd thought was mere packaging material. Flattening the bent sheet, I wormed my thumbnails into the edge and peeled it apart.

Sunk in a beveled well inside was a white-silver disc.

CHAPTER 53

A rush of excitement overtook me. Their CD had been here in the house the whole time, lying on the floor, buried in trash—the one place no one would think to look for it. I plucked it out, held it to the light, appraising it like a jeweler.

So it *had* been Ridgeline who'd broken in to search our house and steal back their FedEx package. Wanting to recover every piece of evidence, they'd taken the envelope, shipping label, and blank CD. But since the cardboard packaging had been missing, they'd assumed I'd figured out what was hidden inside and that I'd moved it to a safe place. So they'd lured me to Keith's, dropped a grenade in my lap, then posed as cops to get me to cough up where I'd secreted the disc. It never occurred to them that I'd taken the packaging for trash and dumped it on the heap on the kitchen floor.

The thrill of discovery was undercut by a thin, warbling siren in the distance. And then another.

I grabbed a wad of cash and the pickup keys from Ariana's purse, then spun in a full circle in the kitchen, sizing up everything, trying to think what else from the house I needed.

What had Ariana asked to take with her before they'd

hauled her out? Verrone's odd words chewed at me: *What? Yes, get it, it'll look more normal. Now, go.*

The sirens, louder.

Ariana's keys in hand, the precious disc padded by the copied documents in my pocket, I ran out the rear door into the inviting darkness. Thank God she'd moved the pickup around back for me. Running across the lawn, rain spitting at my face, I could hear the squeal of tires from the front. Verrone had narrowed the situation to a simple equation: If the cops captured me, she would die.

And so now I fled out the back, along the same route they'd forced her to move. *If anyone's out there, we're all friends heading out for a drive,* Verrone had told her. He needed her to look as inconspicuous as possible. His reply to whatever she'd said came again: *Yes, get it, it'll look more normal.*

I halted. Turned my face up to the raindrops, felt the pitter-patter across my cheeks.

Raining, I thought. *Jacket.*

Play the hand you're dealt.

I spun and sprinted back into the house, my wet sneakers skidding through trash on the sleek kitchen floor. Blue and red lights flashed through the front curtains. Voices, boots stomping up the walk. I ran toward them, to the coat closet by the entry.

Someone shouted, and then a battering ram shuddered the front door. The bottom panels bent in, but the dead bolt held.

I threw open the closet door and peered in. Five hangers, an old bomber jacket, and a jumble of shoes. But no raincoat.

It'll look more normal. More inconspicuous for a woman heading out in a downpour. She'd manipulated them into letting her grab her raincoat. With their transmitter stitched into the lining. A transmitter they didn't know that we knew about.

A transmitter that maybe I could figure out how to track.

Shoes slippery on the floorboards, I careened back into the kitchen out of view just as a sonic boom announced the front door's disintegration. Gable's voice, commanding and husky with adrenaline, "Clear the upstairs. Go-go-*go.*"

The walls shook. Pounding footsteps and shouted directives conveyed not just brisk efficiency but wrath. They were gunning for a cop killer, a murderer who'd shot holes through two of their own.

I flew across the back lawn, leaping up onto the fence and spotting a pair of squad cars slant-parked in front of the grille of Ari's pickup, blocking off the street. Patrolmen climbing out, talking—they'd missed the white flash of my face in the night. I dropped to the silent mulch by the greenhouse, my chest heaving.

One said, "You hear that?"

My knee had struck the slats, a rasp that reverberated like thunder in my memory.

Brush and branches half obscured me. In the windows of both floors, I could see SWAT officers wielding semiautos. Upstairs, a face shielded with tactical goggles tilted toward my office desk, rifled papers fluttering up into view.

Behind me and the fence, the click of a flashlight, and then a beam prowled the branches overhead, ticking back and forth as the cop approached. From the house a voice, heightened against the nighttime quiet, called out, "Sweep the backyard!" and I saw a balaclava-hooded head, moving in concert with the barrel of an MP5, float across the kitchen window toward the back door.

My bloodless fist, cinched around Ariana's useless keys, stood out against the dark ground. Pressed to my kidney, the pistol beckoned. I touched my hand to the grip, then pulled away as if it had burned my palm. What was I going to do? Draw down on a SWAT team?

Crunched against the slats at the base of the fence, my back picked up the vibration of footsteps closing in from beyond. Cobwebs draped across my wet brow. Across the yard the knob of our back door jostled. Directly above me a meaty hand hooked over the top of the fence.

Wedged in the angle where splintering wood met moist earth, I had nowhere left to go. My mouth cottoning, I looked around frantically.

Through a skein of dusty sumac, I spotted the section of sagging fence between our yard and the Millers'. A post had keeled over, leaving a break in the slats. I scrambled on all fours, gliding across the soft mulch.

The cop's boots knocked the fence, and I heard him grunting, trying to pull his weight up for a look. Across the lawn the SWAT officer kicked through the rear door, the knob taking a bite from the outside wall.

Behind me the cop landed on our side of the fence with a *harrumph*. I whistled through the gap onto the

Millers' property an instant before our backyard lit up with intersecting flashlight beams. Rolling to the side, I found my feet in Martinique's flower bed. I scurried across the well-kept back lawn, crossed the stamped-concrete patio in a few strides, and swung into their kitchen through the rear door.

Martinique lowered the salad bowl she was scrubbing with ridiculous yellow kitchen gloves and regarded me, her mouth slightly agape. I'd frozen as well, my feet still on the outside step but my weight forward on the hand gripping the doorknob. Beyond her in the family room, his back to us, Don sat watching CNBC with the volume raised. The only movement was the financial pundit raving about the subprime crisis and the kitchen faucet going full blast, spewing a vibrating column of water. I barely dared to move my eyes to take in the room. To my right, their washer and dryer, the lids heaped with dirty clothes, the day's mail, and Don's laptop carrier. Five steps forward, the door to the garage.

Martinique turned her head, her mouth open to call to Don, but something stopped her.

I mouthed, *Help me.*

Car tires splashed water out front, and blue light came wavering across the sponge-painted ceiling. "The hell you think that jackass got up to now?" Don said, standing and dropping the remote onto the cushion. "I'll go upstairs, see what I can see from the den." He turned, draining his scotch. Not bothering to look up at Martinique and me, he set the glass on the sofa table, said, "This is dirty, too," and trudged to the stairs. Neither she nor I had breathed.

Finally her eyes swiveled to the window, the flash-light beams along the fence line now. For a moment I thought she was going to cry out for help.

But her voice came in a low purr. "I'm not getting involved." Her mouth grim, she set down the salad bowl, walked past me, wafting the scent of almond soap, and pulled open a cupboard above the washing machine. Jangling from a silver hook, the keys to Don's Range Rover. "I have too many dishes to clean to notice a goddamned thing."

She returned to the sink, dutifully pulled another bowl from the stack, and went to work on it, hum-ming. I crossed the space, unhooked the keys, and stepped into the garage.

Then I came back and grabbed Don's laptop. Mar-tinique didn't so much as glance over, but I swore I detected a hint of satisfaction in the set of her mouth.

The garage door opened smoothly, on well-greased tracks. A SWAT van and police cars clogged the street in front of our curb, and the house was inundated with uniforms. Our front and side yards were crawling with cops, too—a marksman had even climbed up to check the roof—but their main focus was bushes, shadows, and radios. The upstairs hall window framed Gable's face; he was glowering out as if picking a fight with the darkness, his gaze passing blankly over the lawn, the street, the black Range Rover creeping from the neighbor's garage.

Signaling like a good citizen, I pulled out and turned left down the hill.

CHAPTER 54

Parked in an alley behind a gas station, I looked at the items I'd carried out of the fray, aligned neatly on the passenger seat. Don's laptop. A sheaf of twice-folded documents, wrinkled from my pocket and moist from rainfall. And the real-life MacGuffin, a white-silver disc.

The golf hat from Don's backseat was tugged down over my scraped-up face, the pistol hidden in the back of my jeans. I'd switched out the Range Rover's license plates with those from a pea green Buick reposing in an apartment carport. I needed to buy time before the theft was noticed, and the Buick's plate frame—ZACHARY AND SAGE'S GRANDMA!—hinted that the owner probably wouldn't be heading out to trip the light fantastic at 9:30 P.M. Boosting cars wasn't bad enough; I'd been reduced to stealing from a granny.

With nervous anticipation I booted up Don's Toshiba and started to insert the CD. But I hesitated with it halfway in. Did I *want* to know what it contained? Once I did, could they let me live? Curiosity tormented me, but I fought it off, withdrawing the CD and placing it back on the leather, where it glared up at me. Whatever was on it would surely open up another world of trouble, and I couldn't afford to have any more distractions between me and Ariana.

The longer I delayed, the greater the likelihood that the cops would catch up to me. Or that Ariana's kidnappers would lose patience with her or find her inconvenient. The smartest move would be to call Verrone now and tell him I had the CD. He'd know I'd lied about the safe-deposit box, but as long as I had what he wanted, I couldn't see why he'd care.

The throwaway cell phone had run out of juice, so I turned on my trusty Sanyo. Jerry had said that calls a few minutes long were tough to track, so I'd keep it short. Rehearsing what I was about to say, I punched in Ariana's number. My thumb hovered over "send." But something wouldn't let me put the call through.

Maybe it was the image of Mikey Peralta laid out in that hospital bed, fist-sized dent in his forehead. Or the crimson halo spreading on the floor beneath Deborah Vance's hair. I wanted desperately to believe that as long as I didn't set eyes on whatever that CD contained, Ariana and I would be safe. I wanted to believe that if I gave the Ridgeline crew what they wanted, we could shake hands and walk away. But the truth I didn't want to acknowledge was what was freezing my thumb over that "send" button. And that reality made itself known now, like a punch to the gut: My wife and I had *already* crossed the point of no return.

With two dead cops, a pair of kidnappings, and RHD and SWAT gunning for me, everything had spun out of control for Ridgeline, as it had for me. There was no way they could still entertain the notion that they could rein this back into a simple frame-up and leave me holding the bag.

Before the plan had derailed, they had needed me alive to insulate Festman Gruber, their employer, from suspicion in Keith's murder. But now Verrone, DeWitt, and whoever else constituted Ridgeline seemed to have switched to full-blown damage-control mode. Their objective now was self-preservation. Which meant acquiring leverage. Covering their asses. And eliminating witnesses. Mikey Peralta's "car accident" and Deborah Vance's "revenge shooting" were pretty good indications of what they planned to do to me and Ariana once our usefulness was exhausted. We knew too much now. We'd *seen* too much. They'd keep Ari on the hook just long enough to lure me in.

Aside from those copied documents, the CD staring up at me was my only ammunition.

If I delivered it to Ridgeline, they'd kill me and my wife.

I looked down at the phone, those ten digits glowing on the screen. Then at the CD on the passenger seat. The phone. The CD. Phone. CD.

It was time to change the plan. To go on the offensive.

The only way to beat them was to outplay them at their own game.

With a renewed sense of purpose, I turned off the phone, fired up the computer, and slotted in the CD. A single PDF file popped up, which I double-clicked. Fifteen pages, charted by the right scroll bar. Tables and graphs. A CONFIDENTIAL stamp, conspicuous yet translucent, halved each page at a diagonal. The cover sheet stated, Festman Gruber—internal document only—do not reproduce, followed by a few paragraphs of dense legal threats.

I clicked from page to page, scanning numbers and columns, waiting for the data to take shape. A graph on the tenth page, labeled "Internal Study," spelled it out plainly enough even for my geometry skills, atrophied since sophomore year of high school.

Three lines charted sonar decibels across various months. The blue one, a steady horizontal, showed the existing legal limits. Another, flying high above the law, indicated the decibels reached by Festman Gruber's sonar system. They peaked north of three hundred decibels, well above even the figure Keith had thrown at me through a puff of clove smoke from his deck chair.

In other words, illegal activity.

A green line across the bottom of the page, far beneath the legal limits, puzzled me. The key labeled it simply *NV.*

The letters tugged at a memory, tripping an image I'd seen in the documents I'd pulled off the Ridgeline copy machine's hard drive. Grabbing the papers, I shuffled past the creepy picture of me, past Keith Conner's phone records, past those money order slips positioned like dominos, finally finding the surveillance shot of the older man with a silver goatee exiting a limousine. The next picture of him included the image I was looking for, a logo painted on the lobby window of the high-rise in the background. The logo was an elegant one: Encompassed by a ring, an *N* quarter-turned like a dial so the letter's diagonal and second upright suggested a *V.*

NV, all tied up in a neat little circle.

So it was a corporation.

I studied the gleam off the limo's wax job, the formidable building, the man's confident bearing. It all seemed to suggest that he was someone high up at NV. The fact that he'd been placed under Ridgeline surveillance, in turn, suggested that his company was a rival to Festman Gruber.

I needed a name.

Beneath the photo was a copy of a cell-phone bill that belonged to a Gordon Kazakov. Several of the phone numbers were underlined, but they meant nothing to me.

I drove off, searching for a Starbucks. In Brentwood that took four blocks. I tucked the Range Rover into the curb in front, close enough to pirate their wireless Internet signal, then neurotically slotted a few quarters in the meter, though it was well past the hours of operation. My eyes swept the window and caught on a wall clock over the espresso machine— 10:05.

Less than sixteen hours until Ridgeline would kill my wife.

The light banter and scent of java from inside struck at my nerves, reminding me how far I'd skidded off the tracks. With the hat brim pulled low over my bruised face, I turned from all that light and warmth and scurried back to the vehicle. Door locked, laptop open, and voilà—a Linksys Internet connection.

Google Images spit out a number of pictures for Gordon Kazakov, the man in the surveillance shot. A few clicks showed him to be the CEO of North Vector, NV of the nifty logo, a Fortune 1000 powerhouse specializing in—surprise—global defense and technology. In addition, he owned two football teams in Eastern Europe, a low-fare airline with a hub in Minneapolis, and a historic mansion in Georgetown. But the most interesting bit of news was hidden in a recent *Wall Street Journal* profile. Though North Vector had made no official announcements, the article suggested that it had a revolutionary sonar system nearing viability.

A competing system that—according to the smuggled document—functioned using not just legal but markedly reduced decibel levels. The comparison, judging by the graph, didn't look flattering for Festman.

The muscles at the base of my neck had tightened into knots so unyielding that they felt inanimate when I reached back to knead them. Closing my eyes, I ran through what I knew, searching out the hairline crack where I could drive in a wedge.

Ridgeline had been hired by Festman Gruber to do their dirty bidding—to make sure that nothing interfered with Festman's defense contracts until that Senate vote went through. But Ridgeline seemed to be growing increasingly distrustful of their employers. They'd started keeping backup records of the illegal activity they conducted on behalf of Festman. They'd even gone so far as to acquire a confidential internal study showing Festman's sonar system to be operating outside legal parameters, a document that, if leaked properly, could probably do more damage to Festman's pocketbook than a Keith Conner documentary.

I massaged my temples, considered the angles. I thought about something Ariana had told me the night we'd received that first menacing phone call and discovered the cameras in the walls. We were huddled out in the greenhouse, running through our lack of options, and she'd said in exasperation, *We don't* know *people big enough to help us.*

For a good time, I stared at Gordon Kazakov's cell-phone bill. Then I called the bold number in the header. Five rings. Seven. No voice mail?

I was about to hang up when a voice answered. Smooth as bourbon.

I said, "Gordon Kazakov?"

"Who is this?"

"The enemy of your enemy."

A pause. "Who's my enemy?"

I said, "Festman Gruber."

"I'd like a name, please, sir."

I took a breath. "Patrick Davis."

"I see that they've been busy on your behalf."

How could he know that? But I was eager to finish the call and turn off my Sanyo again before the signal could be traced. So I got to the point. "I have something you want."

"I'll meet you."

"That'll be difficult," I said. "Don't you live in Georgetown?"

"I'm in Los Angeles," he said. "I promised my wife she could meet Keith Conner. That was before, of course, but I'd booked some business the first part of the week."

My bewildered silence must have spoken volumes, because he said, by way of explanation, "The first day of production was to be Monday."

"Wait a minute," I said. "You were involved with the movie?"

"Son," he chuckled, "I was financing it."

CHAPTER 55

Hotel Bel-Air, tucked into twelve bucolic acres of priceless real estate, was of course where a Gordon Kazakov would stay. With their sheltering trees, private paths, and white-noise brook, the grounds were the embodiment of discretion. The hush-voiced staff had played host to royalty of every definition, from Judy Garland to Princess Di. Marilyn Monroe and Joe DiMaggio used to sneak off here to get away, and now I was doing some nonroyal sneaking of my own, past the dinner patrons trickling out with their eco-farmed furs and bloody lipstick.

Ari and I had come here for an anniversary meal once, though we couldn't afford to stay the night. Intimidated by the waiters, I'd overtipped, which was probably undertipping. We'd sidled out, thanking everyone too profusely, and I'd never been back. Until now.

Having parked up Stone Canyon, I took a path along the brook to dodge the valets. A foursome strolled over the bridge above me, and Keith Conner's name sailed from the low murmur of their conversation as if it were aimed at me. Lowering my face, I kept walking, and so did they. The rain had stopped, leaving the air clean and sharp with the scent of vegetation. Passing three floating swans and as many signs warning of their temperament, I headed under a nearly horizontal California sycamore, crossed a patch of lush grass, and regarded the private stairs leading up to Room 162. Tea lights flickered on each step, a romantic touch, but to me the shifting shadows felt merely ominous. In choosing to trust Kazakov, I'd placed my freedom and Ariana's life in his hands. For all I knew, he'd called LAPD already and they were all waiting for me inside, oiling their semiautos and sipping Campari.

There was much to gain and everything to lose.

Steeling myself, I headed up the stairs. I knocked twice, once, then twice again.

A dry voice came through the wood—"I was just kidding about that"—and then the door tugged open. I tensed, but there was no Gable, no SWAT, no hired muscle, just Kazakov in a white bathrobe and his wife across on a couch, dwarfed by the expansive suite.

He rubbed an eye. "Come in, please. Forgive my getup, but I don't dress for anybody after ten anymore." A handsome man, though he looked older than he had in the photos I'd seen, maybe closing on seventy. "Need something for that?"

He was so matter-of-fact that it took a moment for me to realize he was talking about the bruising on my face. "No, it's fine."

"Come in. This is my Linda."

She stood, smoothing her designer sweat suit, and offered a feminine handshake. She was around his age—noteworthy in this setting—with a graceful demeanor and sharply intelligent eyes. We exchanged a few polite words, preposterous under the circumstances, but she inspired etiquette. Then she glanced at her husband. "You need some tea, love?"

"No, thank you," he said. As she withdrew, he winked at me and reached into the minibar. "Forty-two years. You know the secret?"

"No," I said. "I don't."

"When we're at an impasse, I admit to being wrong half the time. No more, no less."

"I've got the being-wrong part down," I said. The thought of Ariana caught me by surprise here in this lavish suite. I flashed on DeWitt's broad, handsome face, those arms that barely tapered at the wrists, the shoulders that kept going. And Verrone, of the down-turned mustache and the steady, lifeless glare. My wife in the hands of these men. Controlled by them. Breathing only as long as their mood or judgment held.

"You seem shaken," he said.

The time blinked out from the DVD player beneath the wall-mounted flat-screen—11:23 P.M.

Twelve hours and thirty-seven minutes until Ridgeline would kill my wife.

I said, "I won't argue that."

He gestured for me to sit. "Would you like a drink?"

"Very much."

He poured two vodkas over ice, handed me mine. "They play dirty pool, our friends over at Festman Gruber. I know their tricks, as they know mine." He sat sideways at the edge of the secretary desk and crossed his hands over a knee as if waiting for someone to paint his portrait. "It was very much in their interest for this movie not to happen. McDonald's stopped Supersizing after that documentary. If you can get McDonald's to do something, hell, sky's the limit. We needed a star of a certain status for the picture to get the kind of exposure we required. You know how it is. Given our time frame, it was tough to begin with. It's not like A-listers sit around waiting to be slotted into low-budget whale movies." He took a sip, squinted into the pleasure of the alcohol.

I followed suit, the vodka burning my throat, soothing my nerves.

He used his thumbnail to buff an imaginary spot off the lacquered desktop. "Keith Conner was not as much of a lout as you'd think."

"I'm starting to figure that out."

"Movie stars aren't killed quietly," he mused.

"They needed something failproof."

"And low-tech." He gestured with his glass. "Golf driver, was it?"

"I don't even golf."

"Don't understand the game myself. Seems like an excuse to wear bad pants and drink during the day. I did enough of that in my youth."

I looked down into the clear liquid, my hands starting to tremble. After so much menace, the human contact and our quick rapport had caught me off guard. It felt safe in here, which opened me up to what I'd been trying not to feel. The past hours were a jumble, one trauma bleeding into the next. I flashed on Sally, pinwheeling back, mouth open, eruption from her chest. "Someone was shot. Right in front of me. A single mother. There's a kid who right now is . . . is finding out . . ."

He sat there, patient as a sniper. I wasn't sure what I was trying to convey, so I drained my glass and handed him the CD. His eyebrows lifted.

He took the disc, circled the desk, and popped it into his laptop. He clicked and read. Read some more. I sipped and sat back, cataloging everything I was going to do differently if I got a chance to be with my wife again. That last night we'd been together, my thumb drawing a bead of sweat through the dip between her lovely shoulder blades, the quick urgency of her mouth against my shoulder—what if it was a final memory?

His voice startled me from my thoughts. "This internal study shows very different results from those that Festman released publicly and put into evidence before Congress. Three hundred and fifty decibels? That's well into illegal territory."

"The figure surprises you?" I asked.

"Not in the least. We all know it. This just *proves* that they know it." A glance back at the screen. "They stole our data, too. We must have a mole. That will be handled." He was talking to himself; I just happened to be there. His gray eyebrows furrowed, holding an anger he'd so far concealed. "At least they stole *accurate* data." He seemed to notice I was there again. "We have a superior product," he told me. "But innovation takes time. Change is hard. There are alliances. Partnerships. Inertia. We needed to raise awareness, apply the right pressure at the right time. The documentary was a way of doing that. Business can make for strange bedfellows."

"And by 'product' you mean the sonar system that you're developing?"

"More or less. We design transducers and sonar domes for submarines and ship hulls. Just like Festman Gruber."

"Why are yours superior? Because they don't harm whales?"

He chuckled. "Don't mistake me for some manatee hugger. We have a lot of motivations. Saving Shamu certainly isn't at the top of that list. But our system *is* less disruptive to the environment. That's a PR benefit, you see. Which makes it good business. And a good advantage to press. How's your physics?"

"Paltry."

"Okay, here's the shorthand: Festman Gruber's is a traditional sonar system. Low frequency but high output power—think of it as high intensity. The high intensity is what screws up whale migrations, blows out their ears, all that Greenpeace stuff. Of course, Festman denies any link."

"Like cigarette companies and cancer."

"Like smart businessmen. You can't please shareholders airing your dirty laundry all the time. The key is"—he pointed to the laptop screen—"not to get caught with your pants down."

"How can your company's sonar work in such a low decibel range?"

"Because North Vector has developed a low-frequency, high-pulse-rate, *low-intensity* sonar, based on the type used by whispering bats. We overlap signals correlating from multiple sources to increase propagation distance *without* raising intensity. This offers a huge strategic advantage, because even though it's active, it's hard to detect, record, or source, even with specialized acoustic equipment."

"And what could a little arts-and-crafts project like that be worth?"

"About three point nine billion. Annually. For five years." He uncrossed his hands, held them out like Vanna White. "But can we really put a price tag on the well-being of our seafaring mammals?"

I wanted to make a smart reply, but I thought of Trista sitting in her bungalow with those autopsy photos, Keith lingering in the shadow of the Golden Gate to rest a hand on the side of that gray whale, and decided to keep my mouth shut.

He continued, "NSA has an essentially unlimited budget. They need more money, they print it. But they don't like paying twice for the same thing, not in these amounts. Looks bad to the Senate Appropriations Committee. And Festman, see, is in the middle of a long-term naval sonar contract. So despite all our advantages, we're next in line. And this document"—another adoring glance at the laptop screen—"or more specifically the *threat* of this document, is the kind of thing that will accelerate certain processes."

"They can't just say it's doctored?"

"It won't come to that. This battle has to be over before a single shot is fired."

"How?"

"I make sure that the right people in the right positions are aware that if they support Festman, they will be on the losing side. Senators. United States Attorneys. Cabinet members."

"How do you do that?"

"There is no greater power—not bombs, not laws, not parliaments—*no* greater power than picking up the phone and having the right person on the other end."

"Won't the government push back?"

"I am the government."

I said, "You're a private company."

"Exactly."

I nodded slowly. "I keep finding I'm not cynical enough to live in this country."

"Try living in other countries," he said. "It won't convert you to an optimist."

I jabbed a finger in the direction of the laptop. "Can you use that internal study to nail Festman's hide to the wall?"

"That's not what we want."

"After what I've been through, Mr. Kazakov, I'm not sure you can speak for what I want."

"You came to me for a reason, Patrick. I know how to swim in these waters."

I tapped the empty glass against my thigh.

"You never want to humiliate a rival," he continued. "Because then you don't get what you want. You flash your hand, give them a way out. Avoidance of shame is a vastly effective and underutilized motivator. We bury the study. Arrange to clear your name for whatever charges they've drummed up. It all happens quietly, behind the scenes, and we agree on a headline or two that we can all sell and live with. The higher-ups at Festman Gruber won't be imprisoned. They'll just lose. This round."

"And you'll get the defense contract."

"How much," he asked, "do you want for this CD?"

"I don't want money. I want my wife."

"Then let's get you your wife."

"It's not that easy." Standing, I pulled the folded documents from my pocket and tossed them on the desk before him, all those phone bills, wire transactions, bank accounts, and photographs linking Ridgeline to Festman Gruber. "There's much more at stake. And I've got a lot more than just an internal study."

I explained to him about Ridgeline and what I'd determined about their relationship with Festman Gruber. When I told him about Ariana's being taken, his eyes burned with forty-two years of empathy and his hand tightened angrily around the arm of his chair. His wife emerged silently, ostensibly to return the tea service to the counter, but her timing suggested she'd been listening to our conversation. She made sure to catch her husband's eye, and his expression of marital resignation made clear the decision was no longer in his hands. When she retreated to the bedroom again, he nodded at me weightily.

"This," he said, "changes everything." He sank back, rubbed his temples with his fingertips. His silver goatee looked gray in the glow of the banker's lamp. "If Ridgeline so much as catches wind of the fact that you're making a play, they'll clean up, understand? That's what they've been doing. Cleaning up."

I fought off dread, the endless wrong-turn scenarios, the crime-scene imagery.

"I need to know how it works," I said, "if I'm gonna help my wife. Who's involved and at what level? Does Festman's CEO make the call to hire Ridgeline?"

"The CEO?" He waved a dismissive hand. "The CEO isn't even *aware* of this. It's not like in the movies. He lists corporate priorities. Makes a directive. 'Stop that fucking Keith Conner documentary.' That's all. The rest gets brainstormed and implemented."

"By whom?"

"Security."

"Who's Security report to?"

"Legal. Insert lawyer joke here. But that's how it's done."

Kazakov's neutrality—his *casualness*—was chilling.

My voice shook. "So they're the ones who laid the plan? To fuck with me and my wife? To murder Keith? To frame me and take away my life? *Lawyers?*"

"I don't know that Legal would have come up with the plan. But that's who would have approved it."

"Once they'd hired Ridgeline."

"That's right."

"How do I know who's at the top of this particular food chain?" I asked. "Legal?" I spit the word.

"You show up with some information and see who comes out to talk to you."

"Show up? Aren't they in Alexandria?"

"You bet your ass whoever's running things is on this coast overseeing this little imbroglio."

"Won't they just call the cops on me?"

"Maybe," he said. "You'll be betting that they'll want to talk to you first."

"Betting my life and Ariana's."

"Yes."

On the leather blotter rested a satellite cell phone. Distractedly, he reached over and spun it. The Glock was digging into my kidney, so I pulled it free and set it on the coffee table.

He eyed the pistol, unimpressed. "That's useless. This is a power and intel game. You're not going to win it with that. You'll probably just shoot your knee-cap off."

I picked up the glass again, as if it had magically refilled with Stoli. "I want Legal to go down. And I want Ridgeline. The business stuff you can handle however you see fit."

"You've got a long row to hoe."

"That's why I need your help. The only benefit to being stalked by a global defense and technology company is that their rivals are *also* global defense and technology companies."

"That we are. Fire with fire and all that, sure. But what do you expect us to do?"

"They stitched a tracking device into my wife's raincoat. They don't know we know about it. My wife managed to grab her raincoat as they snatched her."

"Resourceful woman."

"Yes, you two would get along just fine. Is there any way to track that device?"

"Not unless you had the signature of that particular signal."

"Like its characteristics?"

"Yes, radio frequency, period, bandwidth, amplitude, type of modulation—all the usual suspects."

"An acquaintance of mine swept our house for us, and he found the thing using a signal analyzer. Would that have recorded the signature?"

"Any signal analyzer worth a damn would have saved the signature in its library. Can you get the analyzer?"

"I have an idea how I might. But I . . . uh, I might need you to offer the guy a job."

"He get fired?"

"Not yet."

Kazakov nodded. "I see."

"I need to make a call. If I turn on my cell phone, can Ridgeline source where I am?"

"This isn't *24*. It takes a good amount of time to track a signal. If they're looking. Keep it to a few minutes and you'll be fine." He gestured to the balcony, but his eyes had already moved back to his copied cell-phone bill, the one I'd used to track him down. As I stood, I noticed that his stare had caught on some of the underlined numbers.

"Whose numbers are those?" I asked.

"Advocates," he said, not elaborating. "May I copy this as well?"

"You can have it."

"You've done me an enormous service. Now I need to do a bit of damage control." He gestured to the sliding glass door again, and I left him to his vodka and satellite phone.

"Help you?" The weak cell-phone connection did nothing to stifle Jerry's indignation. "Jesus, don't you learn?"

"Not quickly."

"I'm hanging by a thread over here after Mickelson found out I swept your house. I told you this shit better not come back on me with the studio, and here I am—an ass hair from fired."

"You said you wanted to get back to real security anyway. I have a job lined up for you with North Vector."

"Everyone's looking for you, Patrick. Cops, press, not to mention whoever you're tangled up in. Forget *fired*. How 'bout aiding and abetting?"

"You haven't watched the news today," I told him. "You don't know I'm on the run."

Beyond the closed sliding glass door, Kazakov sat in his plush white bathrobe, satellite phone tucked between ear and shoulder, gesturing with aggressive precision. I set my hand on the balcony rail, looked out into a tangle of branches. I closed my eyes, breathed in rain and mud, waited for Jerry to decide my wife's fate.

"No," he said slowly. "I guess I haven't. What kind of job?"

"You can sit down with the CEO and pick one."

"The *CEO*?" He was breathing hard. "This better not be a ruse."

"They have my wife," I said. "They have Ariana."

He was silent. I checked my watch, eager to turn the phone back off.

"Tell me what you're asking for."

We talked through the details, made arrangements, and signed off.

Immediately after I hung up, an Asian chime sounded. With dread, I clicked to open the cell-phone message.

BY NOON TOMORROW, YOU WILL LEAVE THE CD WITH THE VALET AT STARBRIGHT PLAZA.

The screen opened to a live shot of Ariana, bound to a chair. The background was blurry, but it looked like a small room. Her hair was loose and wild, one eye was black, and blood trickled from the edge of her lips. There was no sound, but I could tell she was screaming my name.

The feed vanished, replaced by block letters: TWELVE HOURS.

Then darkness.

I turned off the phone. My mouth was dirt dry, and I had to clutch the balcony rail until I could feel my legs back under me.

A memory came, vivid and unbidden—that first time I'd met Ariana at the freshman-orientation party at UCLA. Her lively, clever eyes. How I'd approached on nervous legs, gripping that cup of keg beer. My lame line—"You look bored." And how she'd asked if I was making a proposition, an offer to unbore her.

I'd said, "Seems like that could be the challenge of a lifetime."

"Are you up to it?" she'd asked.

Yes.

Out on the balcony, the midnight cold had found its way through my clothes. I was shivering violently. Inside the hotel room, Kazakov set down his satellite phone and beckoned me.

I pried my hands off the balcony rail and started in.

Twelve hours.

CHAPTER 56

The lobby was spotless and gleaming. Even the marble ashtrays, standing obediently at the elevator doors containing nary a butt, looked as though they'd been polished with a silk handkerchief. It could have been a hotel or a country club or the waiting room of a Beverly Hills dentist. But it wasn't.

It was the Long Beach office of Festman Gruber.

The elevator hummed pleasantly up fifteen levels. A floor-to-ceiling wall of thick glass—probably ballistic—rimmed the lobby, funneling visitors to the bank-teller window of the reception console. The security guard behind the window had a sidearm and an impressive scowl for 8:00 A.M. Behind him was a beehive of offices and conference rooms, also composed of glass walls, with assistants and workers scurrying to and fro. Aside from the dollhouse view, it looked just like any other business, depressing in its sterility. The front barrier muted everything beyond to a perfect silence. All that classified work, taking place right in the soundproofed open.

It didn't seem that the guard recognized me, but the bruising on my face said that I was out of place here among the Aeron chairs and plush carpet. My palms were damp, my shoulders tense.

Four hours until Ridgeline would kill my wife.

"Patrick Davis," I said. "I'd like to speak to the head of Legal."

He pushed a button, and his voice issued through a speaker. "Do you have an appointment?"

"No. Just give my name, and I'm sure he or she will want to see me."

The guard didn't say anything, but his face showed he thought that to be improbable. I prayed that the cops wouldn't be summoned before I had a chance to talk to someone.

Of course I'd yet to sleep. I'd picked up Jerry's signal analyzer from a drop point in the wee hours, and some of Kazakov's unnamed associates were rigging it to plug in to a standard GPS unit so I could zero in on Ariana's—or at least her raincoat's—location. After that I was on my own. I'd have to source that tracking signal and catch up to the Ridgeline crew wherever they were hunkered down before they headed out to our meet point at high noon. Right now I needed something to drive that wedge deep and hard between Festman Gruber and Ridgeline, something to arm myself with to take in to the men holding my wife. There were more variables than I could wrap my sleep-deprived mind around, and if any one of them tilted in the wrong direction, I'd be making funeral arrangements, standing trial, or filling out a casket.

As I waited for entry or arrest, treated to a little piped-in Josh Groban, I watched an assistant walk down a glass-walled hall and enter a glass-walled conference room. Men in suits rimmed a granite table the length of a sailboat. One man, identical to the others, rose from the head abruptly when she whispered in his ear. He glanced through the walls at me, Ariana's life hanging in the balance of his decision. Then he walked briskly into an office next door. Waiting breathlessly for his verdict, I was struck that all the glass wasn't some pretense of feel-good corporate transparency; it was an embodiment of the ultimate paranoia. At any time everyone could keep an eye on everyone else.

To my great relief, the assistant, an Asian woman with a severe bob cut, fetched me and led me back. I passed through a metal detector, dropping Don's car keys to the side in a silver tray that passed them through a scan of their own. But I kept my sealed manila envelope in hand.

Now came the real challenge.

The man waited for me in the middle of his office, arms at his sides. "Bob Reimer," he said, not offering his hand.

We stood centered on the slate rug, regarding each other like boxers. He seemed to fit with the total ordinariness of the setting, a mover and shaker who left nary an imprint on the retinas, as bland as a watercooler in a bomb factory. He was older—fifty, maybe—of a generation that still wore tie clips, carried through on their side parts, said "porno" instead of "porn." I couldn't help but think of those replicating G-men from *The Matrix*—Midwest white, neat suit, not a hair out of place. He was Everyman. He was nobody. Blink and he'd been replaced by an alien, simulating human form. A crushing disappointment, after all the fear and loss and menace, to be confronted with such banality in an air-conditioned office.

He crossed behind me and tapped the glass wall with his fingertips, and it clouded instantly, blocking us from the rest of the floor. Magic.

He went to his desk and removed a handheld wand, which I supposed, in light of my continuing spy education, to be a spectrum analyzer. "Given circumstances, I assume you won't object," he said.

I held my arms wide, and he ran the wand up and down my sides, across my chest, my face, the manila envelope. I resisted an impulse to drive the point of my elbow down through his nose.

Content that I wasn't emitting any RF signals, he slid the wand away in a well-oiled drawer. A framed photograph of an attractive wife and two smiling young boys was on proud display. Beside it sat a coffee mug picturing a cartoon fisherman that said WORLD'S BEST DAD! I realized, with revulsion, that he probably *was* a good father, that he likely carved his life into neat little compartments and managed them with a despot's efficiency. This compartment had all the trappings and symbols of an ordinary family man, but I had the sensation of being in a well-appointed viper's nest, designed to imitate human surroundings.

"You're a fugitive from justice," he said, not unpleasantly.

"I've come to deal." My voice sounded level enough.

"I have no idea what you're talking about."

"Right," I said. "Clean hands up here on the fifteenth floor."

"Why did you come here?"

"I wanted to look you in the face," I said. Though fury had edged into my voice, his expression remained amiable. I took a half step closer. "I can connect you to Ridgeline."

If there was shock at hearing the name, he concealed it beautifully. "Of course you can. Ridgeline is a security company. They handle our international executive protection."

"We both know they've been handling a lot more than that."

"I'm uncertain what you're referring to." But his eyes stayed on the envelope.

The phone on his desk bleated. He crossed and punched a button. "Not now."

The Asian assistant: "There's an investigative reporter team here from CNBC. They say they want a statement on a breaking story."

He crossed his office in four steps, knocked the milky glass with a knuckle, and it grew clear again. More magic.

Across in the lobby stood two men in windbreakers, one toting a massive video camera with CNBC TV emblazoned on the side next to the familiar peacock rainbow flare. "Get rid of—" Reimer's jaw flexed out at the corners, and his gaze swiveled to mine.

"I haven't leaked this yet," I said. "Obviously, or I

wouldn't be here. But I can't speak for what Ridgeline's doing."

"Why would you think Ridgeline's making a move against us?"

I didn't answer.

The assistant again, through the phone: "Would you like me to have them wait out here?"

"No." He shot his watch from the cuff of his jacket. "I don't think we should keep investigative reporters in the lobby to hobnob with the Jordanian contingent due here ten minutes ago." His sarcasm was understated, and all the more biting for it. "Put them in Conference Four, where I can keep an eye on them. Offer them coffee, Danish, whatever. I'll be in with Chris to see them shortly."

His mouth pulled to the side in a straight line, no curl—his version of a smile. "Perhaps we could speed this along? What's this about, *exactly*?"

"As I said. Ridgeline."

"I don't know what stories you think you've caught wind of, but you should know that companies like Ridgeline are a dime a dozen. They're given an assignment, and off they go. They don't even know why they're doing what they do half the time, so it's easy for them to misinterpret instructions, overstep their bounds. They're composed of former Spec Ops guys, and let's just say that type has been known to get a little . . . overzealous on occasion."

The breezy tone, nary a stutter—to him this was all just business as usual. And being here behind the scenes where levers were thrown and accounts brutally balanced, I felt naïve and sickened. I watched his pink lips moving and had to check my disgust to focus on his words.

He continued, "That's why Festman Gruber is very careful to limit its dealings with companies like Ridgeline to specific contracted services, such as executive protection. You need a junkyard dog sometimes, but you also have to make sure that you're holding the leash."

"It would be unfortunate if that junkyard dog maintained records of all its transactions with Festman Gruber." I held up the manila envelope.

I looked at him; he looked at it. He took the envelope a bit more hastily than suited his demeanor, breaking the seal and sliding the sheaf of papers into his hand. A complete set of those documents I'd pulled off the Ridgeline copier's hard drive—payments, accounts, and phone calls tracing the connection from Ridgeline back to Festman Gruber.

His tie, set neatly to his Adam's apple in a broad half Windsor, appeared suddenly too tight. His face colored, accenting the stubble pinpoints beneath that close shave, but he needed only a moment to process the surprise and regain his composure. When he looked back up, he was completely in control again. "Whatever Ridgeline elected to do on their own time, they will answer for."

I just looked out across the floor, giving him rope. There was plenty to behold, a whole world contained in the glass walls—all that respectable industry in constant, efficient motion. The reporters had been ushered into the conference room across the hall. They sat slurping coffee, the large camera with the CNBC logo resting on the table between them.

"We do a lot of business in the international community, Mr. Davis," he said. "We have dealings with over two hundred thousand individuals, last I checked. Many of them in the aggressive professions. We can't account for the temperament of each one."

"But *these* individuals answer to you," I said. "Or they *did*. You're the top dog, at least when it comes to this little scheme. It stops with you, so everyone above remains nicely insulated from the truth."

He didn't refute the point, which felt an awful lot like confirming it.

"You can reach Ridgeline," I said. "You can make them stop."

His bottom lip bowed in just barely, as if he'd tasted something repulsive. "It's safe to say that contact—and loyalties—between our companies has frayed."

"You're not in touch at all?" I asked.

From what Kazakov had told me about the workings of such arrangements, I'd assumed as much. And given the aggressive moves Ridgeline had taken against their omniscient employer, they'd need to stay off the grid as much as I did. But I wanted to confirm the communication breakdown, and I needed to draw Reimer out.

"Regular communication can be a detriment when it comes to matters where both sides require"—a pause as he selected the right word—"prudence. All the more when dealings achieve a heightened level of complication. And now this." He sighed, disappointed. "These documents make clear that Ridgeline isn't interested in upholding their agreements. But that cuts both ways. We are no longer obligated to offer them the customary protections."

I nodded at the papers in his hand. "Looks like they read that one coming."

"This"—he raised the sheaf—"this can be explained away in a few phone calls."

"If your bosses are willing to make them for you. Ridgeline is expendable. My guess is you might be, too. You know what they say: Never be the senior man with a secret."

A cough of disbelief. "Documents can be altered. Put into context. The news waits for *us*." He gave an almost unconscious nod to the reporters sitting patiently across the hall. "You think a few pieces of paper are enough to make my bosses want to hang me out?"

"Combined with the story I can tell."

"You?" He smiled. "We can erase you. Not kill you. *Erase* you. From all consideration. It's not just us, it's whose shoulders we're standing on, which databases we plug in to, which institutions are reliant on our continued success."

"Is this the 'I am the government' speech? Because I've heard that one already."

His lip curled, almost imperceptibly. "Ridgeline, like everyone else"—he waved a hand around— "they're just fish in our aquarium. We tap a little food into the tank, and they come swimming." A faint grin. "But I'm sure a grounded college instructor like yourself can't relate to that."

The words cut deep. My mind moved to Deborah

Vance in her apartment, the vintage travel posters and antique furniture and spot-on style, all selected with painstaking desperation to transport her to another age. Roman LaRusso, agent to the washed-up and disabled, hunkered down in his stacks of dusty paperwork, his view of a brick wall offering barely a craned-neck glimpse of billboard and blue sky. All those faded dreams hung framed on his office walls, head shots with signatures and stale advice from would-bes and also-rans no more qualified to proffer it than I: *Live Every Moment, Don't Stop Believing,* and yeah, *Follow Your Dreams.* I thought of who I'd let myself become by the time this had all started twelve endless days ago—a has-been almost-screenwriter with a marriage on the rocks. Impatient, gullible, desperate for attention, eager to be exploited, to be noticed, to hasten whatever was coming my way. I'd been out of the spotlight, off the stage, consigned to the real world, where I was unwilling to deserve what I already had.

Reimer was watching me expectantly, his words still lingering: *I'm sure a grounded college instructor like yourself can't relate to that.*

"Not anymore," I said.

"No?"

"I don't care about movies or writing or whales or sonar," I said. "I care about my wife."

"They have her?"

"They do."

"Looks like they read you coming, too," he said with a measure of satisfaction. "They're trying to clean up their mess. They will do what they have to do, and they will invent stories and defenses later. I'm afraid that doesn't bode well for you and your wife."

"So you and I are in the same boat."

"The difference is, we can scrape a company like Ridgeline off the bottom of our shoe, and we can use a nuclear warhead to do it. It's all about allies, who's on the other end of the phone. Ridgeline thinks they've built an insurance file in this"—he shook the papers, the first little show of emotion—"but they've done nothing more than arrange for their funerals. You—and they—know next to nothing about something that never happened. They've compiled proof of our dealings, but proof is relevant only if there's a legal inquiry, an arrest, a jury. We will make calls. We will rewrite this. That's what all you fish—circling in your glass bowls, captivated by your own reflections—never grasp. Companies like Festman Gruber, *we* decide which stories get told. Festman Gruber doesn't answer to a bunch of copied documents or a crusading murderer with a bone to pick. Everything will be hung on you. And the fallout will land on Ridgeline."

"Unless," I said, "you've been good enough to give me what I came for."

His eyes darted back and forth, scanning my face. "As in this is being recorded?" He barked a one-note laugh. His grin looked stuck to his teeth. "Bullshit. You went through a metal detector."

"There are cutting-edge devices," I said, "that function using tiny amounts of metal."

"I scanned you myself for RF."

"It wasn't transmitting then. In fact, you turned it on yourself."

He looked down at his arms, his hands, finally focusing on the envelope he still grasped. With dread, he lifted the loose flap. A razor-thin clear square, the size of a postage stamp, remained inside on the gummy strip. Its transparent contact, which had been pulled open to activate the device when he'd raised the flap, was stuck to the envelope. "There's no"—he paused for a breath—"power source."

"It vacuums RF out of the air and converts it to power to run itself."

His gaze moved through the walls, all those cell phones strapped to belts, assistants tapping on iPhones, routers blinking from bookshelves, all that free RF floating around, waiting to get grabbed out of the air he breathed all day up here on the fifteenth floor. A single bead of sweat emerged from his sideburn and arced down his cheek.

"A . . . a transmitter that small, it would need its receiving equipment close by"—he tried on a shrug—"or . . . or there's no way this tiny signal could transmit beyond our front barrier." He pointed to the wall of ballistic glass that framed out the lobby and the outside world.

I knocked on the wall, the glass clouding. My second knock brought it clear again. Across the hall, in Conference Four, the CNBC reporters sat cocked back in their chairs, feet on the table, eating crullers. The guy at the head of the table nodded at me, sucked glaze from his fingers, and made a ta-da gesture at the massive camera.

"Hidden in the camera," Reimer said hoarsely. "That's the receiving equipment." His voice was flat, but I thought it was a question.

"Receiving," I said, "and relay. To a safe off-site location."

"I don't believe it. Besides us, there's maybe a handful of places in the world with that kind of teeth in the surveillance arena. You . . . Where would *you* get technology like that?"

"Where do you think?"

His face shifted, and I believe he understood what fear was for the first time in a very long time.

In Conference Four the fake reporter leaned forward and peeled the magnetic CNBC peacock sign off the side of the camera, revealing the North Vector logo beneath.

Reimer made a noise—something between clearing his throat and grunting.

I said, "There's an internal study on relative sonar levels I managed to get into the hands of North Vector as well."

He blanched.

"That junkyard dog you hired seems to have slipped the leash," I said. "Some of those important calls you were talking about? They're being made right now. I understand that the contract at stake is worth twenty billion dollars, give or take a few billion. I'm guessing a figure like that might go a certain distance toward eroding your bosses' devotion to you."

"Okay," he said. "Okay, let's talk about this. We can still rein this in, get everyone what they need. Listen—" He put a hand on my shoulder, leaving a sweat stain. "You'll need us to mediate this situation with your wife. We're the only ones who have an angle in to Ridgeline. We can hurt them."

"You already told me. You don't know how to contact them."

"But when they emerge." His words were adamant, compacted into hard little syllables. "You need us in the mix. We can undo all this. You need *me*. Even if you *could* convince the cops to jump off your trail and onto theirs, you don't want law enforcement crashing into a hostage house. Not with operators of this caliber dug in. There'll be nothing left of your wife but a bloodstain."

Through the clear walls, I could see the clock in the neighboring office—8:44 A.M.

Three hours and sixteen minutes until—

"No cops," I said. "No force."

A puff of disbelief parted his lips. "Then how?"

"I'll worry about that. You'd better worry about what to tell your higher-ups in Alexandria. And you'd better pick your words carefully—I've found Festman Gruber's corporate culture to be a bit unforgiving."

I left him standing on the rug, a droop in that square posture. When I reached the door, his voice came over my shoulder. It sounded less vengeful than weary, resigned to the carnage to come. "You are way out of your depth," he said. "You can't begin to imagine what kind of men these are. If you take them on alone, you might as well put the bullet in your wife's head yourself."

My hand resting on the door lever, I closed my eyes,

reliving that grainy feed that Ridgeline had sent to my cell phone at midnight. Ariana roughed up, screaming my name soundlessly. The thin line of blood at the edge of her mouth. What else had they done to her? What else were they doing to her right now? He was right, at least in part: I was way out of my depth. Was he also right about where this would all end?

I pushed out into the hall. The North Vector operators stood waiting. As we threaded through the glass labyrinth, workers rose from various workstations and watched us leave. At the elevators I looked back, but Reimer had turned the glass walls of his office opaque, a dark knot at the core, a symbol of my own quickening dread.

CHAPTER 57

I parked Don's Range Rover in a driveway at the end of a perfectly normal residential street in North Hollywood. I called 911 from my cell, told Dispatch I was ready to give myself up and seek their help for Ariana's recovery. I couldn't see any other choice, I said. Not with my wife held captive, due to be executed in fifty-three minutes.

Sitting, sweating, I watched the SWAT van roll up, then the black-and-whites, then Gable's sedan.

Leading with their submachine guns, the SWAT officers came fast and hard, closing on those tinted windows from all sides. A gloved hand yanked open the driver's door, and then MP5 barrels crammed the interior. But I wasn't there.

I was a mile and a half away, parked on a dirt overlook, watching through a military scope that seemed like something out of science fiction, with magnification suited to a NASA telescope. Can see the whites of birds' eyes, Kazakov had bragged.

I could even make out the address on the Post-it I'd adhered to the steering wheel. The address of the single-story clapboard two blocks up the slope from me.

I hustled back toward the boosted Dodge Neon

that an anonymous friend of North Vector had helped arrange for me—Kazakov's final favor. North Vector wouldn't accompany me from here on out. Providing tech support to help take down a rival company was one thing. Saving my wife was another. Bullets, exposure, and liability—the risk of coming out on the wrong side of this one was too high.

But *I* had no choice.

I dialed my cell phone again, and my favorite paparazzo, fresh out of hiding, picked up.

"You in position?" I asked.

"Yup." Joe Vente was wired, smacking his gum.

I'd called him last night, and in return for an after-the-fact exclusive if I lived to give it, he'd agreed to put out the word to his grapevine of colleagues. They'd get to the block just before I did and remain hidden until I arrived. I'd made clear to Joe: The timing had to be just right. I'd go to the house first, before the photographers made themselves known and before the cops arrived. I'd lay out the situation to DeWitt and Verrone, mention that the house was surrounded with recording equipment of every type and law enforcement of every stripe, then pray that would be enough of a deterrent to negotiate Ariana's and my way out of there.

"But," Joe added, "we've got a problem."

The words knocked the breath out of me. Everything had to go like clockwork. If the Ridgeline crew caught wind of anything before I knocked on that door, they'd likely kill Ari and bolt.

Reimer's words floated back to me: *If you take them on alone, you might as well put the bullet in your wife's head yourself.*

If they hadn't put it there already.

"Problem?" Fear thinned my voice. "What problem?"

"Big News caught the story. I don't know how they got onto it, but they're sending crews. And once crews show up, my ilk ain't gonna hold back. You know how we are."

I was running toward the car. "How the hell did that happen, Joe?"

"How's it always happen? Someone paid someone for a tip, probably. You're a cop killer, too, now, so this thing's bigger than the white Bronco. Patrick Davis and the Big Showdown."

I jumped into the car, turned over the engine, and peeled out. On the passenger seat was the fat laptop of Jerry's signal analyzer, the pulse from Ariana's raincoat represented in oddly pretty amplitude waves. A handheld GPS unit was plugged in to the side, the blinking dot laid down on the street beyond the turn I could see just ahead through the dusty windshield.

"Hold everyone back," I said. "You told them it's dangerous? A hostage situation?"

"Of course, but look, the block is crawling. The natives are getting restless, inching in for a peek. It's only a matter of time before someone's spotted."

I floored it, fishtailing on gravel. "Any sign that you've been seen?"

"No, man. All the curtains are drawn. Silence." A beat. "Shit. Here we go. This thing just went live."

"What hap—"

I screeched around the corner in time to see a news helicopter roar up over the ridge, blowing specks of dirt across my hood. Channel 2 News. Up ahead, paparazzi had gone on the move, shuffling from front yard to front yard, high-stepping hedges, and clutching cameras. A few news vans came gunning toward the house from the opposite direction. A second chopper joined the fray above the house. Way below I could hear the faint wail of sirens, the cavalry en route.

It was all going down too fast.

I could barely hear Joe above the commotion: "—movement at the windows. You'd better get here."

"Do you see Ariana?"

"No . . . nothing. . . ."

Guys were running beside my car, snapping pictures of me. TV cameras up ahead, well back from the curb. Joe coming in and out in my ear. ". . . directional mike . . . hear them inside . . . freaking out . . ."

Confused reporters blended with the freelancers, swarming the car. A few houses away, I threw open the car door and shoved out, yelling, "Stay away from the house! There are armed men inside."

A ripple of panic. Shouting. Questions.

Their fear only compounded mine. What if they saw the cameras, killed Ariana, and shot their way out?

I sprinted forward, breaking from the throng, the numbers dwindling as I neared the house. Even paparazzi weren't eager to get in the line of fire. But a few had pushed out into the danger zone. A scrappy woman with hippie hair aimed a camera from behind a telephone pole. A guy in fingerless gloves crouched by the mailbox. His lens had rolled out into the driveway, but he looked too scared to go for it.

I confronted the house. Peeling cornflower blue paint, a broad porch, the rental sign still hammered into the front lawn. It seemed a fiction that the clapboard walls contained such menace inside. Then again, what did I expect? A dungeon with dripping pipes? This is where quiet horrors happened—every day in perfectly nice neighborhoods like this one, behind closed doors and cheery suburban facades.

To my right, Joe was bellied down in a stand of lavender, sneezing and pointing a directional mike, earpiece in, to pull sound vibrations off the front windows. I'd barely noticed him in my dash to the walk.

"What are you picking up from inside?" I asked.

Keeping his face to the dirt, he repeated flatly, " 'What the fuck what the fuck oh Jesus God we're fucked.' "

Sirens came screaming up the hill.

A shadow at the curtain ahead. And then the dark oval of a face. It stared at me. Frozen, I stared back.

"Hang on." Joe cleared his throat, listening. " 'Let's do her and get the fuck out of here.' "

I had the sensation not of running but floating up the walk.

You can't begin to imagine what kind of men these are. There'll be nothing left of your wife but a blood-stain.

I banged on the door. "Wait!" I shouted. "It's Patrick! I have information you need!"

Silence. Locked. I banged away, kicked. "Wait, *wait*! You need to talk to me!"

The door opened, and then a giant hand shot out, grabbed my shirt, and hurled me inside. I pinwheeled across the slick tile, DeWitt's face leering down at me. Verrone was at his side, and two other men with military builds shouldered to the front windows with short-barrel shotguns at the ready. One was red-faced, his knee jittering back and forth. He swung the barrel, sighted on my head. "Let's do him and hot-ass it out of here."

I recoiled from the dead stare of the muzzle, shouting, "You need to know what I've got!"

The sirens, almost on top of us.

A closed door led back to a bedroom. Ariana. I had to tear my eyes away. "Is she back there?"

No answer from the Ridgeline crew.

"Is she okay?" My voice shook.

Sweat beaded DeWitt's forehead. He said, "What the fuck did you do? What the *fuck* did you do?"

I pulled a manila file from inside my jacket and threw it at him. The pages scattered across the floor. Money orders, surveillance photos, all those banking and phone records, the payments for the murders of Mikey Peralta, Deborah B. Vance, and Keith Conner.

"No," Verrone said. He took a wobbly step back. "How?"

"The hard drive on your copy machine."

Verrone shot a furious glare at one of the men by the window, who said, "You didn't tell me anything about a fucking hard drive."

I spoke quickly. "Those documents blaze a trail

back to Festman Gruber. But they also blaze a trail forward to you."

"Who cares?" Verrone said. "We've got the leverage to make Festman throw their weight around on our behalf. They'll have to. Or they'll go down, too. And these aren't the types of guys to go down."

"Right," I said. "Mutually assured destruction. But guess what? I'm not part of the 'mutually.' "

"What does that mean?"

"I'm holding the cards. I've got the disc, too—those illegal decibel levels. And I know what it all means to the parties involved."

"How?"

Very slowly, I retrieved the digital recorder from my pocket. When I punched the button, Bob Reimer's voice filled the room: *These documents make clear that Ridgeline isn't interested in upholding their agreements. But that cuts both ways. We are no longer obligated to offer them the customary protections.*

DeWitt said, "Reimer *knows*? Festman fucking *knows* already?"

The man by the window said, "This piece of shit brought it to them?"

The other: "We've gotta clean up and split. *Now.*"

Verrone paced a tight circle, grabbing at his hair, his yellow face gone gray. He pulled out a sidearm, aimed at my face, the skin fluttering at his temple. I flinched, waiting for the crack.

"You can't manipulate Festman into doing what you want," I said. "Your leverage is gone. I gave it away. And they know it. You're finished. There is no move. This is checkmate."

Bob Reimer's recorded voice continued, *"Ridge-line thinks they've built an insurance file in this, but they've done nothing more than arrange for their funerals."*

The Ridgeline men exchanged a round of glances, eyes darting frantically from face to face, reading the angles, weighing options and loyalty. I could hear the click in DeWitt's throat when he swallowed. Both men at the front windows stepped back from the curtains.

"Cops are here," the jittery one said. "They're gonna set up a perimeter. We can still run and gun. But it's gotta be *right now.*"

From behind his gun, Verrone considered. He took a step forward, placed the cool metal against my forehead, pushed until I sank to my knees. I dropped the digital recorder, but it kept playing. My back-and-forth with Reimer in that air-conditioned office seemed like a game of badminton compared to this.

"You think you're in charge?" Verrone said. "You think you're writing the script? So you made some moves. Put us in a bind. But right now it's just us and you in a room. Why are *you* calling the shots?"

"Because I'm the guy with the cameras on him."

"A couple reporters—"

"No, not a couple reporters," I said. "There are news helicopters in the air. Paparazzi for blocks. SWAT all over. Everyone's watching, documenting. You can't get away. You can't do anything without them watching and knowing."

Play the hand you're dealt.

More sirens neared, then cut off. The rush of news

helicopters overhead. The curtains blocked out the mayhem, but we could hear the cries and footsteps and vehicles, the photographers yelling, someone shouting orders to reposition the cars.

I said, "You don't want to add another murder to what you're facing."

DeWitt looming over Verrone. "The hell we don't."

The barrel shoved harder into my face. I steeled myself, fighting off terror, praying that I'd be alive for the next breath and the one after that, praying that my wife's heart was still beating behind that closed door.

My first word came out a yell—"*Just . . .* just stop. Think. What's the *only* play? Talk to the cops. Cooperate. Turn state's evidence against Festman Gruber. Think of the pull they have. It's your only prayer against those guys. And it starts right now. This instant."

Reimer's voice from the recorder: *"Everything will be hung on you. And the fallout will land on Ridgeline."*

The men had moved in to surround me. My knees ached. My head throbbed. My heart was moving blood so fast I felt dizzy. They towered over me, blank-faced executioners. Verrone's arm was as steady as a statue's. His finger, curled around the trigger, was white at the creases.

I closed my eyes, alone in the dark. There was nothing in the world except the ring of steel against my forehead.

The pressure lifted.

I opened my eyes. The pistol was lowered at Verrone's side. The men parted unevenly. DeWitt's lips bunched around his teeth. It looked like he was biting down hard. One of the others abruptly sat on the floor, and the fourth went back to the window. It was as if a spell had been broken, leaving them dazed and dumb.

I came up, wobbly, to my feet. It hit me that I hadn't heard a sound issue from that back room—not a single shout or cry. "Is my wife behind that door?"

But they all just stood there, guns lowered, stunned.

I blinked back tears. *"Is she alive?"*

Verrone nodded to the man by the window, who reached over and tore the curtain from the track. Light flooded in, striking us. A bleached-out view of camera lenses and tactical goggles and windshields and gun muzzles—the whole world, perched out there, trained on the sudden spectacle. And us, staring through the glass right back at them.

Squinting into the brightness, Verrone put his hands up. DeWitt, and then the two other men, followed suit.

When DeWitt raised his arms, I noticed a streak of crimson running along the underside of his forearm. A drop snaked down, dangled from his elbow.

All at once the shouting from outside was gone, and the thrumming of the helicopters. Through the window I saw a cop at the perimeter yelling into a bullhorn, his mouth partially in view, the cords of his neck straining but no sound at all issuing forth.

I could hear nothing but my heartbeat, the muffled echo of my shouted words. *"What did you do? What did you do to her?"*

And then I was barreling for that closed door,

moving in hateful slow motion. SWAT blew in—I sensed the vibration, the shrapnel spray from the splintering front door peppering the back of my neck, the wood panel flying past my head. I was feet from the closed door, yelling my wife's name. I heard the officers behind me, felt the heat of their bodies, the air moving from their limbs, their shouts. Each strand of the carpet stood out, a sea of fibers stretching between me and my wife. My arm was ahead of me, reaching, veins splitting the back of my tensed hand. Someone struck me low at the calf, knocking me off balance, but I righted myself, still hurtling forward, almost there. The officers hit me at once, high and low, wrapping me up and hammering me down into the floor. My head collided with someone's heel, sending me into a spin, darkness coming on to blot out my last glimpsed image—that door, still closed to whatever bloody sight lay beyond.

CHAPTER 58

I step out of the headmaster's office at Loyola High, walk across the verdant front lawn, and tip my face to the sun. It's July, my favorite month. The gloom has finally burned off. For such an impatient town, Los Angeles likes its summers to come late.

In my hand flutters an offer to teach tenth-grade American literature. I will certainly accept, but I didn't want to do it in the room; I wanted to draw out the sweetness of anticipation, like putting off the bottom half of an Oreo to drink more milk.

I am free of legal trouble. After literally days of grueling interrogation, and with the help of some of those well-placed phone calls Gordon Kazakov is so fond of, I managed to untangle myself from all charges. As Detective Sally Richards might have pointed out, I did have justice, truth, and all that crap on my side as well. Excessive scrutiny actually helps when you're innocent.

Even the lawsuit against me for not punching Keith Conner was dropped. With no more Keith to protect, Summit Films wanted to get as far away from me as possible. You know you're in dire straits when no one wants to sue you anymore. At final tally my legal costs were almost precisely what I'd netted from my screenwriting deal for *They're Watching.*

The movie opened last month, not with a bang but a whimper. On its second weekend, I finally worked up the nerve to go see it. Feeling like a self-abusing pervert in a pussycat theater, I watched from the back row of an empty Valley cinema. It was worse than I could have imagined. Though Keith was afforded some respectful deference, the reviews were understandably blistering. Predictable plot, trite dialogue, bled-dry characters, the pacing pumped to a steroid-rage confusion of edits. It was, in its own way, masterful in its incompetence. Kenneth Turan suggested that the script might have been generated from a software program.

As my name flickered during the closing credits, it struck me that—like so many of those first-round wailers on *American Idol*—I was never really very good at this. Getting fired off *They're Watching* was one of the best things that could have happened to me. I'd come close to throwing away everything that I'd built because I had never bothered to reexamine a childhood dream that I didn't even want anymore.

I'm happier watching movies than writing them.

I'm happier teaching.

Standing on the front lawn, I open my eyes again. I turn and look at the school, and in the reflection of the chapel window I see myself. Khaki trousers and a button-up from Macy's. Battered backpack in hand, dangling at my side. Patrick Davis, high-school teacher. After all this I'd wound up where I'd started.

But not really.

I climb into my Camry. The interior is a bit scorched from the stun grenade, but not too bad, since my face had been good enough to absorb most of the blast. I can't afford a new car yet, but I did have the dashboard buttons and dials fixed, and I've vowed not to punch them anymore.

I hide the job offer in the glove box like treasure and head home, running the 10 west, then cutting up to Sunset Boulevard so I can surf the curves. The air blows through the open window, riffling my hair. I watch the mansions roll by behind their gates, and I don't wonder or care what it would be like to live in them.

My life isn't like *Enemy of the State* anymore. It's not *Body Heat* or *Pay It Forward* either.

It's *my* life.

I stop off and pick up dry cleaning, nodding to the clerk, whose eyes linger a beat too long on my face. People look at me differently now, but less so every day. If fame is fleeting, then L.A. infamy is the blink of a firefly. But still, things are not back to what they were. They never will be. There are night terrors and waking panic and from time to time I still break a cold sweat checking the mailbox or opening the morning paper. And most days, when it's too quiet or not quiet enough, my thoughts drift to my wife, bound and held in the back room of a clapboard house. How she'd tried to fight her captors. How she'd sunk her teeth into DeWitt's arm when he'd gagged her. How, in the grip of blind fear, she'd felt in her heart of hearts that she was going to die.

Sally was honored as a hero at her funeral. Which

she was. More and more I think of heroes as ordinary people who decide to give a damn about what they do, not what they might get. Watching her casket descend, I felt heartsick. I doubt I'll encounter her combination of composure and wry incisiveness again. Her son is being adopted by a cousin. The pension board is reviewing Valentine's case, and it seems unlikely his four boys have as straight a road ahead.

The four men in that clapboard house—none of whom were actually named DeWitt or Verrone—all copped pleas. In return for offering testimony against Festman Gruber, they'll avoid the needle, but they all had to agree to life without parole. I think of Sally and Keith, Mikey Peralta and Deborah Vance, and I am pleased that those men will be eating off trays and looking over their shoulders for the rest of their lives.

If they can be believed, they were the entire team for this job. Ridgeline and the numerous shell companies enfolding it are being vigorously investigated, but from what's trickled back to me, it's been tough sledding once that paper trail hit Bahrain.

Bob Reimer, the face of the scandal, has not fared well. His pretrial motions drag on, and he's looking at special circumstances, which could mean the death penalty. As he forges forward with gray-miened unflappability, prosecutors and media continue to dig into the Legal Department at Festman Gruber. Reimer's well-heeled colleagues are wading through a sea of lesser indictments, and some of them may likely join him in lockdown someday if he isn't executed.

Festman's higher-ups were predictably outraged at everything that had transpired. Their stock price has plummeted, and I bet that hurts the bastards most of all. Without a single public volley being fired, the naval sonar contract moved from Festman Gruber to North Vector. That Senate vote on decibel limits is fast approaching, and Kazakov seems to have a pretty good sense of which way it'll go.

Thank you, Keith Conner. Your life for a cause. James Dean never saved the whales. But in a weird way, you did.

Trista Koan got another movie greenlit. It's about frogs in the Amazon being killed off by global warming, and they have some new kid, a crossover pop star, doing the voice-over. He's not supposed to be half bad. When his last album went gold, he replaced Keith on that billboard outside The LaRusso Agency, and maybe, if he's lucky, it'll still be there next month.

I turn at Roscomare and drive up the hill, passing couples walking dogs, gardeners loading pickups, that McMansion with Tudorbethan mock battlements. Paul McCartney whispers words of wisdom from my banged-up speakers, and then the on-the-hour news breaks in. One of the Lakers got caught with a transvestite in a Venice Beach bathroom stall. I turn off the radio, let the breeze blow past my face and clear all that scandal and prurient interest from the air.

I stop off at Bel Air Foods and walk the aisles, checking items off my mental list, whistling a tune. I'm almost at checkout when I remember. I go back and grab some prenatal vitamins.

Bill rings me up. "How you doing today, Patrick?"

"Great, Bill. You?"

"Never better. Working on the next script?"

"Nah." I smile, at ease in this moment with myself, the world. "I love movies. That doesn't make me a screenwriter."

His gaze lingers on the vitamins as he slides them across the scanner, and he looks up and gives me a wink.

I drive home, pull in to the garage, and sit for a time. To my left, up on the shelf, Ariana's wedding dress is visible through the sealed clear-plastic bin. I open the glove box, remove the job-offer letter, and read it again to make sure it's real. I think about our venerable and flawed kitchen table, the freshly painted baby blue walls of my former office, and, flooded with gratitude, I cry a little.

Juggling the grocery bags, I walk out front to the mailbox. A jolt of apprehension strikes me as the lid drops, but the mail today—like yesterday and the day before—is just the mail. I tuck it under my arm and stand, regarding the house I have fallen back in love with.

Next door there is a Realtor's sign in the Millers' front lawn. They are liquidating their assets to make the paperwork easier. Beyond Martinique's silk drapes, I can see a young couple inside being shown around. Their whole lives ahead of them.

Near the fresh-turned soil beside our own front lawn lie a pair of slender gardening gloves and a trowel. I start up our walk, a baguette sticking out of one of the grocery bags like in a postcard of France. I think about all the things I used to chase for all the wrong reasons. And how by standing still I now hummed with a vitality I'd never known.

On the porch I set down the bags and pull from one the bouquet of mariposas. Lavender. I step forward and ring the bell like a suitor. Her footsteps approach.

Ariana opens the door. She sees me, sees the flowers, and extends a hand toward my cheek.

I step across the threshold, into the warmth of her palm.

ACKNOWLEDGMENTS

I'd like to thank my splendid editor, Keith Kahla; my publisher, Sally Richardson; and the rest of my team at St. Martin's Press, including but certainly not limited to Matthew Baldacci, Jeff Capshew, Kathleen Conn, Ann Day, Brian Heller, Ken Holland, John Murphy, Lisa Senz, Matthew Shear, Tom Siino, Martin Quinn, and George Witte. My UK editor, David Shelley, and his gifted crew at Sphere. Überagents Lisa Erbach Vance and Aaron Priest. My beloved attorneys, Stephen F. Breimer and Marc H. Glick. Rich Green at CAA. Maureen Sugden, my copy editor, for improving my grammar, my diction—no doubt even my posture. Geoff Baehr, my technology guru who at times feels like *the* technology guru. Jess Taylor for early remarks. Philip Eisner, who lent me his considerable reading talents. Simba, my faithful Rhodesian ridgeback, the perfect underfoot writing companion. Lucy Childs, Caspian Dennis, Melissa Hurwitz, M.D., Nicole Kenealy, Bret Nelson, M.D., Emily Prior, and John Richmond for performing various invaluable tasks. And finally Delinah, Rose Lenore, and Natty—my collective heart.

Read on for an excerpt from Gregg Hurwitz's
upcoming book

YOU'RE NEXT

Coming soon in hardcover from St. Martin's Press

The four-year-old boy stirs in the backseat of the station wagon, his body little more than a bump beneath the blanket draped over him, his hip sore where the seatbelt buckle presses into it.

He sits up, rubbing his eyes in the morning light, and looks around, confused.

The car is pulled to the curb, idling beside a chain-link fence. His father grips the steering wheel, his arms shaking. Sweat tracks down the band of flushed skin at the back of his neck.

The boy swallows to wet his parched throat. "Where. . . . where's Momma?"

His father takes a wheezy breath and half-turns, a day's worth of stubble darkening his cheek. "She's not. . . . she can't. . . . she's not here."

Then he bends his head and begins to cry. It is all jerks and gasps, the way someone cries who isn't used to it.

Beyond the fence, kids run on cracked asphalt and line up for their turn on a rusted set of swings. A sign wired to the chain-link proclaims, IT'S MORNING AGAIN IN AMERICA: RONALD REAGAN FOR PRESIDENT.

The boy is hot. He looks down at himself. He is wearing jeans and a long-sleeve T-shirt, not the pajamas he'd gone to bed in. He tries to make sense of his father's words, the unfamiliar street, the blanket bunched in his lap, but can focus on nothing except the hollowness in his gut and the rushing in his ears.

"This is not your fault, champ." His father's voice is high-pitched, uneven. "Do you understand me? If you remember . . . one thing . . . you have to remember that nothing that happened is your fault."

He shifts his grip on the steering wheel, squeezing so hard his hands turn white. His shirt cuff has a black splotch on it.

The sound of laughter carries to them; kids are hanging off monkey bars and crawling around the beat-up jungle gym.

"What did I do?" the boy asks.

"Your mother and I, we love you very much. More than anything."

His father's hands keep moving on the steering wheel. Shift, squeeze. Shift, squeeze. The shirt cuff moves into direct light and the boy sees that the splotch isn't black at all.

It is blood-red.

His father hunches forward and his shoulders heave, but he makes no sound. Then, with apparent effort, he straightens back up. "Go play."

The boy looks out the window at the strange yard with the strange kids running and shrieking. "Where am I?"

"I'll be back in a few hours."

"Promise?"

His father still doesn't turn around, but he lifts his eyes to the rear-view, meets the boy's stare for the first time. In the reflection, his mouth is firm, a straight line, and his pale blue eyes are steady and clear. "I promise," he says.

The boy just sits there.

His father's breathing gets funny. "Go," he says, "play."

The boy slides over and climbs out. He walks through the gate, and when he pauses to look back, the station wagon is gone.

Kids bob on see-saws and whistle down the fireman's pole. They look like they know their way around.

One of the kids runs up and smacks the boy's arm. "You're it," he brays.

The boy plays chase with the others. He climbs on the jungle gym and crawls in the yellow plastic tunnel, jostled by the bigger kids and doing his best to jostle back. A bell rings from the facing building, and the kids fly off the equipment and disappear inside.

The boy climbs out of the tunnel and stands on the playground, alone. The wind picks up, the dead leaves like fingernails dragging across the asphalt. He doesn't know what to do, so he sits on a bench and waits for his father. A cloud drifts across the sun. He has no jacket. He kicks the leaves piled by the base of the bench. More clouds cluster overhead. He sits until his rear end hurts.

Finally, a woman with graying brown hair emerges through the double doors. She approaches him, puts her hands on her knees. "Hi there."

He looks down at his lap.

"Right," she says. "Okay."

She glances across the abandoned playground, then through the chain-link, eyeing the empty parking spots along the curb.

She says, "Can you tell me who you belong to?"